ADVANCED PR

Keeper of the Qu

CH01498340

"Adrienne Dillard has crafted a story that captures the minutiae of life as a lady in waiting amid a story of friendship, faith, and heartbreak in a time of political brutality. This novel brings readers into the heart of Jane Seymour's court, with an eye for detail that is a pleasure to read."

—**Gareth Russell, author of *Young and Damned and Fair: The Life of Catherine Howard***

"Adrienne Dillard's talent lies in her ability to combine a scholarly approach to research with imaginative empathy, and *Keeper of the Queen's Jewels* is her finest novel to date. In a sea awash with tired intrigue and scandal, Dillard's characters shine with brilliant, authentic humanity. The story of Henry VIII's third and most caricatured wife, the supposedly meek and colourless Jane Seymour, is woven with the little-known lady's maid, Margery Horsman, who had a 'great friendship' with Jane's predecessor, Anne Boleyn. The result is a gripping story, filled with natural uncontrived tension, a powerful narrative exploring love and hatred; a perfect balance of historical events informing a deeply human portrayal of two women who form a lasting bond in the fraught aftermath of Anne Boleyn's execution. You may fall in love with Margery, but Jane is fire and ice. This is Jane Seymour as you have never seen her before."

—**Olga Hughes, historian**

"Dillard crafts the complicated past relationship of Margery and Jane with the dead queen with immense skill. The living women, both perfectly depicted, carry the heavy guilt of her death, desperate, in their own ways, to come to terms with their actions that may have led to Anne's bloody end. Dillard is an amazingly gifted writer—and this novel will not disappoint her many readers. It is her best work yet."

—**Wendy J. Dunn, author of the *Falling Pomegranate Seeds* series**

PRAISE FOR

Cor Rotto

"Adrienne Dillard's descriptions of childbirth, breastfeeding, loss, and the marital dynamic all evoke a powerful connection between the reader and protagonist, fostering a sense of relatability that is not often found in historical fiction. The author's raw depictions of these experiences—and so much more—set *Cor Rotto* apart from other novels of the same genre and time-period."

—Olivia Castetter, reviewer—The Pensive Bookworm

"Adrienne Dillard's book is beautifully written and tells the story of such a remarkable woman. Dillard was able to portray the love that Catherine had as a mother and wife in a simple and humble way that it felt like Catherine could be a friend. She was able to bring the life of a royal and a mother of 14 to life in such a respectful and dignified way."

—Heidi Malagisi, reviewer—Adventures of a Tudor Nerd

KEEPER

of the

QUEEN'S
JEWELS

ADRIENNE DILLARD

ISBN (print): 978-1-958725-00-9
ISBN (ebook): 978-1-958725-01-6

Book design and production by Domini Dragoone
Cover image (jewel box) © Morgan Studio, Shutterstock

Published by GreyLondon Press
Gwynedd Valley, PA
www.adrienne-dillard.com

GREYLONDON
PRESS

This book is dedicated to the wonderful people who picked me up when I fell. Without their support, encouragement, guidance, and love, I could never have finished telling this story. They gave me strength when I was weak. They gave me courage when I had none. They are the rocks upon which I've built my foundation:

Catherine Brooks and David Ibbotson, Derek Gilbert and the entire D & S Crew, Olga Hughes, Elena Kuhnhenn, James Nutter, Christine Seabury, Sandra Vasoli, Jeff White, and my dearest family.

To Danielle and her darling little one for reminding me to believe in miracles.

And to my beloved Logan: the prince who was promised.

Historical Figures

THE SEYMOURS

Margery Wentworth Seymour

Edward Seymour (Beauchamp)

Anne Stanhope (Beauchamp)

Harry Seymour

Thomas Seymour

Elizabeth Seymour Ughtred Cromwell

Dorothy Seymour Smith

THE TUDORS

King Henry VIII

The Lady Mary

The Lady Elizabeth

Henry Fitzroy

THE LYSTERS

Michael

Richard (his father)

Richard "Dickon" (his son)

THE MAIDS

Margery Horsman Lyster

Jane Ashley Meutas

Mary Norris

Joan (Jane) Arundell

Mary Arundell, Lady Sussex

Eleanor (Elizabeth) Jerningham

Katherine & Anne Bassett

Mother Stonor (Mother of the Maids)

COURTIERS

John Husee

Lord & Lady Lisle

John Russell

Thomas Cromwell

Thomas Boleyn

Ralph Sadler

Dr Butts

THE GREAT LADIES

Lady Richmond

Lady Rutland

Lady Rochford (widow of Geo. Boleyn)

Lady Salisbury

ARTISTS

Hans Holbein

PEARLS

Innocence

MAY 19, 1536

MARGERY HORSMAN

YORK PLACE

The trembling clerk clothed in the rumpled livery of Master Kingston thrust the gilded coffer into my hands. "The thing is cursed," he whispered, his cracked lips puckering around the word, like poison to be spat out. I knew what was in the coffer before I even opened it: Nan Bullen's most prized possession. On the night before her coronation, I had watched her wrap it in a swatch of silk embroidered with three bulls, the heraldry of her house.

"Nan Bullen is gone," she had intoned, carefully tucking the package beneath the ornately engraved lid. "A queen has arisen in her place. The bulls will always hold a special place in my heart, but from this day forward, I shall forever be the falcon, crowned." Her remark had struck me as odd. I had never heard anyone refer to Anne Boleyn by that name. Who was Nan Bullen?

Sensing my confusion, Anne had peered up at me through long, dark lashes. She fixed her black eyes on my own just long enough to make me uncomfortable, tracing her finger around the whorls of the letter carved atop the coffer. "Nan is my innocence," she explained. "She is the girl I was before I knew I could be anyone else. Nan is my comfort, my protection. Nan is my heart."

"Please forgive my presumption, Your Grace, but how can your heart be gone?" I asked. "Does it not still beat within your chest?"

Anne's hand fell to the curve of her gravid belly, her face rising to meet the warm sunbeam streaming through the leaded window. "I have given my heart to our king," she whispered, a smile playing across her lips. "From here on, *he* will be my comfort and my protection."

That warm summer day faded away long ago, and I had not seen Nan Bullen or the necklace inside her coffer since. "Why have you brought this to me?" I challenged the clerk, who stood, still quaking, before me in his leather riding boots. "This should go to the jewel house; the royal gems are not my duty."

"This piece belongs not to the Crown, but the lady herself." His eyes grew wide; silver plates set in a blanched face. "She begged my master send it to you."

"Why me?"

"She told him you would know what to do." His hand twitched at his side.

"I cannot take this! If the king were to discover it—"

"You speak dangerous words," the clerk hissed, eager to be quit of my company.

I turned away before he could see my tears. Clutching the coffer to my chest, I fled from the corridor to the safety of the maiden's dorm, throwing myself against the great oak door once inside. Fighting hard to catch my breath, I allowed sobs to overtake me. I slid to the floor. The usual twitter of the queen's fledgling ladies had dissipated in the days following her arrest, all the little birds sent home to their mothers, to await a new mistress. I was left behind, my cries echoing in the hollow room, reminding me I was forever alone.

Dejected, I conjured an image of my own mother. Nearly twenty summers had passed since her death. When she left, I was merely eight, and it seemed to me she had been sick for the entirety of my life. I didn't know then how still the night could be without her barking coughs punctuating the dark hours. Looking back, I suspected her illness was far more fleeting than I remembered. I understand now that death never lingers longer than necessary, claiming what is his with stunning immediacy. Before you realize you have exhaled your last, rasping breath, you are gone.

I took fright at the men who came to our home to prepare my mother's soul for its ascension from the Earth and her body for its return to the same. Scrambling away at the earliest opportunity, I sought safety in a cramped, rarely used cupboard situated across the hall from her bedchamber. Burrowing deep beneath the linens stored inside, I inhaled the sweet, creamy scent that seemed to infuse everything my mother touched. The comforting familiarity of it held me in a warm embrace. I swam through the layers of fabric, my head bumping against something frigid and unyielding. When I reached for the offending object, my hands closed around a small metal box. My short-lived triumph at untangling it dissolved when I realized it was locked.

I wallowed within the comfort of my cocoon while the voices of the local priest and physician droned together outside the door; the sound of their shuffling footsteps seemed like the wind, growing higher and dropping lower with each pass they made down the corridor. Eventually, I drifted off to sleep. My father discovered me hours later with the box clasped in my hands, a crust of tears on my face.

"My darling Margery." He heaved a great sigh of relief. "We have been looking everywhere for you."

The years separating me from that wretched day dissolved into the shadows as I considered this new coffer resting in my lap. I thought again of my father. He had offered me a sad smile when he discovered me in that closet, clutching at my mother's jewel box. "Have I told you about the girl named Pandora?" he had asked, slipping his arms beneath me to pull me close. "She had a chest just like this one." I closed my eyes, revelling in his memory. Foolish Pandora—Oh, how she had defied the gods! I was no better. I had allowed hatred and envy into the world as well. Yet somehow, Pandora managed to save hope in her box. Now, I was tasked with protecting the hope remaining in mine: the one possession that belonged to the copper-haired child Anne left behind.

When I lifted the lid, the gold letter at the centre of the string of alabaster pearls winked in the dancing candlelight. *B for Bullen*—I thought to myself—*pearls for innocence*. Caressing them, I felt the heat of Anne's skin. I had to save this treasure for her daughter, Princess Elizabeth. Only then could I right my wrongs against her mother; only then would my guilt be satisfied. Could I be brave like Pandora?

JANE SEYMOUR

CHELSEA

I awoke at dawn to an insistent prodding. "Jane, it's time to prepare. The king will be here soon," my brother's wife urged, tugging on the thick damask counterpane. As the weight of it slid away, a new heaviness settled deep within my bones. Doom clouded the air.

"Not yet, Anne." *Anne.* Her name tasted so bitter on my tongue that I practically spat it out, though the woman I called to was nothing at all like the late queen. *No, not queen—she was never Henry's true wife. She had been a usurper.* People were beginning to call *me* the usurper. Perhaps they were right. Anne Boleyn had been a queen not merely in name only; she was properly anointed, touched by God. The legality of her marriage was inconsequential against the blessing of the Almighty. Today was not meant for those musings, though. His Grace would soon arrive, pink-cheeked and jubilant. I must rise to the occasion.

"The water will get cold if you don't hurry," Lady Anne insisted. "Sybil's had it carried up from the kitchens, so the heat is not likely to last much longer."

"Of course," I agreed, reluctantly. Sir William Paulet's home was luxurious and inviting, but it was also large and draughty. It would not do to catch ill mere weeks before I was to marry the King of England.

I pulled myself up against the bedstead, swinging my legs off the edge. My feet were greeted by the caress of a soft Turkish carpet, laid down purely for my enjoyment and pleasure—a far cry from the scratchy plaited rush mats I was accustomed to, living as Sir John Seymour's plainest daughter at Wulfhall. Yet here I was: the pinnacle of success. At this very moment, it felt more like a precipice. One mislaid step, and I could tumble—a falling star expelled from the sky. *No, she's not yet dead—His Grace could still show mercy.* If he did not, the world as we knew it would be forever changed. *If he could kill one queen, who could stop him from killing another?*

"Jane!" Lady Anne called again with more urgency—this time hidden beyond sight in the corridor. I sucked in a lungful of air, then levered myself out of bed.

A WOODEN BAYNE lined with white linen had been set up in a room at the end of the hall, where my lady's maid met me with a cheery smile. "Good morning, Mistress Jane. I hope you slept well?"

"How could one not when treated to such comforts?" It wasn't a lie in so many words. Nor was it the truth. Sumptuous though my accommodations were, they provided few assurances. It had not been a restful night.

Sybil gestured towards the tub. "I hope it's warm enough still. I've asked the boy to bring more logs. Once you are settled, I shall bring your gown. Would you prefer the crimson or the white?"

"The white," Lady Anne barked, cutting off my reply. "The better to remind His Grace of your innocence. The better to remind him of your purity." A chamberer bustled in behind her, arms loaded with wood for the fire.

Sybil scurried from the room.

"Imagine it!" Lady Anne crowed. "Crimson on today, of all days. How foolish. You'll be leaving her behind." A constant tutor, humming in my ear since the earliest days of my courtship with the king, the woman had been loath to relinquish the position.

"But Sybil has been with me since Wulfhall." My voice cracked on the last word, my beloved childhood home seeming a world away.

"That life is over, Jane. Remember? Besides, you will have new maids after the wedding." Her voice dipped low, "Hopefully, ones with a bit more discretion."

"She meant no harm," I insisted, keen to defend a servant who had shown nothing but loyalty since the days when I was nothing, nobody.

"They never mean any harm." Avoiding my gaze, she busied herself with a stack of washcloths.

"I am sorry for Sir Richard. How fares your mother?" I gnawed at the inside of my cheek. The skin was tender, puckered from so much chewing. "She must suffer with her husband in the Tower. Is there anything I can do?"

"She is tolerable," Lady Anne clipped. "I am sure his arrest meant nothing. A mere feint to disarm the people. Richard Page would never be disloyal to my mother with that *harlot*." The word fired out like a shot, ricocheting off the limewashed walls.

"The king's letter said there was unrest over our relationship. A ballad was made to mock me." My brother Tom had played the cloyingly sweet melody after supper one night. I wanted to bash his lute against the footstool.

"There is always a ballad." She sighed, turning back to me. "My mother's husband is in the Tower because of you, not Anne Boleyn. Imprisoning one of your connections makes it look as though they carried out a proper investigation, rather than wiping out your rival's supporters. He will be out soon enough. Along with that dreadful poet, Thomas Wyatt. Now, get in."

I pulled the satin nightgown—a gift from the king—over my head, tossing it to the floor. Lady Anne furrowed her brow at this small act of defiance before crouching down to rescue it. Just as she had warned, the water had grown tepid. I slipped into its embrace without flinching, the heat from my contempt enough to warm me. Lady Anne dipped a finger into the tub. She gave me a look of exasperation. "Maid!" she bellowed. "Bring more hot water.

Sybil scrubbed until my skin felt raw, then left me to stew while she set out my clothing in the next room. I stared silently at the river outside the window, my insides pitching and churning like the tide rocking against the shore. Anne Boleyn would be mounting the scaffold now; death was close at hand. *Had I brought about her undoing?* In the distance, a cannon boomed. When the ordnance sounded a second time, my belly clenched against the roar. A gush of scarlet bloomed in the water around me.

Lady Anne paled when she spied the bloodstains on the cloth that lined the tub. Having gone down to the kitchens during my washing, she had only just returned to inform me everything was ready for our celebratory feast. "What's this? What have you done?" Her voice trembled. "This is an ill-omen."

"Never mind, it is just my courses. There could be no better proof of my fertility." My reply rang dismissive, but the words scorched the back of my throat. Contrived confidence belied the bitterness behind them. "Instruct Sybil to put away the white. I prefer green, like the king's livery."

HIS GRACE ARRIVED arrayed in his finest, crowned with a blue velvet cap. A jaunty white feather tucked into the brim lent a festive air. Never had I seen a man who revelled so much in his cuckoldry. My brother, Edward, would have rather died than admit his former wife's adultery. He shipped the lovely Katherine Filliol off to a nunnery where she withered away, alone and abandoned. Only after her body was stiff in the ground did he turn to Anne Stanhope. *Henry Tudor's wife should have gone to a nunnery.* I savoured the thought in my mind, letting it drop away unsaid, then turned my attention to the king.

We had all gone down to meet him at the river's edge. Every Seymour available crowded around the pier as the royal barge docked and the king disembarked. "Mine own dear sweetheart," he sang, setting a course straight for me. I willed myself to be brave, composing my expression.

"Beloved king," I cooed, sinking into a low curtsy. "You have come bearing welcome news?"

His Grace's smile hid the echo of a sneer, his lips tight and twisted. "I could not bring sweeter words than these: at long last, the whore is dead."

Dread tickled the nape of my neck, its skeletal fingers skipping upon my skin. I forced the corners of my lips up. "Praise God that our king is a just and righteous one."

The king's face lit up, and my brother, Tom, gave a great laugh. "Oh ho!" It was fleeting, but I caught a spark of rage in His Grace's eye.

"What is the meaning of this, Tom?" Harry demanded, appalled by our brother's outburst.

"Show some respect to your sovereign," Edward seethed. Our mother looked as though she had just swallowed a leech.

Tom reddened. "No offense intended, my gracious prince." He delivered a conciliatory bow before explaining, "I only jest at this solemn banter that seems so contrary to the occasion. The Lord has blessed us with a splendid spring day, our manifold enemies have perished to the depths of Hell, and we have all come together to celebrate my sister's impending nuptials. Rather than linger by the river with dour faces, we should frolic among the flowers and crush a cup of wine with great bacchanalian abandon. What say you?"

His Grace stared stonily at my brother, then slowly cracked a grin. "How right you are, Tom. All is forgiven." Harry breathed a sigh of relief, but Edward retained his peevish scowl. "On your advice, I should like to take my darling bride on a stroll through the gardens," the king continued. "Then we shall drink to our marriage and the smiting of these vile traitors, may they rot forever."

"Edward…Anne…" I nodded towards my eldest brother and his wife. "Would you please be so kind as to accompany us?" My hand grazed the king's sleeve as he slipped my arm through his; the fabric was damp with sweat.

Lady Anne knelt low in reverence. "It would be our dearest pleasure," she replied delicately.

MORNING DEW STILL clung like a lover to delicate rosebuds heavy with expectation of the warm months to come. So too did the king cling to me, his body close enough that his feet nearly trod upon mine. I felt pinned to him as we made our way down the winding path. He stopped for a moment to stroke the naked bulb on a rose bush, groaning in irritation when it did not open at his prodding. "Tom said there would be flowers," he muttered.

"It is still early in the season yet." I drew his hand away before he inflicted further harm. "In the coming weeks, the rose's cocoon will burst open in all its glory. In the meantime, the knot garden beyond the terrace is in full bloom. Would you permit me to show you?"

His Grace brought my palm to his lips. He wove his fingers through mine, twisting my arm behind my back to pull me in for a kiss. His lips tasted of honey and sweet berries; a lingering reminder of the rich breakfast he had devoured while Anne Boleyn breathed her last. Pushing away all thoughts of the woman who came before me, I lost myself in the moment. An uncertain longing stirred within me. The years had been lonely, and I had all but given up on ever receiving the affectionate caresses of a paramour. The king broke contact before I did. "Not yet," he murmured to himself without meeting my gaze. "You always set me to rights, darling Jane. That is why God has placed you in my arms," he continued, raising his voice so our companions could hear him. "Take us to these flowers you speak of."

I had discovered the knot garden the morning after arriving at Chelsea. Mother and I attended lauds in the chapel at daybreak, then decided to take a walk like we always did at Wulfhall. When we came out on to the terrace, I saw the blooms and was immediately smitten. I had gone back every day since to study the arrangement of flowers and herbs, my fingers itching to dig in the soil. It was here where I took His Grace, hoping he would be as charmed.

"Ah, now this is what I was looking for. How beautiful it is."

"See the edging of hyssop, Your Grace?" I enthused, heart in my throat. "It plays up the colour of the marguerites and the scent of the daffodils. I have always wanted to do something akin to it back home, but our gardener refuses to change any of his plans."

"You shall have whatever your heart desires from now on," the king broke in, his face alight with pleasure. "When you come to my palace at Hampton Court on the morrow, we shall speak with my man."

"Tomorrow?" My guts clenched as they had in the tub. I was not meant to leave Chelsea until the following week.

"For our betrothal," he answered, grinning. "Edward, come share in our joy."

Before I could say more, my brother and his wife approached. They had kept a leisurely pace behind us to offer privacy. Hearing his name, Edward hurried forward. "Trouble, Your Grace?"

"No, dearest brother, all my troubles are over. Now, let us move on to the house for that cup of wine."

Mother waited for us on the terrace. She cast her gaze from Edward to me, desperate to uncover what we might have spoken of in the garden. I offered no hints. Better for the king to tell her. His Grace did not appreciate being upstaged. I had no intention of making that mistake.

Dinner was a lavish feast, each dish carefully curated to impress the sovereign. Fifteen courses, including capons in a creamy sauce, tender veal, and lamprey pie, all vied to tempt him from the main attraction: a roasted peacock dressed in its feathers. Though everyone ate heartily, I found myself picking at my plate, my stomach sour. It was all too much, too soon. "Has my cook displeased you, my love?" His Grace asked. I shook my head, offering a feeble excuse: too much excitement had dampened my appetite. I could not tell him that as I looked around the table at my family's faces, all I saw was death. Edward with a spike through his head; Tom hanged by a rope; and Harry, the brother between them, flayed open for the crows. All of them ruined if I was not careful.

Mother stepped in to rescue me. "Jane wants to be sure she can fit those beautiful gowns you had made for her. Besides, every girl is nervous before her wedding."

"I would not mind a plump bird in my nest." The king cackled at the jest, then his voice grew cold. "I have found lean women to be cruel and unyielding."

I countered his remark with a hungry smile. "You have inspired me, Your Grace. I find that what I crave is a nice fat quail."

CARNELIAN

Courage

MAY 1536

MARGERY HORSMAN

YORK PLACE

E verything came rushing back the moment I opened my eyes. The coffer. The cannons. The pearls. I reached under the bed for the piss pot and retched black bile over the delicate cabbage roses etched inside. Yesterday's events still felt raw. I had only just stashed the silver coffer in my trunk when the first cannon thundered. One shot, then another, each clap of ordnance renting another jagged piece from my tattered soul. My queen was dead.

Unable to face the emptiness outside, I laid back against the pillow, yanking the quilt up to my chin. My eyes ached. Rather than joining the boisterous diners in the great hall last night, I had stayed in my room, sobbing until exhaustion lured me into a restless sleep. The usual cacophony of court had been too much to bear; everyone going about their lives as if nothing were amiss. There was safety in that, I supposed. I had always struggled to conceal my true feelings, a failing that could prove dangerous.

I hid beneath the covers until a rap at the door drove me from my bed. A muffled voice seeped under the crack. "Margery? Are you in there? It's Stonor."

"I shall be but a moment!" I shouted, remembering that Mother Stonor was a bit hard of hearing. I ran to my trunk and threw open the lid. Digging through the fabric, my hand brushed the silver coffer. An ominous draft ruffled the hairs along my arm. Unnerved, I yanked out the first kirtle I touched, then shrugged it over my shoulders, lacing it up as I scuttled towards the door.

"Margery, I'm so pleased to...Oh!" Mother Stonor's face fell when she saw my clothes. "No. No. That's no good. You cannot wear that."

I looked down to see if I had missed an eyelet, but the fastening appeared secure. "What's wrong with it?"

"Well, it's black, dear," she reproached, perching her hand on her hip.

"The queen is dead. I thought..." My voice trailed off at the obvious inference.

Mother Stonor gave a backward glance before shouldering me back into the room. "No, girl, a traitor is dead," she whispered, fingers working quickly to unlace what I had just tied. "We need a more suitable colour. Something that won't offend the king."

"Does such a thing exist?" These days, the man was liable to execute his own shadow.

Mother Stonor jerked the straps on my kirtle. "What is the matter with you?" she snapped; all forbearance gone. "Have you not yet learned?"

My cheeks flushed at the rebuke. "But it is just us here. Surely you cannot believe she was guilty?"

"I believe our king would do nothing without cause." She measured her words carefully. "And if anyone should deign to request your opinion, I would suggest the same answer."

Sufficiently chastened, I gulped back a retort. She was right. We had all become careless in service to Queen Anne; our words bold and unguarded. Mother Stonor held my linen smock down while I pulled the kirtle over my head. I returned it to the trunk and fished out a replacement, careful to keep the coffer buried beneath the rest of my clothing.

"How about yellow?"

"Yes, that will do. Now let's go. Master Lloyd is waiting for us."

Slipping through the crowd in the courtyard, I spied relief on more than one face. I caught a peal of laughter from a flock of grooms congregated near the gate. "Imagine Smeaton, waiting all night in the marmalade closet!" The boy who made the comment was riddled with pockmarks. "He was the one getting a taste of something sweet," another boy hooted in response. Laughter smeared their hideous features. An older man with stringy grey hair reached across the fence to cuff them both on the ear. "Enough of that, you little wretches. You're needed in the stables," he growled before dragging them away.

"Marmalade closet?" I bristled. "What nonsense is this?"

"Everyone has a jape," Mother Stonor huffed, continuing her determined march. "Pay it no heed."

"Smeaton's dead because of me," I murmured under my breath.

She stopped to stare at me. "What did you say?"

"Nothing. I said nothing."

MASTER LLOYD WAS shouting orders from deep within one of the closets when we arrived at the queen's wardrobe. A clerk stood nearby, furiously scribbling on a sheet of parchment. His quill stopped scratching when he saw us. "Master Lloyd!" he called out, flipping a lock of hair out of his eyes.

The Yeoman of the Wardrobe stuck his head out the low doorway, his velvet cap knocked askew. "Happy you could find the time to join us."

"Our apologies, Sir. Mistress Margery was feeling a bit..."

"Not my concern," Lloyd interrupted. "You," he jerked his thumb in my direction, "in here, now." I hurried to join him in the cramped quarters. "We need to pull out the garments delivered to Anne Boleyn last month. Since they haven't yet been worn, they will be given, by the king's gift, to Mistress Jane Seymour."

"Yes, Sir." The thought of Jane wearing clothes sewn for Queen Anne caused my throat to constrict. My breath hitched.

"After you are done, I need you to pull out the coronation apparel. We will send it to Skutt to be taken apart and refashioned for the next." Lloyd retreated with a batch of linen nightgowns slung over his shoulders. "Send these to the laundry," he muttered to the clerk.

Mother Stonor craned her neck around the doorway and asked if she could help. I shook my head. She returned with the clerk's parchment, against my protests. Together, we sifted through the queen's order from the tailor. I recalled helping with the request. Master Skutt had come to the palace with his fabric swatches, and we spent the day passing them through our fingers, exclaiming over the soft velvet and buttery smooth silk. She had chosen several practical gowns of tawny and black in velvet, satin, and damask, along with three embroidered cloaks to match. After Skutt left, Queen Anne turned regretful, calling him back again the next day. "I would also like one in purple damask and cloth of gold, lined with—oh," she had hesitated. "Silver," I supplied with an encouraging smile. "It will set off your hair."

I had done no more than my duties required. Still, I felt a shift after that day, a metamorphosis in how we related to one another. Perhaps it was due to what happened between Skutt's first visit and his second. The strained confession I gave when the queen caught me weeping over a verse her brother wrote in Madge Shelton's book of poetry. "George is spoken for," she told me. "But we shall find you a husband, I swear." All those years of waiting for the king's divorce had made her sympathetic to my plight. I was nearing my thirtieth year with no hope of a match in sight. To my great shame, her kindness came a week too late. I had already turned treacherous.

Often the most treasonous words are spoken, not out of calculated malice, but rash impetuousness. Out of sheer resentment and frustration. The damage becomes apparent only after things begin to unravel. "Marc Smeaton is over-familiar with Her Grace," I remarked to the Vice-Chamberlain one evening, after hearing the queen praise the musician's latest composition. My pride had been wounded by the rapid ascension of this son of a carpenter. What hypocrisy. I was the daughter of no one, given my place at court by those better than me. We were one and the same. Yet, I begrudged every crumb sent his way. Smeaton had caused no harm to me, save revelling in the attention lavished upon him. Attention I coveted. The interrogations began soon after my careless words. Thomas Cromwell was already skulking about while the queen and I met with the tailor.

Mother Stonor's voice startled me from my thoughts. "Margery? What of these sleeves?"

I glanced over at the pair she held aloft for inspection. Honeysuckles and acorns had been worked in gold throughout the ivory satin. "The queen never wore them, but surely the king would not gift them to Mistress Seymour. That design was conceived for Queen Anne. Set them aside for now."

Master Lloyd and his clerk returned in the afternoon with a trio of grooms; each one was dressed in Master Kingston's colours and weighed down with a parcel. "Leave them there." He jabbed a finger towards an empty corner. The grooms filed in and dropped their packages, then scattered before the yeoman could rope them into more work. "I'll be reporting this to your master," he shouted after them. The clerk smirked behind his hand. After an appraising glance around the wardrobe, Lloyd nodded in approval. "Well done then, ladies. I've another job for you."

All the colour drained from Mother Stonor's face when I pried open the first crate. "No, I—" she stuttered. I reached out to steady her and felt her arm tremble beneath my hand. "She wore that on the scaffold," she finished in a low voice.

"Go on. I can take care of it." I looked to Master Lloyd for support. He sighed but waved her on. Mother Stonor retreated, shoulders wilting.

Setting my jaw, I turned back to the task at hand. I started with the crate Lloyd opened last, saving the first one until the very end. Inside, Master Kingston had carefully packed away everything that provided Queen Anne with comfort during her imprisonment. A hollow ache settled deeper into my chest with each item I drew out: books still marked with her stopping place, a gold chalice once touched by her lips, the black velvet gown she wore to the trial. By the time I returned to the first crate, darkness had fallen. I reached in, pulling out a gable headdress trimmed in pearls. A dark spot near the peak caught my eye, so I held it nearer the candle for closer inspection. The stain was the colour of rust—a droplet of blood.

JANE SEYMOUR

HAMPTON COURT PALACE

Tom's incessant foot-tapping grew louder with each moment that passed. "Lord Jesu hear my prayer," I whispered into my hands, appearing oblivious to his irritation. I felt his eyes boring through me, but he made no move to approach. I sank closer to the floor, my knees aching against the crushed velvet of my gown. The chaplain shuffled past, his robes swirling a cloud of incense around my head. Heated words cut through the hush of the chapel and then the slam of a door. Silence fell again. My lips formed the words a second time, "Lord Jesu, hear my prayer." I remained prostrate until my heart slowed, and I could no longer feel its thud against my chest.

Mother was pacing the corridor when I exited the chapel. She didn't notice me right away, but I saw her. Had her posture always been so stooped? Had her hair always been so grey? She was once a famed beauty in her youth—a poet's muse. She seemed almost a ghost now. When had that happened? Was it before or after Father's death? Nearly half a year gone, and it still felt as though he could return at any moment. She seemed to sag further when she finally spotted me. "Jane, they are waiting for you."

"That may be, but Tom's behaviour is unacceptable. I was at prayer." My voice came out more plaintive than I wished.

"Edward sent him," she countered, brows knit tight with worry. "The royal barge is here."

My brother's lanky form came into view near the riverbank. His charcoal-coloured doublet was chased in gold—austere, yet sumptuous at the same time. Most importantly, it hid the slight depression in his shoulder—a defect gifted from our ancestors. He was exchanging pleasantries with the boatman, stopping short when he caught sight of me. "There she is." Despite a genial smile, his voice had an edge to it. I took his proffered arm and mounted the barge carefully, so as not to lose my leather slippers to the depths below.

"Where is Lady Anne?" I glanced back at the manor. "I thought she was joining us?"

Edward shook his head. "No, this is to be an intimate affair. I shall be your witness. The king will bring his own. And Cranmer, of course."

I bit my lip to hold back the tears that had suddenly formed. A betrothal was supposed to be joyous, celebratory. Mine would be held in secret like it was shameful. Just like Anne Boleyn's betrothal. "Not even Mother?" I asked hopefully.

Edward sighed, my questions irritating him. "Not even Mother."

PREVIOUSLY, I HAD travelled to Hampton Court by horse, as one amongst a passel of maids, moving in slow stages through the English countryside. By barge, the journey seemed far more pleasurable. The clop of hooves was replaced by the more soothing sounds of the tidal rush and birdsong hovering overhead on the river. When we drifted nearer the shore, a curious starling flew aboard, perching herself on the rail. She offered a shrill melody before spreading her wings, taking flight once again.

We arrived at the water gallery before the sun crested the sky. His Grace stood just inside the brick gatehouse, flanked by Archbishop Cranmer and Charles Brandon, the Duke of Suffolk. Buoyed by my arrival, he bounced on the balls of his feet. His cheeks were rosy, his eyes twinkling. One would have never known that less than twenty-four hours ago, his most entirely beloved wife had been put to the sword.

"Welcome, my lady." The duke pulled me from the barge, the buttons on his coat straining to contain a distended paunch. Suffolk was one of the first to revile Anne Boleyn openly. A lifetime of devotion to the king insulated him from rebuke during her ascendancy, but he still had to bite his tongue while the light of royal favour shined upon her. Now that the light fell elsewhere, he basked in triumph.

His Grace clasped my hand, placing a wet kiss on the back of it. "My entirely beloved bride, I am so pleased to see you again. I feel as though I have waited an eternity for this day."

I dipped low. "As have I, Your Grace." I *had* been waiting for this day since the moment I set off from Wulfhall, determined to make my way at court. I had a different groom in mind back then. Not the aloof bore my mother wanted me to marry, but certainly not the king either. He had been deeply in love with Queen Catherine then, hadn't he? No, perhaps not, upon reflection. Better I married the bore. Safer. Whatever had become of Will Dormer? His haughty mother would choke to see me in such finery as I now wore. Not good enough to be her daughter, yet good enough to be her queen. The king misread my stifled giggle for excitement.

"I am pleased to see your happiness," he tittered, cheeks flushing deeper.

"And I yours, my king."

Outside the water gallery, the servants were busily fishing pike out of the ponds. "Shall I send some down to Chelsea?" he asked.

"Mother would love that, Your Grace," Edward cut in. "She loved the fish pie we ate when you visited yesterday. We are all becoming fat off the hearty food your cook makes. It has been a treat to have him."

"Think nothing of it, dear brother." His Grace caressed the bulge at his waist. These late months, he had seen far more banqueting than sporting.

Suffolk and my brother surged ahead, leaving Cranmer to drift behind. He quickly sidled up to His Grace, eager to spill praise in his ear. I did not fear the cleric, nor did I particularly dislike him. He made me uneasy. I expected a man of the church to show fealty to God, above all others, but Cranmer's loyalty bent like reeds in the wind. I trusted him not. Marriages he made and unmade on a whim all seemed to end with a dead woman. If I displeased the king, my marriage could be unpicked like a misplaced stitch just as easily—a quick jerk, the rip of a seam, tattered and frayed. And what of me? Queen Catherine, God rest her soul, had the whole of Christendom, while Anne Boleyn had the support of some of the most powerful families in the realm. I had fewer allies and none so mighty.

"Are you ready, my love?" We had finally arrived at the entrance to the king's new lodgings.

I tried to sound light as the spring. "Yes, of course."

The palace's inner corridors seemed far less populated than they should have been for a royal visitation. I had not anticipated a crowd, but I'd not imagined it would be so sparse. His Grace acknowledged my bewilderment with a comforting pat on the hand. He had sent them away, he assured me. He wanted to have me all to himself. I followed him through the inner court, past the cloister green, and into the gallery. Workers scurried ahead of us, chiselling away the entwined letters marring the linenfold panel walls. A lonely *H* hung precariously overhead; its companion *A* gouged out with a carpenter's pick.

Our betrothal ceremony was held in the royal closet overlooking the chapel. While the archbishop prepared, I stared up at the marvellous ceiling above, a sea of golden stars etched upon a field of dazzling blue. Edward slipped quietly behind me, giving my arm a gentle squeeze to let me know they were ready. The king stood beside Cranmer, eyes alight with hunger. "I, Henry," he began, his voice soaring to the roof beams. He twisted a ring upon my finger. A stone—the colour of fire—sat in the middle of five petals fashioned out of fine gold. My mother had a similar gem. "A carnelian for courage," she would tell me as she pinned it to her gown before rushing off with Father to another court banquet.

Then it was my turn. I repeated the words with little feeling, as if by rote. "I, Jane, plight thee my troth."

Vows over, the king gestured towards the door, and our witnesses fled with knowing glances regarding what was to come next. After the door closed, he advanced. Mother had prepared me for this moment. "Once you say the words, your body will no longer be yours. It will be his to command and control; to inflict pleasure or pain. Let him do as he must, and perhaps he shall be good to you. All you must do is part your legs and pray for a son," she said. Pinned against a pillar, I fought the impulse to slink away from the king's grasp, instead planting my feet firmly between his.

"Oh, Jane." His breath was hot in my ear. A guttural moan surfaced from deep within. He shifted his weight, wedging a knee between my thighs, and then covered my mouth with his own. I closed my eyes, imaging the golden-haired William Dormer. Dull though he was, the Lord had blessed him with the most desirable lips. They were plump and smooth—not like the king's, thin and tight. I lost myself in the thought of his hands probing and caressing, the remembrance of yesterday's arrival of my monthly courses coming too late.

"No, we mustn't," I yelped, pushing the king away. He removed his hand from beneath my skirt, blanching at the discovery of a thin streak of scarlet on his fingertips. "Pardon, Your Grace. I thought we would wait until the wedding."

"No matter," he muttered, face twisted in disgust.

"It will soon be over," I promised. "And then perhaps we shall conceive once we are wed."

The king nodded, still staring down at his hand as though its very existence offended him. "I need to wash up. Wait for me in the privy chamber."

When he strode away, I turned back towards the chapel; the winking of the stained-glass window in the sunlight caught my eye. It was a depiction of St. Anne. She was laughing at me.

IN THE GREAT hall, Edward's eyes sought mine. How I hated when those dark orbs darted to and fro; always searching, prying. 'Have you accomplished your task?' they wanted to know. I shook my head. He would ask me to explain on the journey back to Chelsea, but what concern was it of his? This was the business of women. Besides, his time to meddle had come to an end. He got me into the king's bedchamber; he need not know what went on there.

"I hope you are finding the accommodations at Chelsea to your liking?" Suffolk boomed, shattering the awkward silence.

"Yes, Sir William has gone out of his way to show us every comfort. It is a lovely home."

"I haven't been since Thomas More lived there. They say he tortured heretics in a shed by the stables." He took a deep pull from the flagon in his hand. Ale, I surmised from the look of his flushed cheeks.

Edward broke in, "Let us only speak of light matters this day."

"I saw no evidence of that, my lord," I snapped at the duke, despite my brother's obvious discomfort. More had been a saintly man, a pious Catholic. Mother and I had spent the day of his execution eschewing all sustenance and praying for his soul. "My sister and I explored that shed and found it to be quite peaceful. Perhaps they are mistaken?"

Before Suffolk could answer, the king arrived. He had changed his clothing, from his doublet to his hose, as though the ones he wore before had been soiled. He took his seat at the head of the table, gesturing for us to join him. Two grooms appeared carrying platters piled high with cheese and roasted meat. Another followed behind them with a basket of bread and a dish of stewed pears. I could not remember the last time I had cinnamon. Some special occasion, I supposed. The scent of it warmed my belly.

I ate in silence while His Grace discussed the feast being held tomorrow at Windsor to celebrate the Order of the Garter. A vacancy had opened earlier in the year. When the arrests were carried out, I was sent to Sir Nicholas Carew's home at Beddington. During my stay, the man spoke of almost nothing but the election. I thought Carew would have been happy at his elevation. I was mistaken. "They all think I was chosen to spite that arrogant sot," he complained of George Boleyn, who's star had already begun to fall alongside his sister's. "Never mind the king's promise to give it to me years ago." I felt no pity for the man or his pride—at least he still had his head.

After the meal, the king made great protest of the many things requiring his attention, his polite way of letting us know our audience had come to an end. I honoured him with a deep reverence. He had trouble meeting my eye when I rose. Nausea washed over me. I had been caught wrong-footed, through no fault of my own, by the very thing that should have brought comfort to the king—a woman's blood being a promise of sons to come. I swallowed the fear in my throat and thought of the ring on my finger. A carnelian for courage. In the roil of my belly, fear became rage.

MARGERY HORSMAN

YORK PLACE

M aster Husee lurched out of the dark recess of the corridor, sending me wheeling back against the stone wall. "God's Blood, you startled me!" I panted, clutching a stack of linen tightly against my chest. "Where did you come from?"

John Husee grinned at my oath, his crooked teeth gleaming in the torchlight. He carried a crate under his arm. "Cherries?" He pulled out a handful of the plump red orbs. "You prefer the sweet ones, right?"

"Cherries?" I repeated, bewildered. "What are you doing, wandering the corridors in the middle of the night?" I knew the answer before the question had finished upon my lips.

"Lady Lisle sent me." He showed his teeth again. The first time I had seen Master Husee's smile, I knew why he was the Lisle's most trusted servant. Warm and soothing, that grin invited one to share confidences they would have otherwise taken to the grave.

"Of course, she has." I popped a cherry into my mouth. The sweet flavour burst across my tongue as I worked carefully to dislodge the pit.

"You are always amply rewarded," Husee crowed. I threw him a look of annoyance for his impertinence. Married to the king's uncle, Lady Lisle was always very generous to those willing to turn her favours. In the past, I had been the recipient of birds, marmalade, vegetables. She gave me enough cramp rings to repel sickness for an eternity. Thankfully, she had also offered up a steel casket as a reward for a kirtle I wheedled out of Queen Anne months ago. All the rings had gone inside.

"There is nothing to be done until after Whitsun, when the new royal household is installed," I countered, still unable to bring myself to call Jane the queen. My mouth went dry every time I attempted it.

"No, too late." Husee scratched at the scruff on his chin. It was newly grown and greyer than the hair on his head. My fingers slipped unbidden beneath my hood, smoothing my own strands. Husee noticed, teasing me with a wink. "Call me flattered that you care so much for your appearance when I am near."

Heat bloomed on my cheeks. "What I call you cannot be said in polite company," I shot back, both pleased and abashed by the attention. "Now, what can I do for your mistress this time? I am afraid to say her credit might not hold the value it once did. She appeared only too eager to please Anne Boleyn in days past."

He nodded, shifting the crate to his hip. "There have been troubles between my master and Edward Seymour, as well. You'll have to go to Cromwell. He is the only one who can ease the way."

"And you cannot?" Asking for a kirtle or fabric for a hood was one thing. Seeking an audience with the king's Master Secretary was another matter altogether. That was far beyond my power and Husee knew it. Even if one could get into his presence, there was no guarantee he would look favourably upon the suit.

"I did, but he would not help me. Said it was better left to the ladies." He chewed his lip. "So, Lady Lisle bid me ask a lady for help. She wants her daughters in the new queen's household."

"Of course, you chose me to be that lady," I groaned. "You ask too much this time. Those positions are already spoken for."

"Please, Margery?"

The way he said my name—his pleasure in tasting it in his mouth—won me over.

"Fine, now go. I'm busy and important." I bared the tip of my cherry-stained tongue in mock indignation. Husee gifted me with another winning smile before slipping into the darkness.

I DROPPED THE linen at the laundry before returning to my room. Silence reigned over the dormitory, leaving me with nothing but my thoughts for company. After changing into my smock, I pulled a lute from under the bed. The delicate wood face was scarred, and a few of the pegs bent, but it had been a gift from my father. When loneliness called, I often sought its company. I dragged a cushion to the window and sat with my feet drawn beneath me, plucking the strings until the ache in my fingers overcame the sorrow in my heart.

Since I saw it yesterday, I had been unable to stop thinking about the droplet of blood on Queen Anne's hood. I turned again to the gruesome image. It was like a rotted tooth I couldn't stop pushing with my tongue, renewing the pain with each persistent nudge. Unlike the tooth, which could be pulled for relief, I could not pluck the disturbing visions of Anne's death from my mind. She wasn't coming back. Neither was George. Clever, cutting George with flickering eyes of fire. I had been foolish to think I could capture his attention. He desired only Jane Rochford. Now she was left with nothing but his name.

John Husee was as different from George as a man could get. His eyes were the colour of a summer sky, and he possessed an enduring agreeableness that never seemed to waver in the face of adversity. He was the sort of man my father would have wanted for me. The sort of man I should have wanted for myself. Had Lord Morley known what fate was in store for George, he may have chosen another husband for his daughter. Surviving George's death had certainly caused me to reconsider my desires.

I played the same chords, over and over, until I grew tired. Tucking away the lute, I padded over to my trunk. The necklace was still there, beneath the folds of my gown, safely hidden in the silver casket. How long until someone found it? I needed to get it to the only remaining Boleyn I trusted, Mary. Unfortunately, I had not seen Queen Anne's sister since she turned up at Woodstock with a swollen belly two years ago. She was banished, never to be heard from again. Surely, she couldn't have gone far. England was but a small island, her secrets easily breeched.

Pulling the trunk lid closed, I retired to bed with Mary and the necklace on my mind. Yet, it was John Husee stalking my dreams. I awoke in the early morning hours with more certainty than I had felt in a long time. Husee's work for the Lisles brought him into contact with all the court circles. If anyone could find Mary, it was him. Better still, he owed me a few favours. I found myself only too eager to see him again.

ON ANY OTHER day, the great hall would have thrummed with activity, but I discovered only a handful of grooms gathered at the end of a long trestle table set up near the front of the room. Two of the young men had their heads bent close, a fog of whispers hanging between them. I slid into the open spot across the table and helped myself to a chunk of cheat loaf. The dark-haired groom eyed me suspiciously as the fair one shoved a dish of butter in my direction. "I thought the women had gone home?"

"Most of them," I replied through a mouthful of crust. The butter did little to moisten the bread, and I nearly choked on the crumbs. Clutching at the nearest tankard, I gulped back the remaining dregs of small ale inside. It tasted bitter but wet my throat enough to stop the cough.

"Hugh, she drank your ale."

The fair groom's blue eyes danced. He shrugged. "I was done with it anyway."

Feeling a blush warm my cheeks, I moved to rise from the table. "I'm sorry, I shall be on my way."

"What can we do for you, Mistress …?" Hugh's voice trailed off as he groped his memory for a name.

"Margery," I supplied, settling back into my seat. "We have not met before, though your livery looks familiar."

"We work for Harry Parker, but I'm sure you didn't come here looking for him," the dark-haired groom snapped.

"That's enough, Wat." Hugh kicked him under the table.

"I seek the Master Secretary. Have you seen him?"

"What do you want with him?" Wat growled.

Hugh jabbed at his partner again before supplying a more helpful response. "He is at Windsor with the king. Our master said they would be returning soon for the wedding."

"Did he say who else may be coming?" Harry Parker was brother to George's wife, Lady Rochford. If she had been summoned back to court, he would be among the first to know.

Wat said, "No" at the same time Hugh replied, "Not the Earl of Northumberland." This time, Wat delivered the kick.

I stared at Hugh, goading him to finish the story. The earl must have been the cause of their earlier whispers.

Wat heaved a sigh, "He collapsed at the feast. They stopped everything until he came back 'round again." His voice deepened, "He hasn't been the same since that woman's trial."

Hugh threw him a look of disgust. "She had a name, Wat."

"You won't hear it out of my mouth," Wat barked.

Poor, frail Henry Percy. None of us had failed to notice how gaunt he appeared the last time he was at court. It still came as a shock when he crumpled to the floor after the guilty verdict was passed. Was it due to illness or perhaps distress at the queen's fall? I was not the only one who remembered the young earl mooning about the royal apartments, trailing after a certain vivacious young woman before she caught the eye of the king. Their intense romance had been short-lived. If only Percy had been allowed to take her to wife. Nan Bullen would still be alive, ruling over the frigid northern counties and driving the wild Scotsmen from our borders.

I changed the subject before anything further damning could be said. "Can I count on one of you to find me when Master Secretary arrives?"

"We're leaving on the morrow." Hugh jerked his thumb in the direction of an elderly groom hunched over the end of the table, shovelling porridge into his mouth. "He may help you."

"And why would I help you?" the man grunted in return, a wet glob flying from his lips.

"Does your wife sew?" I asked, an idea quickly taking shape. "Master Skutt will be after another seamstress. I could put in a good word."

"Truly? My Maude?" He dragged a fist across his mouth, wiping away spittle. "She is an expert needlewoman, and we could use the extra money."

Rising to leave, I threw a linen napkin in his direction. "Send for me when Master Secretary returns, and I'll deal with Skutt. You have my word."

THREE DAYS LATER, the old man was waiting for me in the courtyard outside the wardrobe. I sent Mother Stonor ahead and then followed him around the corner, away from prying eyes.

"He was walking with the Spanish ambassador—Chapuys, I think his name was," he mumbled. "I heard them talking about the king's daughter. The true one, not the bastard. They were headed towards the presence chamber. If you hurry, you might catch him before he leaves."

I squeezed his gnarled hand. "I cannot thank you enough. I must go now."

"Don't forget about my Maude!" he shouted after me.

Pushing past the laundress and several pages, I tore across the yard, only slowing when I reached the corridor leading to the royal lodgings. I ducked inside, catching a tangle of voices coming from down the hall. Cromwell's tone was low, the ends of his sentences lost in the ambient noise, but I heard his companion's high, thin voice. Most of their conversation, conducted in rapid French, was lost on me, but I recognized a few words. As the groom said, they were discussing "Mademoiselle Marie." The ambassador also seemed to be congratulating Cromwell. Only when I heard him say concubine did I understand. He was applauding the man for his part in taking down Anne. I gripped the wall to steady myself against a rush of disgust.

Unable to move closer to the king's rooms without an invitation or the accompaniment of his consort, I slipped back out into the sunlight, sending up a prayer the men would exit the same way. I lingered outside until curious stares compelled me to move along. The instant I made up my mind to leave, the door swung open, and my quarry appeared. Bereft of his compatriot, he strode past me with a blinding purposefulness that indicated a long list of urgent remembrances. Waylaying the secretary meant risking his displeasure, but he had been absent from court as of late, and I did not know when I might get a second opportunity. I took a deep breath. "Master Secretary!"

He halted so abruptly, his cap slipped forward, covering his brow. A furred black cloak swished around his legs as he turned to seek out the source of disruption. "Ah, Mistress Margery, I thought that was you." His dark eyes peered down at me over the scarlet bulb of his nose. I knew he hadn't seen me, and yet the lie was almost convincing.

My words flew out. "I deeply apologize for the intrusion, Sir. I promise not to take but a moment of your time."

"I am sure you won't." He pulled his cap back into place. "What can we do for you?" He stared intently as I made my case for Lady Lisle's daughters, never once allowing a hint of annoyance or impatience to cross his face. Nary was there a flicker of warmth, either. In the past, I found the king's servant to be genial, if not always obliging. Today, he seemed detached, disinterested. He waited until I finished my speech before brushing it off. "Please remind Master Husee that the queen's household appointments are not up to me. The Mistresses Bassett will be submitted for consideration along with all the other eligible young ladies, yourself included."

"Myself?" It had not occurred to me that my position was insecure. "I thought…"

"You know, of course, nothing is ever certain?"

"Of course," I echoed, feeling as though the world had gone off-balance.

"I wouldn't worry too much," he went on. "The king knows you have been a loyal servant."

Loyal to whom? I wondered. Surely not Anne Boleyn, who died because of my careless words. Nor not the crown either. When the Vice-Chamberlain hunted me down for further questioning, I dissembled and denied until he moved on to the other maids. I had not shown fealty to either side. "Thank you, Master Secretary," I mumbled. "It has been a great honour to serve."

Cromwell nodded. "We shall speak soon, Mistress Margery."

Watching him walk away, a sharp pain grew in my chest. King Henry's court had been my home for longer than I could remember; the life I had before no longer existed. My mother was dead. My father was dead. I had nowhere else to go.

I MOVED THROUGH the palace dazed, going through the motions yet never entirely committing myself wholeheartedly to the day's tasks. I sent linen to the wrong apartments. I gave Master Skutt the wrong bolt of velvet and neglected to make good on my promise to speak to him about Maude. The clerk screamed at me for knocking over his inkpot. By the time Master Lloyd sent me to supper, I had thrown the wardrobe into utter disarray. Walking out the door, I heard the clerk muttering to himself about the former queen's poor choice in servant.

Mother Stonor waited for me outside the great hall. Mercifully, her husband, Sir Walter, was along, so she seemed oblivious to my sour mood. We sat together at one of the lower tables, while the courtiers recently returned from Windsor occupied the ones closer to the dais. We received the more elaborate fare served during the king's residency, but I did little more than pick at the rich dishes. Instead, I watched the Stonors banter and jape in the way only couples who had grown comfortable in warm, loving unions could. He carved her meat, and she wiped the crumbs from his beard. They giggled at a memory from long ago and commiserated over the stubbornness of their daughter. If Mother Stonor were dismissed from the household, she would have a port of safety, and I envied her for it.

I sat quietly at the table until an opportune moment for escape presented itself, allowing me to slip out unnoticed. Rather than returning to the desolate dormitory, I headed outside to spend the remaining golden hours of sunlight in the garden. Halfway down the path, I heard a familiar voice calling my name.

"Hello, Master Husee." I took in his ruffled breathlessness, the heaving of embroidery across his broad chest. Sweat glistened at his brow.

"I have been trying to get your attention since you entered the hall. You walked right past my table."

Shame enflamed my skin. "My apologies, I have been a bit lost in my own world."

"Have you spoken with Cromwell?" he interrupted before I could offer more excuses.

"Yes, I saw him this morning."

"And?"

His hopeful gaze caused the pain in my chest to flare anew. "He is not minded to aid Lady Lisle's daughters."

Husee groaned. "I feared as much. Thank you for trying, at least."

"You are welcome. I only regret I could not be of greater assistance."

"Nonsense." He grinned. "You are one of the few ladies here I can rely on." He dipped a shallow bow and then turned to walk away.

"Master Husee," I cried. "It is me who needs your help now."

Husee turned back, his brow furrowed. "What is it?"

"If I should lose my place here, could you …" I halted, measuring my words. "I mean, would you speak to Lady Lisle on my behalf? Find me a place in her household?"

"It would be my honour to do you this favour. Though I highly doubt you will be dismissed, I can say that you would be in good company, for there is another of your former peers in her household."

"Truly?" Tears of relief pricked my eyes. "Who do you mean?"

"The last queen's sister, of course. Mary Boleyn has been in Calais since her banishment. She married a man of Lord Lisle's retinue and goes by the name Stafford now."

JANE SEYMOUR

CHELSEA

O n the river, Edward pestered me for details of my moments alone with the king. I refused to divulge anything. Fury clouding his vision, he did not understand that I did it for his own good. *Anne Boleyn killed her brother with secrets!* I wanted to scream at him. Instead, I met his icy stare with my own until he slunk off defeated. George Boleyn would have been spared if not for his unnatural closeness to his sister, and my brother knew that better than anyone. Had he already forgotten the details of Thomas Wyatt's revelations in the Tower? His tales of the siblings' laughter at the king's dress, the king's poetry, the king's impotence? I would not be so foolish.

Unsatisfied, Edward compelled his wife to coax it out of me. Lady Anne saw the truth as it was and put an end to it. Whether she grew tired of his nagging or imagined herself occupying the same precarious position as George's poor widowed wife, I'll never know. She became even more protective, hardly daring to leave my side. Whatever the reason, I saw her presence as a welcome barrier and invited her to keep me company in the solar.

We worked on an altar cloth for St Mary's, the church near our manor at Wulfhall. With my needle dipping in and out of the fine lawn cloth, I thought of all the services I attended there: funerals and baptisms, masses, and weddings. I should have been standing before that very same altar, speaking my vows. Alas, it was not meant to be. God, and the king, had called me to a higher honour. The humble church where I spent my childhood, and might have married William Dormer, would not be grand enough for a royal wedding. Nor would it be a suitable venue to baptize my child, should the Lord see fit to bless me with one. "A knight's daughter is not supposed to become queen," I mumbled to myself.

The bright snip of Lady Anne's shears cut loose the thought. "Have you decided who you would like to have in your household, Jane?" she asked, tucking a spool of thread into the basket by her feet.

"You are supposed to call her 'Your Grace' now," Elizabeth chirped uncharitably from her cushion across the room. My sister had grown accustomed to her precedence over me after her marriage to Sir Anthony Ughtred; she was incensed by Edward's edict commanding her to return home to serve in my train. I planned to send her back to Yorkshire once I became queen. She was a widow with small children to raise; she belonged with them.

Mother pulled out the needle pinched between her lips. "That's enough, young lady," she scolded. "Be kind to your sister. She will be the one best placed to help you. Sir Anthony left your family with very little to get by."

"It is not as though I need reminding, Mother," Elizabeth sniffed. "Besides, I sincerely doubt Jane will accomplish much on anyone's behalf. The king has been led by the nose through two marriages already. He will not do it again."

"Not true." Dorothy's timid voice almost went unheard under the clamour of our own. Both Elizabeth and I turned to stare at our youngest sister, who sat below the window in a puddle of sunlight. "Edward said the king promised him a title. That must have been Jane's doing, right?"

Her innocent hopefulness burrowed under my skin. I made no reply and instead turned my attention back to the pile of fabric in my lap.

"No, it was not," Lady Anne answered in my stead. She gave me a sympathetic look before going on, "Enough of this. The king will be here shortly, and he'll have no interest in this line of conversation."

"What conversation?" asked Tom, peering around the corner with a wide grin stretched across his face.

"Never you mind," Mother tutted.

"Well, you better finish it up," he replied playfully. "Because His Grace is here."

I MADE MY way to the hall, shame and fear overcoming me at the thought of those dizzying scenes from my betrothal. A nervous twitch rippled through my belly when I remembered His Grace's look of disgust in the chapel. Inciting the king's anger this early on did not bode well for our marriage, and I wondered if he had come to break it off. The prospect of that was equally alarming. Who would want me then?

"There she is!" the king bellowed as he crossed the room to greet me, a great bluster no doubt made to distract from the presence of a slight limp in his walk. Pity flared inside my chest. Knowing better than to mention his leg before an audience, I made a mental note to ask after it when we next found ourselves alone.

"Welcome again, Your Grace." I swept a deep curtsy. "I trust you have been well since we last supped together?" I marvelled at the lack of awkwardness between us; he was clearly pleased to be in my company again.

"Yes, but we have had much and more to do. Crum, here, has kept me going all hours, making ready for your arrival."

At the mention of his name, the king's Master Secretary perked up. "I have come with His Grace today to discuss your household appointments." He shifted an armload of parchment. "Summons will need to go out no later than tomorrow morning if they are to convene by the second day of June when you will be shown as Queen."

"Must I decide so quickly? I had hoped to have some time to think on it more." Master Cromwell smirked. "Surely, you have thought on it for months already."

The king jumped in. "It matters not. We have already settled upon most of the names. All that's left is to confirm them. Now then, another draught of this strong Rhenish wine would do much to fortify me. Sir Edward, would you be so kind?"

My brother refilled the king's cup and then motioned him aside. After a brief whispered exchange, the sovereign nodded his agreement before returning his attention to Cromwell. "Sir Edward has suggested we move to a room with greater privacy." He gestured at the door.

The chamber overlooking the gardens was one of the most extravagant in the house. Hung with Sir William Paulet's costly tapestries and containing a treasure trove of manuscripts, paintings, and furniture, it was also the most unused room in the house. However, it didn't appear that way today. The chamberers had been in before us, as evidenced by the cheery fire blazing in the hearth and the vase of fresh-cut lilies on the table, making the room feel warm and inviting.

Once we settled, Master Cromwell charged ahead with the list of names he had prepared. He began with the great ladies, those who would take precedence over the maids and serve me on special occasions, such as feasts and processions. Included amongst their number were the Duchesses of Suffolk and Richmond, the Marchioness of Dorset, and the Countess of Rutland. I had met them intermittently throughout my time at court but did not know them well. Still, the appointment of Lady Richmond was the only one that made me nervous. She was a near kinswoman of the Boleyn family, and her marriage to the king's bastard, Henry Fitzroy, was made at the behest of the woman who came before me. I wondered if she would give me any trouble.

Next, the secretary moved on to the maids. "You are allotted six, with one extra for the wardrobe," he informed me.

I flinched at the king's lofty suggestion to return most of the women he had just dismissed. "Surely, they are at no fault for that woman's misconduct. Do you not agree they are worthy of reward for their quick report of her behaviour?" he asked. I did not. I wanted virtuous, loyal servants, not ladies who would tell tales about me to serve their own purposes.

"We have Joan and Mary Arundell, Anne Parr, and Mary Zouche. Jane Ashley will return, and Mary Norris will come over from the Lady Elizabeth's household," Cromwell said. "Mother Stonor can stay on Mistress of the Maids, but we need to address Mistress of the Wardrobe. Margery Horsman has been serving in that position, but I don't know that you would like her to continue."

"Why wouldn't I?" Margery was a diligent and reliable young woman, if not always wholly in command of her emotions. Still, she knew the role well, and our friendship went back to the days of our service to the king's first wife.

Cromwell glanced at the king. Seeing that His Grace was more entranced by the distant view of the river than our conversation, he ploughed ahead.

"To speak plainly, my lady, Sir Edward Baynton found Mistress Margery most unhelpful during the recent investigation into the treasons at court. Having been one of the first to report her suspicions about the musician, she inexplicably went mute when he began his inquiries. Apparently, a great friendship arose between her and the former consort in the interim. I suspect she may have been bribed."

Bribery indeed! Anne Boleyn would never stoop to such a thing. More likely, Margery was one of the few maids honouring her oath of service. "Perhaps Sir Edward misconstrued her behaviour. Her actions may have come about more out of fear than villainy," I replied in an even tone. Battles should be chosen carefully; I was not about to turn this into a quarrel. "I would like to offer her a second chance if it so pleases His Grace." Beneath the table, I curled my fingers around the king's hand.

"Yes, of course," he sputtered, his attention finally drawn away from the boats passing beyond the window. "That which pleases you, pleases me, dear heart. Give my lady whatever she desires, Crum."

"As Your Grace wishes. To that end, let us offer the Lady Rochford her former position—If we indeed are to be handing out appointments based upon the need of redemption." He turned a cold eye to me.

"Splendid idea, Crum. Her willingness to return *would* demonstrate approval for the justice delivered upon her husband."

My mouth went dry. Had not the poor woman been through enough? It was far too soon; she needed time to mourn properly. I addressed the king with a simpering smile. "Your Grace," I cooed, stroking his arm gently. "Being as I am in such awe of your wisdom; I wish for nothing more than to conform to your desires. I welcome Lady Rochford's return most wholeheartedly. I merely wonder if we should give her more time to come to terms with her husband's great betrayal. Perhaps she could re-join us before we go on the summer progress?"

Cromwell's eyes bore through me.

The king brought my hand to his lips. "Is not my bride the kindest woman at court?" He aimed his question at the secretary, but his eyes rested upon me. He brought his hand to my face, caressing the curve of my cheek.

Not to be outdone, Cromwell offered an alternative. "Then perhaps another Boleyn family member? Do I recall a niece?"

King Henry's expression hardened. "Mary Stafford's daughter is too young. It would be most unsuitable."

Hoping to save him from further irritation, I changed tact. "Wouldn't it be lovely, Your Grace, if your eldest daughter served me?"

A scowl stormed the king's face. "No! Absolutely not!" he barked. "She will not step foot in my court until she admits the truth of my marriage to her mother and recognizes me as head of the church. I shall not reward her insubordination. I have already warned you not to overstep, Madame."

I looked to Cromwell for help. He had gone white, his long fingers knotted together. He glanced away. "I am deeply sorry to be the cause of such offense. I merely thought, with her great enemy gone, the Lady Mary would be a wonderful ornament to your glorious court. Please forgive me," I pleaded. How I hated to deny the princess her title.

My contrition did not move his Grace. "You will defer to me, Jane," he replied coldly. "Just as my obstinate daughter will do, or she will find herself reduced to the same state as her great enemy."

My hands grew damp against the cool damask of my skirt. Only a monster could condemn his child to death. My own father had always spared his daughters the worst punishment, never dealing us anything more than a few stern words. "I am yours to command, Your Grace." I willed myself not to cry. Neither the king nor his ministers would ever be privy to my tears.

"It is settled then. Mistress Margery shall stay on, and we will return to the matter of Lady Rochford in a few months," Cromwell broke in, resolving the tense silence. "Now, there is the matter of your badge and beast. His Grace has suggested a panther since the existing leopards can be easily adapted to curb costs. With the work being carried out to remove the former consort's symbols and a coronation on the horizon, the royal treasury is under great strain. You understand, I am sure?"

"I have had another thought, Crum," the king interrupted. "The badge should be a phoenix. We are rising from the ashes; all our hopes reborn." He slammed his fist on the table. "There can be no better symbol."

Cromwell's quill scratched across the parchment: panther, phoenix; his scrawl all thick lines and sharp angles. "And the motto you have chosen?"

Gazing at their expectant faces, I realized the motto I had settled upon would not do. It seemed too forceful and imprudent, considering the king's remonstrance. It sounded too much like his last wife. I needed a safe and submissive motto, one that underscored my desire to please the king. Taking inspiration from the wedding vows I was soon to be repeating, I composed a replacement, as sovereign and secretary stared back at me. "How about, Bound to Obey and Serve?" I answered, for I would be constrained to do both whether I willed it or not. At least by my brother, if not the king. Without a doubt, Edward was eavesdropping outside the door, sore that his opinion was not required.

"A most excellent motto, my lady. Would that everyone in the realm would follow your example." Cromwell was unable to hide the admiration in his voice.

"We shall have it emblazoned on everything: plates, cups, bed hangings..." the king bellowed. Raising me from the chair, he planted a kiss on my fingertips. I tried not to flinch at his touch. "There is much yet to accomplish, so we must go. I will send a barge tomorrow to carry you to York Place, where we shall finally be married."

"I look forward to it." I swept a low curtsy. Maybe it would all be easier once I was queen. Perhaps I would succeed where Anne Boleyn had not.

MARGERY HORSMAN

YORK PLACE

J ane Seymour returned to court in much the same way she fled it mere weeks before: travelling by royal barge under cover of darkness, her furtive arrival kept hidden from the people to contain any murmurings against it. But, as it was with most secrets at court, it was ill-kept. By the next afternoon, most of the household had become aware of her presence, and the news was eagerly passed from one famished ear to the next.

John Husee told me he had been down at the quayside when the barge docked, taking delivery from a merchant carrying a package from the Lisles. "Wine and quails," he explained with a raised brow. Like I cared what bribes his masters had shipped over. Impatient, I urged him on. "I can stop, if you have somewhere else you need to be," he goaded.

"Tell me, Husee!" I stomped my foot but was still glad to see him despite my annoyance.

He adopted a conspiratorial tone. "She was wrapped in a cloak the colour of night, bundled off the barge, and up the king's privy stair so quickly, I thought I imagined the whole affair."

I shared his sense of bewilderment at the surreal unfolding of these events. Only nine days had passed since Queen Anne's execution. After we parted ways, I sought out Mother Stonor in the private apartments she kept with her husband on the king's side, looking for both comfort and reassurance.

"Is everything all right, Margery?" she asked, swinging the door wide to let me inside. "I was just going out to meet our new mistress, but I can spare a moment."

"Oh—I did not realize the summons had gone out. I never received one."

The distress in my voice drew her attention from the goblets she was filling for our refreshment. She held my gaze, a line of worry creasing her brow. Setting the ewer of wine back on the table, she said, "Do not fret, child. I am certain it will come."

I offered a half-hearted smile. I had not been a child for many years, but perhaps I still was in her eyes. Regardless, the mark of affection left a curious warmth in my chest. "I'm sure you are right," I answered, accepting the goblet she held aloft.

Mother Stonor moved to a chair by the window, her soft slippers trudging across the rushes, wafting the citrus tang of juniper into the air. I settled into a cushion near her feet, and we sat quietly, sipping our wine in the sunlight. It reminded me of the peaceful afternoons I spent growing up in the Countess of Salisbury's household. I had loved perching close to the great lady, listening as she read aloud from a book of psalms. The insistent clang of the abbey bell battered the glow of the memory.

"Goodness, I have to be going." Mother Stonor lurched from her seat, panic-stricken by her forgetfulness of the time. Trundling past, she snagged the half-empty goblet from my hand.

Rising from the cushion, I crossed the floor to make my exit and found myself biting back a sarcastic remark about Mistress Seymour's impatience. A woman had been put to death by Jane's haste to be queen; God forfend we should keep her waiting. I thought better of it, keeping my mouth clamped firmly shut instead. Mother Stonor had already reminded me once this week to be watchful of my words. "Shall I see you at vespers?" I asked instead.

"Of course. And try not to worry so much, Margery."

ON MY WAY back to the dormitory, I passed Lady Lee in the corridor. She wore a vacant expression, her eyes devoid of the playful light I had always seen in them. When I smiled, her lips parted to return the greeting. They froze somewhere between a grin and a grimace as if she had forgotten how. She quickened her pace, her face falling blank again. Before I could utter a word, she was gone. It surprised me little to find Lady Lee in such straights, considering her brother's predicament. Thomas Wyatt had been carried up in the maelstrom surrounding the queen's fall, and though he did not follow the other men to the scaffold, he still languished within the Tower walls. For him, the danger had not passed.

Turning the corner, I was brought up short by the sound of a familiar voice down the hall. The maids were finally returning to court. Racing to the door, I flung it open to find a flustered Mistress Ashley chastising a pair of chamberers lugging an oversized trunk between them. "No, not there. I want it by the other window."

"Is everything all right in here?"

"It will be once these two figure it out," Mistress Ashley moaned. "Not that one—the other one!"

The chamberers exchanged a grievous look, then dropped the trunk with a heavy thud. One of them rolled his eyes, edging past us through the doorway. The other nodded before giving me a parting smile. "Always a pleasure, Mistress Margery."

"What was that about?" Mistress Ashley demanded, pulling the tawny velvet hood from her head. She tossed it on the nearest bed, then kneaded her temples.

"Nothing, he has been delivering coal for my brazier. I have hardly spoken to him," I replied dismissively. His greeting was of less importance than the looming possibility my secret would be quickly discovered by the dorm's returning occupant. I tried to decipher her plans. "Did you receive a summons? Are you back for good?"

Her eyes combed our surroundings. "Long as our old friend Jane pleases His Grace." Left unspoken, the likely result of his displeasure seemed to dim the light of the room.

She flinched when I reached up to tuck a wayward strand into the knot of ochre hair at her neck. "She will. I am sure of it," I soothed, despite my uncertainty. I needed her to leave so I could move the necklace, but I could not staunch the flow of words. I blamed the nerves. "I am pleased to see you again. The silence has been deafening."

"You should have savoured the solitude. Pretty soon, you will not have a moment to yourself."

"Perhaps not. There has been no summons for me. I am expecting my dismissal at any time."

Mistress Ashley grimaced. "Is that it?" She gestured at the folded sheet of parchment at the foot of my bed. "A page came while you were gone." It seemed so innocuous lying there, nothing more than ink and fibre. My hands grew clammy at the sight of it. "Well, go on then," she urged.

Without stopping to think, I ran over and cracked the seal. The page trembled in my grip. "She wants to see me after vespers."

"For good or for ill?"

"It does not say."

"You cannot wear that hood." She frowned. "I have already been told to put away my French ones. Have you any that are gabled?" To my great horror, she darted towards my trunk, yanking the lid open before I could stop her.

"Stop!" I pushed her away. "Stay out of there." Jane Ashley was the last person I wanted to find the necklace. She hated Anne Boleyn ever since the queen and Lady Rochford had conspired to get her exiled from court and taken to mocking her with the name Mistress Marchpane. Mistress Ashley never forgave her for it, and neither did she forget. I had yet to see a piece of the sweet she loved so much cross her lips since.

"What do you have in there? A pair of vipers?" Arms folded across her chest, she glared at me from the safety of her bed.

"I have just spent hours straightening it," I lied, wiping away the sweat that had beaded above my lip. "I never meant to push. Did I hurt you?"

She grabbed her hood, wresting it back on to her head. She turned from me. "Forget it. Let us go to supper."

Heart sinking, my eyes skimmed the burnished latches of my trunk. The cursed treasure inside would have to wait.

I DEVOURED SO much food in the great hall, I feared I might burst before making it to the chapel for our evening prayers. I took a portion from each tray that came to our table, inhaling each morsel as if it were to be my last. Afterward, the food gurgled and roiled like a cauldron on the fire as the minister's droning monotone and the stench of bodies in the chapel filled the air. I kept checking the queen's closet, hoping to catch a glimpse of her, and perhaps a foreshadowing of what awaited me when the service was over. Her seat remained empty. Wherever the king kept his paramour in the palace, she was safely out of sight.

Fleeing after the last "Amen," I hurried off to wash my face and change my hood before my audience with the future queen. If even the slightest chance of retaining my position remained, I had no intention of losing it with such a silly mistake. Mistress Ashley had not yet made it back to the dorm by the time I was ready, so I sat in the shadows, gathering my thoughts. Perhaps I could bury the necklace somewhere on the grounds in the morning? Though I was alone, there simply was not enough time to do it now without arousing suspicion. All too quickly, I was due see my new mistress. I found some comfort in knowing that an answer to at least one problem was soon to come; I could worry about the path beyond after. My heartbeat slowed. I took a deep breath, then stepped out into the corridor.

"Mistress Horsman? I have been waiting for you." He stood in the darkness between the torches. When I gasped, he stepped into the light. "Forgive me for the fright. Sir Edward Seymour sent me to collect you. Her Grace is awaiting your attendance."

"That is quite all right. You are not the first to surprise me in a dark hallway, and I am sure you will not be the last." I sighed, thinking of Master Husee. "You seem familiar, but I do not think we have properly met. You know my name; would you kindly share yours?"

"Please, call me Michael." The skin around his eyes crinkled when he smiled. They were grey as London fog and framed by long dark lashes. Beneath them, a smattering of freckles decorated the bridge of his nose; lower still, he sported a full beard the same rich chestnut as the tousled hair peeking out from beneath his cap. Handsome, he was, but more importantly, he seemed to exude a quiet tenderness in the delicacy of his features. I fought an overwhelming urge to embrace him.

We started down the corridor. "Do you serve the king?" I inquired. He towered over me, and I struggled to match his stride.

Noticing my difficulty, he slowed. "Occasionally. I have a son at home in Herefordshire, so I try not to spend too much time away from him. The king has been very gracious in allowing me to serve at court when I am able."

"It is wonderful you get to see him so often. At least he still has his mother when you are not there. Does she ever come to court with you?"

Michael drooped beside me. He cast his gaze towards the floor, staring down at the stonework. Silence filled the space between us. After a few paces, he glanced over at me, his eyes bright and wet. "No, she died giving birth to our son."

"How awful. I am truly sorry for your loss. Was it long ago?" I felt a rush of guilt for prying into the sadness of a stranger, but I had always been drawn to the darkness of mourning. Losing my mother at the commencement of my earliest living memories left me with an insatiable curiosity for the details of another's grief. When and how had it happened? Was it an untimely tragedy or long expected? What scent or sound, touch or taste conjured the spectre of their loved one, stirring that familiar ache in their heart? Those were the questions for which I craved an answer, in the hopes that, somehow, it would quell my overwhelming sense of loss.

"Three winters ago." Michael halted abruptly outside the courtier lodgings. I hadn't noticed we had gone past the hallway leading to the queen's rooms. Seeing confusion upon my face, he gestured at Sir Edward Seymour, who was leaning rather stolidly against the wall, one shoulder slung lower than the other. "Her Grace has not yet been installed in her apartments, so she is staying with her brother. He will take you from here." He dipped a bow to us both, then turned to leave.

"I hope to see you again, Master—" I paused. He had not told me his family name.

"Michael. Just Michael," he called over his shoulder. "All the best to you, Mistress Horsman."

Sir Edward said little beyond the range of polite conversation during the short walk to his apartment, preferring to always stay a few steps ahead. Not that we had much to say to each other, for when it came down to it, while we were both glorified servants, his status had grown alongside his sister's, reaching an echelon to which I would never be admitted. That notion might have troubled others in my position. It suited me fine. I once desired a man with money and a title. Neither of those things saved him in the end. Any regard I may have had for those trappings died the day he did. But who was Sir Edward to have usurped such authority? What made his opinion better than anyone else's? Nothing that I could see.

Sir Edward's cool demeanour noticeably warmed nearing the doorway where his wife was waiting. Though Anne Seymour had a reputation for being demanding and overbearing, one would certainly never believe it by the gaze of adoration they exchanged. Sir Edward placed a gentle kiss on her cheek, excusing himself while she ushered me inside. Cromwell had told Husee, this was the business of women. He was leaving us to it.

Having never been asked into any courtier lodgings before, I had no basis for comparison; nevertheless, the opulence was staggering. Underneath the ornately carved walnut furniture lay several plush Turkish carpets. Rich velvet arras tied back by twisted gold cords hung on the walls, and flickering beeswax candles danced above the tables, casting a warm glow over the room. The atmosphere felt soft and close, like a womb. I struggled to catch my breath, wondering if it had been furnished in anticipation of the Seymour sister's new title. How presumptuous of Sir Edward to arrange his apartments with such finery ahead of the sovereign's latest consort. Whatever the case, my pondering was cut short by the arrival of the woman herself.

Jane looked plumper than I remembered. Her features had grown rounder since she was last at court, and even her chin had begun to recede into the flesh growing around it. Yet, she had not gained enough that she had gone to fat. Truthfully, the added weight made her appear more attractive, content. When Queen Anne was at her most joyous, we always had to let out her gowns. During the worst of times, we cinched the waists tighter. Towards the end, she seemed so painfully thin I feared she would waste away. Though we hid it the best we could, I remained ever mindful of what lay beneath the padding and heavy fabrics. Her replacement needed none of those habiliments.

I froze when she entered the room, unsure of which reverence to give. A nod? A curtsy? How low? Last month, we occupied the same station. I would have offered her none. Since then, her position had changed considerably, though she was not yet crowned. Sensing my hesitation, she offered a bit of guidance, "Get the first one out of the way, and the rest will come much easier."

"Yes, Your Grace," I quipped reflexively, sinking so low I nearly lost my balance.

"Well, I do not require you to be quite that dramatic, but you have done it, and there is no need for further awkwardness between us."

"But there isn't—"

"Margery," she interrupted my lame protests. "Let us be honest with each other, as we always have been. Now, please rise so I can see you properly."

I rose, shifting my gaze from the floor to her face. "My only wish is to serve."

"I know," she replied, tugging a stray thread hanging from her gown. The movement drew my attention to her sleeves, and I recognized them instantly. They were black satin embroidered with gold acorns and honeysuckle. "I want you to serve me."

"Truly?" Was she toying with me?

She dropped into a nearby chair. Thrumming her fingers on the upholstered arms, she stared at me. Drawing a deep breath, she began, "Your loyalty was to the Boleyns, I know. Perhaps more for George's sake than his sister's. Oh, do not deny it, I was there and saw the way you looked at him." She waited for my swell of defiance to pass before proceeding. I had refuted the charge for so long, my reaction had become instinctive. "Not that I owe anyone an explanation, but I want you to know I never wished for their deaths and can assure you it was not done at my behest. Yet, they are gone, and I cannot change that."

"It is more my fault than yours. It was I who told Master Cromwell about Marc Smeaton. Though there was nothing truly to tell." While it pained me to admit it, the confession made me feel lighter once it was out.

"No, that burden is not yours to carry. There was already—" She held up a hand as if to stop herself. "None of that matters. Do you want to stay, Margery? Can you be loyal to me?"

Honouring her request for honesty, I gave it. "I will try."

"I believe you." She rose from the chair. The gold embroidery on her gown winked in the candlelight. "Is there anything else you would like to tell me?"

"Your sleeves…Skutt made them for her."

"Yes, I thought as much." She walked towards the bedchamber where Lady Seymour had retreated at the start of our meeting. Disappearing briefly, she re-emerged with her brother's wife in tow. "Lady Seymour will see you out."

I leaned into another curtsy. This time it was not as deep. "Thank you, Your Grace."

"Put your faith in me, Margery. I will do my best to shield you from harm."

Much as I desired the position, it made getting the necklace to Calais and Mary Stafford insurmountable. I wanted to believe Jane, now more than ever. Yet, how could she ever protect me? There was no safety in this realm; the preceding weeks had put that notion to rest forever more.

DIAMONDS

Faithfulness

JUNE 1536

JANE SEYMOUR

YORK PLACE

K ept in seclusion since my arrival back at court, I spent the long days
holed up in my brother's over-extravagant apartments, watching
the hours drag past. Edward offered up his vast array of thick, leath-
erbound manuscripts for my enjoyment, but studious as he was, I never
developed a taste for it. Preferring more earthly pursuits, I longed to feel
the dew-soaked grass beneath my feet and the warm caress of the sun
on my neck. Trapped within the stifling bowels of my brother's velvet
drenched rooms, I settled for embroidery. Needle in hand, with a stretch
of empty fabric before me, I retained some modicum of control. The use
of colour and design was my choice, and no one else's. I decided which
stitches went where and whether the finished product would be used in
the church to honour God or for more secular purposes. It was not much,
but it sufficed.

As the young women chosen to serve me wended their way back to
London, I pounced on the opportunity to meet with them privately upon
their arrival, in hopes of easing any lingering tension and uncertainty. I
was no longer one of their number and wanted to set clear expectations
and boundaries. Anne Boleyn's court had thrived in the ambiguous void
between mistress and servant. I would brook no such liberties. Drawing an
unbreachable line between myself and my maids seemed the safest course
of action. At the same time, I worried about alienating them. Distance

cultivated both deference and indifference. I dreaded the latter. My maids need not venerate me, though their respect was imperative.

"In whatever way you choose to rule them, do not nourish their fearful nature," Lady Seymour counselled when I summoned the first girl to our chambers.

"Fear? Why should anyone fear me?" I balked.

"You were once an equal, privy to opinions never dared muttered to those above. They may expect reprisals. You must assure them the past is forgotten."

Her advice looming large, I drew each maid into my confidences, and by the time my audiences finished, I felt more assured of their loyalty than I anticipated. Still, I never dared forget how quickly their allegiances flew from Anne Boleyn to me. One morning, they were all sighing at her knees; the next, they brought me comfits and wine. Both had tasted rancid.

The harrowing month shuddered to an end, and my life began anew in the small closet where I would forevermore say my prayers as the queen consort to Henry Tudor. We exchanged marriage vows in a candlelit ceremony at dawn, witnessed only by my brothers and the Archbishop of Canterbury. Afterward I knelt in supplication at the altar, fervently praying that this second royal wedding conducted by the churchman would bear sweeter fruit than the first. Later, when the king asked for what I prayed, I answered, "For nothing more than your good health and well-being, Your Grace. Long may you reign."

We processed to the great hall with less pomp than would accompany a funeral. I felt ashamed. Though none of the courtiers would have dared say so aloud, I suspected many of them found our hasty marriage distasteful. How could they not? Any reasonable person would have waited for the memory of the condemned to pass, but King Henry was not a reasonable man; he had proven so again and again. Still, time waited for no man, much less a disgraced queen. There were heirs to be gotten, and if I wanted to continue in this world, I had better conceive sons.

When I entered the hall, the noise died away, and all eyes swivelled in my direction. Malice lurked behind fewer simpering smiles than I had anticipated. Most of the watchers appeared merely exhausted. Those seated joined the rest on their feet and then, in chorus, bobbed in reverence to us. "Good people," the king blustered. "Recent events have dealt a terrible blow to both my family and the realm. A woman with cruel intentions bewitched her way into my heart, and her ill-workings brought great danger to those I hold dear. In my distress, I have not been of a mind to take on another wife. Alas, my Privy Council's persuasive urging has convinced me of its necessity for the protection and quietness of the realm. I have followed their advice and my heart. And so, it is with great pleasure that I present to you my entirely beloved bride."

My cheery expression belied the uncertainty I felt. It was discomfiting to have the attention of the whole court and their stares boring through me. Never again could I melt away into the crowd. Taking my husband's proffered hand, I dutifully followed him to the dais, where we took our seats beneath the canopy of estate. Up here, the goblets were gold, the napkins made of Holland cloth. During the ensuing feast, the nuptial gifts were presented, and I found myself flushing with an odd mixture of embarrassment and pleasure as the names of my manors—all one hundred and four of them—were read out for everyone to hear. Just as quickly, a stab of guilt turned my guts to water.

Noticing my wan face, the king leaned close to whisper in my ear. "Is something the matter, my love? I know it can all seem a bit overwhelming at first."

"I wish the rest of my family could be here, is all." I looked to Edward, who was seated at a nearby table with his wife and Tom. It had been his orders that kept them home. He did not want any distractions.

"Yes, of course, you do," the king said, stroking my hand. He knew what it meant to long for a missing parent, his mother having died during his youth. "We will invite them to court soon to celebrate with us. They shall have the finest lodgings and a banquet held in their honour. I wish to thank them for the beautiful gift they have given me in you." He looked so childlike, so eager—as if he would give me anything in the world, I needed only ask. All I wanted was to love him. To look upon him and feel adoration in my heart rather than despair. Maybe it was possible yet. Perhaps I was wrong, and Anne Boleyn deserved her death. Perhaps it was me who was unreasonable, not the king. Maybe I had been given this chance to help restore the Princess Mary to her rightful place. I should have been rejoicing, rather than stewing in ungrateful wretchedness.

"Thank you, Your Grace," I mumbled, my skin flushing. "Mother would love that."

The king kissed my fingertips. He then pressed my palm to his face, his beard stiff and wiry against my skin. "Give yourself to me, Jane, and you will want for nothing ever again." Before I could reply, the heralds sounded, announcing the king's painter. "Hans, we have been expecting you," His Grace quipped, flinging my hand away, all tenderness swept aside in an instant.

Master Holbein strode into the hall, elegantly weaving through the crowded tables, a massive cup worked in gold cradled in his arms. When he reached the dais, he hefted the piece on to the table, then stepped back, bending neatly at the waist. A breath later, he straightened, triumph upon his face. "A gift from the king," he said. For a foreigner, his accent was oddly refined; he sounded more English than German. It was an affectation, no doubt cultivated by his many years on our island, serving in the cultured household of Thomas More and the royal court.

I turned my attention from the painter's heavy-lidded eyes to the cup looming before me, a gasp escaping as I took in the exquisite detail. The main piece was banded with intricate scrollwork, a nude bust carved into the centre; masks in relief decorating either side. Below, two shimmering fat pearls hung beside an enormous diamond settled between the golden petals of the Tudor rose. Encircling the base were more of these roses, each cupping a smaller stone. A matching lid, crowned with mermaids and cherubim, fit seamlessly into the top. Our entwined initials were worked into one of the bands. My newly chosen motto was engraved on both the lid and the stem, reminding me of all that I had promised: obedience and servitude.

"How extraordinary," I breathed, tracing my finger across the scrollwork. The chill of the metal on my skin jolted me back to a sunny afternoon of my childhood when I stole into the chapel for a taste of the communion wine. Why I had done such a thing was still beyond my comprehension, but for whatever reason, I was compelled to investigate this seemingly magical chalice that could change wine into Christ's blood. When the chaplain had been summoned to quiet the cries of the bereaved wife of one of our tenants, I seized my opportunity.

I had expected something akin to the single piece of Venetian glass Mother owned—a goblet gifted from her aunt, the Countess of Surrey. At the very least, it would resemble the pewter tankard from which my father drank his ale. The vessel I found was nothing like I had imagined. It was simple and unadorned; a plain wooden cup that warmed my hands. The chaplain caught me, just as the rim kissed my lips. To distract him from my unfulfilled quest, I challenged the state of this holiest of grails. Why was it not finer? In his infinite wisdom, the chaplain replied with a question of his own, "What need does a carpenter have of gold?"

In the cradle of this recollection, it struck me: these gifts were a seduction.

"Are you pleased?" my husband prodded, dragging my attention away.

"Yes, of course," I replied, my words counterfeit.

"I'm happy to hear that. Now, it is your turn to please me."

CONTRARY TO WHAT some might have believed, I had never lain with a man before my wedding. The king was far too concerned about our future children's legitimacy to dare risk a premature conception. "I learned that lesson with my daughter, Elizabeth," he told me at the beginning of our courtship. He named her a bastard several months later. Neither had I been with anyone else. I had rarely garnered any more illicit attention than a perfunctory smile or nod in all my years at court. Yet, I was not afraid for all my inexperience when the king took my hand and led me from the great hall.

Margery Horsman was waiting when I arrived to claim my suite of rooms. She followed me to the bedchamber, proceeding to remove the layers of fabric adorning my body, leaving only the silk chemise underneath. The king, accompanied by a band of courtiers, appeared in the doorway before she could cover me with a robe. "Everyone out!" he thundered, slamming the door. They all skittered out of sight, my maid following closely behind. He wasted no time as we took to the bed. Shoving my chemise up around my thighs, he drove into me. Mother had said there would be a sharp pinch, so I was surprised when none came. After a few half-hearted thrusts, I realized he had gone limp. He collapsed then, heaving in frustrated anger.

I laid there quietly, feeling the immense weight of him atop me. The force of his frayed breaths pushed me deeper into the mattress. Running my hands up his sweat-slicked back, I curled my fingers through his damp hair, and waited for him to harden.

He started again, slowly at first. Quickening his pace, he found a rhythm. Soon he began to grunt and moan. I yelped at the pain. It only seemed to stoke his lust. He poked urgently, hungrily, until at last, he gave a great shudder, crying out the last name I expected. "Anne!"

It should have hurt, hearing that. I felt nothing more than the deep ache between my legs. Offering no consolation, he rolled away. I found myself wondering if he even realized what he had said. "Thank you again for my beautiful gifts," I murmured. "No one has ever been so generous to me."

"Think nothing of it." The king stared absently at the ceiling above us, where a gilded falcon glittered in the candlelight of the sconce beneath it. Swinging his legs off the bed, he rose with a grunt. Shrugging his shirt over his broad shoulders, he grabbed his purple velvet robe from the foot of the bed. He slid his arms through the sleeves, then knelt for a stiff, dry kiss. "I shall be back for supper."

True to his word, he returned that evening in a merry mood. He arrived wearing an effusive grin and a richly embroidered gown, studded with blue and green jewels. The days were growing longer with the warmer weather, and I relished the knowledge that soon we would spend more time outdoors. In my excitement for the coming pleasure of afternoons in the field hunting and hawking, a shadow of uncertainty darkened the mood. Who would accompany me on these outings? On most occasions, the king would be there, but I needed an attendant of sufficient rank to join me when he could not; someone pleasant, sweet, and above reproach.

"What has you so occupied, my queen?" The king settled into his place at the head of the table. He lifted a folded linen napkin from the table, straightened it with a snap, then threw it over his shoulder with practiced ease.

"Nothing of any great import, Your Grace." I draped my own linen carefully, ever fearful of staining my new dress. "I was merely reminiscing about the summers we spent chasing deer in the park surrounding Wulfhall. My sisters and I had such fun. 'Tis a great pity they will not be able to join me this year."

The king speared a roasted plover with his knife. Cupping his hand beneath to catch any escaping juices, he moved it to his plate. "And why should they not? I see no reason to exclude them." He dipped his fingers into the washing bowl again before eating the bird.

I tore a hunk off the loaf of bread lying on the table between us. It was soft and spongy, unlike the manchet I usually ate. "Elizabeth has gone back home to Yorkshire, and Edward is nearing the end of his negotiations for Dorothy's marriage. I do not expect either will spend much time here—at least for the near future."

My husband chewed thoughtfully, turning the question over in his mind. He swallowed, then drank deep from his cup before answering. "How about Suffolk's wife? Or perhaps Dorset or Rutland's women? You have plenty to choose from."

"Yes, but—" I played for time, crafting the right words.

The king set down his knife. Wiping his fingers, he turned his attention to me. "What, Jane? I am listening."

"Well, I worry about encouraging any undue familiarity. I would be more comfortable with someone closer to my rank."

"There is no one closer than a duchess," he scoffed. "Besides, it has never been a problem in the past."

"It hasn't?" Had the man forgotten that his last wife was brought low by such intimacies with her subordinates?

The king gawped at me. "And who do you suggest, then?"

"Perhaps Lady Mary would be suitable…"

The king burst into a deep belly laugh. He howled until his face grew ruddy with the effort, fat tears rolling down his cheeks. "Oh, Jane. That was an admirable effort," he panted, laughter ebbing away. "But until my daughter gives me what I want, she is not welcome at my court. I would rather send her to the scaffold."

"You cannot possibly mean that," I gasped, horrified by the very thought.

"I mean every word of it, I assure you." The king's face tightened, his eyes narrowing, all mirth gone. "I have given that girl every chance to amend her ways, to show me the respect a daughter owes her father. She will not. She begs men—*my men*—to support her disobedience against my will. Master Cromwell, the privy council, all subjected to her desperate entreaties and mewling letters. It ends now. Once Parliament meets, I shall send her my terms. If she disagrees, she will find herself keeping company with her mother in the grave."

I bit my lip hard against an angry retort, tasting the sharp tang of blood on my tongue. I made my gambit and lost. I would receive no further warnings. Noble as it was, and no matter the depths of my loyalty to her mother, my efforts to bring Mary back into the fold were going to get us both killed. "Your Grace, I—"

"I prefer to finish eating in my room," he snarled to the chamberer. Tossing his napkin aside, he turned his ire to me. "We leave for Greenwich on Friday. Have your household ready for travel. Until then, I bid you good night, Madame."

MARGERY HORSMAN

YORK PLACE

Queen Jane had seemed calm, almost serene, while I fussed about, pulling off her gown and kirtle. When the king burst in to collect her maidenhood, she held her ground without a quiver of hesitation. It seemed an incredible show of bravery to me. What virgin did not quake at the thought of her husband's first prodding? Or was it merely my own dread of the act that caused me to think so? Regardless, all pretence of courage had faded away by the time she called me back later that evening to prepare her for bed. Her puffy eyes and swollen lips belied the secrecy of her tears.

Lady Anne Seymour met me at the door, hovering nearby while I worked. She watched me help the queen into her nightgown and then comb the tangles from her straw-coloured hair. The lady's mouth fluttered open more than once, but she kept her peace until I finished my tasks. When I stepped out into the corridor, arms laden with pieces to go back to the wardrobe, the words came. "Speak of this to no one," she hissed. Though my quickly nodded assent was to appease her, I would have kept the queen's misery to myself even without her prompting. My duty bound me to obey. Still, there was something even more compelling driving my discretion: pity. The roots of it had taken hold that day in the Seymours' presence chamber, when I saw the queen wearing those beautiful sleeves made for someone else. The furtive tears, shed on the day of what should have been a great triumph, served to nourish the seedling.

In the days following, the last of the maids straggled into court. Trunks and carts, loaded with the trappings of their fine new wardrobes, followed behind in a steady stream, throwing the dorm into utter disarray. The weeks of solitude had made me wistful for the return of the noisy chaos of my compatriots. Now that my wish had been fulfilled, I was finding it somewhat overwhelming. No matter where I stepped, I managed to tread upon someone's gown or cloak, and nothing ever remained where I left it, each slipper or hood seeming to disappear into some unseen realm. Worst still, my efforts to hide the necklace were waylaid at every turn.

I managed to smuggle the thing out to a hole I had dug in one of the gardens but could not bring myself to lower it into the ground. It felt too funereal. Soon after, I happened upon a loose stone in a wall near the river stair. That plot came to undignified end when Husee appeared out of nowhere, startling me enough to require a change of undergarments. Another, involving one of the wardrobe's empty cupboards came to naught when Master Lloyd set his clerk to a reorganization program. News that we were to move on to Greenwich for the Whitsun festivities only made things more difficult and I was far too busy to carry out further plans. For the time being, my trunk would have to do. Mercifully, the rest of the maids were similarly preoccupied.

The preparations for such a progress created an enormous burden. Every night, I collapsed in exhaustion. An unending stream of servants bustled throughout the palace, dismantling entire rooms to be packed and loaded on a train of carriages and sent ahead to the next destination. This included most of the royal wardrobe. Of the queen's portion, I took charge. The brevity of our excursion would make things especially taxing. Just when it seemed as though everything had finally been put into place, it would be time to pack it all back up again. Knowing we would be at Greenwich for less than a week made the effort feel ever more painful.

When Mother Stonor arrived to collect me for Master Lloyd, she surveyed the dorm with disgust. "This is unacceptable. You ladies were born of great and ancient houses, not sheep farmers. Clean this hovel." When I knelt to pick up a stray nightgown tossed to the floor in haste that morning, she slapped it out of my hand. "Not you, Margery, you're needed at the wardrobe. Mistress Norris," she called out to my bed mate, "you'll finish packing Mistress Horsman's trunk."

"No, thank you," I yelped, my face burning. They all turned to stare. Mistress Ashley smirked at me from behind her hand. "You have enough to do, don't trouble yourself."

"Nonsense," Stonor barked. "It is nothing more than she can handle. If she cannot manage, Mistress Ashley will."

Mary Norris' gaze flitted from Mistress Ashley's face to mine. Sensing my unspoken desperation, she addressed Stonor with a radiant smile. "That won't be necessary. I will help Margery."

MASTER LLOYD HAD worked himself into a frenzy by the time we arrived. We found him pacing, red-faced and breathless, before a line of open parcels. "I wasn't expecting this delivery from Skutt until our return, but it has come today and cannot wait. The fabric will wrinkle if we leave it too long."

Stonor gave me a gentle push. "I shall be back for you later," she said, dipping out the door.

I pulled a kirtle from the first crate; it was made of satin dyed a lush peacock blue and edged with tiny seed pearls. "Some of these pieces are jewelled—it must have taken months to finish them. I do not recall this order."

"They were made for Queen Jane, not that other woman." Lloyd gave a dismissive wave. "Please get everything hung. The porter will be here in a few hours to load the trunks bound for Greenwich."

The urgency of my task left little time for fretting, but the moment I stopped to take a breath, I had a vision of Mistress Norris rifling through my trunk, and a sudden sense of panic overtook me. As a rule, I tended to keep my belongings tidy. I treasured what little I had, knowing I would never be able to replace it. Service in the royal household meant I was well-fed and slept with a roof over my head, yet I did not earn much in the way of an income. I'd not had a new gown, outside the queen's livery, in ages. The rarity of such pleasures compelled me to keep most of it safely packed away. However, I had left a few things strewn about, and the items that had gone astray earlier in the week were sure to turn up when the dorm was restored to order. It seemed unfathomable that Mistress Norris would not open my trunk. I only prayed she was not as nosy as some of the other maids.

When Master Lloyd released me from my duties, I sprinted back to my room. As expected, the clothing had been picked up and put away, the beds had been made, and fresh rush mats covered the floor. A clean kirtle and one of my best gowns were draped across the stool next to my bed. The spot where I kept my trunk was empty.

"There you are! Everyone else has already gone down for supper." Joan Arundell stalked into the room, pulling the hood from her head, a curtain of gold cascading over her shoulders. She collapsed on her bed with a grimace, tucking her skirt around her legs before laying back. "Have you anything for a toothache? It throbs," she groaned miserably.

"In my trunk, perhaps. Do you know where it is?"

Joan rubbed her jaw. "Last I saw, Mistress Norris was putting your slippers in it. We found them under another maid's bed. It was the oddest thing. How did they end up there? No wonder you could not find them." She tried to laugh. It came out more like a moan. "Anyway, the porter came 'round soon after to take our stuff to the baggage carts. I have not seen it since then."

Her indifference offered a small measure of comfort; the maids would have been scandalized to discover the necklace. Yet, I could not be sure Mistress Norris had not seen it, or worse—taken it. "I am heading to the great hall now; I will ask if she remembered seeing my clove oil."

"You won't find her there. Both she and Mistress Ashley are sleeping on the queen's pallet tonight. They will take their meal with Her Grace. You'll have to wait until tomorrow when we swear our oaths."

RATHER THAN GOING to the hall for supper, I headed outside, hoping to find my trunk. I hadn't even crossed the courtyard before Master Husee slunk out of the shadows. "Margery, wait!" he called.

"Not now, I am in a hurry." Dodging his outstretched hand, I scrambled across the cobblestones, just out of reach.

Undeterred, Husee pursued me through the stone archway. "I heard you met with the new queen. Did you tell her about Lady Lisle's daughters?"

"Of course not, you fool!" I blazed, wheeling around so quickly we nearly collided. He lurched aside, stumbling on the uneven stones.

He straightened himself, the amiable smile sliding from his face. "I am greatly sorry to have offended. Please forgive me. I shall not bother you again." He turned to leave.

"No, I am the one who should be sorry. That was appallingly rude."

He paused, watching me with unease. "If I am a nuisance, you need only tell me."

"It's nothing you've done," I sighed, inwardly tracking every precious moment that ticked past. "I'm trying to find something that was loaded on the baggage train. If I don't hurry, I'm going to—"

"Miss it?" he interrupted. "You already have; it left nearly an hour ago. What were you looking for?"

Damnable Hell! I was too late! Blinking hard against a swell of tears, I whirled away before he could see me cry. "Nothing important," I answered, willing my voice not to waver. "I must go now, Master Husee."

"Margery? Margery!" His shouts melted away as I dashed into the encroaching dusk.

By the time I returned to the dorm, the last candle had already been snuffed out. The maids were tucked into their beds, soft snores curling in the darkness above them. My bed, the only one that remained empty, stood in the shadows like a forlorn sentinel. It was too late to call for assistance out of my gown, but it mattered not. I spent many years lacing and unlacing garments. I could do it with my eyes closed. My practiced fingers did their work, and then I slipped quietly beneath the thin blanket, giving myself up to the gloom.

The night unspooled like an endless thread. I tossed and turned, lost in a world of my own dreaming: a garish land of stone cells and severed heads. I awoke in the murky dawn, resigned to whatever punishment awaited me, as an escape from this fearful purgatory.

"Hurry up, Margery," Mistress Arundell chirped from across the room, her troublesome tooth seemingly amended for the nonce.

We processed to the queen's rooms, the more senior ladies in front and me at the back, our trains trailing behind us. Queen Jane had given strict instructions on how long they were to be, along with orders as to how many pearls we were required to wear. Demanding though she could be, not even Queen Anne was as controlling. It affected me very little since my livery was provided. On this occasion, however, I wore my best gown, recently refashioned to Her Grace's specifications. The tailoring had been a gift from Master Skutt, a reward for introducing him to Maude, his newly hired needlewoman.

The queen, splendidly dressed in crimson satin and cloth of gold, awaited us in the presence chamber. She sat like a great lump of stone—her gaze fixed upon some distant point above our heads. The warmth and friendliness, so evident the last time we met, had been hidden beneath a cold, impervious mask. Was it self-preservation or a reaction to news of treachery? I felt the bile rise in my throat.

Mistress Norris rushed over to join our row. Studiously avoiding eye-contact, she squeezed in ahead of me. Though I desperately wanted to ask her if she had found me out, I did not dare. Instead, I took her stiff demeanour to mean the worst.

Slowly, the line crept forward. The rustle of damask filled the chamber as each maid swept a curtsy then repeated the oath, binding them to honourable service. Queen Jane looked down upon them from her throne while Lady Anne Seymour danced attendance nearby, measuring the length of fabric trailing our gowns. Lady Rutland shuffled the dawdlers along. When Mistress Norris retreated, I hurried forward. Dipping low to the ground, ensconced in a puddle of grey satin, I repeated the words. Afterward, I stared up at that bloodless regal face, searching for reassurance. Her Grace gave nothing away. Whatever she thought of me, or this spectacle, was locked away deep inside.

JANE SEYMOUR

GREENWICH

A mere fortnight after the spilled blood of their mistress stained the scaffold stairs, Anne Boleyn's maids pledged their fealty to me. It happened almost effortlessly; there were no tears, no outbursts, no angry words. Still, the weight of our shared betrayal sat heavily upon me. When each girl knelt before the throne, I found myself gazing at the woven tapestries on the wall, desperate to hide the shame in my eyes. Edward's first wife had used a similar tactic to preserve her dignity at the family table, after rumours of her infidelity began filtering through our household. Except, our wall-hangings weren't nearly so luxurious, and no one was convinced. I still wondered whether she had been faithful to my brother. Had she deserved her exile?

Making our way to the privy stairs after the ceremony, Lady Anne was cheerful. "Well, that went easier than expected."

"If you can forget all that came before this day," I replied darkly, remembering the expression of utter desolation on Margery Horsman when she recited her oath. She had gone ghostly pale. Her delicate chin trembled so much the words clattered out of her mouth. Margery would not forget; of that, I was certain.

"Stop it," she snapped. "Be grateful for the king's favour and pray it lasts, for if it does not…" She worried the ruby brooch at her breast, nervously scuffing her thumb across the centre jewel. There was no need for her to continue. We both knew the unspoken truth.

"It will be all right, won't it, Anne? That woman—I am nothing like her. She was insolent, and cruel, and…and…" I struggled to catch my breath.

"Vile," she finished softly. "Yes, my dear sister. That is what we must tell ourselves. And everyone else."

In the light of a mild summer morning, the spectres of the past faded into the murkiness behind us. The king and his retinue awaited on the river stair, the hulking form of the royal flagship, *Great Harry*, glowering above them. The carrack's bronze cannons gleamed in the sunlight, the red and green streamers adorning all four masts whipping in the breeze. "There you are, Jane!" His Grace bellowed over the eager murmuring of the courtiers surrounding him. "The barge will be here for you shortly. We shall see you again at Greenwich quite soon." He gave a brusque wave before climbing aboard, disappearing into the bowels of the ship with his men snaking behind.

The *Great Harry* had disappeared beyond the horizon by the time the royal barge arrived. It had been scrubbed clean, all traces of the crowned falcon pried off or painted over. A new sigil had been worked in alongside the king's—a phoenix. My phoenix. I hated it on sight. The bird was a grim reminder of the destruction worked in service to my elevation. It felt like an insult—a bastardization of the Seymour wings that had represented our house for generations. My husband had commandeered it for his own, remaking it in his image. I was losing myself piece by piece.

Crowding on to the barge behind me, the maids settled in, and we got underway, our smaller vessel following the path of the king's mighty one down a winding river of blue. I stared out across the Thames, marvelling at the press of onlookers cheering as we passed. A few threw their hats into the air, one unlucky fellow losing his to a gust of wind. He clawed in futility as it swirled above him before it was carried far beyond his grasp. The bank of the river curved. We approached the great London Bridge, and the stony turrets of the Tower came into view.

"Don't you dare look at it." Lady Anne's fingers snaked into the opening of my sleeve; our knitted grasp hidden within the folds of silk. I turned my gaze to much safer shores on the opposite bank, searching for the crenelated towers of our destination: the Palace of Placentia.

We feasted well at Greenwich, that first evening I sat abroad as Queen. Dishes piled high with portions of venison and lamb, dripping in their juices, were brought out after a course of baked rabbit flavoured with rosemary and onions, served alongside root vegetables soaked in wine and basted with a honey glaze. Afterward there were strawberry tarts with cream, custards spiced with cinnamon and nutmeg, and sweet comfits. I could not remember the last time I ate as much; my stomach was so full that the simple act of drawing a breath felt impossible. The next evening's meal brought even more luxuries: a roasted boar hot from the spit, duck baked in a tangy citrus sauce, and savoury dolphin pie. At the end, the king and I shared a bowl of cherries—a special gift from Lady Lisle.

"More like a bribe," he whispered, breath hot in my ear. "Whatever that man of hers promises, you are not to let her daughters into your service. You would do well to keep Husee out of your rooms altogether. He's a genial lad, I'll admit, but there is no end to his mistress' demands. You give Lord Lisle one office; she will ask for another, more lucrative, one. Nothing is ever enough for her." I suppressed a smile at this piece of unsolicited advice. Had he forgotten I had been at court long enough to know all about Honour Lisle and her limitless ambition?

As if he had been privy to our conversation, Master Husee chose that moment to catch my eye from across the great hall. He doffed his cap, sending a quick nod of recognition, before turning back to one of my ladies. Judging by her broad grin and flushed cheeks, they looked to be having a most stimulating conversation. When Mistress Horsman passed behind my chair, I tugged on her sleeve. "I need you to deliver a message of gratitude to Master Husee. Please tell him the king and I thoroughly enjoyed the cherries, finding them to be the sweetest ones we have had this year."

"If it pleases Your Grace." She blushed, bustling away.

The king simmered beside me. "You think you are wiser than I, wife?" he growled. "You disregard my counsel?"

When I turned, his lazuline eyes were blazing with fury, those rosebud lips pursed small and mean. "I would never dream of such ill, my dearest husband," I soothed in a honeyed tone. "I sent Margery to disrupt the

over-familiarity Master Husee seems to be enjoying with one of our ladies."
I pointed at the two carrying on, oblivious to Margery's approach. "See
how she leans towards him, stroking the hollow at her throat as he speaks,
lapping up every word? Easily charmed, that one."

"Well, aren't you clever?" He sniggered.

Catching his fingers in mine, I brought them close for a kiss. "I shall
not tolerate any misbehaviour."

"I'll come to your rooms later." His colour deepened. "On the morrow,
you will be proclaimed queen; tonight, you shall make me a son."

The taste of cherries returned to the back of my throat.

WHEN THE FESTIVITIES were over, and the court had gone to bed,
my husband arrived. Dismissing the maids, he took me hastily, as though
he feared his vigour might not last if he tarried too long. Having already
broken my maidenhead, the king gave me minimal pain, but neither did
he provide much pleasure. All was over before it had hardly begun. *Was
this what the poets sang about?* This time, he shouted no names, performing
his duty in near silence. Resting his hand upon my stomach afterwards,
he bent to kiss my forehead. "Do not think to fail me," he muttered
against my brow. There was no place sacred; his threats followed me into
every refuge.

In the morning, we processed to the chapel for the Whitsun Mass.
When the archbishop raised the host, he called on England's people to
pray for me. King Henry had announced to the realm that Anne Boleyn
was queen in much the same way. The remembrance of it sickened me, and
I gripped the arms of my chair to steady myself. In doing so, I accidentally
grazed the king's sleeve.

"Soon, Jane." He brushed my hand aside. "Cromwell has held the Imperial Ambassador off this long, but I have promised to speak with him next.
He is eager to push an alliance with his master now that black-hearted
woman is dead."

Which wife did he mean—Catherine or Anne? I wondered. "Will I see
him after?" I asked instead.

The king heaved a deep sigh. "Yes, he asked for an audience with you. If his womanly nagging does not vex me in the next hour, I am inclined to grant it."

"I would be most honoured, Your Grace."

Rising from his seat, he offered a pointed warning, "I know you will not embarrass me, Jane."

Eustace Chapuys seemed almost puzzled to find himself on this side of the royal apartments. "Don't forget, he has not been in these rooms since they were occupied by Queen Catherine," Lady Anne whispered, placing a supportive hand at my elbow. "His master ought to be thrilled that a woman more like his aunt once again shares the throne. You know, Master Chapuys visited Catherine's sickbed. How distraught he was to have missed her final breaths. Still, he is very eager to meet you. After all, you were the one to vanquish the queen's great enemy."

Would he still be so keen if I told him the truth, that while I happily sowed seeds of discord in the king's mind, I never once dreamed the fruits would be so deadly?

"Your Grace, it is a great pleasure to see you again," the ambassador enthused in his stilted English. He planted a dry kiss on my cheek before continuing, slipping in and out of his native tongue, "*Félicitations* on this most happy of occasions." At this turn of phrase, his lip curled into a smirk. "I am sure—*sans doute*—you remember who last claimed that *honneur*? *La plus heureux*? How ironic it is that you should be the one to bear that reality, and how very *un*-happy that woman turned out to be." He watched me, sizing up my understanding. Though I was not fluent in French, I knew enough. Edward spoke it often at home, having picked it up during his youth on the continent. I understood the ambassador perfectly but also saw the advantage in pretending as though I did not.

"Thank you, Master...pardon...*Monsieur* Chapuys," I stumbled, fixing an abashed smile upon my face. "I am most honoured by your kindness."

Chapuys wrinkled his brow. "My master is pleased beyond measure that his beloved brother, the king, has found such a virtuous and goodly wife. He remembers your brother's time in his service fondly. My Lord Seymour always showed himself to be *très dévoué*—that is to say, most dutiful."

"You flatter us, kind sir. Are you thirsty? Can I have some wine brought to you?" I gestured at the cluster of maids gathered around the king; the Arundell girls shrieked at some jape His Grace was telling.

"*Non, merci*, there is nothing I need. I only wish to say how wonderful it is—the satisfaction of the people for this new marriage—how they rejoice at the restoration of *la Princesse Marie*. And a great blessing that you should have such a *fille sans accouchement*. I know you will find more consolation and happiness from her than—perhaps—any you may have with the king."

The ambassador tread dangerous waters. "My apologies, *Monsieur*, my French is lamentable, to say the least." Darting a cautious glance at the king before going on, I attempted to steer the conversation in a safer direction. "I look forward to welcoming the *Lady* Mary to court once she and her father are again in perfect harmony."

"*Oui*, but of course you do." Annoyance flitted through Chapuys' raven eyes. He quickly recovered with a polite smile. "The Emperor is certain that Your Grace will endeavour to bring such peace and harmony to pass that you should be known as Queen Jane the Pacific."

When I opened my mouth to respond, the king approached. "Jane, my beloved, you look quite speechless." Turning to the ambassador, he continued, "You will have to forgive my wife, Chapuys. You are the first ambassador to whom she has spoken, and she is not yet accustomed to such audiences."

"There is nothing to forgive, Your Grace," Chapuys replied coolly. "We were just discussing your daught—"

The king cut in before the ambassador could finish. "Queen Jane the Pacific, a most apt name for Her Grace," he mused. "For, besides being blessed with a gentle nature that is much inclined to peace, she would not for the world wish me to be engaged in war, lest we be separated too long. Isn't that right, dearest Jane?" His hand shot out as he spoke my name, his long fingers dancing lightly across my waist; he never ceased reminding me.

"Yes, Your Grace." A safe refrain I found myself repeating so often that if I were to be cut open, one might find it etched upon my heart.

MARGERY HORSMAN

GREENWICH AND YORK PLACE

Q ueen Jane was still at morning prayers when I arrived at the royal
apartments with the gown chosen for the journey back to Westminster. Both Joan Arundell and Mary Norris attended upon her during the
night, but only Mistress Arundell was left behind to greet me.

"You're early," she called over her shoulder as she leaned across the
queen's table to straighten the napery. "Have you eaten anything yet? I do
not think Her Grace will notice if you help yourself to a bit of bread. She
is certainly not eating it."

"You know the Queen notices everything. Or have you already forgotten the incident with your sister's veil?"

Mistress Arundell pulled a face. "Lady Seymour and her measuring
stick."

"She goes by Lady Beauchamp now," I reminded her, slipping past
to lay the gown on the bed. My fingers worked quickly to smooth the
creases that had begun to mar the satin. It was a delicate fabric and notoriously difficult to clean. "Mistress Norris will have to help me. I do not
want your butter-greased hands anywhere near this satin. You shall send
Lloyd into fits."

"The girl won't be thrilled about that." She lifted the ewer of wine to
her nose, sniffing it appreciatively. "Hmm…Gascon. What I wouldn't give
for a taste."

"Well, you won't be getting any." I shot her a grievous look, my heart thudding wildly. "Why should Mistress Norris be troubled? I have had naught to do with her." It was true, but our separation had not been of my choosing, and I spent the sleepless nights since fretting over what she might have told our companions.

When my trunk had finally been returned, I was overcome with great relief to find the necklace still hidden inside. My comfort dissipated when I realized the silver coffer had been opened. Had Mary Norris poked through my belongings or was it someone else? If so, then who? And why weren't they talking? In a place where knowledge was currency, it was perilous not to know your debtor. I had watched for tell-tale signs from the others, but none surfaced. The normalcy of it all felt unsettling. Ominous.

Mistress Arundell sighed. "Norris told me you spoke ill of her father. That is why she asked Stonor to switch beds when we arrived."

I thrust my chest forward, hands clenching at my sides. "I would never speak of the dead that way. Henry Norris was never anything but—"

The door swung open with a thud. "Think on how you want to finish that sentence, Mistress Horsman," Queen Jane cautioned, striding into the room from her prayer closet, the hem of her linen nightgown billowing in her wake. Mary Norris shrank behind one of the great ladies, her raw eyes appearing all the darker with the colour drained from her face.

Crashing to my knees, I stared hard at the floor, a flood of stinging tears blurring the vivid colours of the tiles below. "Your Grace, I only meant to say that Henry Norris was never anything but kind to me. I would never say anything to besmirch his memory."

When I looked up, the queen's face was devoid of emotion. Her tone was quiet, resigned. "Sir Henry Norris besmirched his own memory by engaging in treason, and you all would do well to remember it. Wouldn't you agree, Mistress Norris?"

The maid stiffened, fingers trembling around the girdle book in her hands. "Yes, Your Grace," she squeaked.

Fitting the queen into her voluminous layers of sarcenet and satin, Mistress Norris dared not look at me. She fled once the final pin was in place. "Wait!" I cried, chasing after her. "Please talk to me."

"Leave me alone, Margery. I want no part of your schemes."

I waited, praying she would return for an explanation or apology, but all I heard were footsteps retreating down the hall. Belatedly remembering I had left the queen's washing behind, I headed back to retrieve it, only to be stopped short outside the bedchamber door at the sound of raised voices.

"...most sensible response you could have given. What did they expect you to say?"

It was the queen's sister-in-law.

Lingering in the silence that followed, I debated whether to intrude. Just when I decided it had gone on long enough to make my entrance safely, my fingers stretching towards the door, the queen's reply came.

"I want them to trust me. How can they do that when I must say the most detestable things? Poor Mistress Norris. Could you not see her pain? She will never forgive me."

"She must. And she will!" Lady Anne Beauchamp snapped, the slab of oak between us failing to soften the edge in her voice. "Your maids will be back at any moment. Please compose yourself, or we will have the devil to pay if the king finds out you are weeping over a convicted traitor."

Leaning in to catch the queen's next words, I felt a firm grip yank me back. "What are you doing, Margery?" Mistress Ashley hissed. "Spying is Cromwell's game. Did he put you up to this?"

"Of course not." I pushed her hand away, smoothing down the fabric that had puckered in her grip. "I forgot the queen's laundry."

Mistress Ashley shook her head. "A fine excuse for your lurking. Haven't you caused enough trouble today?"

Mistress Arundell approached before I could respond. "Margery, Mother Stonor is looking for you."

I offered my thanks but kept my eyes locked on Mistress Ashley's. The maid's lips twisted into a smirk, and then she gave a trite little wave. "See you on the barge, Margery."

THE MID-SUMMER SUN, glinting off the glassy surface of the Thames, simmered against my skin but did little to warm me against the icy tension that had settled over the queen's barge. The morning's events set every-one on edge, quieting even the most voluble among us. The respite from the chatter gave me an opportunity to consider what I had heard outside the royal bedchamber. I always suspected the queen's behaviour was a ruse or pretension. Never would I have guessed it was to distract from her distaste of all that had happened. This discovery made me surer of my charge. Anne Boleyn and the men truly *had* been innocent. I would protect her jewel at all costs.

Mulling things over, I sat alone at the back of the barge, the expanse of damask-covered bench beside me left empty and uninviting. Crowded together in the front, the other maids saw the festivities before I did: the lords in their ornately decorated barges, the gleaming guns on the king's ships, and the green and gold streamers whipping high above us on the parapets of the White Tower. I was treated to the detritus littering our wake: the brightly coloured rubbish that had come detached from the barges, plumes of smoke polluting the air after the naval report, and a sense of foreboding that radiated beyond the Tower walls despite the fes-tive streamers. My only advantage came as the procession drifted past the Imperial Ambassador's pavilion when Monsieur Chapuys sent out two boats of musicians to serenade the royal couple. The musicians joined our cortege as we sailed by them, and their sweet music followed me to London.

At York Place, Mother Stonor honoured Mistress Norris' request to remain with her new bed mate, and it was decided I would sleep on my own since I had been employed in the royal household longer than the rest. This deference should have pleased me; only, it felt a bit like punish-ment. Masking my true feelings behind a gracious countenance at Stonor's announcement, I hurriedly unpacked my trunk while the other girls were preoccupied. When my fingers knocked against the cool metal of the coffer, I resolved to find a safer hiding spot before the summer progress com-menced My nerves were not fit to handle the worry of smuggling it halfway across the realm.

In the morning, the remaining dregs of hostility towards me seemed to melt away in the excitement of the staged pageantry of parliament's open-ing. We joined the queen in the gatehouse, high above the parade's route, to watch the king march out. Riding before him, holding the cap of maintenance aloft, was His Grace's bastard, Henry Fitzroy.

"Why look you so glum, Lady Richmond?" I asked, noting how the corners of her mouth turned down when her husband rode into view. "I have heard rumours that His Grace means to make Fitzroy his heir until…" I nodded towards the other side of the gate where Queen Jane was taking in the scene below with Lady Anne Beauchamp. "That must be welcome news in your household?"

Lady Richmond fussed at the girdle beads slung low around her waist. "Fitz is not well, Margery. Astride that horse, he looks fit, capable, and ever so…" Her cheeks flushed.

"Handsome?" I finished, offering a conspiratorial grin.

"Yes, that." She smiled back, and then her mirth fell away again. "Outwardly, he appears hearty and hale. At night he is wracked by such coughing as I have never heard before. He tries to hide them from me, but the laundress dropped one of his handkerchiefs in the corridor, and the colour of it was more crimson than white."

I thought of Mother, and my heart constricted. How many bloodstained handkerchiefs had we burned after her death? Too many to count. "It grieves me to hear that, Lady Richmond."

She blinked back tears. "Hopefully, it is nothing serious. Fitz is young yet, and we have many happy years ahead."

"Try not to worry." I patted her on the arm. "I am sure you are right. In time, this will all seem a bad dream." The lie left a bitter taste on my tongue.

TWO DAYS BEFORE the feast of Corpus Christi, Queen Jane called me back to her rooms after being dismissed for the evening. Mistress Norris was sent to collect me, and she didn't appear too pleased about it. When she spoke my name, it was the first time I heard it from her lips since she fled from me at Greenwich. She recoiled when I leaped to attention, like a dog eager for her acknowledgment, but said nothing as she led me out the door, two paces ahead.

When we were clear of curious ears, I summoned the courage to speak. "You must know, and yet you do not tell. Why?"

The maid halted, keeping her back to me. Torchlight quivered above us, casting golden pools upon the rich linenfold panelling. The fabric constraining her ribs heaved. I counted one, two, three breaths before she answered. "I do not know what you are talking about." She began to walk again, faster than before.

Speeding ahead, I grabbed her by the shoulders and spun her around to face me. "Look at me, Mary! Please!" The tears came hot and fast, salty tracks staining my cheeks. Somewhere in the distance, a door slammed shut with a heavy thud. We scanned our surroundings for intruders. Finding none, our eyes met again. Hers shone bright, with rage or with sadness, I was not sure.

"I can't, Margery. I just can't." She crumpled to the floor. "I saw nothing. I swear, I saw nothing." The carpet of rushes swayed with the force of her sobs.

"Oh, that's all right. Get up, get up," I soothed, lacing my arm through hers. I pulled Mistress Norris to her feet, then straightened her hood. "Please don't cry. I never meant to frighten you."

"It is not you who scares me," she sniffed. "It is *the king*. He killed my father."

I looked again for eavesdroppers. The hallway remained empty, but that did not mean no one was listening. "Say no more, I understand. Just promise you will keep my secret."

Her fists rubbed away the tears. "I want to, but I cannot swear it. What if he kills us both?"

I tucked a stray hair behind her ear. Patting her shoulder, I draped her veil there. "Did any of Queen Anne's ladies suffer for her transgressions? No. If the king were to find out, it is only I who will be punished." Internally, I wondered if this were true.

Then she voiced what I had not dared, "But six were punished for no transgressions at all."

There was nothing I could say in return. She was right, of course, but the thought was so terrifying, I forced it from my mind. By the time we reached the royal apartments, I had managed to convince myself the maid would not tell—perhaps not to spare me, but because she feared the king's wrath. Whatever her motives, I felt safer. For now.

We found the queen hunched over her table, examining a pair of sleeves. Several other pairs sat in a pile beside her, awaiting scrutiny. "Mistress Horsman, I am glad you have not gone to bed yet. I need an errand of you."

I slid into a curtsy. "I am at Your Grace's command."

"On the morrow, I want you to go with the Master of the Jewelhouse to the embroiderer, Ibgrave. He is to do some work on these sleeves and one of my kirtles, and I do not trust our dear Sir Antony to give him proper instructions. I have a design in mind, and I want it exact. Can you do that for me?"

"Yes, Your Grace. But I shall need—"

"An escort, yes," she interrupted. "I have asked a member of my brother's retinue to take you. You know Michael Lyster. He brought you to my rooms before."

I nodded. "I remember."

"Good, now return to your room, and I will see you after lauds. I shall explain it all then." She dismissed me with a flick of her wrist.

THE QUEEN HAD already dressed by the time I arrived the next morning. The gown she wore was one remade from Queen Catherine's stores. When I sent it out to Master Skutt, I had been sceptical he could do much with it—the fabric was threadbare in some areas, and the cut was hopelessly out of fashion—but it came back more beautiful and richer than before. The silver woven throughout the cloth shone brightly against the indigo dye, and the neckline—raised higher and tight—bore the weight of a habiliment studded with opal and diamond quatrefoils. Not even Anne Boleyn wore anything so fine when she was queen. On Jane Seymour, it was transformative. For the first time since she came to court, I wondered if perhaps we had underestimated her allure all along.

Having waited on Her Grace through the night, Mistress Norris was still in attendance, studiously ignoring me while I received my instructions. I stole a furtive glance in her direction, hoping for any sort of sign that she had taken on board my pleas for discretion, but she gave nothing away. I hoped it a harbinger of her silence. With nothing forthcoming, I turned my attention back to the queen.

The seriousness with which Her Grace treated the embroidery pattern last night led me to believe it would be something intricate and overly complex. I was taken aback when it turned out to be rather ordinary, little more than a pair of wings encasing her first initial emblazoned in gold thread. Her most insistent reminder was that she wanted Ibgrave to stitch *I*'s rather than *J*'s and that the kirtle he was already working on should have precisely 1,562 pearls. No more and no less. Such an arbitrary number with no explanation. I realized then that it had less to do with her confidence in Sir Antony Denny or the embroiderer's ability and more to do with her desire to be in control, to have something and someone she could influence and command. Her power seemed so weak, when compared to the other side of the throne.

When I re-emerged into the presence chamber an hour later, I found Master Lyster waiting for me. Curiously, my heart jolted at the sight of him. *How strange*, I wondered. *I hardly knew him.* He bent at the waist, removing his cap in reverence, then popped back up with a small smile on his face.

"Lovely to see you again, Mistress Margery. I trust you have been well?"

We exchanged the required pleasantries, winding our way through the palace's dim halls, before stepping out into the dazzling morning sunlight of the courtyard. In the stables, Sir Antony Denny was mounting a black rouncey laden with saddlebags.

"Let's get a push on, Lyster," he snapped, his bushy forked beard wilting in the summer heat. Now that June was half over, the cool respite of the early hours had grown shorter, making all and sundry more peevish than ever.

We trotted through the gates and into the city at a leisurely pace. The caress of the sun drew a slick of sweat down my back. I kept to the middle, with a man on each side to protect me from the press of people swarming the street. A gang of bedraggled boys approached Sir Antony to beg for coins, but most filtered around us going about their business. The crowd thinned as we travelled further from the busy markets, and by the time we arrived at Ibgrave's shop, the streets had grown bare. Only a stunted old woman with milky eyes haunted the empty alleyway, a dingy grey dog panting at her feet.

Master Lyster dismounted first, then helped me to the ground. He motioned for me to wait before digging into the small leather purse hanging from his neck. He pulled three farthings from inside, slipping them into my hand with a nod towards the woman. While he worked with Sir Antony to free the saddlebags from the rouncey, I delivered his gift to the woman. She repaid me with a toothless grin as the coins clattered into the bottom of her cup.

Inside, the pale, spare Ibgrave eyed me with the weariness of one accustomed to the demands of an exacting mistress. He took my instructions with sparse commentary, his quill scratching out the queen's directives in great looping swirls. When Sir Antony opened the bags to lay out the jewels, the embroiderer insisted upon a triple-count of the inventory, all of us counting aloud as he slid the gems across the counter. Then, he divided the pearls into two casks: 28 to use on the king's doublet and queen's sleeves, 1,562 for her kirtle. He made me count them again after the separation. Finally satisfied that each item was present and accounted for, Ibgrave drew up several receipts before shooing us out the door.

The journey back to York Place seemed to take longer, but I did not mind. I found myself enthralled by the rush of the mob around me: the servants haggling with the merchants, the cutpurses slinking through the crowd, and the children chasing after a brightly coloured ball that rolled down the cobbled street. The business of life out here appeared so much more important than the trivial pursuits we entertained ourselves with at court. How contradictory it seemed that I felt safer beyond the stone walls of the palace than inside them.

"How is the queen faring these long days?" Sir Antony asked, startling me from my trance. "Any sign yet?" Smirking, he rubbed his belly vigorously in case I missed his meaning.

"Forgive me, good sir, but I am not at liberty to discuss Her Grace's personal matters." My stomach began to sway with the trot of my horse. A lump of bile rose in my throat.

"Oh, come now," he groaned. "All the maids talk. Why should you be any different?"

Master Lyster rushed to my defence. "Leave her be. Besides, the queen would not yet know, herself, if she were with-child. The wedding was mere weeks ago. I doubt she has even missed her courses."

"Well, she had better hope she misses them soon. Just the other day, the king showed himself disappointed to have rushed so quickly into matrimony, when he spied two plump partridges flitting through the garden." A wink accompanied this vulgar wit. "If our new queen should find herself as incapable as the last two, she just may end up going the same way."

Master Lyster flushed. "This is no proper conversation for a maiden, Sir Antony. On my honour, I must ask you to desist."

"Have it your way." Sir Antony sagged in his seat. "It would be a sad thing, in truth. Sir John Seymour was a great knight. I would hate to see his daughter come to the same sticky end as the Earl of Wiltshire's."

Master Lyster said nothing in return, and the three of us kept the silence until we passed through the palace walls. Leaving the stables, I heard the heavy tread of boots thudding up behind me. I whirled around, expecting to find Sir Antony chasing me down now that I was alone, but found Master Lyster's kind face staring back instead.

"I must apologize for Sir Antony. He is harmless but often forgets his audience."

"It is quite all right. I have been asked far more uncomfortable questions in far more unsavoury company."

"How unfortunate." Master Lyster frowned. "I suppose it goes with the position, though."

I nodded. "It can, and yet I always manage to survive."

"I am glad to hear it. Take care of yourself, Mistress Horsman." He tipped his cap, then turned back towards the stables.

"Call me Margery!" I shouted after him.

JANE SEYMOUR

YORK PLACE

The colour drained from Edward's face. "Francis Bryan and Nicholas Carew have been taken for questioning."

Anne Seymour lurched to her feet at the mention of her husband's associates, sending her chair clattering to the floor. "What has happened? Are we in danger?" She ran to the comfort of his arms, burying her face in his velvet doublet. My brother stared at me over the curve of his wife's hood, his brows creased with worry.

"This is about the Lady Mary, isn't it?" I asked, setting down my wine cup. The sweetness of the last swallow still burned the back of my throat. "The king was in a rage, screaming himself hoarse this morning, over her letter." The remembrance of his fury made my heart race as it had earlier during the storm. "She begs to no avail. How much further must she debase herself for his forgiveness?"

Edward led his wife to a cushion by the window, easing her down gently. He returned to my table. Their devotion to each other never failed to beguile me. The ever-strident Lady Anne virtually melted in her husband's presence, turning to him for all things. I could not recall her ever speaking to him in a sharp manner, though she spared almost no one else from her bite. For his part, my brother honoured her veneration, treating her as his very equal in a way I had never seen a man treat his wife. It was as if, in their joining, the sun was always at its apex—man and shadow became one. It was the sort of marriage I was never destined to have.

"We must lightly tread where she is concerned. Bryan and Carew stand accused of preferring the Lady Mary to any children conceived by you. We know this to be false!" He slammed his fist on the table. My plate trembled under the force. The sight of my uneaten food further stoked his displeasure. "What is this? Are you no longer eating?"

Lady Anne straightened under my blistering gaze. "He knows you have been fasting."

Shoving the plate aside, I glared at Edward. "I am not fasting. You have seen me take food with the king." *And plenty of it—His Grace desired a plump wife in his bed, this time around.*

Leaning forward on his elbow, Edward rubbed his chin. "So why do you not eat on your own?"

"It is penance for her guilt," Lady Anne trilled.

Edward sat back, sighing. "Stop, sister," he said, not unkindly. "That woman's death is not your fault. You did not—" he stopped. "None of us could have expected it would go so far. Stop punishing yourself. Besides, it does nothing to aid your fertility. Queen Catherine destroyed her chances for a son with all her bloody fasting."

"What happens with the king's daughter now?" I deflected before he could force me into any promises. "And Bryan and Carew?"

Edward plucked a strawberry from my plate. He bit into it. Chewing, he considered his answer. "I could not say. The king rails against her one moment then sobs over her mistreatment by that harlot the next. His Grace seems adrift with uncertainty, and that is when we are most vulnerable." He paused to take in my reaction. Emptying my face of emotion, I refused him the satisfaction. "In the morning, he is sending Norfolk and Sussex to secure her submission, by force if necessary. If they are unsuccessful, well…"

The Lady Mary would die. The very marrow of my bones ached with certainty. The king cried over Anne Boleyn's careless words, but it was he who tortured the girl. He who held the means of her destruction. "Perhaps I could—"

Edward banged the table again. "You will say nothing! The king has already suggested to the Spanish ambassador and others that he regrets rushing into this marriage. Do not give him cause for action. You will do nothing, save your duty as a wife."

Regret? Ha! I could tell the king a thing or two about regret. And what of my duty as a queen to protect the weak and innocent? We were taught better than this! I wanted to shout these thoughts at my brother. Still, I knew in my heart that he was not as cold as he tried to appear. He was scared; we all were.

Kneeling at my prie-dieu before bed, I prayed fervently for the Lady Mary's deliverance. *Lord Jesu, please help her to see she must give in,* I sobbed silently. *Absolve her soul for what she must do and absolve mine for what I cannot.* Sleep-deprived and filled with worry, I moved through the next day's processional as if in a dream. Suffocating crowds of well-wishers pressed against us during the journey to Westminster Abbey. I took no comfort in their joy. From my perch amid the soaring stone arches, I stared down at Dr Sampson performing the mass. His words rose to surround me, and yet I took none of the message in. All I could think of—watching him glide across the colourful pavement before the high altar—was Anne Boleyn treading on the swirls of glass and stone to receive her crown.

THE KING KEPT himself from me that night and then the next. I grew suspicious of my maids, searching the face of each one that came into my rooms. Had one of them overheard my conversation with Edward and tattled? Treason, treachery, foulness; I had seen those vices hiding within in their pretty gowns before. They had turned on Catherine. They had turned on Anne. They could turn on me.

"They might," Lady Anne sniffed when I finally divulged these disturbing thoughts to her. "But were you not feeling pity for these same girls mere days ago? Fretful they would hate you?"

"I must be going mad."

She tucked a wayward strand of hair beneath my coif. "You are not the only one."

His Grace came to me on the third day, and it became instantly apparent why he had avoided my rooms: he was limping again. I felt a surge of relief and then shame. Was this emotion derived from a sincere affection for him, or did his infirmity flood my defences? He seemed so pitiful, hobbling into my privy chamber, reduced somehow, despite his height and girth.

"I am pleased to see you again. I worried that I had done something to displease you."

He sank into the chair next to mine with a great sigh. "Of course, you have not displeased me, Sweetheart," he grunted, heaving his leg on to a nearby footstool. "Why ever would you think that?" His gown shifted, revealing a pale brownish stain on his hose—dried blood.

"You did not come to my rooms last night." I took a seat beside him. "You must forgive me, but I crave your company so."

My words generated the desired effect and the king's face relaxed. His head dropped forward, resting in the cradle of his thumb and forefinger; his blue eyes snapped shut, and then he heaved a few laboured breaths before responding, "It is that intransigent, disobedient daughter of mine. She gives me no rest."

"The Lady Elizabeth?" I supplied. Wishful thinking on my part; it would be so much easier if it had been the truth.

The king gave a bellowing laugh. "Would that be the case; she is still young enough to correct. Mary is grown now and has too much of her mother's Spanish blood in her veins."

Buoyed by his jest, I ventured the actual question on my mind. "What will become of her if she does not obey?"

The warmth in his cheeks leached away, his lips contorting. "Perhaps I shall allow Norfolk to make good on his promise to beat her head soft as a baked apple."

Swallowing back the sick in my throat, I reached for his hand to soothe, comfort, and tame. "The Lady Mary will change her heart, Your Grace. How could she not? For you are the most gracious and loving father she could ever hope for."

Lady Anne caught my eye when I looked away. Her head tilted just enough to indicate her approval. I had performed well, but the play was not over. Turning my attention back, I grazed the back of his hand with a kiss. The king twisted in his seat, pulling me close to rest his lips upon mine. The suddenness of it startled me, and my face heated with embarrassment. My ladies were watching.

Breathless, he pulled back. "I will visit again," he promised, struggling to his feet. "Very soon. When my leg has healed." Striding towards the door, he called back over his shoulder, "Forget about Mary. She is as good as lost to us." In this, I could not obey. Her mother's death had relieved me of my service, but never of my loyalty.

After days of closed-door debates and discussions regarding the king's daughter's fate, my brothers arrived bearing news. "There are some who insist the Lady Mary's claim is right," said Tom, picking at a spot on his shirt. Gravy by the look of it. "They concede the marriage to her mother was unlawful, because who would dare contradict the king on this point? Their argument is that it was made in good faith, and for that reason alone, she remains the true heir. At least until you provide a son."

"Will they help her?" I wondered aloud, giving it little credence even as I said the words.

Tom just laughed. "Have the last five years taught you nothing? King Henry would never allow it, purely out of spite."

"This is why *you* are not on the Privy Council," Edward snapped. "You don't know when to shut up." Much as our eldest brother had cared for the Lady Mary when her mother was queen, he was now of a differing opinion than those brave supporters. I blamed his relationship with Cromwell. The man had ignited a change within Edward, lighting a fire in his heart for this new and strange way of worshipping. He yearned to leave the old traditions and their adherents—like the king's daughter—behind. Still, he refused to countenance Tom's uncouth remarks, even if he agreed with them.

Back and forth, the tumult raged in these sessions. I witnessed none of it but felt the upheaval swirling within. A raging fire of emotion scorched a path through my body, and on more than one occasion, I awoke in the middle of the night, soaked in sweat and trembling. "Only a nightmare," I assured my ladies. They would send for Margery Horsman to bring me a fresh nightgown and new linen, all while politely ignoring my obvious distress. Except for Margery. "Are you well, Your Grace?" she whispered in my ear, tucking my sodden hair back under the nightcap. "Shall I get Lady Beauchamp for you?" I always declined. Lady Anne would tell Edward, and I needed none of his worrisome reprimands.

This distressing purgatory of abeyance continued until the feast day of St Alban when everything changed.

"Lord be praised, I have word from Hunsdon." The king wore the expression of a lunatic, eyes wide and unblinking.

Making a great show of pausing my embroidery to give him my full attention, I stalled for time, my mind scrambling to compose an appropriate response for whatever he said next. "Happy news, Your Grace?" It was more of a prayer than a question.

"Wonderful! More than I dared hope." He gestured for me to join him at the table, calling for wine to celebrate. While the steward hurried out to find some, Mistress Ashley set out a dish of candied plums and sugared almonds for our pleasure. The king stuffed a piece of fruit into his mouth like a man who was starving. He gulped it down, then devoured a second one before going on. "She agreed to it." He smacked his lips. "All of it."

"All of what, Your Grace?" Best to plead ignorance until I was certain what would please him.

"Jane, listen!" He gave me a contemptuous look. "She acknowledges me as her sovereign and submits to my laws. *All my laws*. She repudiates the bishop of Rome, recognizing my sole authority over the church," he continued, ticking the points on his fingers. "Most importantly, she finally deigns to accept that my marriage to her mother was unlawful and incestuous." He shuddered on this last one as if the thought was too much to bear.

"This *is* wonderful, Your Grace. What does this mean? What shall we do?"

"What do you suggest we do?"

His question startled me. Was this a trick? I hurriedly weighed the risks in my mind. The last time I spoke up for Mary, I had been brutally rebuffed, but that was before her capitulation. Perhaps His Grace would be more open in the changed circumstances. Still, I must tread carefully. "Bring her to court, Your Grace. In your exalted presence, she shall relearn how to be an obedient daughter."

My answer brought forth gales of laughter. "You sound like my councillors, Jane!" When his amusement finally subsided, he got to his feet. "I must think on this," he said, bending to stroke my cheek. "Forgiveness is such a burdensome thing."

I clutched his hand before he could pull away. "May I write to her, Your Grace?"

The king studied me for a long, painful moment. He nodded his assent. "I believe she has earned this small courtesy, but mind what you say to her. She is easily influenced."

ON ST PETER'S Eve, we went to the Mercer's Hall to see the setting of the city watch. In the encroaching dusk, the flames of thousands of torches flickered and pranced like nymphs on a river of light. Dressed in scarlet surcoats covered with shining silver armour, the Lord Mayor and the sheriffs rode ahead while a jubilant band of Morris Dancers and minstrels made merry behind them. The houses from Westcheap to Aldgate were awash in every colour imaginable, each cheering the parade with a welcoming party of lively faces and enthusiastic chants. How marvellous it was to see such joy after so much misery. Watching the spectacle, my sorrow melted away, and I remembered the promise our chaplain made when I was just a girl: God can make all things anew.

This must be His doing.

When we returned, enlivened from the heady celebrations, the king asked me to wait up for him. There was something he wanted to give me. I dressed for bed quickly, eagerly dismissing my ladies when he reappeared.

"What is this?" I asked when he placed the folded parchment in my hand.

"It is from Mary." He grinned. "To you."

I opened the letter with great anticipation, despite the twinge I felt at realizing the seal had already been broken.

To the Queen's grace, my good mother.

Tears sprung to my eyes, blurring the words on the page. *Oh, Mary. I am not sure I know how to be your mother.*

"I have decided that we will go to her. If she shows herself truly repentant, then she will join your household after the summer progress."

Desperate to believe him, I chose to accept the promise wholeheartedly. "Can we leave after morning prayers?"

"No, but it will be soon," he replied, taking the letter from my hand. "Time enough to prepare a gift, so you must think about what you would like it to be."

The answer was simple, and it came without hesitation: Mary deserved a diamond.

GARNET

Strength

JULY & AUGUST 1536

MARGERY HORSMAN

YORK PLACE

"Of what do you dream, my little queen?"

Mother had never looked more beautiful, her hair a crown of spun gold and skin the colour of fresh cream. She threw her head back in rapturous laughter, twirling me around until we collapsed in a dizzy heap upon the soft earth beneath our feet. Above us, the clouds sailed upon a vast indigo sea.

"Do you want a garden filled with the prettiest blooms? How about a palace of playful children? And a knight, courageous and true, to call your very own?"

Giggling, I reached for her hand, and caught nothing more than air. Down I fell, into the void. The cold darkness rushed up to steal my breath away.

I awoke with a start, drenched in sweat, the sound of my pulse thudding in my ears. Struggling to pull myself up, the memory of my mother's scent engulfed me, sending me crashing back to the bed with an anguished sob. She had been stolen from me once more.

"Another nightmare, Margery?" Mistress Ashley's round eyes peered anxiously at me from beneath her nightcap. Thrashing through my misery, I had not heard her creeping through the rushes to my bedside.

"It was nothing more than a forgotten wish. Go back to sleep. We have much to do in the morning."

JOAN ARUNDELL HAD been looking forward to St Peter's Day. It was all she spoke of in the week leading up to the holy day. "There will be a great pageant and jousts. And oh, how long it has been since I danced." A tortured sigh always accompanied these musings, and then she would opine, "We are never merry here. All we do is pray and sew."

"Some of us pray while we sew," her younger sister, Mary, giggled in response, sending the two of them to blows over who had the worst marriage prospects. In truth, it had all become a tiresome routine, but the sentiment was not without merit. Queen Jane's household *was* far more subdued. When Anne Boleyn was queen, her rooms had been alive with music and dancing. There were always young gallants traipsing through to entertain us with poetry or masking, to flirt and tease. Most of the dalliances that occurred were harmless games of courtly love, but occasionally the pursuit led to marriage negotiations.

Or broken hearts.

While Queen Anne had seen it as her duty to broker profitable alliances for her maids, Queen Jane—thus far—seemed reluctant to do so, an unfortunate development for any young lady who came to court seeking a husband.

Remembering Joan's earlier enthusiasm, I felt a pang of guilt for my nocturnal turmoil when she stifled a yawn as she shuffled wearily out to the quayside for the day's first entertainments: a mock sea battle. We watched in awe as the four ships—three small foists and a great carrack—parried with gleaming guns, the sharp crack of ordnance ringing in our ears. Bit by bit, the foists closed in on the carrack until one was close enough for her passengers to board. In the ensuing melee, we heard a ragged scream, "He's gone overboard! He's gone overboard!"

"What's happened?" Queen Jane shifted uncomfortably next to the king; her question nearly swallowed by the sound of gunfire.

His Grace brought up a hand to shield his eyes from the sun. Searching the water, he said, "I think one of the men fell between the ships."

The queen's voice rose. "Why haven't they stopped? He is sure to have been crushed!"

Before the king could respond, a loud groan issued from one of the foists bucking in the water. The ship rolled from side to side, the sailors abandoning their positions to seek refuge in the depths below. "She has lost a piece," he said finally. "I think she is going to sink."

"Please, Your Grace, you must stop this. I cannot watch anymore." The queen's face was ashen.

The king glowered at the scene on the river, his sport spoiled by the tragedy unfolding there. After a tense moment, he called one of the lords over. "My wife has had enough. Send one of your boats out to pull those men from the water."

"Yes, Your Grace." He scuttled off as we took our leave.

Back in the maid's dormitory, a sense of gloominess imbued the air. "I do not care to celebrate any longer. I think I shall just stay here the rest of the day." Joan Arundell flopped on to her bed, sending something clattering to the floor.

"What was that?" Crouching to search among the rush mats, I found the object—a coin of lead—hidden below one.

She shrugged when I held it up for her inspection. "Oh, it's just one of my weights."

"Your weights?" Mistress Norris arched her brow. "Whatever do you use that for?"

"I sew them into my skirts. They lay smoother that way," Joan replied, examining the hem of her gown. "By the saints, it's torn! Can you mend it, Margery?"

The silver coffer winked menacingly when I shoved it aside to collect the sewing kit from my trunk. In the whirlwind of the last few days, I had almost forgotten it remained there. Almost, but not entirely. Mary Norris had kept her peace thus far, lulling me into a false sense of safety. There was no telling when she might crack. *Where could I hide it?* Since that morning on the barge, there had been no answer forthcoming, but the lead coin resting in my palm gave me an idea.

THE TASK ITSELF was simple; carrying it out proved difficult. After St. Peter's Day, the festivities at court slowed to a crawl, which meant the other maids had little to occupy their time. When they weren't with the queen, they were holed up in the dormitory, cursing the heat and their restlessness. While their hours of leisure time swelled, mine dwindled. Only those deemed essential knew about the planned visit to the Lady Mary. As Mistress of the Wardrobe, that number included me. While my compatriots lazed their days away, indolent and idle, I bustled from errand to errand.

I was on one of these assignments from Master Lloyd when the Countess of Salisbury stopped me outside the great hall. It was the first time I had seen her since her return to court. "Margery, how good it is to see you." When she embraced me, warmth spread throughout my chest. Lady Salisbury had once rescued me from the depths of despair. She knew how to mend the lost and the broken.

"The same to you, my lady. How long has it been?"

Hand to her heart, she drew a deep breath. "It was so long ago—you were just a girl then. Yet, here you are, a woman grown. Time slips away so quickly." Her eyes grew wet at the sentiment.

"Please don't cry, my lady. We had many happy days," I pulled her hands into mine. They still felt soft, but there were more wrinkles and spots than I remembered—scars left behind by the passing years. "How is your family? Your sons? Ursula?"

Lady Salisbury's smile was cheerless. "Ursula is well. She has another baby on the way. Her sixth." She brightened at this, but the joy was fleeting. "Henry and Geoffrey are good sons, as always. Reginald gives me no rest."

"You must be so frightened, my lady." I once witnessed one of King Henry's tirades against the countess' son, and the memory of it still haunted me. "This break with Rome has—"

Lady Salisbury pressed a finger to her lips. "Say no more, dear girl, or we will all be worse for it."

"Yes, of course. I cannot imagine why I said that—I know better."

"Remember what I taught you? *It is hard to bite our tongue, but it is something that must be done!*" She laughed as she recited it, but we both knew she had not taught me the rhyme for pleasure.

"It seems I had forgotten. I won't do so again," I promised.

"You have always been such a clever girl. What a pity your father is not here to see it—his beloved daughter, serving the queen. He would be so proud of you."

"Thank you, my lady." I choked back a sob, my voice cracking. "I wish I had more time with him. Fortunately, he left me in the best possible hands."

Lady Salisbury squeezed my arm. "He was a great asset to my household. We were all the poorer for his loss." She sighed. "I remember the day he brought you to the manor, after your mother died. You were so small, even for your age. The other children in the nursery fell in love with you immediately. There is just something about you that always draws people in."

I brushed off her compliment. "They only feel that way because I give them what they need. Be it information, favours, or even a kind word. It isn't me they desire. They merely love what I can do for them." I had learned that lesson early on. Being amenable in nearly every situation had opened more doors for me than true affection ever could. I became jaded, playing the game, but never losing sight of my place in it. I saw through the courtiers who sought my company, and so far, only one seemed to genuinely have a fondness for me.

As if reading my thoughts, Lady Salisbury changed the subject. "John Husee tells me he sought your assistance in getting Lady Lisle's daughter a position?"

I instinctively tucked the hand that wore my most recent acquisition from the man's employer into the folds of my gown. "He is very persistent," I agreed. The gold ring he had passed to me felt as though it were burning a brand around my finger. "I am afraid there isn't much I can do to help him at this time. All the positions have been filled, and there are unlikely to be any openings. At least not until one of us marries." It would embarrass me to admit that I sometimes daydreamed that the ring had come from Husee himself; a token of promised matrimony that might never come.

"That is what I told him as well; everything in due time. Should his badgering ever become less than friendly, you be sure to let me know." She laid her hand on my cheek. "Alas, I have detained you long enough. We will see each other again very soon, I hope."

I waited until she took her leave before heading into the hall. Stepping through the doorway, I felt a tug on the hem of my gown, then heard an awful tearing sound. The Arundell sisters, passing on their way to the gardens, burst into gales of laughter at my misfortune. "I forgot to tell you," Joan gasped through howls of merriment. "There is a bent nail in that door. Now your skirt looks like mine!"

Mother Stonor shook her head when she saw the damage. "Go take care of that," she commanded. "I will finish here. If we don't see you at supper, one of the girls will bring you something to eat."

MARY NORRIS AND another maid were leaving as I arrived back at dorm. "Would you like us to stay and help?" the maid asked when I showed her the gash in the black taffeta. Mistress Norris looked away, choosing to inspect the silver pomander hanging at her waist rather than meet my gaze.

I politely brushed them aside, assuring the girl I had it in hand. After they were out of sight, I gleefully hurried into the emptied dorm. My first thought had been to sew the necklace into my gown. When I stitched the weight back into Joan Arundell's hem, I realized my folly. The pearls were thick and far too heavy for the fabric. However, Joan's reasoning for the weight stuck with me, her words tumbling around in my head for hours afterward. The answer had come the next morning when I dressed the queen. While the rest of the maids eavesdropped on the conversation between Her Grace and Lady Anne Beauchamp about our upcoming journey to Dover, I wrestled with the ties on the queen's bum roll.

I had two such rolls given to me by Queen Anne, who had preferred the comfort of having these bolsters tied around her hips to the unwieldy cage of a farthingale. One was for everyday use, the other I kept for formal occasions. They were both made from fine lawn cloth and stuffed with wool, full and sturdy enough to hide my secrets.

Working quickly, I unpicked the seams on either end of the roll, pulling out the barest amount of stuffing. Fearing scratches from the wool, I placed the necklace in a linen handkerchief, using embroidery thread to wrap it tightly, before feeding it through the open seams. I pushed the stuffing back inside, manipulating it around the package to hold it in place securely. Sewing the first end shut, I squeezed the roll to be sure of my work. Mercifully, I felt nothing more than the firm bolster of fabric inside, so I finished stitching up the rest, feeling relieved and rather pleased with myself. The coffer was another matter. It had to be sacrificed.

I pulled off my gown, grabbed the gap's torn edges, and widened it with a quick tug. I mended a portion of the gash with a trail of half-hearted stitches, just enough to make it look as though I had tried, then gathered the coffer up inside the pile of fabric. I put on a fresh gown after packing the newly augmented roll in my trunk. Grabbing the balled-up pile of taffeta, I stole out into the deepening twilight.

I was mere steps from the wardrobe when he called my name. "Mistress Horsman, what are you doing out here? Everyone else is in the great hall."

"Except you, Master Husee," I parried, disarming him with a smile. The band of gold encircling my finger gleamed in the fading sunlight.

"I am on my way to the ships."

"What has Lady Lisle sent this time? More cherries? Perhaps some peasecods?"

Husee grinned. "Velvet. She is most unhappy with Skutt's work on her last gown, so she wants him to remake it." He glanced down at the bundle of taffeta in my arms. "I think you both are in need of him."

"Yes, I need to get this inside straight away." I pushed past him. "Let me know if I can help with Master Skutt."

"Will that cost me another gold ring?"

Whirling around to fire back an angry retort, I found him bent over, shaking with laughter. "You are not as amusing as you imagine, Master Husee."

"You used to find more pleasure in my jests. What has changed?"

Everything and nothing. "Listen," I began instead. "If Lady Lisle wants one of her daughters at court, she will need to approach the queen herself. The king wants to inspect the defences at Dover in a few weeks. Tell Lord Lisle to sue for permission to come over. He can bring his wife, and with enough charm, she will do more to help her cause than you or I can."

"Margery, you are a gem." Husee attempted to kiss my hand, but I pulled away to avoid lessening my grip on the real treasure hidden in my arms. "When do they plan to be at Dover?"

I struggled to recall the earlier conversation between Queen Jane and Lady Beauchamp. The details were hazy. "I will write Lady Lisle all she needs to know. Meet me here this time tomorrow?"

"I have commitments outside of London," he replied wistfully. "I will send Corbett instead. He handles Lady Lisle's correspondence."

Disappointed as I felt, there was little time for farewells. Over his shoulder, I saw the distant form of Mother Stonor ambling into view. "I will look for him. I must go now, Master Husee," I said, fleeing. Once inside the wardrobe, I rushed to the back room where the crates from the Tower were stored. I slipped the silver coffer into the nearest bin and somehow made it back to the main room as Mother Stonor opened the door.

"I thought that was you, Margery. Were you able to mend your gown?"

I shook out the rumpled mess of fabric. "It was worse than I thought. I am going to have to send it to Master Skutt."

JANE SEYMOUR

HACKNEY AND YORK PLACE

T he spires of London were still bathed in the eerie light of a silvery moon when we set off for Hackney. The place had been chosen carefully: near enough to the city should the whole thing go awry, yet far enough to give the appearance of compromise. The ongoing battle with the Lady Mary had been hard-won. Still, the king wanted to show his daughter he was gracious. Forgiving. I came to realize rather quickly the choice had more to do with His Grace's other daughter—the thought of seeing Elizabeth made him physically ill.

I was surprised the first time he awoke sickened in my bed, reaching for the piss pot like a woman heavy with-child. The bouts occurred more frequently the closer the day came. *He's nervous to see the Lady Mary*, I thought. This possibility endeared him to me, feeding my growing affection. *He has loved her all along.* My brother, Tom, disabused me of the notion.

"He is afraid of running into Anne Boleyn's bastard. Or, God forfend, one of her supporters foisting the child upon him in front of an audience," he told me, shaking his head as though I were the most ignorant creature.

"Love blinds us all," I muttered in return, shamefaced by my gullibility.

"Then may the devil take it, for I want no part."

Despite Tom's blasphemy, I refused to undo the progress I had made by lingering on this knowledge. Elizabeth was not my concern. She was fed, she was clothed, and that was enough. Mary was different. She was the true heir to the throne. At least, she was in the eyes of the Heavenly Father, if not her own sire's.

Anticipation grew as we moved through the lush woodlands, drawing nearer the home Thomas Cromwell had recently returned to the king. Before that, the Duke of Northumberland haunted its halls. Perhaps it would have also housed that poor orphaned imp left behind at Hunsdon if only the duke had fathered her. How different all our lives would have been if Cardinal Wolsey had not impeded his marriage to Anne Boleyn.

Lady Bryan appeared somewhat frayed when she welcomed us at the door. She swept an effusive curtsy, then bustled us into the hall to await her charge. We were a small party, accompanied only by a handful of attendants, yet I panicked that the girl would be overwhelmed. When the Lady Mary finally entered the room, I realized my doubt had been misplaced, for she carried herself with a bearing so regal she seemed to be her mother reborn.

The very sight of her robbed the breath from my lungs. She had transformed from the last time I saw her. Where there was once a vibrant, lively cherub, now stood a slight waif of a woman—all her soft curves and brilliant shine worn away by rough treatment. Though this change was unsettling, it reassured me to see the steely determination in her piercing blue eyes.

"Your Grace?" Her tone sounded gruff and deeper than expected, underscoring my shock at discovering a stranger in place of the girl I remembered.

The king stared at her with an expression of slight bemusement. He, too, couldn't quite comprehend the young lady standing before us. In his mind, he had given her up for dead, but here she was resurrected; her words of contrition having had the power to give life. They stayed like this, eyeing each other suspiciously until the king suddenly returned her reverence with a deep bow. "Beloved daughter, it has been far too long."

The Lady Mary relaxed then, shedding her stiff demeanour like an old cloak. Her whole face lit up, the corners of her lips twitching into a meek smile. "Thank you for coming all this way, Your Grace."

"Let us dispense with the formalities," the king chided, wrapping her tightly in his arms. "You may call me Father."

Mary was so slight, I feared his bulk would crush her, but she emerged unscathed with an air of triumph. When she shifted her expectant gaze towards me, I hesitated, afraid to move without my husband's approval.

The king sensed my reluctance. "I would like to present my wife, Jane. The one true queen."

She flinched at this. Hiding her face from me, she dipped another curtsy. "It is a pleasure to see you again, Your Grace."

I wanted to rush over, embrace her like the king had. Instead, I hung back, saving it for a more private moment. "The pleasure is all mine."

Lady Bryan returned. "I thought Your Graces might appreciate a rest from your journey, so I have had your rooms prepared. Dinner will be served shortly."

THE MEAL BEGAN in near silence, all of us dancing delicately around tender wounds. After the first uneasy course, Cromwell broke the tension by asking Lady Mary about the horse he sent ahead of our visit—a reward for her obedience. Her face flushed with pleasure. "He is beautiful, Master Cromwell."

"Lord Cromwell now," the king corrected. At the end of the table, Edward went rigid. He did not bemoan the secretary's recent barony, but he deeply resented the king naming Cromwell Lord Privy Seal. He felt that position should have been his.

"My apologies," Lady Mary stumbled. "I did not know."

Annoyance flashed across Cromwell's face. "'Tis quite all right. Your Grace intended no offense, and so I took none. In any case, it will not be official until parliament concludes."

"Do you like to ride, Lady Mary?" I redirected, hoping to avoid further unpleasantness.

"Yes, Your Grace." She brightened. "Though I still have much to relearn. Before *Lord* Cromwell's generous gift, I was in sore need of a suitable mount."

Cromwell choked back a laugh. Was it her emphasis on his title or the unintended sexual innuendo he found so humorous?

"I have a gift too," the king barked, not to be outdone. "A thousand crowns, for whatever small pleasures you desire. And that is merely to start. From here on, you shall want for nothing. You need only ask."

"It would be wonderful to have a new gown." Lady Mary gazed at him in wonder. She must have longed for this day. Yet, my happiness for her felt poisoned with sadness and regret. She should never have been brought so low to feel such joy at this trifling generosity. The king's meagre offer was hers by right of birth. How disgraceful that she must beg for small comforts.

The king beamed. "Say no more. It is already done. Once we are through here, I would like to discuss your return to court."

SOMEWHERE BETWEEN THE final course of sweetmeats and Lady Mary's arrival at our chambers, the king changed his mind. The time was not right, he explained. We were leaving for Dover soon, and then it would be the summer progress. Her rooms at York Place were not ready, and the ones at Greenwich had fallen to some disrepair. He wanted to hold a feast in her honour, and that took planning. He had a great many reasons, none of them sincere.

There was little I could do to soothe Mary's dashed hopes, but I still had a gift to give her. Trembling, I unwrapped the parcel. "Lady Mary, I know this modest token cannot erase the past. However, it is my dearest hope you will be reminded of the strength of your future when you look upon it."

Lady Mary gasped when I slid the ring—an oval shaped diamond, bezel set into a circlet of brilliant gold—on her finger. "Your Grace, I..." she stammered, the words catching in her throat. "This is too much. I have nothing to give in return."

"I ask for nothing more than your friendship."

"Then we shall always be perfect friends." She leaned into my out-stretched arms.

"The jewel belonged to your mother," I whispered. Her body went limp in my embrace; her soft sob stifled against my neck. *Don't let him see you cry,* I prayed silently.

When she pulled away, her eyes were wet. "I shall treasure it always."

We spent the rest of the evening and the next day together in such pleasure that one would have never known there had previously been strife. Lady Mary was an enthusiastic gambler, besting me at both cards and dice. Overcoming her father proved a bit more complicated, but I was secretly thrilled by her nerve. She never willingly allowed his win.

The king's renewed promises to bring his daughter to London grew more effusive as our visit wound to a close. "Very soon," he enthused, kissing her cheeks as we prepared to take our leave after vespers. "I will send Cromwell to you at Hunsdon before the week is out to appoint your estate. Write up a list of those who would serve in your household, and arrangements will be made."

Lady Mary gave him a broad smile. "Monsieur Chapuys has already given me some counsel as to whom I should—"

"*Monsieur Chapuys* shall mind his own counsel," the king snapped. "You will heed Lord Cromwell's advice in this matter."

Lady Mary held his gaze. "By your command, Father." Turning to me, she said, "I will hold you in my prayers until we meet again."

That evening, we journeyed back to York Place. The king and Cromwell rode ahead of us, conferring quietly as their horses kept pace with each other. My brother and his wife drifted behind to keep me company. Edward made little effort to hide his irritation at being excluded from the conversation. "Do you think they are discussing the Imperial Ambassador?" he asked.

"I would not know, Edward."

At the city gates, the king reined in his horse, gesturing for me to catch up. "I have been discussing a letter Cromwell received from the Lady Rochford," he said. "It seems she would like a position in your service."

THE CHAMBERER HAD a bath waiting when I finally returned to my rooms. "Jane Boleyn? Are you certain?" Lady Anne repeated. I slid into the steaming water, the dirt and grime from my skin swirling across the surface. She perched herself on a stool beside me, tapping her fingers nervously against the ledge of the tub. "Edward has heard nothing of this."

"The king said she begged Cromwell to find a place for her. When I argued that all the positions had been filled, he told me there might be a vacancy." Despite the heat, a shiver skimmed the length of my skin, raising goosepimples.

Lady Anne got to her feet. "A vacancy? But who?" When I glanced up to answer, the slight swell beneath her kirtle caught my attention. *When had that happened?* Unaware of my growing alarm, she began to pace.

"Anne, your belly!"

Her hands flew instinctively to her womb. "Edward wanted to wait until we were certain," she replied sheepishly.

"And are you?" Against my intention, the question came out like an accusation.

"The child hasn't yet quickened..." she trailed off.

I forced a smile, stifling my resentment before it could escape and drown us both. "Don't fret, dearest sister, I am pleased to hear such joyous news. We shall pray for your safe delivery."

The tension in her shoulders eased. "Thank you, Jane. You are far too kind."

I opened my mouth to reprimand her use of my name but stopped myself. She spoke to me as a sister, not as her queen. *I will not stoop to pettiness.* "Have there been whispers?" I asked instead. "Anyone behaving strangely?"

"My attendant, Mistress Jerningham, keeps a watchful eye. She has never mentioned anything out of order. Surely the king would tell you if he were moving against one of your ladies?"

The arrival of Margery Horsman, arms laden with clean linen, stopped my tongue. *My husband had shared none of his movements against Anne Boleyn.*

Taking my silence as her cue, Lady Anne turned her attention to the maid. "Mistress Horsman, please inform the others in your dormitory that Lady Rochford is returning to court." A look of panic flashed upon Margery's face. Lady Anne ploughed ahead, ignoring it. "You, and they, are to treat her with the utmost respect, as a woman in her position deserves. There will be no gossip, nor mention of her husband or his family. Do you understand?"

Margery nodded. "Yes, my lady." She turned to help me from the tub.

Taking her proffered hand, I rose, quivering as the chilled water dripped down my body. When she leaned in to wrap the linen around me, I pulled her close, pressing my lips tightly against her ear. "I am counting on you to tell me everything you hear." A whisper lighter than a feather, carrying the weight of a corpse.

MARGERY HORSMAN

YORK PLACE, GREENWICH, AND DOVER

M aster Sadler's interrogation felt like an attack. What was the nature of my relationship with Lady Margaret Douglas? *Nock.* Did she ever confide in me? *Draw.* How about Lord Thomas Howard? *Loose.* Had I seen them together? *Nock.* Did they communicate through Mary Shelton's poetry book? *Draw.* Was I aware of a secret betrothal between them? *Loose.* Each question was an arrow, and I the target.

I desperately wanted to give him the answers he craved, but Cromwell's most trusted servant proved hard to read in the weak candlelight. Sir Edward Baynton used the same tactic to examine me when the lady in question was Anne Boleyn. Sitting in the darkened room, hands gripping the arms of my chair, the memory of that terrifying day pulsed through me.

"Is there anything you *do* know?" Sadler asked after my final plea of ignorance. He shoved his papers away in disgust, sending a feathered quill clattering to the floor.

"If I had more information, I would happily share, Master Sadler." I shrugged apologetically.

Sadler closed his eyes. He drew a sharp breath. When he opened them again, his face split into a grin that seemed oddly unsettling. "Of course, Mistress Horsman. I am sure you recall those early favours from my master and would do anything you could to satisfy them."

No, I had not forgotten about Martin Hastings' farm lease. It was a gift I never seemed to finish repaying; a crippling debt for a cousin I hardly knew, brought up yet again to force me into saying something that suited Cromwell's needs. The last time Sadler mentioned Martin's name, George Boleyn ended up in the Tower. "Yes, Sir," I mumbled. "May I be excused? The queen will need me soon."

"Yes, go." He nodded at the door. "Send Mary Norris in."

Returning to the dorm, I was met with a flurry of new questions, this time from the nervous maids. "It is nothing to worry about," I assured them. "We haven't done anything wrong."

Mary Arundell chewed her lip. "Is it the queen? Is she in trouble?"

"No, I think not. Master Sadler asked about Lady Margaret, the king's niece."

Jane Ashley uttered a small gasp, fleeing the group for the safety of her bed. She grabbed her abandoned prayer book, opening it to hide her face from our curious stares.

"Tell us!" Joan Arundell cried.

Mistress Ashley pretended not to hear. She set the book in her lap, closed her eyes, and began to pray quietly. We all stared helplessly at the spectacle.

"Mistress Norris, Sadler wants you next." Mary shrank back at my words. She gave a weak nod and followed me from the room.

"If he asks about the necklace, I will confess. I swear it." Her voice was emotionless. She seemed to care not whether the information she imparted might cost my life. I said nothing in response, instead offering up a silent prayer her interrogation would proceed as mine had.

After the door closed behind her, I remained in the hallway, staying behind to challenge my fate if she exposed my secret. The flames in the wall sconces flickered with every whispered murmur that escaped. Their gambolling revealed nothing meaningful. An hour passed, each minute swollen and lingering. The air thickened with the heat from a nearby hearth. Colourful tapestries on the wall closed in, stifling me. I waited, and I prayed. When the candle above me sputtered to its end, the door flew open, spitting out my companion. Mistress Norris' face was splotchy, her eyes scarlet. She shook her head violently at my reproachful stare. "He does not know."

Lady Anne Beauchamp was more upset by my tardiness than the queen. When I arrived at the royal bedchamber, flustered and perspiring after my exchange with Mistress Norris, she admitted me with a peevish huff. "You are late."

Queen Jane sat at the dressing table, gazing at herself in the glass. Her reflection looked up, taking in my dishevelled state. "You are dismissed, Sister." She pulled the coif from her head. "Mistress Horsman can take care of my hair tonight. The king is planning to visit, so do not worry about sending in any other maids."

Lady Beauchamp touched her belly. "Perhaps this shall be the night you conceive," she remarked, gliding from the room.

I caught the queen's eye in the glass, then realized my impertinence. "Excuse me, Your Grace. I should not have done that."

"Never apologize for looking me in the eye." She held up the gilded comb in her hand. "Go gently. Lady Beauchamp always pulls. I often wonder if she does it on purpose."

"She would never!"

"No, you are right. She is merely a bit strident on occasion." The queen smiled behind her hand. "Now, what news do you have? What did Master Sadler want?"

LESS THAN A month after carrying the queen's train into mass at Westminster Abbey, Lady Margaret Douglas was taken to the Tower, imprisoned for daring to promise herself to the man she loved. Lord Thomas Howard aimed too high when he sought to marry the king's niece and found himself occupying his own cell within the fortress. I wondered if it was the same cell where George was detained, both men abandoned and discarded by their closest kin. Parliament ended, spilling ink upon Howard's death warrant, and freeing the king to commence the much-longed-for progress to Dover.

We set off from Greenwich, moving overland through the countryside, with a train of carts and carriages following behind. Upon our arrival at Rochester on Wednesday afternoon, we were informed that Fitzroy, the king's bastard, was ill. I went to bed that night expecting a swift return to London on the morrow. Instead, Mother Stonor awakened me at dawn with instructions to dress the queen for her next audience at Sittingbourne. By Friday, we were at Canterbury, with our destination on the horizon.

We rode through the imposing stone curtain walls of Dover Castle on Saturday morning, a flock of gulls crying overhead. Beyond the welcoming contingent of soldiers, clad in the king's livery, crenelated towers rose to meet the sky. In the brilliant sunlight, the jewel tones of the leaded glass windows were blinding. Bringing up a hand to shield my eyes, I saw that the shimmer was coming from the golden phoenix in Queen Jane's badge. *Windows like these must have been commissioned some time ago.* The realization sickened me.

"Mistress Horsman, you look a little peaked." Michael Lyster reined his courser beside me. The horse whickered in irritation.

"It is this heat." I smiled wanly. "All I need is a drink."

"Find me in the great hall during supper. I shall have an ale waiting for you." He whistled at the horse, digging his heels to spur on the animal. I watched with interest as he joined the boisterous group of men surrounding Lord Beauchamp.

Mary Arundell disrupted my gawking. "Who was that?"

"I think he works for the queen's brother. He served as my escort when I took Her Grace's pearls to the embroiderer."

"Michael Lyster does not work for Lord Beauchamp," Mistress Ashley trilled. "He serves under the king, and his father is Chief Baron of the Exchequer. He is a widower—a *desirable widower* at that. Perhaps he is interested in Margery?"

"No, that's not it," I replied, remembering the sorrow in Michael's eyes the day we met. "Besides, I have no money for a dowry. What would he want with me?"

"Never underestimate yourself, Margery," Joan Arundell quipped, a mischievous arch to her brow. "This time last year, Jane Seymour's future appeared bleak, but now she is queen. Who would have ever believed it?"

JANE SEYMOUR

DOVER, CANTERBURY, AND GREENWICH

At Dover, the ocean rose to meet the sky, stretching out before us like a ribbon of blue. Far from the sweltering, fetid air of London, bracing coastal winds licked at my face, salting my skin. Beneath the chalky white cliffs, an armada of ships teemed with activity. Joining the royal vessels were those that had come from across the channel carrying Lord Lisle and his retinue. The courtier had wormed his way into securing an audience with the king, so I was urged to greet the lord's wife beforehand. It was a meeting I did not relish.

During our time together as ladies-in-waiting, I discovered early on that Honour Lisle could be brash and bold. Though she seemingly operated within the bounds of decency, her forcefulness often teetered towards the edge. She wanted the best of everything: the costliest gowns, the choicest produce, and the most lucrative positions. She would beg, borrow, and possibly even steal to get them. At least that was the sense I got the last time I was in her company. But perhaps that was unfair, I reasoned. *I hoped.* In truth, I pitied Lady Lisle in her need to continuously remind those of us at court she still existed. How lonely it must be so far from friendly faces.

I found her waiting in my designated presence chamber an hour before the appointed time. She stood near my chair of estate, running her fingers over the embroidery worked into the violet upholstery. Startled, she attempted to cover her blunder with an elaborate curtsy—one that she had obviously practiced with some care—but the feigned contrition only served to annoy me further. "They told me I could wait in here, Your Grace. If there has been a mistake, I will happily point out the groom who erred."

"That is unnecessary, Lady Lisle. We would hate to cause any unpleasantness when we have been welcomed with such pomp here at Dover, wouldn't you agree?"

Lady Lisle's face fell. "I meant no offense, Your Grace. It's just, well—" she faltered. "I suppose I would want to know if it had been one of my grooms."

"Are your servants known for their impertinence? What must it be like in the wilds of Calais?" I added with dramatic effect.

From the corner of my eye, I saw Mary Arundell stifle a giggle. Mother Stonor's well-aimed jab straightened her.

"Calais is by no means wild," Lady Lisle began, and then she paused. "It seems I have begun on the wrong foot, Your Grace."

"It appears that way, my lady. We are willing to start over."

She took a deep breath. "Thank you for inviting us, Your Grace. It is a great honour to see you again."

"And you as well, Lady Lisle. Now, what is it you would have of us? That is what this audience is about, is it not?"

Lady Lisle pulled at her sleeves, her slender fingers twisting the fabric nervously. I recognized the pattern, spring blooms wrought in cloth of silver. There was a kirtle made of the same material in my wardrobe, one of Anne Boleyn's leavings. I had worn it only yesterday at Canterbury. "If it pleases Your Grace, I hoped to find a place in your household for my daughters. Katherine is the elder at nineteen, but Anne trained in one of the most distinguished households in France. If Your Grace required it, I am certain Madame de Riou would be happy to send her recommendations."

Lady Lisle chittered away, praising her younger daughter's accomplishments, all the while oblivious to her case's unmaking. The more she described the girl, the more the girl indeed began to sound like another Anne—the Anne whom no one at court wanted to remember.

I held up my hand to stop her. "My lady, it would seem you believe Anne to be more prepared for service, yet she is the younger daughter. By how many years?"

"She will be fifteen in the autumn."

Sweet relief poured over me. "You are aware, having served in the royal household yourself, that Anne is far too young to accept at this time?"

"Your Grace, with her experience—"

"We are truly sorry, Lady Lisle, but we dare not make an exception. In any case, the point is moot, as there are no vacancies. When, and if, a position becomes available, we would happily consider your elder daughter. Until then, there is nothing to be done."

Lady Lisle stared at me wordlessly. After a few tense moments, she knelt a curtsy far less refined than the first one. "Thank you for your consideration." Her voice was terse, filled with hurt. "I wish you a safe journey back to London."

I expected the refusal to be more satisfying, but it left me feeling unmoored. I had dashed a girl's hopes with one small word for no other reason than dislike of her mother and fear of my husband. And yet, how could I possibly have allowed it? At best, the king would be upset to have a reminder of his last wife. At worst, he would enjoy it and take her to bed. Or further. *Lady Lisle would love a crown on her daughter's head.* No, Anne Bassett was not coming to court, and neither was her sister.

FOR ALL THE ceremony that accompanied it, supper turned out to be a solemn affair. Piqued by her failure to secure her daughter's place, Lady Lisle sulked over her roasted boar. By contrast, her husband was his usual affable self. Arthur Plantagenet was the illegitimate son of His Grace's grandfather, the fourth King Edward, and shared the former monarch's taste for merrymaking. Still, for all his good intentions, he was unable to conjure more than a few half-hearted chuckles out of his royal nephew. The king was pleasant—if distracted—appearing for all the world as though he would have rather been elsewhere.

He revealed the source of his distress when he retired to my bedchamber later that evening. A letter from St. James' Palace had arrived while he was inspecting the ships: Fitzroy lingered near death. He paced the room like a caged lion, muttering curses under his breath until he collapsed in exhaustion. He slept fitfully, twisting himself up in the sweat-soaked linen, while I laid awake staring up at the oak tester, shivering in the cool night air. When I managed to doze off, he rolled over, slinging a heavy arm across my body, pinning me in place. We stayed locked that way until rays of sunlight began filtering through the leaded glass windows.

The king issued a loud snore as I slipped out of his embrace. Padding lightly across the floor, I knelt at the prie-dieu in the corner, murmuring a silent prayer for the sick boy: *Lord Jesu, please send comfort to your child, Henry Fitzroy, in his hour of need. Henry must not lose another son; the agony of it would be unspeakable.*

A sharp rap at the door stirred the king from his slumber. He lurched towards it, disoriented and stumbling. "Who's there?" he shouted.

"Sadler, Your Grace," came the muffled reply.

My husband yanked the door so hard it bucked on its hinges. "What do you want?"

Ralph Sadler entered wearing a furrowed brow. "Your Grace, the Duke of Richmond, Henry Fitzroy—"

"I know my son's name," the king spat. "What news of him, you fool?"

"I regret to inform Your Grace that he died shortly after midnight. They sent a rider only after it was certain."

The king's ears darkened beneath his nightcap. "Thank you, Master Sadler. Please send for my chamberlain. I shall need two gowns of black waiting in my rooms."

He carefully latched the door behind Sadler's hurrying figure, tracing his fingers over the intricate lock in silence. With pursed lips, he moved to the wash basin, where he splashed cold water on his face. He caught his reflection in the glass, pausing to stare back at his own hollow eyes. "What have I done to deserve such punishments?" he seethed. "Why must I be brought so low?" Gripping the basin, he ripped it from the wooden stand and sent it hurtling through the air. Water exploded against the stone walls. A chunk of rock crashed to the floor. "Why, Wife? Why?" he screamed.

I shrank from his fury, taking refuge behind the bed. The rush mats on the floor scratched at my bare feet, leaving painful welts. I refused to cry out.

In a rush, he was on me, crushing my shoulders against the wall, his breath hot in my ear. "You will give me a son, Jane, or I shall call down the hounds of Hell against every Seymour in this forsaken place. God so help me."

"Yes, Your Grace." I willed my voice not to tremble.

He pulled away, dropping his hands to his side, fists clenched tightly. "See to it that you do, for I fear what might become of you if you do not." Without a backward glance, he stalked out the door.

Fearing the late hour, Margery Horsman arrived in anticipation of her summons—before I had time to gather myself. Thus, she found me curled up, staring at the puddled water on the floor. "Your Grace?" she asked tentatively, picking up the pewter wash basin, hesitant to touch me. "Are you hurt? Can I help you up?"

My breath made ripples in the puddle. "Please give me a moment, Mistress Horsman. I never intended anyone to see me in this manner."

Margery knelt beside me, lowering her face to mine. "I would heed any command from Your Grace, but I feel I must insist on disobedience in this instance." She held out her hand.

I allowed the maid to help me to my feet, shame overpowering me. In my former life, I could have hidden away, sobbing until my eyes grew swollen. I could have raged. I could have screamed. I could have displayed any emotion I felt in private. Now that I was queen, the highest woman in the land, I had no right to privacy—or such selfish indulgences as weeping.

"That's better, Your Grace, none the worse for wear." Margery pulled slivers of river rush from my hair. "Would you like me to get Lady Beauchamp?"

"No." I stopped her hand. "You mustn't tell anyone of this, Mistress Horsman. I beg—no, *command*—you never to speak of it."

"I shall take it to my grave," she promised. "I will be back with fresh water for Your Grace's basin, and then we will begin anew."

"Thank you, Mistress Horsman. When you return, please bring my black brocade gown. We are in mourning."

WE RETURNED TO the St Augustine monastery at Canterbury on the journey back to Greenwich. The prior, Thomas Goldwell, was a pleasant and dutiful host, but his guests arrived far more subdued on this second visit. After supper I made my excuses, retreating to the chapel for prayers. I trusted only the Lord to safeguard my secrets.

I sensed the king's arrival before he made his presence known, the rustle of taffeta as my maids bowed and scraped, sounding a warning he was near. I pretended not to hear it, remaining on my knees at the altar, head bowed. He crouched next to me, smelling of mint, and sweat, and incense. "Jane," he whispered, dispensing with any intention he had to join me in prayer. "I apologize if you feel I spoke too harshly at Dover. It was heartache causing me to lash out—grief for my only boy." A quiet sob accompanied the last word: boy.

"Your Grace has nothing for which to apologize. I am the sorry one for having not yet conceived Your Grace's much longed-for heir." *Had I truly deserved his wrath?*

He issued a blast of bitter laughter. "Perhaps I will never have a son, and then we shall be plunged once again into the brutal wars that plagued my ancestors."

"It is early days for us yet, Your Grace. My brother and his wife have only just now conceived, but their wedding was over a year past."

"Yes, well, that is all fine and good when you are young," he balked, his voice growing louder with each word. "I do not enjoy the same luxury of time."

"I promised Your Grace a son, and I intend to succeed where others have failed," I replied evenly, claiming responsibility for a promise that had never been mine. Those vows were given to the king by my brother, Edward, and his friends.

The king rose. "I fear I may have made this marriage in haste," he huffed. "When you finish here, send for me."

Had he not commanded it, I would never have sent for him again.

AT GREENWICH, THE king set aside his mourning clothes, all responsibility for his son's funeral and disposition falling to the Duke of Norfolk. He quickly returned to the business of ruling, meeting with both the French and Spanish ambassadors before we set off again on the summer progress. Cromwell often visited, bringing with him some matter or another requiring His Grace's attention, but on the night before we set off, it was I who requested an audience with the Lord Privy Seal.

He looked different than he had when I last saw him. His hair had been trimmed and topped by a fine velvet cap with a garnet cabochon sewn into the crown. The jewel reminded me of Queen Catherine's badge, the pomegranate. She had often worn the deep red gemstone in honour of her homeland, Granada. Was he making his allegiances more apparent now that the Boleyn's were gone? It was they who had always supported a French alliance, never Cromwell.

"Thank you for seeing me, Your Grace," he said, as though it had been he who called this meeting. "I hope you are faring well in your new role?"

"Of course, my lord. All has gone better than I could have wished," I answered.

If Cromwell sensed dishonesty in my words, he politely overlooked it, countering with a smile. "Your Grace had the benefit of many years in the household of the Dowager Princess of Wales. Though she was never legally queen, no one could argue that she did not rise to the honour while holding the title. She was the very model of piety and charity."

"I would agree, my lord, and strive to follow her example."

Cromwell nodded. He glanced down at the roll of parchment in his hand before returning his gaze to me. "An admirable pursuit, Your Grace, but I would urge caution. The king will not welcome any reminders of his brother's widow."

"Catherine's memory is unavoidable." I moved towards the window embrasure, out of earshot of my gawking maids. "Regardless of what I do, the king has two very potent reminders of the other women who have called him husband."

Cromwell's sparse brows jumped in surprise. "Is that why Your Grace called me here?" He tapped the parchment roll against his palm.

"Yes," I began, then stopped. "No, actually, I wanted to ask your counsel."

He leaned closer, hungry for whatever morsel I was about to confess. "I pledge to give Your Grace my best."

"How do I make the king happy?" I whispered.

Cromwell pulled back, the slight twitch in his lip revealing his disappointment. "The answer to that is simple: you must put a boy in the cradle."

"I have heard this refrain before!" The abruptness of my retort attracted concerned stares from the brace of maids sewing near the hearth. Ignoring them, I lowered my voice. "Even if I were to fall pregnant today, there would be months of waiting until the babe comes. What must I do until then?"

He considered me thoughtfully. "Your Grace must heed the advice of Daedalus."

"The father of Icarus? I must apologize, my lord. My knowledge of Greek stories is lacking. My father did not deem them suitable for a daughter."

"An unfortunate belief amongst most fathers, I am afraid." He sighed. "Daedalus was a craftsman hired by the king of Crete to build a labyrinth, where he could imprison the dangerous beast born of his wife's liaison with a bull. Unfortunately, Daedalus found *himself* trapped in the labyrinth instead, when he helped an enemy of the king defeat the beast. To escape, the craftsman fashioned wings from wax and feathers, a pair for his son, Icarus, and a pair for himself. The father set out first, warning the son to stick to a middle path. If he flew too low, the damp sea would weigh down the feathers, and if he flew too high, the sun would melt the wax."

I could see where the story was headed. "So, which was it? The sea or the sun?"

Cromwell smiled. "It was the sun, of course. Icarus grew complacent soaring high above the clouds, forgetting how dangerous it was."

"I am sorry, my lord. I do not see how this parable helps in any way."

"I shall put it plainly, Your Grace: there is great danger in striving to make the king happy. For when you reach that point, where you believe you have accomplished this impossible task, you will be lulled into a false sense of safety. And that is the most dangerous place to be."

I stared at him in astonishment, unable to form a response to such a blunt warning.

"Now, I must be off." Bowing, he tucked the parchment under his arm. "I have a message from Lady Bryan I must deliver to the king."

His swift diversion untethered my tongue. The knot of worry in my stomach tightened. "Is it about the Lady Mary?"

"The letter is regarding her sister, I am afraid. The Lady Elizabeth has grown out of her wardrobe, and Lady Bryan begs for replacements."

"Is the girl well besides?" I found myself asking.

"Lady Bryan mentioned that she suffers great pain with the coming of her teeth, but that is to be expected."

A memory of my younger sister, Dorothy, drifted into my thoughts. How she sobbed when her teeth broke through; desperate wails that only our mother's comforting touch could ease. For all the experience Lady Bryan had, it could never compete. *Poor Elizabeth—nothing more than an innocent, motherless child.* I had been so neglectful. "Whatever the child needs, I will gladly send from my stores."

"Are you certain, Your Grace?"

The words vomited out, falling like sickness from my lips. "Only if the king is so inclined."

Cromwell gave me a knowing smile. "The sun is less likely to burn when you mind the middle path, my queen."

MARGERY HORSMAN

CHERTSEY AND AMPTHILL

ecrets are like rabbits—my father used to say—*they tend to breed.* Honesty had always been a matter of life and death to him. He saw lies as cancer upon the soul. I was an innocent then, unable to appreciate the myriad of reasons people had for hiding the truth—not all of them wrong. When Queen Anne's beloved Purkoy died, we kept it from her for days. We knew she would be devastated over the loss of the little dog. Thinking back on it, I was thankful for the lie because it meant Anne Boleyn saw fewer days of heartbreak during her unfinished life. Finding Queen Jane on the floor, in a miserable heap, seemed to me the same sort of secret. Still, my father's adage proved accurate: my collection of secrets—for good or for ill—was growing.

A fortnight after that day in Dover, we set off on the summer progress. Moving through the verdant rolling hills and lush, ancient forests, I left all thoughts of my own secret, safe in its linen and wool cocoon at York Place, behind. Freed from my burden, I was further comforted by the change in my mistress. The sultry afternoons spent in the field, chasing stags, and flying hawks, were like a balm for her sorrow. Riding out on a fine white palfrey, back arched, bow and arrow a perfect extension of her limbs, she was the goddess Diana in human form. Years spent hunting with her brothers deep in the Savernake Forest had crafted her into an earnest huntress, and she revelled in the joy of it.

The celebratory mood continued indoors with all manner of feasting and cheer. At Chertsey, the king sent his musicians to enliven our spirits, and for the first time in Queen Jane's reign, there was dancing in her chamber. Had the cause of Her Grace's pain been resolved, or had she merely resigned herself to its inevitability? For all the trappings marriage to King Henry brought, it also wrought a particular sort of unhappiness. If I had not known otherwise, I would wonder if all marriages were so fraught.

Determined to press his suit for Lady Lisle's daughters and conclude some murky business for her husband, Master Husee trailed along with the court, following us from Chertsey to Woking, Ampthill to East Hampstead, then on to Grafton and back again. In the field and at the table, he kept close to the royal party. Husee was always angling for an opportunity to bend the king's ear or discuss his mistress with the queen. Much as I liked the man, his guilelessness often grated me. How could he not see? Despite whatever fair words Her Grace offered Lady Lisle, she remained unyielding.

Returning to Ampthill after a morning hunt in the nearby forest, I threaded my way through a pack of horses slung with the day's take. Cringing at the crimson-soaked slaughter, I tugged the reins, pulling my skittish mare from the scent of blood and death. Rather than joining my brethren at the head of the column, I peeled off in the direction of the castle, with hopes I would manage a private moment to change my clothing before being called to help the queen do the same.

Beneath the gatehouse, an austere carriage waited. Two porters lugged a trunk out of its yawning doorway. The larger of the two tugged the handle causing the smaller one to lurch forward. "Come on, you," he grunted at the boy. "On to the queen's lodgings." The boy staggered under the weight. I watched them leave, then hurried to stable my horse.

Back in the castle, I changed quickly with the chamberer's help, donning the tawny gown Queen Jane always complimented. "Whose carriage is down there?" I pointed to the window overlooking the courtyard. The girl shrugged. She dumped my filthy basin water into her pail. "Did you see who came in?" I tried again.

"No, Miss," she answered finally. "No one but you."

Anchoring my hood into place, I attempted another look. This time, the carriage was trundling through the gate, beyond the castle walls. Within minutes, the king's sumptuous purple hat rode into the frame. I pulled away from the leaded glass, snatched my sewing off a nearby stool, and rushed towards the royal apartments.

Unsure of who I expected to find in the watching chamber, the emptiness that greeted me disappointed. Despite the cheery fire dancing in the hearth, the cavernous room stood barren, devoid of warmth. The woven curtains covering the windows swayed on a draught. Spying a tray of fruit on the sideboard, I bit into an apple, wincing at the tart tang of its flesh. I cursed at the juice that spilled down my chin, leaving wet splotches across the top of my gown. A chorus of voices filtered beneath the door. I blotted the spots with my handkerchief.

"Mistress Horsman, we wondered where you got off to." The queen strode in, tucking a stray tendril of hair beneath her hood. Colour flushed her cheeks. "Finish your apple and meet us in the raying chamber. No need to bring anything. Mistress Stonor has already sent for the russet damask." She disappeared through the privy chamber door before I realized I had forgotten to curtsy.

"That hue suits you," the queen continued as though we had never parted when I slipped in behind her. "I was always too pale for it—such a pity."

"A lot of good it has done me, Your Grace." Dust rained over the rushes when I pulled the riding gear over her head. "I fear I shall die an old maid."

She dunked a square of linen in the silver wash basin. "Don't fret, Margery." She scrubbed the dirt from her face and neck, and then washed between her thighs. Bent over, her breath came in short blasts. Naked of shimmering jewels and fine fabrics, she put me in mind of a common milkmaid. "I am ready for my hose," she said, tossing the linen back into the basin.

Piece by piece, we returned her queenly glory: silken hose, satin kirtle, and damask gown. I tied her hair back, then settled a heavy collar of diamonds around her neck. "Is this new, Your Grace? I do not recall seeing this before."

She ran her fingers over the gemstones. "The king bought it for me. How do you like it?"

"Beautiful, Your Grace." *Was it a gift to assuage his guilt?*

"That reminds me, Margery. I wanted to ask you something—"

Another voice interrupted. It was low and mournful, hauntingly familiar. "There were once falcons in those windows. Now, they are gone."

I spun around, knocking a silver comb to the floor. It screeched against the tile. My mouth went dry.

The queen got to her feet. "Lady Rochford, we expected you at Greenwich." She extended her hand in a peace offering. "How good of you to come early."

"My father had business with Lord Cromwell." Lady Rochford ignored the gesture, her gaze alighting on the diamonds instead. "I did not wish to bother Your Grace, but he thought it an extravagance to pay a second carriage when one could carry us both."

"Unfailingly practical, our Lord Morley." Queen Jane said kindly. "It is no trouble at all. We will have a room made up."

"Thank you, Your Grace. I will await instruction from the Lord Chamberlain." Lady Rochford bobbed a curtsy and started towards the entryway, pausing before she stepped through. "My deepest apologies for bursting in on Your Grace." Her cheeks burned with shame. "Having been so long from court, I seem to have lost my manners."

"We have already forgotten, Lady Rochford. Waste no more regrets on it."

Lady Rochford nodded. "My regrets could flood the Thames," she sighed, slipping out of sight.

The queen and I stared at each other wordlessly, neither of us sure how to react to what had just transpired. After a moment of tense silence, I bounded into action, grabbing her gabled hood from the dressing table. "Shall we finish, Your Grace?"

JANE SEYMOUR

AMPTHILL

Beside me, the king groaned with pleasure. "Have you tried the venison, sweetheart?" He prodded me with an elbow. "The most tender by far this year. Wouldn't you agree?"

I had yet to touch the dish, my attention elsewhere. "Delicious," came my distracted reply. *Where had she gone?* I wondered. *Where was the wraith that appeared unannounced in my raying chamber?*

"Eat, Jane!" the king snapped, catching my full attention. "This is your kill, after all." He dabbed primly at a spot of grease near the corner of his mouth.

Spearing a hunk of charred flesh from the trencher, I fought back a wave of disgust. While I knew my husband meant the red buck shot during the morning hunt, I could not help thinking of George Boleyn. The meat tasted of death.

Scanning the hall again, I spotted my quarry beneath the minstrel gallery. In her black widow weeds, Lady Rochford was nearly lost in the surrounding shadows. She was propped against the panelled wall, nursing a cup of wine, a faraway look in her eyes—hollow grey eyes that had cut right through me only hours before. Still, she seemed lost, unsure of how to act. Slipping in like that, unannounced, would have been perfectly acceptable behaviour—had her husband's sister still been queen.

When the music slowed, and the dancers changed partners, one of the men broke away. Lady Rochford visibly relaxed as he neared her, a hint of relief creeping into her face. It took a moment to come to me, but then I recognized him: Henry Parker.

"I see Lady Rochford has been reacquainted with her brother," the king remarked, sounding pleased with himself. "No doubt, he will help her settle in."

"It is too soon. She is still in mourning." I thought of Mother, all alone in a house full of servants. She wept for months after Father's passing. Refusing to eat, she hid away in her chamber, sobbing quietly in the place where he had once lain. My sister, Dorothy, told me that when she crawled into the bed with her one night, Mother said she could still smell him on the bedclothes. She begged us not to launder them, and we obeyed her wishes for as long as we could. On the day we washed the sheets, her wails could be heard echoing through the Savernake.

"The black? Nothing more than a display of her newfound wealth," he scoffed. "Crum told me Wiltshire was incensed when I demanded he increase her yearly allowance to a hundred pounds. He took me for a fool. I knew the price of her jointure—I paid half of it."

"Losing his children that way," I gnawed my lip nervously, "their treason, I mean. It must have been difficult." I halted, afraid to continue this line of reasoning.

"His anger is displaced." Tossing his napkin over the trencher, the king waved a page over to clear it. He leaned back in his chair. "His quarrel was with those children, not me. They are a blotch upon the Boleyn name."

Knowing better than to argue, I changed the subject. "Are we to go hawking tomorrow? My brother's goshawk arrived this afternoon. I am eager to see how she does."

The king stroked his beard, weaving his fingers through the faded copper strands, which seemed to turn greyer by the day. "Mayhap, I have much to do while Crum is here. The commissioners have returned from Catesby, and he wants to discuss it. We also need to go over plans for the coronation. He will be bringing the warrant for the jewellers—have you decided who will be your keeper? It might be just the position for Lady Rochford."

I glanced over at the lady in question. She was in the same spot, alone now, hunched over with her face buried in her hands. The flickering light of the torches almost hid the shudder of her shoulders. How could I possibly ask the poor woman to dress me in her dead sister's jewels? "I have something else in mind for Lady Rochford, dear heart." Trying a tactic that had worked on him before, I traced my fingertips down his arm. He shivered at my touch. "I would like to promote Margery Horsman. Since she dresses me every morning, it would be most convenient to have my jewels in her care." The king began nodding. "But only if Your Grace thinks it wise," I added. "I defer to your counsel."

He kissed the tips of my fingers. "If that is what you wish, darling Jane. Alas, I must bid you adieu. There is much requiring my attention, and so I return to the privy chamber." With great effort, he heaved himself from the chair. "Please, do not let it hamper your evening. We shall re-join once I am through."

IT WAS NEAR midnight by the time the king arrived at my chamber. I wanted nothing more than to sink beneath the covers but felt compelled to lavish attention upon him in return for getting my way earlier. Having prepared to perform my wifely duty, I was surprised to find him in a more reflective mood. He wanted to unburden himself first.

King Henry spoke of Queen Catherine and the dawning of their union—how impossible it had seemed at the time. "I was never intended to be king," he mused dreamily. "When Arthur died, clearing the way, I believed God was showing the world he favoured me instead." Because of this bounty, he felt he owed it to Arthur to marry his widow, despite the misgivings gnawing at his heart. His voice pitched and dipped, alternately cursing Catherine for her obstinance, then scorning his ministers for the way they forced him to treat her. Back and forth, he vacillated until my hand itched to strike him across the face. I wanted to scream at him for driving such a godly woman to her grave.

For Anne Boleyn, there was no such pity—she was evil incarnate. She deceived him and seduced good men to eternal damnation in Hell. "And she had no beauty to recommend her," he scoffed. He derided her French manners, demeaned her supposed cleverness, even sneered at the way she had played her lute. Everything she ever said or did or cherished was heartily ridiculed by a man who grew smaller in my estimation with each word dribbling from his lips. And yet, I swallowed his bile like a starving penitent, burning inside while I soothed his wounds with a tender hand, knowing all the while that to do otherwise would condemn me to the same fate as his previous wives. To argue would be akin to screaming into a storm—dangerous and utterly futile. When he cupped my chin and whispered, "I thank God for you, Jane. You would never do such terrible things," I felt a pall settle over me.

Purging these grievances had a restorative effect, stirring the king's amours, and soon we were abed. He laboured atop me, grunting and wheezing. The ghastly spectres of Catherine and Anne watched over his rounded shoulders in judgment. Unable to shake their ever-looming presence, I closed my eyes and endured, holding my breath to keep the foul stench of his leg wound out of my nostrils. When the fingers of dawn clawed me from a fitful slumber, I awoke to find him staring down at me with a beatific smile. "Forget Crum's papers, I feel like taking the falcons out today."

THE BIRD TOOK flight from Edward's outstretched hand with a violent shriek. He grinned. "She is lighter than expected." He watched the skies with unrestrained glee, a roar of laughter escaping when the goshawk returned with a limp mouse hanging from her beak.

"Well done, my lord." Michael Lyster hurried over with a tiny leather hood to cover the bird's eyes. "That makes four. Shall we try for bigger prey? Would you like me to call for the falcon?"

"That is enough for now," he replied, giving the bird over for return to the Master of the Mews. "I want to watch His Grace's hunt." I followed his gaze across the field to the distant figures of the king and Thomas Cromwell. Master and servant seemed to be enjoying themselves immensely, and Edward loathed being left out. "Would Your Grace care to join me?"

"Did I give you leave? What if I have not finished?" I tried to keep a straight face but fell to laughter at his shocked expression. "Edward, I am only teasing you. Of course, we can go to the king."

My brother smiled wickedly. Wading through the lake of grass, he confessed, "Have I ever told you how much I hate that I must defer to you now? Had I known you would be so insufferable, I might have rethought tempting the king with you."

Said in jest, his remark contained more than a grain of truth. Though he was much too polite ever to say it, Edward took special pride in being the eldest. No matter the benefits he reaped from it, my elevation must have a stung. Such pleasure it gave me to know this. "Yes, well. Had you not been so fixated on the rewards, you might have given me to someone less capricious, rather than selling to highest bidder." Contented by his shocked expression, I turned to other matters. "How is your lady wife? We have missed her at court."

"Growing rounder and more disagreeable by the day," he snorted, looking away.

"Such a happy condition, though. I find myself more envious than I care to admit."

Edward twisted a gold button on his doublet. "What do you think they are planning?"

Looking up, I spied the king slapping Cromwell on the arm. His lips peeled back in a wide grin. "He said Cromwell wanted to discuss the Catesby monastery."

Edward frowned. "The prioress has been hounding Cromwell to spare them. The king cannot be thrilled to hear that."

"Why not?"

"When the commissioners visited in May, they returned with promising reports on its good order. The king still insisted upon closing it down. Cromwell showed him the first letter from the prioress, taking up their cause. His Grace said he would think on it but ended up sending the commissioners back to turn the prioress and her nuns out. She was more obdurate than he anticipated, and three months on, the nuns still have not left."

A most unwelcome revelation. The embers of my rage rekindled. "I thought the dissolutions ended with Anne's death. Was it not part of the Boleyns' crusade of supposed reform?" The king had made it seem like it was *her* doing. It was *her* fault the abbeys were closing; *her* fault that his daughter was treated so poorly. He lied about Mary; had he lied about the abbeys as well?

Edward tugged at my hand, bringing me to a jarring halt. "Jane, we have been together since the day you came red-faced and squalling into the world, and never once have I known you to be stupid." His voice was deep, tight. "If claiming wilful blindness will satisfy your conscience, then do as you may, but be wary of deceiving yourself."

Shaking off Edward's grip, I tried to mirror the grin I had seen on the king's face, desperately hoping an air of confidence would smother the flames in my chest. "If it is money the king wants, perhaps I can perform a miracle that will please everyone." Edward shook his head in warning. I forged ahead. "Your Grace!" I called, nearing my husband and his companion.

"What is it, dear Jane?" The king moved towards us, Cromwell shuffling behind with an armload of rolled parchment.

"Edward has just kindly reminded me of my charitable duties—which, I am ashamed to admit, have been utterly neglected," I replied breathlessly. "I know it has been customary in the past for queens to grant bequests to religious houses in thanksgiving, but I yearn to go further because I feel as though Your Grace has made me the most blessed queen in Christendom."

The king raised his brow, intrigued by my proposition. "What do you have in mind, my love?"

"Well, if Your Grace would permit it, I would like to purchase one of the abbeys set to close. It doesn't have to be a large or very wealthy one. I merely want it ran by a sober and pious prioress."

Silence fell as we awaited the king's response. After a tense moment, Cromwell spoke up, "Her Grace's offer might solve the issue of Catesby. It is certainly worth considering."

"Perhaps, Crum. Perhaps." The king brushed us off, fleeing towards the snowy white gyrfalcon dancing in its cage. He called loftily over his shoulder, "I shall chew it over, darling Jane."

Cromwell bowed, indicating that my audience had come to an end. Beckoning my ladies, I marched across the field with all the dignity I could muster, my impotence before them leaving behind a bitter taste. Anne Boleyn would never have allowed herself to be humiliated that way, swept aside like last night's crumbs. *And Anne Boleyn is dead*, a voice screamed inside my head, *so you must suffer what she would not.*

WHEN WE BROKE our fast the next morning, my husband informed me that he had tasked his surveyor, James Nedam, with my coronation preparations. Using the king's design, Master Nedam and his carpenters were to build a high walkway leading from Westminster Hall through the palace and across the road, into the abbey. Rather than process through the streets like Catherine and Anne, my route would be high above it, where everyone could see me. Nedam would also erect buildings for the various household offices in charge of making the banquet's food and pastries, complete with fresh paint and plaster, and tinted windows featuring my badge.

Discussing these plans sent a frisson of excitement through me, strong enough to push my frustration over Catesby out of mind. The king was obviously not keen on entertaining—nor further discussing—my offer, but at least I had escaped punishment. The coronation would go ahead—this was a promising sign.

Further to the construction at Westminster, the king had commissioned a jeweller from Holland. The man would be granted a license to hire an astounding number of journeymen to make my jewels and devices. "Six of them! Can you imagine it?" he crowed. "You will be encrusted in gemstones."

"Is that necessary?" I thought of the poor nuns at Catesby and their brethren, turned out to wander destitute and hungry, all in the king's pursuit of their riches. Wearing finery tainted by their subjugation was more than I could bear. "Surely there are enough suitable pieces in the jewel house already."

The king's face constricted. "Are you not pleased?" he grumbled, the corners of his mouth turning down.

Fumbling for an excuse, I began reciting the costs: the works at Westminster, the food, the entertainment, new gowns for myself and my ladies, trappings for the horses.

"Darling Jane, these are my gifts to you. Leave the figures to me." He leaned in for a kiss. "Sir Antony Denny has sent your jewel coffer ahead to Windsor. Holbein wants to see the collection before he sets down new designs." He wanted the artist to refashion a few pieces, specifically an initial pendant worn by my predecessor. He could not bring himself to utter her name.

"I will inform Mistress Horsman of her promotion."

"Very good," the king replied, peace restored once again. "And what of Lady Rochford?"

I had given this much thought. As the wife of a traitor, Jane Rochford had been stripped of her husband's properties. Still, she retained his title—both a blessing and a curse. The stipend she received from George's father was not nearly enough to cover her household expenses. She needed higher salary and generous bouche of court to ease the financial burden the title entailed. "I would have her in my bedchamber."

"A privilege indeed." The king cocked his head. "Are you certain?"

I had already practiced my answer. "Yes. I want to keep my eye on her."

RUBY

Sacrifice

SEPTEMBER & OCTOBER 1536

MARGERY HORSMAN

F uriously flicking a fan about her face, Joan Arundell leaned against the open window to catch an errant breeze, groaning in pleasure when it danced across her dewy skin. Freed of her bulky velvet hood, wild tendrils of golden hair fluttered in the current, settling limply across the nape of her neck.

With an annoyed grunt, Joan's sister barged into the embrasure, her elbow delivering a sharp rebuke. "There is more than enough room for us both," Mary Arundell whined, dabbing her forehead with a handkerchief. "Will this infernal heat ever end?"

"Rain is coming." I anchored my needle, tossing my sewing to the floor in frustration. Heat and sniping aside, my mind swirled like a tempest. The storm began the morning Queen Jane called me to her chamber at Ampthill and asked me to be her jewel keeper. My heart filled with pride—how pleased my father would have been to see me raised so high. This joyful news buoyed me through a month of endless bickering in the maid's dorm, then it all came crashing down last night when Her Grace informed me of our meeting with Master Holbein. The king wanted the artist to remake some pieces, including one that had belonged to Anne Boleyn. The very same necklace I had stashed away at York Place.

"You have been saying that for weeks." Mary Arundell draped herself against the window. "What makes you so certain? Mrs Coffin says Anne

Boleyn cursed England while she was in the Tower. She swore there would be no rain until she was free."

"Oh, do shut up," Mistress Ashley snapped. "No one wants to hear your nonsense."

"I shall not suffer insults from the likes of you." The younger Arundell sister quivered with indignation, the pitch of her voice growing shriller with each word. "You are only miserable because Lady Rochford has returned. We are all aware of the trouble she caused you. Mrs Coffin told us everything!"

Mistress Ashley snorted. "Don't presume to flatter yourself." She flopped into a nearby cushion with a languid moan. "That happened a lifetime ago—I've already forgotten it."

"Then you won't mind if we call you Mistress Marchpane?" Joan Arundell countered.

This resurrection of long-dead ghosts launched me to my feet. "That's enough!" I needed an escape—to plan, to think. "Stonor wanted to see me before vespers. Please try to settle this before we return. I cannot stand to hear any more of it!"

Out in the courtyard, the air felt heavy as wet lamb's wool. It pressed at me from all sides. Sweat pooled in the hollow place above my lip. In all my years, I had never known a summer so cloying and thick. Was Mrs Coffin right? Had Anne Boleyn placed us under a curse? No, that was ridiculous. The woman was no witch. Fear muddled my thoughts. Only the truth could loosen the tethers of my guilt. Perhaps the time had come to confess.

Exiting the stone gate, I heard church bells peal in the distance—the chapel calling the parishioners to prayer. I considered returning to the palace to attend service in the queen's closet but quickly decided against it, joining the crowd headed into the church instead. Once inside the soaring stone walls, I broke away from the group, seeking refuge in one of the alcoves. In my haste to dash behind one of the imposing marble tombs, I nearly toppled over a pair of leather slippers. "Forgive me, I did not see you there," I whispered to the kneeling figure. Though the woman's face was hidden, there was something familiar about her that gave me pause. Still, I had no desire to disturb whomever it was. "I shall find another place."

The woman staggered to her feet. Motes of dust swirled in the sunlight around her skirts. "You may stay. I was just leaving." Her detached gaze sent a chill through me.

"Lady Rochford, I was not expecting to find you here."

"Nor did I, and yet here I stand." Her eyes were puffy from lack of sleep, and the tight pinch of her lips suggested tears were not far behind. She was on the verge and fighting it.

"May I escort you to the palace?" The walk back was sure to be long and uncomfortable, but it was my duty to offer. If not for her sake, then for George's. Mercifully, she demurred.

"No, I prefer to be alone." She made it no further than a few paces before turning back, her face gripped with sudden fury. "Did you tell Cromwell those disgusting lies about George, Margery? Were you angry with him? Angry with me?"

The words tumbled out before I could stop them. "No, I loved George." Too late, my hand flew to my mouth. I had lived with the shameful secret since the Chateau Vert pageant, all those years ago. Before the world had turned upside down. Backed against the wall, I had watched the gowns of brocade and silk spin across the dance floor, their bright colours blooming like petals. George and I had been laughing together. At what, I have long since forgotten. He leaned in, smelling of mint and leather. The musk of him still occasionally lingered in my nostrils. "Beautiful, isn't she?" he asked.

At first, I thought he meant me, then I followed his gaze. My lungs deflated, withering away inside me. I could not breathe. I could not speak. He was staring at Jane Parker. The same woman standing in front of me, wearing a mask of desolation. Her tone was resigned. "Love makes us do terrible things."

"I could never lie about George." That much was true, and yet I was not innocent in his death. The allegations against him had not come from me. Still, the blame was mine. My pettiness towards Marc Smeaton caused his death. Oh, how I wished to take those words back.

"I know not why, but I believe you," she replied softly. With a final tilt of her head, she departed, my tenuous resolve to return the necklace vanishing with the rustle of her skirt.

MISTRESS ASHLEY WAS pacing the cobblestone walkway when I emerged later, depleted from my prayers. "Where have you been? The queen and Master Holbein are waiting for you."

Dashing through the courtyard, I struggled to keep panic at bay. Would they suspect me? I searched my memories for the page's words. What message had he delivered with the necklace? *Master Kingston told him I would know what to do with it.* Had I gotten it wrong? Was I supposed to return it with her other possessions? *No, it wasn't Kingston*—I remembered then—*those were Anne's words.* I wanted to cry out to her—ask her what she meant—but there would be no more answers from Anne Boleyn or Nan Bullen, now nor ever again.

Skidding to a stop outside the queen's presence chamber, Mistress Ashley grabbed my hand. "Wait, I must tell you something."

"Hurry," I gasped, my breath coming in ragged spurts. A sharp pain spread beneath my ribs.

"Whatever you see in there…" She struggled to find the words. "Whatever they show you…" A bead of sweat trickled down the bridge of her nose, splashing down on the heaving swell of her chest. "Try not to show your surprise."

"What do you mean?" Thudding wildly, my heart felt close to bursting.

"Never mind, Margery, they are waiting." She locked her arms around me. "I took care of it. Find me after, and I shall tell you everything."

Staggering out of her grip, dizzied by the heady scent of her perfumed sweat, I gathered my bearings with a deep breath and headed into the chamber on faltering legs.

Glancing up at the herald's announcement, Queen Jane gave me a sharp look, then turned back to the sketches laid before her. Master Holbein was hunched over in the next chair, hastily scribbling on a torn bit of parchment. His hands moved swiftly, the pen dancing across the page. When he paused to offer a smile, I stole a peek at his work. Beneath his blackened fingertips, the image of a pendant was taking shape. From a distance, it appeared to be an ornate square. Upon closer inspection, I discovered crossed lines in what should have been the void. Staring at it longer, I realized that it wasn't a square and cross at all, but interlocked initials: H for Henry, I for Jane.

"Do you like it?" Master Holbein asked eagerly. "Her Grace has not yet chosen a centre stone. However, we have decided to use Mistress Boleyn's pearls at the base. Three is a perfect number, don't you think? For the Trinity." He pointed at the prism of jewels spread out across the end of the table.

Mistress Boleyn's pearls? No, it couldn't be! I rushed over; my stomach knotted with dread. Garnets, sapphires, emeralds, and more glittered in the candlelight. No pearls. Beyond, a gilded casket lay open, a tumble of overturned boxes beside it. With great trepidation, I peered inside. Upon the scarlet silken lining, it lay coiled, like a serpent ready to strike: a strand of milky pearls curled around a lustrous golden *B*. I stared at it, feeling as though I were floating high above my body. The queen's voice sent me hurtling back to the ground. "Margery, is something the matter? Master Holbein asked you a question."

Try not to show your surprise, Mistress Ashley had said.

"Please excuse my rudeness, Master Holbein. The heat has made me a bit faint." My body swayed in response.

Holbein jumped from his chair, reaching out with steadying hands. "Shall we call for a physician?" The deep pools of his eyes bore down on me. They were the last thing I saw before the darkness swept them away.

I AWAKENED DISORIENTED, my surroundings bare and unfamiliar. I remembered speaking to Master Holbein in the presence chamber. Everything after felt fuzzy, distant. How had I ended up here? The room was small, devoid of fine furnishings. Besides the cramped bed, there was a table dressed in flickering candles and a wooden stool in the corner, but little else. At least there was a window.

Throwing off the threadbare blanket, I swung my legs to the floor. The first steps were tentative. Growing more surefooted, I crossed the room. Beyond the diamond-shaped panes, the sky loomed black and dreary. Flecks of rain began to appear; light at first, but soon fat drops pelted the glass. When I wrenched open the window, the scent of it poured in, earthy and sweet.

So much for the curse of Anne Boleyn.

The thought of her stirred my memory, seizing me with a sick realization: the necklace. It was there, in the jewel casket—but how? Suddenly, it all became clear: this was a holding cell until they could take me to the Tower. In a fit of panic, I thrust my head through the window. The deluge obscured the ground, showing nothing more than an eternal plunge into darkness. It was too far down. I would never survive the fall.

I yanked my head inside when a short rap sounded at the door. I instinctively touched my hair; it had become unbound while I slept and was now dripping with rainwater. "One moment, please!" I cried, frantically searching the blanket for my hairpins.

"Margery, let me in."

Mistress Ashley. Breathing a sigh of relief, I dropped the bedding and ran for the door. To my great astonishment, I found it unlocked. "Oh, praise God, it is you."

"Of course, it's me. The others are too afraid." She bustled in carrying a tray loaded with bread, cheese, and ale. Placing it carefully on the small table, she wiped her hands on her skirt, regarding me with dark eyes. "That was some performance. I almost believed it myself."

"It was not an act, I assure you."

"I suppose not," she replied with a trace of disappointment. "Nevertheless, all worked in your favour. Half the court thinks you have been stricken with the plague." The corner of her lips twitched.

Reaching for a cup of ale, I threw it back in one long gulp. It seared going down but quenched my raging thirst. "Almost wish I had been."

"It would have been a far worse fate if I had not stepped in. What in God's name were you thinking? How did you even get that bedevilled necklace?"

"How did *you* get it?" The ale was creeping up into my throat. I reached for the piss pot beneath the bed.

Mistress Ashley crossed to the window, closing it tight. "You cannot be too careful." She narrowed her eyes. "Is this why your hair is wet? Did you think to jump?"

"Please answer the question," I begged.

Flicking the water from her fingertips, she perched on the edge of the stool. "Do not play the fool, Margery, I have known since the day

you shoved me away from your trunk—such odd behaviour from you."
She frowned. "After you left with Michael Lyster to see the queen, I dug
through it. Imagine my surprise to discover such a scandalous secret." She
flushed, pleased with herself.

I stared at her dumbfounded. She knew all along and never once had I
suspected it. "Yet you said nothing? Why?"

"I was terrified and not looking to get caught up in whatever you
were doing. Until Mary Norris came to me. Ralph Sadler's interrogation
unnerved her. She was too scared to go to Cromwell, so I promised to take
care of it. By that point, you had stashed it in your bum roll. I panicked
when I couldn't find it, then Stonor mentioned what an awful mess you
made sewing up the tear in your gown—that was even stranger than the
shoving! I pieced it together after I overheard the wardrobe clerk tell Antony Denny he found the silver coffer."

I felt a stab of anger at the delight she seemed to take in my unmasking—
how elated she was to have bested me. "So, you decided to act. What then?"

Mistress Ashley ignored my churlish tone. "I switched our rolls while
you were dressing the queen. See, I am wearing yours right now." She
tugged up her gown, determined to show me.

I held up a hand. "I believe you. No need to prove it. How did it get
into the queen's jewel casket?"

With a sniff, she released her skirts in a colourful cascade of embroidered satin. "I am still shocked by the ease of it, truthfully. Everything was
so chaotic with preparations for Dover. I knew it would be my only chance.
Denny seemed rather pleased when I arrived with it in hand. I told him you
found the pendant while helping Lloyd. That it got separated from the coffer and mislaid when Anne Boleyn's belongings came back from the Tower."

I could not believe what I was hearing. My emotions pitched from rage
to bewilderment. Then I felt something else—a shiver of relief. The choice
was no longer mine to make. "I wish you would have come to me first."

"And risk you doing something foolish? No." Mistress Ashley shook her
head. "There has been enough death—do not let Anne Boleyn be yours."
She averted her gaze but was not quick enough to hide the distress glinting
in her eyes.

"Master Kingston sent it. I never sought this duty out." I had been a faint-hearted, weak-willed fool. Why had I ever believed I could do it?

"Now it is at an end." Mistress Ashley rose from the stool. She gestured at the tray of food. "Eat all of it. Dr Butts will come in the morning to see how you fare. Be your liveliest, cheery self, else they shall never let you out of here. Plague is rampant in the city, so they are taking no chances."

I held my tongue as she walked away. She may have saved my life, but I refused to thank her for betraying me. I was not sorry for hiding the necklace and would not give her the satisfaction of pretending otherwise.

JANE SEYMOUR

WINDSOR

Rain lashed against the window in a wicked fury. Standing in the embrasure, I watched it run down the glass in fat rivulets. Swollen pools formed on the ledge before trickling to the ground far below. Overnight the cold set in, creeping through tiny crevices in the walls, necessitating warmer fabrics than the silks I brought on progress. Fortunately, the wardrobe at Windsor was kept well-stocked, and something more suitable was quickly found. Mother Stonor sent Mary Norris to dress me in Margery Horsman's absence and she arrived at daybreak, quailing under the weight of a heavy brocade gown. Consumed with worry for Margery, I spared no thoughts fretting over its previous owner, slipping into the garment as though it had never graced any other body but my own. Afterward, I resumed my vigil by the window, awaiting the doctor's verdict.

Throughout the summer an outbreak of the plague had raged through London's streets, its flames licking hungrily beyond the bounds of the city. The progress kept us ahead of contagion, but my maid's collapse was a troubling signal that the scourge had finally caught up. Much like the sweating sickness that claimed the lives of my two youngest siblings barely out of the cradle, the plague struck without regard, carrying off the young and old, the frail and healthy, the rich and poor alike. It was a dreadful disease and one I feared more with each passing year.

The yeomen posted outside my bedchamber were under strict instruction to turn away those deemed nonessential. The fewer bodies in my presence, the better; the less chance I would be exposed if my maid did indeed turn out to be infected. I tried to entertain myself as the morning stretched on—prayers at the prie-dieu, a reading from my book of hours, stitching a blackwork collar—but could not escape the niggling doubts in the back of my mind. It had been so unlike Margery to turn up the way she had, flustered and tardy; worse still, ignoring Master Holbein as though he were a petty servant. If she was not sick, what was she hiding? And why had she keeled over at the sight of that blighted necklace?

A curious emotion had overtaken me when Sir Antony unveiled the thing. Expecting to feel some sort of distaste when I saw it—a desire to have it gone or broken to pieces—I found myself fighting off an inexplicable urge to stuff the pearls down my bodice. I wanted to hold them close, hide them away for the daughter of their disgraced owner. It had been visceral, undeniable—akin to falling under a spell. In truth, Margery's collapse had been somewhat fortuitous. It stole the attention away from the struggle raging inside me, a battle pitched plainly across my face.

The gilded casket was bundled into my bedchamber in the ensuing chaos, its miniature drawers shoved hastily into place. Rising from my bench beneath the window, I went to it again, drawn to the treasures hidden within. Beads of amber and carnelian occupied one drawer. Held up to the candlelight, their russet glow seemed to shoot sparks of fire. In another drawer, a ruby cabochon and diamond pendant winked at me from its velvet-lined cradle. The gemstone gleamed like liquid, dark as blood. I drank in its beauty, imagining the same colour dripping from the wounds of Christ during the crucifixion. His sacrifice for our salvation. Could I be so courageous? When I lifted the lid of the casket, peering into the topmost drawer, I found my answer.

The pearl strands were coiled around the pendant, which rested upon a trio of larger, tear-drop-shaped pearls. When I pulled the necklace out, the teardrops swung loose, twisting on the loops that attached them to the bottom of the golden *B*. Holbein wanted to use the pearls in his new design. The thought of it repulsed me. I was not meant to wear them, nor could

I bear to do so. In my hands, they were smooth as ivory and warm to the touch—like they had just come off a body. They quivered as though alive, startling me for a moment until I realized it was my flesh trembling. Held in their thrall, I missed the insistent knocking.

"Your Grace?" The guard stuck his head through the doorway, greeting me with a frown. "Forgive my intrusion, I feared the worst."

Cramming the necklace back into the casket, I bequeathed a bashful smile over my shoulder. "We are all right, thank you. Is that Dr Butts?"

"Yes, Your Grace." He stepped back, allowing the doctor into the room. "Let me know if I can get you anything else."

"Nothing at this time, thank you." I dismissed him.

Dr Butts waited until the guard was gone to dip a perfunctory bow. "Sorry to keep Your Grace waiting. I wanted to be sure of the diagnosis before coming."

"And?" I urged, forgoing the formalities.

"Having examined Mistress Horsman, I can say with great confidence I see no indications of the plague. She claims to have been felled by the heat, and I see no reason to doubt that. This rain may be the first we have had in some time, but there has been an unseasonable abundance of moisture in the air, making it feel much warmer than usual. Tell me again what she was doing when it happened."

"She was running back from the chapel, late to our meeting with Master Holbein," I replied, leaving out the necklace. "It happened moments after she arrived."

The corners of Dr Butts' eyes wrinkled with his reassuring smile. "Ah— that lends much credence to her claim. I see nothing to fear, Your Grace. I will continue to observe your maid. However, it should be safe for you to come out of hiding."

"Thank you, Dr Butts." I returned his smile. "You cannot be too careful."

"Quite true, Your Grace, particularly if there are signs that one finds oneself in the family way." He leaned forward, eagerness staining his features.

"Please don't let me keep you, Dr Butts."

Amusement flickered in the doctor's eyes. "Always a pleasure, Your Grace," he replied, bowing again. The yeoman let him out the door.

The rain had died down by the time I escaped the bedchamber, but it was still too soggy and cold for an afternoon stroll through the garden. Longing to be out in the fresh air, free from the confines of the stuffy palace, I settled for a brisk walk in the long gallery instead. Upon returning to the privy chamber, I found my brother slouched in a chair by the fire, one leg dangling lazily over the armrest.

"Good to see you, Tom." Taking a proffered cup from Mistress Ashley's hand, I perched on the edge of the seat opposite him. The girl blushed at the flirtatious wink Tom aimed in her direction. "Mistress Ashley, do you remember that story I told you about the steward's daughter at Wulfhall?" I asked casually, taking a sip of the sweet wine.

"That's not fair, sister!" Tom laughed as Mistress Ashley scurried away. "I had no idea who she was at the time. Besides, they all look the same with their clothes off."

"Well, you know who my maids are, so you had best stay away." The last thing I needed was Tom bedding one of them. He managed to keep from getting a bastard off his past dalliances, but there was no telling when his luck would run out. I did not intend for it to end with one of my ladies.

"You weren't always so quick to spoil my fun." Tom stretched his long legs out towards the hearth; his lips turned down in a petulant frown.

"I wasn't always Queen, either." I hoped my baleful stare conveyed more than I could say. *Do not make this more challenging than it already is, Brother.*

"No but being Queen has not made you any more innocent. I know what you are doing."

"That's more than I know," I scoffed miserably. Each step taken in the last year seemed like the wrong one—starting with the foolish notion of attracting the king.

"Do not play me for a simpleton. I know you aren't pregnant." Tom laughed.

"Pregnant? Who said that?" Wine splashed over the rim of the cup as I stiffened, claret droplets spilling down my fingers. I quickly flicked them off before they could stain my gown.

"Dr Butts seems to think you did."

"I never said that!" *Meddlesome old man.* "He asked, and I very pointedly ignored the question."

Tom sat up. "Well, he has taken it as an affirmation and has already been in the king's chambers with his suspicions."

"What do I tell him?" I tried to keep the panic from showing in my voice, but Tom knew me better than anyone. There was no hiding it from him.

"I am certain you will think of something." Leaning forward, he kissed my forehead, then lurched to his feet. "I must be off. His Grace will be here soon for supper. Careful, he is in a mood."

BEFORE I HAD time to muster much of a defence, the king arrived with Ralph Sadler nipping his heels. Sadler, who usually handled Cromwell's business with unflappable ruthlessness, appeared ruffled, anxiously shuffling through the papers in his arms. "What shall I tell Lord Cromwell, Your Grace?"

"Tell your master it is well he should repair to London for the election." Snapping his finger at the chamberer lurking in the doorway, the king tilted his head towards the basin in the servant's hand, indicating he was ready to wash. "However, the Charterhouse is not ordered as we would have had it. Cromwell was told long ago to put the monks out of the house, and though they may now be reconciled, we are loath to accept it due to their longstanding obstinacy."

"By Your Grace's command," Sadler confirmed quickly. "And what of the coronation?"

The king's gaze swept over my belly. He turned to the basin; his silence punctuated only by the splash of water. Drying his hands on a towel, he spoke firmly, "We shall have an answer for you anon—see us in the privy chamber after supper."

With Sadler's dismissal, Joan Arundell and Mary Norris stepped forward to take their places, exchanging a worried glance at the courtier's receding form. I shot them a look of warning.

A troop of servants descended upon us, carrying platters loaded with roast venison, stewed apples dusted with cinnamon, and honey-glazed turnips. Staring at the food, I could not help thinking of the poor brothers of the Charterhouse. Yet more monks put out of their homes, craving sustenance, both physical and spiritual. Our bounty felt obscene in comparison.

The king stared at me as I picked at my plate. "Are you ill, Sweetheart?" He speared an onion pearl, eating it straight from the knife. The sound of his teeth dragging against the steel made me cringe.

"Nothing so serious," I replied, tucking my hand into the curl of his. "I merely worry for Margery."

His Grace gave my fingers a light squeeze before releasing them to snatch a mug from the cupbearer's tray. "Butts assures me there is nothing to fret over." He took a swig of ale. "His concern lay with you."

"But all is well with me," I replied, shaking my head. "See?" I shovelled a turnip into my mouth, chewing enthusiastically, despite the fact it had grown cold.

The king laughed, a hearty guffaw that shook his jowls. A few days ago, his barber had taken a razor to his beard, and it still had not completely grown back in. Beneath the thin spray of hair, his face looked doughy and white. "I am pleased to hear that, especially if what Butts says is true. Are you indeed with-child, Jane?"

Gulping down the mush of turnip, I took a sip of wine to stall. "Perhaps, Your Grace," I answered finally, offering a weak smile. "It is still too early to know. My courses aren't yet due for another week."

"Ah, then we wait in hope." Taking the napkin from his shoulder, he dabbed at his mouth, then pushed himself from the table. "I hate to leave you this way, but I have business to attend. Shall I return for cards later?"

"If you please. I do hope everything is well. Why did Master Sadler ask about the coronation?"

The king's face darkened. "Mistress Horsman may have escaped the plague, but it rages unabated in Westminster. Worse, it has struck in the Abbey. I fear we must put the celebrations off until all sickness has passed. I plan to summon the privy council to discuss it further."

Disappointment surged through me. Though I had expected this news since Margery's collapse, receiving it still felt like a slap. Fearing the plague as much as the king, I knew it was right to be cautious, but I worried it would not be the last time my coronation was postponed. "Whatever you think best, my king."

MARGERY HORSMAN

WINDSOR

They kept me in the dingy cell for an additional seven days after my initial examination by Dr Butts. When he arrived the morning after my collapse to poke and prod, I was at my merriest, hearty, and hale as I could muster. Despite my lack of appetite, I heeded Mistress Ashley's advice, devouring every scrap of food from the tray she brought. Nothing more than a crumb left behind. Butts was pleased with my miraculous recovery. The king and his council proved harder to convince. His Grace's abject terror of anything suggesting illness was notorious, and he would not suffer to let me anywhere near his person until my health was proven beyond doubt. Dr Butts called on me every morning and, after a week passed without further symptoms, he released me back out into the palace to mingle with the rest of the court.

Fury kept me warm, those first days on my own. The gall of Jane Ashley to sift through *my* belonging. And then, to behave as though she had done me a favour. No doubt she expected something in return. With no one to keep me company, revenge occupied my every thought. I spent hours dreaming up ways to repay Mistress Ashley with her own coin, each idea growing ever more outlandish the longer I was confined. As the lonely days stretched on and melancholy took hold, I lost the hunger for vengeance. By the morning of my release, I was ready to forgive all trespasses for the price of a mere kind word from anyone besides the cursed doctor.

The maids waited for me—their eagerness spilling beyond the walls of the dormitory in laughter and shouts—as I made my way down the corridor towards them. After a mad rush of kisses and warm embraces, they grew quiet, reticent. The world had changed while I was hidden away, they said. The whole north of the country was up in arms and threatening to march our way.

The news came as no surprise. After an unending parade of changes wrought by the king's whim, how could the people stand to take any more? Their sacred rituals and holy days were stolen, places they went for comfort and succour gutted and torn away. While she lived, Queen Anne bore most of the blame—an easy target for their wrath—but the number of shuttered monasteries had only increased since her death. Aided by Cromwell, the king's avarice reigned supreme, and I feared we all would pay for it.

The queen's rooms were subdued in the days following; any residual mirth leftover from our summer progress washed away in the autumn rain. All music and dancing, having finally been restored, was put away again. Instead, we spent the long hours on our knees in the chapel. Watching Queen Jane's lips move, her face placid and serene, I wondered for whom she prayed. I knew from our time together in Queen Catherine's household that she kept to the old ways, but her allegiance now belonged to her husband, the king. Did she pray for him? Or were her secret words, whispered into the ears of the Lord, in support of the rebels? One evening after compline, I sought the answer when we retired to her chamber to prepare for bed.

I waited until the last chamberer rambled out of the room, taking my time unlacing the queen's kirtle before easing into the conversation. I found my opening when Her Grace, freed from her binding garments, slumped over the dressing table with an emphatic sigh. "Is it the king, Your Grace? Are you fearful for him?" The queen burrowed further, another gasp emanating from the crook of her elbow in reply. She laid that way while I loosened the ribbons tethering her hair, the flaxen waves cascading around her face. When she finally sat up, her visage was even more white than usual, like that of a corpse.

"Fearful for him or of him?" She caught my eye in the looking glass, a pregnant pause filling the air. "Never mind, do not answer that."

"Forgive me, Your Grace. That was too forward." I threw the embroidered nightgown over her head to stifle her piercing gaze. She tugged it down, re-emerging through the neckline with a rueful expression.

"Mistress Horsman, we have been acquainted long enough for you to know how I feel about the monasteries. What can I do? My husband is head of the church, and his word is law. I dare not speak out."

"Surely His Grace must love you more than—"

The thud of the door saved me from saying her name. Heat flared on my cheeks.

"The Lady Rochford and Mistress Norris, Your Grace," the herald called.

The queen nodded her assent, turning back to me. "Love? Is that what you call it?" She gave a derisive snort. "From what I can see, having a man's love means very little."

"I would not know, Your Grace." Staring down at my hands, I heard the swish of fabric as Lady Rochford and Mistress Norris entered and made their curtsies.

When I raised my head, the queen was wearing a bright smile. "As I was saying, Mistress Horsman, a man's love is a fine thing. Are there any you have a mind to marry?"

Avoiding Mistress Norris' curious stare so as not to give the game away, I watched Lady Rochford remove the warming pans from the bed while I scrambled for a reply. "I had not thought of it, Your Grace." The lie rolled effortlessly off my tongue. In truth, I had thought of it countless times. "My father died before he could arrange a match."

"Ah, yes, I sympathize." Her voice quivered, full of emotion. "I have often wondered what my father would make of my marriage—a match he would have never dared aim for."

"What fortune to have brothers who could arrange it for you."

The queen found my response amusing. "Did Edward pay you to say that? It sounds like a sentiment from his own lips."

"Decidedly not, Your Grace." I returned her wry smile. "My dowry would then be extraordinarily rich indeed. Now, is there anything else I can do before I leave you in Lady Rochford's capable hands?"

"That will be all for tonight. I would like your assistance on the morrow.

The king has heard reports that upwards of twenty-thousand rebels have gathered at Lincoln Cathedral, and the protests are turning violent. Two men have been lynched already with more bloodshed threatened..." Her voice trailed off; all cheer lost with the harsh reminder of the terror moving through the north. "In light of all this, His Grace has grown concerned about his daughters, so he has ordered them to court. It is my pleasure that both young ladies should receive a token upon their arrival."

"A token, Your Grace?"

The queen peered over her shoulder at the bent form of Lady Rochford. She lowered her voice, "I shall explain more when we meet again."

UTTER CHAOS HAD erupted by the time I returned the next morning. In the privy chamber, a swarm of men, buzzing in consternation, had gathered to beg an audience with the queen. At the head was Lord Beauchamp, pacing with such intensity that he failed to notice me slipping silently through the yeomen outside Her Grace's inner sanctum. Sneaking a peek through the closing doors, I caught an amused smirk playing across Michael Lyster's face. He winked as the oak slabs slammed shut. The flirtation stirred my belly, but I felt a twinge of something else. Was it guilt? An image of Husee's face jolted my thoughts.

Queen Jane was already out of bed, kneeling in prayer at the prie-dieu. Two chamberers bustled around her, stoking the fire, and making up the bed. The prior evening's attendants were gone, replaced by the Arundell sisters. They sat side-by-side beneath the window, staring glumly at a book of hours held between them. Mary breathed a sigh of relief when she saw me, nudging Joan with barely restrained glee. Setting aside the book with great enthusiasm, they jumped into action, each one taking an item of clothing from my arms.

"When Her Grace finishes her prayers, we will need to move quickly. They are braying at the door out there."

"Lord Beauchamp tried to burst in first thing, but she sent him away." Mary's almond-shaped eyes rounded in disbelief. "She told him he did not belong in here."

Joan pinched her sister's arm. "Quiet, you. Her Grace stirs."

"Mistress Arundell," Queen Jane stood, the nightgown gathered around her bare feet. "One of you, anyway," she went on, gesturing at the two of them. "Tell my brother there is no need for such theatrics. We shall address him after we have broken our fast." Mary scampered towards the door. The queen called her back again. "Upon reflection, perhaps it is best to leave that bit at the beginning out."

Mary's face flushed. "Yes, Your Grace. Anything else?"

The queen shook her head. "Your sister and Mistress Horsman can handle it from here."

Mary curtsied before sprinting through the doorway.

JOAN AND I set about dressing the queen for the day. As we finished attaching her sleeves, a servant arrived with a tray of food. Her Grace picked at the offering, shoring up her strength before facing the impatient courtiers amassed outside. "I have not forgotten our task, Margery." She rose from the table. "Once we are through with the unpleasant business at hand, I would like for you to return to the wardrobe to fetch me something that belonged to Mistress Boleyn."

"Anything in particular, Your Grace?" *She already had Anne Boleyn's necklace. What more could she possibly want?* I wondered, uncharitably.

Sensing my mistrust, she placed a reassuring hand on my shoulder. "I shall leave that to you. It must be something that would provide comfort to her daughter, nothing that should cause disquiet."

The sadness in her eyes melted the chill in my voice. "I know of just the thing," I answered, thinking of Anne's girdle book. I was certain she wore it into the Tower, but we never found it during our catalogue of her possessions. When we arrived at Windsor, Mistress Stonor told me that her belongings had been removed from the royal apartments before Queen Jane could see them, so perhaps it was here.

Sucking in a lungful of air, the queen squared her blue sarcenet-clad shoulders before striding into the privy chamber to greet the waiting men.

JANE SEYMOUR

WINDSOR

E dward was the first to approach. He bowed reverently, eyes cast to the floor, and the rest of the men followed suit, a sea of black caps bobbing before me. "You have brought an army to our rooms, Brother. What could we have possibly done to warrant such attention?" A prickle of fear burrowed into the hollow pit of my stomach. Had I made yet another mistake?

His lips curled over even, white teeth. "We have come to swear fealty, Your Grace." Honey seemed to drip from every word. He goggled at me momentarily, waiting for an effusive acknowledgment of gratitude. When none came, his voice took on a tone of irritation. "Obviously, we have arrived prematurely." Turning to dismiss the company, he waited until all but Michael Lyster exited, then motioned for his friend to entertain my ladies while we talked in private.

"What is this all about, Edward? What has happened now?"

Edward's gaze melted into one of pity. He reached for my hand, and I instinctively recoiled, his touch burning my skin. Hurt flashed across his face. "You must stop that, Jane. No one is going to accuse us of impropriety."

"You cannot be sure of that." I glanced in the direction of our attendants. The three of them seemed immersed in a conversation of their own, none paying attention to our furious whispering. "The Boleyns probably believed that too."

"That family believed a lot of things, but they could have never imagined you would be named regent," Edward countered with a satisfied smirk.

"I have heard no such thing."

He groaned in exasperation. "I thought the king would have told you last night. Has he not been sharing your bed?"

"Edward!" I warned. The king had not been to see me since my courses made their unwelcomed return, but that was none of my brother's concern. It was bad enough the king complained to all and sundry that he would never have children by me. I refused to lend credence to the claim, despite the pain it caused me. How could I conceive when on the few occasions he visited, he had trouble maintaining his manhood? The fault did not lie with me.

"Well, despite your lack of…" He gave my stomach a pointed glance. "…His Grace has decided to entrust the kingdom to your hands when he leaves for Ampthill to muster the troops. It is quite an honour, so I hope you won't make a mess of it."

"I appreciate your confidence," I answered drily. "When does he plan to leave?"

"In a few days. Lord Hussey has fled like a beaten dog with his tail tucked between his legs, and the rebels at Yorkshire grow stronger, having united behind their newly anointed leader, a lawyer by the name of Robert Aske. He is calling it a *pilgrimage*," Edward scoffed. "They march under the banner of the five wounds of Christ."

Red, like the blood of Christ—I thought of the ruby cabochon in the drawer of my jewel coffer—*a sacrifice*. Like the Saviour, these men gave their lives in the hopes that the king would return to the church, that the monasteries would be reopened for their brothers and sisters, that there would be an end to the heresies. "Are you accompanying the king to Ampthill?" I asked hopefully, a plan forming in my mind. If the worst should happen to the king, could I restore the monastic houses as regent? *Not with Edward here to subdue me.* Quickly as the disturbing thought flitted into my mind, I shook it away. It was treason to imagine the king's death.

"Yes, both Michael and I are to go." Glancing over my shoulder, he emitted a gasp of laughter. "Would you look at that?"

I spun around to see what Edward found so humorous and discovered both of my ladies staring rapturously at Master Lyster, enthralled at whatever tale he was weaving for them. "Why is that amusing?"

"It's not, really—I only laugh because Michael has been asking about your jewel-keeper."

"Margery? Why?"

"I wondered the same, though I suppose she does have a certain charm," he mused, eyeing her simple gown and unadorned hood. "I assume he intends to wed her—*or bed her.*"

I gaped at my brother. Men were dying, and he was attempting to broker a marriage. "Edward, see to the king. Find out if he intends to visit before you leave for Ampthill."

A scowl crept into Edward's face. "Oh, fine. Come along, Michael," he called. "We have been dismissed."

Margery stared wistfully after Master Lyster. "Your Grace," she began in a distracted tone.

"If you leave now, you may catch up to him," I snapped, waving her off.

"That's not what I meant," she flustered in return, giving me a startled look. "I merely wanted to beg leave to complete that errand Your Grace asked of me. I hope I have not offended."

"No, of course, you haven't," I answered, regretting my rebuke. In truth, I could not blame her. Michael had always been exceedingly kind and spoke with a quiet dignity that attracted people to him. Had he not already married by the time I came of age, I might have looked to him for a match. He certainly would have been preferable to William Dormer and his overweening mother. But Michael had been desperately enamoured with his beloved Bess. Her death devastated him to a degree from which I was never entirely sure he would recover. To hear he was inquiring after Margery caught me completely unawares. Perhaps it was something worth pursuing, but not until our people in the north country were satisfied. "Go to the wardrobe, see if you can find what I desire. We shall reconvene after vespers.

THE MAIDS OF honour sat dutifully at my feet, reading, and sewing while the day's petitioners drifted through the presence chamber. A few wanted worldly things, like a license to import wine or a buck from the park at Greenwich, but the vast majority pled for intercession. Without the religious houses, who would help them feed their families and treat their illnesses? Who would listen to their confessions and offer them absolution? What of the poor? And where would their brothers and sisters in Christ live? I listened carefully to their stories—the daily struggles they fought—doing my best to fulfil their pleas, but I could not shake the nagging doubts occupying my thoughts. *Where is the king? How could he do this to his people?*

By the time His Grace arrived, all the petitioners had drifted away forlorn and unsatisfied, and my inner turmoil had reached an untenable pitch. The admonitions I so desperately wanted to say, but could not express, churned on my tongue like the tide of salivation that presaged vomit. I hid this torment beneath a veneer of civility—kneeling and scraping as I always did—but the mask grew harder to maintain the farther His Grace tread down the path of self-righteousness.

"They presume to tell me, *their prince*, whom I can and cannot promote? Or who is fit to advise me? These farmers—this *rabble*—think they know the word of God better than I?" he roared. "I am *Fidei Defensor*—Defender of the Faith—and there is no earthly creature with greater knowledge of it. How dare they seek the rights bestowed upon me, *their sovereign*, by the very God they claim to speak for?"

On and on, his bile poured over me, hot and putrid as the fires of Hell; violent words searing scars upon my heart. Unlawful treachery. Wilful ignorance. Beastly. Abominable. Traitorous. At last, I could take it no longer. I threw myself to the floor, my knees collapsing upon the frigid unyielding tiles. I lurched forward, clutching at his hands in desperation. "Please, Your Grace, pity them," I cried. "Perhaps this is a sign from God that these dissolutions have gone too far. Gracious, generous prince, I beg you. Restore their abbeys. Grant them peace."

The corner of his eye twitched as he stared down at me, his gaze a wintry rime, chilling me to the bone. "You shame yourself, Madame. Get up." He yanked me to my feet. "We think it best you concern yourself with other matters. As well you remember, the lady afore you meddled all too often in our affairs of state. Look what has become of her in consequence. It would be a great pity if you were to share her fate."

"Forgive me, Your Grace. I speak only in concern of your well-being." I failed to hide the tremble in my voice. The room came back into focus then, the horrified faces of my ladies surrounding us. My panicked gaze darted from one to the next, searching for Lady Anne, searching for Margery Horsman, searching for any safe refuge. Instead, I found a pallid-faced Lady Rochford swaying in terror and the crazed glare of my brother, Edward. *Get up!* he mouthed.

"I will not repeat this, Jane, so heed my advice—and *heed it well*." The king was speaking slowly now, enunciating every word to make his meaning clear. "Your role as queen is simple: welcome me to your bed and play mother to my children—the ones I have already and the ones you will conceive for the security of our realm. You will dance and sing beside me at our court revelries, but you will not lift your voice to give any opinion I do not request. Fulfil these duties, provide me with a son, and we shall be perfect friends. Do you understand? I want so much for us to be in harmony. Please refrain from disrupting the peace, as I find I do not have the stomach to seek another wife."

Blinking hard, I refused to avert my gaze, holding my head high in defiance. I would stay silent, as he asked, but I would never keep still.

Edward lingered behind when the rest of the retinue ebbed from my rooms in the king's wake. "Have you lost your mind?" he hissed.

"Not here, Edward." I waved off my curious maids with a feigned smile. "I do not need you making things worse."

"What in God's name would possess you to do such a thing?" he pressed on, ignoring my warning.

It was a fair question, and one I was not entirely sure how to answer. "You did not see their faces, their distress. You think it merely a matter of bending the church to the king's will, but it is not the church who suffers. When His Grace and the Pope tilt at each other, it is the innocent who are run through with the lance."

"That is where you are wrong, my sister," Edward replied sadly. "No one who rises against their king can be called an innocent. I once thought that name fitting for you. Now, I can see I have been labouring under a delusion."

"Do not preach virtue to me, Edward. We lost any claim to that title months ago. Now, if you will kindly excuse me, I have other business to attend."

Edward stepped aside, dipping a reluctant bow. "Tread carefully, Your Grace."

MARGERY HORSMAN

WINDSOR

"Margery, what are you doing? My clerk has finally put things to order, and here you come to muck it all up. I do not appreciate—"

"Master Lloyd, have you seen Anne Boleyn's girdle book?" I popped my head out of the closet, hood askew from my fruitless hunt. I found satin slippers, cloth of gold ribands, countless silk stockings, but no girdle book in sight.

Lloyd's long fingers pinched his brow. He cast about his memory for an answer. "I'm sure it went to the Tower with her. Was it not in the parcels Kingston sent back?"

I shook my head. "Do you think he kept it?" The mere thought put me on edge. I could not bear to imagine anything of Queen Anne's in that doleful prison. Though her body remained within the confines of the Tower, I took comfort in knowing it lay in the chapel, at least; entombed on hallowed ground.

"Kingston was given strict instruction to return all the lady's goods. If it didn't come back, one of her maids must have taken it."

It took a moment for his words to sink in. Then, a bolt of understanding: *Kingston!* Anne's conviction meant her property reverted to the Crown, and none of her ladies would have dared taken anything belonging to a man as dangerous as King Henry. If one of them had it, it must have been smuggled out by Kingston. I choked back a sob of joy so as not to raise

Lloyd's suspicions. I could not be certain of the constable's intentions, but I began to wonder if Kingston had given me the necklace in hopes of creating a relic.

"I have no doubt we shall find it at York Place when we return," I replied, steering the conversation out of dangerous waters. "In the meantime, Queen Jane has asked for a token to give the Lady Elizabeth. I was hoping to give her the girdle book, but perhaps she is still too young for that."

"We have a few wooden dolls the tailor used to model gowns he made for the girl." Lloyd brightened, suddenly eager to please. "Would that be suitable? One of them is still wearing a cloth of silver gown commissioned by Mistress Boleyn."

While not strictly what the queen had asked for, I supposed it would have to do.

Arriving after vespers, I found the queen in her bedchamber. She sat quietly by the window, watching the sun settle into the horizon. Her jewel coffer lay open on the great tester bed, a rainbow of gemstones tossed about the gold lover's knots worked into the velvet counterpane. Mistress Ashley bustled out the door with a look of despair, a wad of soiled handkerchiefs clutched in her hands.

When the queen turned to greet me, her eyes were swollen and red. She wiped the tip of her nose, sniffing miserably. "Have you found something?" I gingerly held aloft my offering, stifling my breath in hopeful anticipation. She took it from my hands. "My mother used to give us her fashion dolls when she finished with them. I grew out of the dolls rather quickly, but my younger sisters often came to blows over them. I think Dorothy keeps one in her trunk still."

"My mother was too ill to sew. I often imagined what it would have been like to wear one of her creations." I wasn't sure if my mother even sewed, but I left that part out.

The queen nodded. "You have much in common with the king's daughters—that is why I have asked for your help. My mother has been a constant guiding presence, so I do not know what it is like to pine for her in the same way you do. The same way Mary and Elizabeth yearn for theirs."

"I was so young. I hardly remember her."

"Yes, but you shall never forget the longing you felt." She pointed at the cache of jewels. "Now, if those were your mother's, which item would you choose?"

My eye immediately went to the clump of pearls in the topmost drawer. I dared not suggest it. The king would never condone that. *The doll would have to suffice for Elizabeth.* Taking a hasty inventory of the pieces on the bed, I dismissed the lot of them, most having been worn by Anne Boleyn when she was queen. I pried open drawer after drawer until I found what I wanted: an onyx pendant shaped into a cross. Queen Catherine had worn it to Blackfriars during the divorce trial. She had been magnificent that day—her testimony emotional and defiant. It was her finest hour in a season of heartrending disappointments. "This is the one," I placed the jewel in the queen's hand.

"A fine choice—onyx offers protection when facing adversaries." Her fingers traced the outline of the cross. "My own mother taught me that gemstones, much like flowers, have a language all their own. A carefully chosen jewel can speak volumes without ever saying a word."

"Your Grace's mother sounds like quite a woman."

"The muse of poets, she was." A hoarse bark of laughter escaped her throat. "Mother never let us forget it."

WHEN I LEFT her, the queen had seemed in better spirits. By the time I arrived the next morning, a more profound pall had settled over the royal apartments. For two days, fear reigned supreme, while we waited in earnest for the delivery of the king's reply to the rebels' grievances. And then news came back that the uprising appeared on the verge of collapse. Plans for the king's visit to the muster at Ampthill quickly unravelled, and all thoughts of naming the queen regent vanished into the morning fog.

In the ensuing calm, I found myself letting down my guard, growing unmindful of strangers stalking the grounds of the palace. I was returning from the wardrobe, occupied with the flapping of my cloak in the bitter autumn wind when the man cornered me. Clad in a muted grey doublet and muddy black hose, I might have easily mistaken him for one of the many servants accompanying the noblemen that attended upon the king, except he had a desperate look about him that made me uneasy. Acknowledging him with a silent nod, careful not to meet his stare, I hurried past on nimble feet. I felt the tug before I heard his voice, a gravelly rasp that tore through the heavy air.

"I have been looking for you, Mistress Horsman," he said, yanking me backward, the hem of my cloak caught in his fist. "I was told you had the ear of the queen, and I need your help."

I spun away from the man's grasp, my foot slipping on the damp stones. "Who are you? What do you want?" I tried to disguise my fear by matching his tone. The words came out in a high-pitched whine that instantly gave me away.

His face flushed. "I never meant to scare milady. Name's Ascue, by the way—Christopher Ascue." He opened his fingers, allowing my cloak to flutter to the ground. "The abbess of Clementhorpe sent me, but the queen's council won't let me speak to Her Grace. Master Husee told me to seek you out. He said you were a favourite."

How like John Husee to compliment and unwittingly wound me in the same breath. I backed up to take the full measure of Ascue before answering. Upon closer inspection, he appeared far less dangerous. His presumption still put me out. "What do you want?" I asked again.

Removing his cap, he proceeded to twist it nervously in his hands. "The abbess asks the queen to save her house. The townsmen are doing their best to keep the king's commissioners out, but they can only do so much. She is willing to pay. Three hundred marks, she's offering."

Townsmen? No. If they were trying to keep the king's men out, they were rebels. "Where did you say the house was?"

"Yorkshire," he replied hopefully.

My heart sank. "I am sorry, I cannot help you. You must take this back to the queen's council." When I turned to go, he grabbed at my cloak again. "Please, Miss!"

Ducking low, I lurched forward to escape his clutches. I didn't get more than a few steps before knocking into something warm and solid. A familiar voice rang over my head. "She said she could not help you. Now, leave her be, or I shall summon one of the royal guards." When I heard the scurry of footsteps retreating, I lifted my gaze to find a pair of grey eyes staring back.

"What are you doing here, Master Lyster? I thought you went back to your estates?"

"Do call me Michael, I insist." He grinned, gesturing for me to walk beside him. "The king countermanded the order. No need for my troops when the men at Lincolnshire are all going back to their homes."

Shivering against the chill, I pulled my cloak tighter around me. "That man said there were rebels at Yorkshire. He wanted me to intervene for one of the religious houses there."

Michael ran his hand against the scruff of his beard. "We have heard whispers that the men in York were not as satisfied with the king's answer. I was hoping it was nothing more than a rumour, but each day brings more disturbing news."

I thought of the king's daughters at Hunsdon. If the rebels marched on London, would they try to take them by force? "I wish the king had sent for the Lady Mary and the Lady Elizabeth sooner. I hate that they are so far from court. What if the worst should happen?"

"Never fear," he assured me. "Edward says they shall arrive within the week."

"Forgive me, I just keep thinking that if they were my children—"

Michael stopped me. "Please do not apologize. I admire your concern for them." He put his hand to his heart. "I would be most honoured to have you fretting over my children."

His compliment brought a nervous flutter to my stomach. "How is your son?" I asked, remembering that Michael had mentioned him the first time we met. "Is he in a safe place?"

"Fortunately, Chabnor is nearer Wales than London, so I have no doubt he is far beyond the reach of the rebels. He is doing well. Growing wilder each day. He needs a mother to soothe the savage beast within." He laughed. "How do you fare with animals?"

"Me?" I yipped, feeling my face grow warm. "I haven't been around children much, to be honest. And I never had any brothers or sisters on which to practice. I have many skills, but I am afraid childrearing is not one of them."

"No one is born knowing how to raise a child. It is something one must learn, often through trial by fire." He held open the door, and I found myself surprised to realize we had already arrived back at the palace. "Farewell, Margery. Always a pleasure."

Watching him stride away, I found myself imagining what it might be like to share his bed, carry his child in my belly. He was kind enough, attentive when we spoke, and chivalrous when the need arose. But so too were most men when they were courting. *Are you honourable, Michael Lyster?*

JANE SEYMOUR

WINDSOR

Brittle dawn heralded the coming of the king's daughters. They arrived together. Grasping hands, they disembarked the protective womb of their carriage into the anxious chaos consuming the court. Far away at East Riding, the fire of rebellion moved through Yorkshire, consuming everything in its path. It raged from Hull to Doncaster, conscripting the enthusiastic and unwilling alike. When the rebels took Pontefract, they forced Lord Darcy from the safety of his castle into the conflagration—at least that was what he claimed when the king's herald came calling. Further afield, the Duke of Suffolk arrived like an angel of death: spilling rivulets of blood in his effort to quench the flames. Still, the fire burned on.

The Lady Mary wore her grief like a shroud. Wraithlike, she stalked the halls of the palace, haunted by the memory of times gone by and the nightmares of the present. The spectre of her mother loomed largely, and I could not help wondering how the Spanish Infanta would have handled such a revolt. Doubtless, she would have pled on behalf of the pilgrims as I had but would she have been slapped down like a dog as well? Only the Lord in Heaven knew. I thought of that indomitable queen when I placed the onyx crucifix she wore into the outstretched palm of her daughter. Mary gasped when she saw it, her diminutive fingers tracing the edges of black stone.

"Are you certain, Your Grace?"

Never had I been surer of anything in my life. "It is yours. I want you to have it."

"His Grace compelled me to write the emperor, you know," she whispered after a lengthy silence. "I was to tell him I believed my mother's marriage unlawful, affirming the renunciation of my inheritance." She brought the pendant to her lips, then pinned it to her bodice, close to her heart. "I pray for her forgiveness each night before I sleep."

The Lady Elizabeth, with her burnished curls and piercing umber gaze, was far more circumspect in my presence. This surprised me not, for she was hardly out of the nursery; her mother little more than a distant figure, quivering on the edges of an unrefined memory. She knelt as she took the doll from my hand, her dark eyes regarding me soberly. "Thank you, Lady Mother," she said in a low voice filled with such sweetness it made my heart hurt. Her mere presence rendered me breathless, my guts roiling with guilt. The blinding pain only subsided after she was taken away in the arms of her new maid, Mistress Champernowne. In an act of self-preservation, I kept both far from my rooms.

For all that Elizabeth observed from a distance, she was far from neglected. I commanded my chamberlain to give her the most sumptuous rooms and sent the best dishes from my table. Delicately nibbling at the portions, she watched her elder sister with ill-contained envy. Sitting opposite me with her back to the girl, Mary was spared these hungry looks, but they did not fall beneath the king's notice.

One night after supper, His Grace pulled Elizabeth on to his lap. No longer fearful that the child would stir remembrances of her mother, he plied her with fatherly affection. Mary tried not to let her stung feelings show, but I caught her gazing forlornly at the ring encircling her finger. Decorated with images of the three of us and a Latin inscription extolling the virtues of obedience, the jewel had been given by the king upon their reconciliation. It pained me to see her take such comfort from a gift I knew to be false. Though her father was the one to claim the glory, the gift indeed came from his minister's pocket. The commission had been Thomas Cromwell's doing, but the king was so besotted when he saw it, he insisted upon giving it himself. "Crum can find something else," he had said dismissively.

I wondered at the king's public coddling. For months he left Elizabeth languishing at Hunsdon without proper attire, her household disordered by the demotion and death of her mother. All that time, Lady Bryan's pleas for her charge falling upon deaf ears, and now such love as I had ever seen between father and daughter. *We are all pieces on a chessboard to be acknowledged and played at his every whim.*

"Are you familiar with a man by the name of Ascue?" His Grace asked when he came to my rooms later that evening, cheeks ruddy from the strong Rhenish wine.

"I do not recall, Your Grace." I moved closer to the fire, hoping to ward off the chill seeping through the windows. Outside, a brutal wind howled, rattling the stained glass. "Perhaps he was one of the petitioners? I can send for my chancellor if it would please you."

The king stared moodily at the flames. "I see no reason to do so since it was he who brought the matter to my attention."

What else have I done wrong? I picked up my embroidery ring, feigning nonchalance. "I hope it is nothing serious."

With a swipe of his hand, he sent the wooden ring skidding across the floor. Dust motes swirled around it, ruining the clean, white linen. A clap of thunder rumbled above the roof. "I warned you not to interfere. Now I hear tales of you taking bribes from the abbess of Clementhorpe?"

"I swear, Your Grace. I know nothing of Ascue or Clementhorpe, for that matter." Tears pricked behind my eyes. What did he mean by this? I searched my memories for the names he mentioned but came up empty-handed.

"This man—Christopher Ascue," he continued, "spoke to your maid, Margery Horsman. He offered up a payment from the abbess of the nunnery in Clementhorpe with the understanding you would speak to me on her behalf. Three hundred marks, no mean sum."

"I made no such promises," I replied slowly, calmly. "If Mistress Horsman did so, it was without my knowledge or consent. I shall see to it she is appropriately punished." I watched his face for signs of disbelief. None came. He sat still as stone.

At length, he rose from the chair. Bending to retrieve the embroidery ring from the floor, he placed it delicately in my lap before touching his lips to my forehead. "No need. Margery denied Ascue and sent him to your council to plead his case."

"I am relieved to hear it." *Relieved to have passed another test.*

"Treachery abounds this fearsome court, dearest wife. You would do well to remember it." He trailed a finger along the curve of my jaw, and I felt him stir beside me. An errant branch scratched at the window. "Enough talk of these deceits. The bed grows cold without us, and I am still in want of a son."

THE KING WAS already up and sitting at the table when I finally awoke, bleary and disoriented from another restless night. "Good morrow, my queen," he greeted absentmindedly, turning back to the dispatch in his hand. He took a bite of bread, then threw back the dregs in his goblet, wiping his mouth with a dainty flourish. "Join me, won't you? It is still warm, but only just."

Throwing the covers back, I swung my feet to the floor. The chill of the tile seeped through the rushes, sending me scrabbling for my slippers. I found them near the hearth, cosy and inviting. Padding to the table, I pulled my dressing gown tight around me. "News from the north?" I asked carefully.

He gave me a sidelong glance as I helped myself to some apple slices and a small wedge of cheese. "Norfolk writes that thirty-thousand rebels met him at Doncaster, more than five times his number. After a parley with their leader, who he soothed with sweet words and fair promises, a deal has been struck. Robert Aske will send two delegates to treat with me in person, and the rest will disperse, for the time being."

The turmoil in my stomach quieted with this hopeful report. "I am glad to hear it and will do everything I can to welcome them."

"No need, Cromwell will take care of all. Besides, you will be far too occupied during their visit."

Guts lurching, I returned the cheese to my plate. "Might I ask what shall consume my attention?"

The king arose from his chair, smiling. "I have been neglectful in commissioning your portrait, so I have recalled Holbein to court."

"A portrait? Does this mean the coronation is back on?" *Surely, it would not proceed until I conceived an heir.*

"All in good time. This portrait, coupled with one I have commissioned of myself, will serve as a message—a reminder of our majesty and the security of our dynasty." Leaning in for a kiss, he gripped my shoulder tightly. "How beautiful you would look, round and full with-child," he cooed, hot breath tickling my ear. "Let us pray that my seed takes root and blossoms in your belly. Perhaps then you would not question my desire to bring these traitors to heel, no matter the cost."

"By your command, my dearest husband." I refused to look at him.

I was still fuming over the king's words when Margery arrived to dress me. In her arms she carried a crimson velvet gown, garnished with diamond and gold quatrefoils. "Stop," I commanded. "Set that aside and bring me something else. I have an occasion in mind for that gown."

Startled, Margery dipped a curtsy. "Which gown would Your Grace have?"

I shook my head. "Whatever you bring will suffice. I would like to keep that one here with me. The king plans a portrait, and there is much I wish to convey through my attire." *Crimson blood and diamonds for faithfulness. Gold for justice.* "Could you also see if there is a hood to match?"

"There is, Your Grace, but Anne Boleyn wore it." Averting her gaze, Margery busied herself, hanging the frock from a hook near the bed.

"No matter, bring it. Sleeves too—with pomegranates on them—if you can find some."

I watched her scurry from the room, then moved to my jewel casket. I knew which piece I wanted the moment I opened the drawer: the ruby and diamond pendant. *Sacrifice and the Blood of Christ.* I rubbed the tip of my finger against the cabochon, drawing strength from its fire. Another jewel glinted in the sunlight, catching my attention. Queen Catherine's brooch: IHS for Jesus, picked out in diamonds and hung with three teardrop pearls. *Innocence and the Trinity—Father, Son, Holy Spirit.* "Perfect," I breathed.

I would be silent, but never still.

SPINEL

Hope

NOVEMBER & DECEMBER 1536

MARGERY HORSMAN

WINDSOR AND RICHMOND PALACE

T he Lady Mary slumped as her father's voice thundered through the room, rattling plate, and courtier alike. "Two hundred thousand pounds, and for what? Provisions, gonnes, and munitions—all to defend my realm from herself. Such discourteous creatures these men are, to tell their sovereign what is right and good. These vast sums from the treasury would have been better spent protecting us from foreign invasion. I expected enemies on all sides—the Emperor or France—never from within. Can you believe this intransigence? And now, they think to send me an envoy. Well, how grand for them to have been raised to such heights. What say you to this outrage?"

With a pleading glance towards the queen, the lady opened her mouth to reply, but the words dried on her tongue.

"Surely the Lady Mary defers only to Your Grace's opinion on the matter," Queen Jane answered swiftly, drawing the king's attention from his daughter. She gave him a kindly smile, patting his hand under the table. "Obedience is one of her greatest virtues, wouldn't you agree, my love?"

The endearment sounded strange in my ears. I could not remember the last time I heard the queen refer to her husband in that manner. Had she ever? She seemed distant as of late, keeping her own counsel since the day I brought the old queens' attire. Why would she trot out their things for a portrait? I found it morbid and ill-conceived, but who was I to question it? *Nothing and nobody.*

The king speared a chunk of pear with his knife. The creamy flesh of the fruit glistened in the candlelight. Chewing, he stared down his daughter. "I am considering a marriage proposal. Two, actually. While my own people rise against me, professed enemies vie for the honour of your hand."

The Lady Mary's spine lengthened. She leaned in, cautiously eager. "Truly, Your Grace? Master Chapuys says—"

"I have told you before. I care not what that man thinks," the king interrupted, his lip curled in distaste. "Yet, his master has suggested a match with the Infante of Portugal, Dom Luiz, so I am compelled to bear him for the nonce."

Despite her father's irritation, the lady brightened, a tentative smile creeping into her face. "How wonderful that would be. Had I to choose for myself, I would pick no one else." She bit her lip, the curves of her cheeks flushing with delight.

"Perhaps a spring wedding? Once the yule festivities are over, of course," the queen added gingerly, careful in her phrasing.

Jane Ashley and I exchanged a worried glance. I had not witnessed the dressing down Her Grace suffered begging the king to show the rebels mercy, but Mistress Ashley was there. "Ghastly," she told me afterward. The event so frightened Mistress Norris that she spent the night sobbing. When Stonor came for her the next morning, she pled illness to avoid showing her tired and bruised eyes.

This time, the king dismissed his wife's remark with little more than a sigh. "Let us not be too hasty in this matter. Dom Luiz may have much to recommend him, but he is beneath you. I am more inclined to the Duke of Orleans. France is the greater kingdom, and one day its throne would belong to your children. Imagine it, Mary, our countries united once more, ruled by the son of a Tudor."

The Lady Mary frowned, deep furrows etching the fine plane of her brow. She swallowed hard, no doubt measuring the cost of her response. Finding the price for dissent too high, she demurred quietly, "Yes, Father. It would be a wonder, indeed."

"That's my girl," the king enthused, reaching out with a bejewelled hand to grasp her delicate wrist. She flinched at his touch, and he pulled away, regret flaring in his eyes. "Crum shall keep you apprised of the negotiations," he added curtly.

"Shall I be leaving?" The Lady Mary's voice was edged with sadness.

The king turned away, preferring the dancing flames in the hearth to the endless azure pools of his daughter's eyes. "Now the ingrates have dispersed and all danger is past, it is time for you and your sister to return to Hunsdon."

THE FOG WAS thick as stew, heavy with swirling droplets of ice, the day the envoys arrived with demands from the north. "An open parliament to be held in York, recognition of the church's rights and privileges; no more dissolutions and no more Cromwell," John Husee told us one evening as we trampled across the frozen lawn.

"How is it you always know so much, Master Husee?" The tinkling notes of Mary Arundell's laugh hovered in the air like flakes of snow.

"I observe and listen. More importantly, I make friends." He grinned, those white teeth gleaming in the moonlight.

"A man will tell you only what benefits him. A friend will tell you all his secrets," I recited, trying my best to imitate the deep timbre of his voice.

"How well you know me, Mistress Horsman." Husee laughed, and I felt my heart lurch with yearning. Quickly tamping down the emotion, I slowed my pace to put distance between us.

Mistress Arundell noted the manoeuvre; her brow arched impishly. "How is it that one so charming as yourself is still in want of a wife? Our dearest Margery is unattached if you are interested."

Mercifully, neither could see the heat emanating from my face. "Master Husee is married to his duty. Lady Lisle is a demanding mistress. She would never countenance competition for his affections." Unkind though it was, my retort stirred nods all around.

"Speaking of weddings—has a date been set for yours, Mistress Arundell?" Mistress Ashley asked, giving me a look filled with pity. For months

I had cursed her presence, terrified of what she might ask from me, but no demands ever came. This small act of kindness—another one of her interventions—made me question my perception of her. I often heard the other girls remark that living so closely in the dormitory was akin to being in a large family. Perhaps this was how it was with sisters. One moment enemies and next, the best of friends.

While Mistress Arundell breathlessly regaled us with details of her upcoming nuptials, Husee drifted back, falling in-step beside me. "You are quiet, Margery. I hope that didn't bother you?"

"Why should it, Master Husee? It is not the first time they have japed at my expense, and it won't be the last time." He opened his mouth to reply, but I stopped him with another question. "Do you think the king will give the pilgrims what they want?"

Husee shook his head. "Giving them a parliament, maybe. Perhaps even reopening a few religious houses. But he will never restore power to the Pope, nor would he return the Lady Mary to the line of succession. He is even less likely to set aside Cromwell. The rebels deceive themselves if they believe he would go so far."

"Will he pardon them, do you think?" I shuddered at the thought of further bloodshed.

"Depends on how much they are willing to grovel."

Grovel they did, their compliments and proclamations of the king's mercy and goodness sparing them the sharp edge of the axe. Still, the treaty was tenuous, balancing precariously upon empty assurances and reticent pledges of better behaviour. The envoys departed with the Duke of Norfolk's retinue wearing hopeful, triumphant smiles, but only time would tell if the king's promises would hold.

WITH THREATS OF plague and insurrection finally abated, King Henry pronounced it safe to abandon the stronghold at Windsor. The servants began their scourge, scrubbing and purging the palace even before we disembarked. Our retinue moved in slow stages through the snow-covered countryside, icy November winds tearing at our fur-lined cloaks. The cold seeped into the very marrow of my bones, chilling me from the inside out, and it was several days before I again sensed warmth on my skin.

At Richmond, the queen spent her days closeted with Master Holbein while he continued working on the preparatory drawing for her portrait. Watching him, I marvelled at the way each line he drew pulsed with life. Like an alchemist, he transformed the simplest ingredients—primed paper and a handful of chalk—into pure gold. "It puts me in mind of Pygmalion," I gushed when he revealed the finished piece.

Holbein raised his bushy brows. "You are familiar with the classics, Mistress Horsman?"

"Just Ovid," I replied, abashed by his attention. "My father used to recite tales from *Metamorphoses* to me."

"How fortunate you were." Seeing the twinge of sadness in my eyes, Holbein rushed his next words. "And I thank you for the compliment. Not everyone appreciates my work."

"Who wouldn't be moved by such beauty? The details are exquisite." The possibility seemed almost like sacrilege.

"When a man commissions a portrait, he does it to show himself to the world. Often, the version he wants to portray is not the true one. He wants all his flaws hidden away beneath layers of paint. Sadly, I do not dabble in miracles, merely art. My paintings are little more than mirrors."

"Even the king's portraits?" I asked dubiously. Would he dare contradict the king's vision of himself?

Holbein laughed, holding his palms out as if in penance. "Only my wealthiest and most powerful patron could tempt me to turn water into wine."

I watched the queen throughout this exchange, wondering if she found the artist's remarks blasphemous. She gave nothing away. Only later, when we were alone in her bedchamber, did she ask me who Pygmalion was.

"He was an artist during the time of the ancient Greeks, known for creating a sculpture so beautiful and faultless, it came to life," I answered, judging it prudent to leave out the finer details of Pygmalion's disgust at the immorality and shamelessness of the daughters of his city. How he poured his outrage into his art, carving a figure of the perfect woman. How the statue so enchanted him, he fell in love and made offerings to

Aphrodite that she would find him a bride who would be its living likeness. Pygmalion was too much like the king, moulding and shaping his wife like marble.

The queen lifted her arms, allowing me to pull her silken undergarment over her head. When I slipped it off, I noticed the rose-coloured marks etching the skin of her stomach, scars from the thickening of her waist. Having the care of her laundry, I knew her blood had come without fail each month, but more than babies could make the belly grow. Fear and loneliness, guilt, or grief—all played their part. Her vulnerability stirred sorrow within me. Despite the vision presented in her portrait to the world beyond, Jane Seymour was not made of stone.

"'Tis a great shame you were not matched with a nobleman. Your father must have hoped for it, training you as he did," she said suddenly, still staring vacantly at the window as if there were more to see outside than the inky void of the night sky.

"Perhaps, Your Grace. He left my care to the Countess of Salisbury after his death. He wanted her to raise me like a true lady. She secured my place here at court when I turned fourteen and I worked my way up." I crossed the room to return her jewels to the coffer. Anne Boleyn's pearls taunted me when I lifted the lid. "My father may have wished it, but he never had enough money to tempt a man into marrying me." With my back to the queen, I carefully slid her ring of spinel on to my finger, admiring the way the deep red stone shimmered in the candlelight. How different my life would have been, funded by jewels like these. Threatened by such dolorous thoughts, I tore the ring off and shoved it back into its drawer, damming a wave of self-pity.

When I turned around, the queen was waiting for me at her dressing table. Unfurling her hair from its trusses, I began to comb. "He is not a nobleman, but there is a man who has made known his interest in you, Margery." She checked my reaction in the mirror's reflection.

"Oh?" I feigned preoccupation with a snarl in her blonde locks.

"My family has known him for many years, so I think I could speak to his character. He is a good man—honest and forthright. Had my parents thought to match me with him in my youth, I would have gladly accepted."

Catching her eye in the mirror, I offered up an appreciative smile. "That is wonderful to hear, Your Grace, but I am afraid I do not have anything to offer a groom. My father did not leave money for a dowry."

"Master Lyster has assured me he has no need of that, but I would not send you to your marriage without a gift of some kind. I shall speak to the king about it before we leave for Greenwich."

It was true then. Master Lyster *did* want to marry me. *But why?* Why would he want me? And why was the queen so willing to help? Overcome by her generosity, I fell to my knees in supplication. "Thank you, Your Grace. I fear I have done little to earn this kindness." Every despicable act flooded my mind at that moment, filling me with remorse and guilt. My careless words had caused death and pain. Because of me, Lady Rochford's husband was taken from her. I had no right to one of my own.

The queen stood. She cupped my elbow, guiding me to my feet. "I command you to stop this nonsense, Mistress Horsman," she said in a kind but firm voice. "It is nothing more than a reward for your commendable service. I am merely fulfilling a promise made before my time."

Anne Boleyn's promise. Would she have kept it if she knew I was to blame? "Please forgive me," I whispered, but it wasn't to the queen standing before me—it was to the queen who once was—and the men who died with her. I prayed my words reached beyond the grave.

JANE SEYMOUR

YORK PLACE AND GREENWICH

The king eased himself on to the bed. Grunting with pain, he swung his legs off the floor. Sneaking a surreptitious glance at his hose, I saw no outward sign of blood or pus but caught the faintest scent of infection lingering in the air. Crawling up behind him, I accidentally brushed the wrapping covering his wound. He recoiled with an indignant yelp. "Careful there. It has flared up again."

"Is it the weather, Your Grace?" The king's wound often festered without warning, but the affliction always seemed to worsen with the change in seasons. Cold and heat posed particularly marked discomfort, so it was not surprising given the bitter chill in the air. Even the Thames, that mighty tidal river, had frozen in protest of winter's cruel touch.

"Only God himself knows why this affliction never ceases to torment me. Of course, the doctors say they have done all they can. What is the point in them, anyway?" he growled. "The treatments I devise have far better results."

I slid my hand between us, nestling it in the hollow dip of his back, an area he often complained of when his leg troubled him. Fingertips gingerly tracing his skin, I found the knot and began to knead. He moaned in pleasure, his body relaxing into my palm. Any other wife might have done this out of compassion or charity for their beloved. I did it out of duty, numb to the intimacy of it.

Since that harrowing day at Windsor, when I dared chance the king's piety, I had done my best to be the queen he wanted: meek, submissive, quiet, and conforming. I honoured my motto in all ways, forever bound to obey and serve. My only rebellion was hidden, codified in a piece of art. The king was too well-sated by my good behaviour to notice. During the one occasion he joined my session with Holbein, his eyes crept over me with an appreciative glance, settling upon the brooch at my breast. "Is that what you created with that harridan's pearls?" he asked. Scanning my face, the artist replied with a simple '*Yes, Your Grace,*' and turned back to his drawing. Holbein never commented upon my attire or the fact that I wore the relics of two dead women. He knew well the language of symbols, though he never spoke it. He kept my secrets, just as he had done with those he painted in the past. For that, I would always be grateful.

Watching the king as he lay eyes closed, back arched against me, I wondered again how he could so easily forget. Queen Catherine wore that brooch many times throughout her reign, even commemorating it in a miniature she commissioned. Yet, her husband failed to recognize it. Worse, he believed the three pearls hanging from it came from the neck of her sworn enemy. The gown and hood I chose had been worn by Anne Boleyn when they struck the medal celebrating her second pregnancy. Yet, the father of that lost child failed to acknowledge it. In his mind, their deaths erased them from existence. Would it be the same for me when I departed this life? Were we as interchangeable as those pearls, trotted out to adorn the wife who would come after us?

The king squealed in pain. "Not so hard! It is tender."

I pulled back, unaware of how rough my touch had become. "Forgive me, Your Grace. I got carried away."

"I preferred it when you called me sweetheart." He pulled me in for a kiss. His hand caressed the curves beneath my nightgown. "I know we are not meant to until the end of Advent, but shall we try again? A son for the new year?"

Please, God, let it take this time. Only a son could save me from oblivion.

Afterwards he gazed at me from the other side of the pillow. "I invited that lawyer, Robert Aske, to Christmas. I must hear from his own lips the causes of this rebellion."

Are you sure that is wise? I wanted to ask. The king had used nothing but abusive language towards the poor man, and now he wanted to court him? Entertain him with feasts and yule-tide merriment? Instead, I said, "Benevolent as always, Sweetheart. Would you extend this same grace to your niece, wretched as she is at Syon?" Since her release from the Tower, poor Margaret Douglas had languished, forgotten at the abbey.

"Despite my sister's pleas, I have not forgiven the Lady Margaret for her rash behaviour. I refuse to give her the satisfaction," he huffed. Cruel and unyielding, like the winter-tide.

Sensing a shift in his mood, I changed tack. "There is something I would ask of you—a favour for one of my ladies."

"What is it, dearest one?" he asked, keen to please after our coming together.

"Michael Lyster has approached me for the hand of Mistress Horsman. The match is suitable, so I have granted my permission, but there is a hitch. Mistress Horsman does not have funds for a jointure. Since you have graciously contributed to such things in the past, I am hoping you will be moved to do so again."

"Would this please you?" He searched my face—looking for sincerity or motive, I was unsure.

"Mistress Horsman has been loyal and diligent in her work. She should not be punished for the misfortune life has dealt her. As someone who also lost his parents during the bloom of youth, I thought you might agree."

The king kissed me again; his thin lips pressed tightly against mine. "Then it shall be as you wish. Mistress Margery will have land from one of the dissolved abbeys in Lincolnshire. Crum will draft a warrant before New Year."

A spoil of war, to do with as His Grace saw fit. At least it was going to someone who deserved it, rather than a ravenous courtier.

THE CHRISTMAS CELEBRATIONS began in earnest with the arrival of the new Lord Mayor of London. After an elaborate knighting ceremony in the king's presence chamber, the gathered party processed out into the courtyard, where our horses were waiting—saddled and ready—for the journey to Greenwich. Behind the Lord Mayor with the mace proudly raised, we rode through the city; the king and I together, the Lady Mary a few paces after. Along Fleet Street, the friars stood in copes of gold, censing as we passed, curling fingers of fragrant smoke dissipating into the frosty air. The Bishop of London and the abbots of Waltham and Tower Hill met us at St Paul's Church. Our arrival was heralded by the angelic voices of the choir, who were no doubt freezing in their robes.

After a solemn mass inside, we returned to the cheering crowds braving the bitter cold without. From the churchyard to London Bridge, parish priests bestowed blessings as our horses trampled by on the gravelled streets. Above, rich gold arras and tapestries fashioned in the most brilliant colours brightened the grey sky. Cresting the bridge, a ribbon of white unspooled beneath us, the Thames snaking off into the distance, farther than the eye could see. When we crossed the river, I looked back at the Lady Mary. She grinned merrily in return, cheeks rosy and luminous. What a change it was from her visit in the autumn. What a difference it made, feeling included, feeling beloved, feeling worthy of consideration. Finally, she was firmly in the king's graces, the one place she always longed to be.

Our rooms at Greenwich were ablaze with light. Flickering candles danced in every window, while the logs in the hearth sputtered and popped with wild enthusiasm. It was a welcome sight after hours in the saddle, shivering beneath mounds of velvet, brocade, and fur. The only thing that could have sweetened it was a steaming meat pie glistening with gravy. But we were still in the throes of advent, so our meal consisted of a vegetable pottage and crusty loaves of bread. In truth, my appetite was not what it once was, and I was glad of the simple fare. I settled into bed that night, thankful and satiated but apprehensive of what the arrival of our honoured guest from the north might bring.

Thomas Cromwell was waiting in the privy chamber when I emerged the next morning. My brothers stood on either side, anxious as a pair of brides. "Good day, sister," they said in unison. Cromwell looked on between them. Edward bristled when the advisor asked for a moment of my time, indicating he meant to have it out of their hearing. The scowl was nearly imperceptible, but I knew my brother's features as well as my own. He was not pleased.

"Lord Beauchamp, Master Seymour, I thank you for the warm greeting. If you wait in the presence chamber, I shall join you shortly." As they exited—one brother slumped with disappointment, the other pridefully erect—Cromwell cleared his throat, directing a pointed glance at my ladies. "Mistress Horsman may stay. The rest of you can see yourselves out," I instructed, glancing at each one of them.

"Well noted, Your Grace, as there is a matter to discuss with the lady you have chosen to stay behind." Cromwell gestured: an accusatory finger pointed at the maid beside me.

Margery went rigid, her body swaying under the power of his gaze. I worried she might faint again. This was not the way I intended to tell her, scaring her half out of her wits, but we had not yet a chance to discuss the king's gift. Unsure how she felt about the dissolutions, I prayed she would hold her tongue if she found the bequest against her conscience.

"Firstly, the king would like to extend his sincere congratulations on your impending nuptials, Mistress Horsman. Master Lyster has frequented the court for many years, always showing himself a loyal and dedicated servant, and we think you shall be pleased to call him husband. To that end, the king wishes to contribute the recently acquired Newbo Abbey to your marriage portion, in appreciation of your service to the crown." A wolfish smile stretched across Cromwell's face. He drew out his next remark. "Particularly your assistance during last spring's troubling events. We might never have thought to investigate Marc Smeaton's behaviour without your report, so thank you."

My maid went white. She swallowed hard. "Please tell the king his exceeding generosity humbles me." Her voice cracked, and she gulped again, wetting her lips. "I am a most unworthy recipient."

There it was again—calling herself unworthy, undeserving. I wondered at her reaction when we discussed Lyster's proposal; now I understood. She thought she was to blame. I wanted to wrap my arms around her, tell her that Anne Boleyn and those men would have fallen with or without her help, but how could I? It was not safe. "Thank you,

Cromwell. Will there be anything else?" I asked, hoping to bring this uncomfortable audience to a merciful end.

"Yes, though I must confess it is not official business. I simply wanted to remind Your Grace that Robert Aske shall be here in a few days, and it would be in all our best interests if conversations with him were kept to cheerful topics. Your Grace might want to refrain from discussing the uprisings in the north, and perhaps, religion altogether."

"Is that an edict?" I kept a straight face. Inside, I seethed.

"Of course not, Your Grace. I would never presume." Cromwell smiled again. This time it was more humane—sympathetic, even. "A mere friendly suggestion, that is all."

Had it been enough to bring one wife down? Was the man losing his taste for it? "We shall take it under advisement, Lord Cromwell."

After he was gone, Margery turned to me. "Are there nuns at Newbo? Will they be forced out because of me?" Her eyes, bright as polished green beryl, shone with unshed tears.

"Not at all." I reached for her hands. "I have asked my brother, and he assures me no nuns have been displaced. The abbey was all but abandoned many years ago." While not strictly true—there had been an abbot and six cannons pensioned off—I saw no reason to distress her further.

"How can I ever repay you?"

"Let the past go, Margery," I replied, wishing I could heed my own words. "Be kind, do good deeds, and we shall consider the debt satisfied." The door flew open, and our palms slid apart.

A harassed yeoman stuck his head in. "Lord Edward Beauchamp and Master Thomas Seymour want to know if they can come in now."

My brothers did not even wait for me to wave them in.

"Well, what did he say?" Edward's brows were knit with worry. He nervously shifted his weight from one foot to the other. The gold chain hanging from his neck clinked softly against a button.

Tom threw up a hand. "Not in front of her," he hissed, eyeing Margery suspiciously.

"Mistress Horsman is discreet. You can say whatever is you need in front of her. Now, what is this all about?"

Edward rolled back on to his heels, relaxing his defensive posture. "Cromwell told us he was coming to warn you about Robert Aske's visit. We thought—"

"You had done something foolish again," Tom interrupted.

"Could you both have a bit more faith? I have done nothing to stir rebuke—this time, at least—nor do I plan to act in any way that might embarrass or anger the king, so have no fear."

Uncertainty passed over Edward's face like a shadow. "I thought to go home to my wife. Now I am not so certain. She takes to her chamber after New Year." His voice faltered.

"I will be here," Tom said suddenly. "She is my sister, too—I can offer support." He shot Edward a confident grin. "And Bryan will be here, as well," he added. "We have it in hand."

"Sir Francis? The man Cromwell calls the Vicar of Hell?" Edward mused doubtfully. "What could go wrong?"

MARGERY HORSMAN

GREENWICH

Mary Arundell's quiet sobs breached the borders of my dream. Unwilling to part from my hard-won—if fitful—slumber, I desperately clung to its threads as it fled, leaving me adrift in the ocean of black that filled the dormitory. A pair of entwined figures solidified as my eyes adjusted to the darkness. Cradling Mary in her arms, Joan whispered reassuring words. She stroked the cascade of wheaten hair falling over her sister's heaving back. "Please don't cry, Mary. Everything will be well, you will see. This marriage shall make you a countess. Won't you enjoy taking precedence over me, for once?"

"I wish it were you instead." She drew a ragged breath. "You are the elder and should be married first. Besides, the earl is nearly as old as Father. Wouldn't you be more to his liking?"

"How ignorant you are to the world, little mouse. A man like Sussex wants a beautiful girl, ripe with youth and inexperience. Those days have faded for me. My golden years have gone like ash on the wind."

It is not too late for you, Joan. We were of an age, the two of us, older than the rest of the girls in the household. *Our lustre may have faded, but we are not yet ashes. The time has come for me, and one day it will come for you.*

FOR ALL HER disquiet, Mary shone radiantly during the morning meal in the great hall. Joan, haggard from the night's confessions, drooped over her bowl, shoring up the sticky contents inside with her spoon. If anyone else knew what had happened, no one let on, but Mistress Norris and Mistress Ashley launched themselves from the table the instant Mother Stonor approached. "Are you coming, Mistress Horsman? The queen awaits."

HAVING COMPLETED MY duties in the royal apartments, I took a detour through one of the courtyards on my way back from the wardrobe. I found myself in a knot garden blanketed by heavy snow. The crunch of my boots echoed in the hushed silence, a whistling magpie my only companion. I stopped to watch the bird alight, tenderly grasping a bare branch above me. It regarded me curiously, no doubt interested in the shining bits of gold on my hood, and then it was gone, swallowed up by the leaden sky overhead.

I slipped between a pair of iron gates, wandering out to the pathway that followed the riverside. It felt strange seeing it so empty, all the boats having been grounded when the water froze. The quayside, usually teeming with noise, was a bleak sight to behold: no fishermen, no merchants, no signs of life. I was standing at the river stair, taking it all in, when Master Husee loped into view.

"Mistress Margery, what are you doing out here? Where is your escort?"

"I was waylaid heading back from the wardrobe, thinking of how the river appeared when we rode through London. 'Tis a wonder to see it this way, so still and calm. I had to have another look."

Shielding his eyes from the sun, Husee took in the sight. "Wondrous and irksome." He laughed, a great guffaw that sent a nearby flock of crows skittering down the foreshore. "I am having the worst time getting Lady Lisle's goods to her."

I suddenly remembered a bit of gossip I had overheard at Richmond concerning his employer. "I hear she is with-child. Please send my heartiest recommendations to her."

"Thank you. I shall. It seems you are due congratulations, as well."

My pulse pounded under his gaze. Was it the nip in the air or the heat of his stare causing my knees to tremble? "Yes, I am due to marry at the end of the coming month."

"I am glad to hear it. Will you be keeping your room? Lady Lisle is still looking to place her daughters."

When the words left his lips, I understood. Anything that had been—or could be—between us was nothing more than a wish or far-fetched dream. I felt silly, yet it did not pain me like I thought it would. Instead, pity overcame me. Poor Husee had sworn his fealty to Honour Lisle, and there would never be room in his life for any other woman.

BACK IN THE dormitory, the maids were giddy with the prospect of the revels to come. The sacrifices of advent could be challenging for those accustomed to the excesses at court, but I often felt renewed by the prayers and the fasting. Still, I joined in their excitement, thinking of all I had to celebrate.

An hour to midnight, the queen summoned me to her bedchamber to prepare for mass. I brought along a cloth of gold and silver tinsel gown, lined with the softest fur. Swirling loops of the tiniest seed pearls sprayed across the bodice in flourishes beneath a habiliment of diamonds. In it, the queen looked angelic, ethereal.

Once she was changed, she sent me to the jewel casket to select a few pieces to complete the ensemble. I laboured over the decision, digging through the drawers for something perfect. At length, I decided the diamonds were sumptuous enough on their own and settled upon a tablet of blue and green enamelled gold. Paired with delicate matching bracelets, it was just enough; anything more would have appeared garish.

We processed to the chapel carrying lit tapers. Pinpricks of candlelight illuminated the dark corridors. It looked like the stars had fallen from the heavens, spilling across our path. The service was lengthy but beautiful and uplifting. The story of the Christ Child was one that never failed to move me, the saviour of our kind, born in the humblest of circumstances. It was a miracle, the likes of which we would never see again. Singing *Gloria in Excelsis Deo*, our voices rang out in prayerful adoration.

After a few hours of much-needed rest and reflection, the festivities began in earnest. In the afternoon there were Morris Dancers and mummers with a visit from a troupe of actors. One of their number, a man dressed in blue and white motley with bells on his slippers, approached Mistress Norris with an open hand. "Alms for the poor?" he asked sweetly, a mischievous smirk teasing the corners of his mouth.

"You do not look impoverished to me, my good sir." She regarded his costume appreciatively.

"Not I, not me!" The man howled with laughter. "I am Sir Peter, the richest man you see!"

Mistress Norris gestured at the men surrounding us. "Look around, Sir Peter, what do you see? Peers of the realm and nobility."

Mary Arundell, trying desperately to keep her composure at this joust of wits, elbowed me. Biting her lip, she looked fit to burst.

The man made a show, taking in the crowd with an appraising eye. "Nothing but peasants," he judged with an exaggerated flick of his wrist.

"Then what, pray tell, are you, Sir Peter? A worldly knight?"

He rocked back on his heel, extending one leg with a flourish. The bell on his toe tinkled with the movement. "I am a lord, simple girl—the Lord of Misrule. Can't you tell by my suit?" Regarding her with pity, he pulled a coin from his hat. "Perhaps you need this more than the poor." When Mistress Norris plucked it from his outstretched hand, he turned to me. "Alms for the half-wit?"

Finally, Mary Arundell could hide her amusement no longer. She bent over, clutching the fabric of her skirt, her body shaking with laughter.

"Fits! Fits! She is having fits!" the fool cried, pointing at her hunched form. "I think the lot of you belong in bedlam."

"I couldn't agree with you more, Sir Peter the Lord." Mistress Ashley sniffed in mock contempt.

"Ah! Kindred spirit." The man sidled up to her, a winsome smile revealing the chip in his front tooth. "Tell me, my lady, what is your tale?"

She threw her head back dramatically, hand by her brow. "Plagued by fools."

"Plague!" he yelped, bells ringing as he leaped aside. "Must go now, no time to waste!" he called over his shoulder, scurrying out of sight. Returning a few moments later, he made his bows. "Gracious ladies, I do thank you for humouring me. Happy Christmas to you all."

Mistress Norris tossed back his coin, and I added a few more to his cupped hand. "Happy Christmas to you, Sir Peter."

When the man smiled again, the chip was gone, his once jagged bite now perfectly straight. Noting my surprise, he gave me a wink. "Tis naught but a show, my lady."

Mistress Ashley giggled, watching him dance away. "Did you see his dimples? We should have given him more coin."

High above the crowd, a trill of music—light and airy—summoned us to the feast. The great hall was in its glory; lush boughs of evergreen and ivy draped in great swags from corner to corner. Golden tendrils of flame writhed in the torches, casting a soft glow over the rows of trestle tables loaded with silver platters of food. The table near the dais held all manner of sugar sculptures: St George and the dragon, a castle surrounded by dainty turrets, even a phoenix in honour of the queen. Mixed amongst the statues were candied almonds, comfits, and sweet dates.

Mistress Ashley shuddered when I pointed out the marchpane cakes. "Foul stuff," she groaned.

"Ah, yes! Mistress Marchpane. I had almost forgotten the Boleyns called you that." Spiteful and petty, I regretted the comment instantly, but part of me enjoyed the stricken look upon her face. Much as I hated to admit it, I still resented her act of betrayal, taking Anne Boleyn's pearls from my trunk. Reminding her of the late queen's taunt felt vindicating in some small way.

The clamour of voices rose all around me, but the chaos fell away when I saw Michael Lyster across the hall. He was standing on the fringes of a mob surrounding Thomas Seymour and Sir Francis Bryan, watching in bemusement as the two men brayed at some joke. Unobserved, I took him in. When he caught me staring, his face broke open with joy.

He disentangled himself from the group, easing away with a sheepish grin and promises to re-join them before the night was over. Striding past, he gestured for me to follow. I glanced up at the dais, where the monarchs sat enthroned beneath the cloth of estate. Sitting beside them was a man I did not recognize. His dark hair was closely cropped, and he wore an ornately embroidered coat the deep scarlet of fresh blood. The king leaned in close, listening intently as the man spoke, oblivious to the servants bustling about the table. Queen Jane turned to say something to the Lady Mary and saw me floundering with uncertainty. She dismissed me with a smile. Released from my responsibilities, I ran after Michael, heartbeat pounding in my ears.

He awaited me in the deserted corridor, one foot propped against the wall, an arm slung low over his waist. I hesitated, wondering if I should have a chaperone. Was this proper? Quickly as the thought came, it faded away, leaving behind an acute desire; a hunger to be wanted, to be chosen, to be claimed as his own. I had been lonely for an eternity. "I waited so long for you, Michael."

He moved closer, closing the distance between us effortlessly. "I was preparing our home for your arrival. If you want it? If you want me?" He looked nervous suddenly as if it had just occurred to him that I might have changed my mind.

"In truth, I have thought of almost nothing else." I reached for him, my fingers finding the curve of his jawline.

Catching my hand, he gave it a gentle squeeze. "Wait, there is something I must say before you commit."

"Nothing could dissuade me," I assured him, despite the worry clawing at me. Had I made a mistake?

"I care for you, Margery—deeply. You have awakened within me emotions I believed long dead." He stalled, struggling to find the words.

"Just tell me, Michael. Whatever it is, it cannot be worse than what I have already endured."

He swallowed hard, nodded. "Truth is that my first wife meant everything to me. She was my beloved, and I may never stop grieving her. I swear that I will always honour and cherish you, provide and care for you. However, I cannot promise to love you as you desire or deserve."

"Ever?" The word was soil in my mouth, bitter and stale.

"Perhaps one day, but I do not know when, or if it is even possible." He looked miserable as if this admission pained him much more than he could articulate. "If the burden is too great—"

I pressed my finger to his lips, stopping him. "Michael, I understand grief. It has been my constant companion for longer than I can remember. You never have to justify or excuse yourself to me. I only ask this: is there hope?"

Kissing the palm of my hand, he offered a mournful smile. "With you, there is always hope."

"Then we shall take each day as it comes, whatever it may bring." My mother said the same words when we learned her life was dwindling towards its end. The days that came after were often brutal and relentless, and yet she was worth every one of them. The anguish upon Michael's face convinced me that he was too.

JANE SEYMOUR

GREENWICH

T he Lady Mary and I met at dawn to celebrate lauds together in my private chapel. She was in high spirits, despite not having slept since the midnight mass, chattering excitedly about the New Year gift she commissioned for her sister, the first of value she had ever been able to give her. A few weeks ago, Cromwell petitioned the king to increase her allowance for the term, and she was inordinately thrilled to share her bounty. "They are the tiniest pair of sleeves, made with cloth of silver," she whispered, settling upon the cushion beside me. "Perhaps next year I can afford a gown to match."

Returning to the presence chamber after the service, we were met by my chamberlain. He was harried and breathless. Master Aske had arrived, and my husband was on his way.

The king strode into the room with a boldness that belied the great bodily pain he had been experiencing since our frigid ride through London. I knew he wanted to make a good show during the festivities to remind his courtiers of the largesse at his disposal and the power behind the throne, but even I was surprised by how convincing he was. Wanting to appear particularly imposing in front of Aske, he was clad in his most sumptuous gown: purple velvet and cloth of gold, sable trimmed and encrusted with jewels. A wide-brimmed hat, decorated with an enormous red spinel brooch, completed the ensemble.

"I am pleased you are both here." He planted a kiss on the Lady Mary's cheek and another on my lips. "We shall show this Aske a united front. I want to soothe him with our grace and benevolence. I want to awe him with our dominance and our might. When he returns to the north, there shall be no more talk of rebellion, for he will preach the strength of our dynasty."

The Lady Mary tugged at the hem of her sleeve, anxiously twirling the fabric between her fingers. "You have already promised a full pardon. I thought you invited Master Aske to understand the grievances of the people better?"

"My darling daughter." The king brought his arm around her, crushing her close to his side. "You have been away from court far too long, and there is much you still do not understand. Trust in me, and all will be well."

Through the palace we marched, the Lady Elizabeth joining our entourage as we passed her rooms. She struggled to keep up, so my brother lifted her into the air, planting the girl on his shoulder in one swift move. When I looked back at Thomas, he was grinning, proud to be carrying out this special duty.

I anticipated the king summoning Aske to his presence chamber, an intimidating and often unwelcoming venue, so I was surprised and inwardly relieved by my husband's desire to meet the rebel leader on neutral ground. This act of mercy signalled his willingness to listen to the man, regardless of his irritation with the rebels. In it, I saw a glimmer of the king I once knew, and it gave me hope.

A vibrant sky, cloudless and blue, hung over the courtyard. I prayed it was an augury, prophesizing success. We waited in nervous anticipation, our feet stomping out the minutes as we tried to warm ourselves against the bracing wind. And then he came, riding through the gate on a rouncey the colour of leaves in the autumn. He dismounted when he saw us, walking his horse the rest of the way as a mark of respect. Dropping the reins, he bowed low, close to the ground as he could go. "Your Majesty does me a great honour. I am unworthy of such a greeting."

Flushing with pleasure, the king lurched forward, enveloping the man in a warm embrace. "Welcome to court, Master Aske. We are thrilled to have you join our family as we celebrate the birth of our saviour. My wife and daughter have especially been looking forward to your visit." Breaking away from the man, he beckoned me closer. "This is Jane, our beloved queen."

Aske bowed again, placing a dry kiss on my proffered hand. "'Tis the honour of my life, Your Royal Highness."

"Thank you for coming, Master Aske. The honour is all ours."

This show continued as both the Lady Mary and the Lady Elizabeth stepped forward to receive his greeting. Mary appeared particularly entranced by Aske, her upturned face beaming rapturously. I could not recall ever seeing her look at a man in that way—alight and flustered by the first stirrings of desire. Had she never felt such emotion before? Cloistered away as she was at Hunsdon, I imagined not.

With the formalities completed, we returned to the palace, where preparations for the evening's festivities were well underway. We processed through the corridors, the bustling activity around us grinding to a halt. All eyes followed the king and his visitor. Waving the attention off, His Grace led us to the royal lodgings, where we could continue our discussions in peace. At the privy chamber entrance, the king gathered his favourites, leaving the rest of the retinue to stare forlornly as the great wooden doors slammed shut behind us.

Inside, Master Aske claimed a seat near Sir Francis Bryan, and I found myself comparing the men sitting across from me. They were near in age, and both suffered from blindness in one eye. Where Sir Francis hid his injury—the result of a splintered lance—behind a patch of black leather, Aske wore his like a badge of honour, displayed for everyone to see. Aske's demeanour was gentler, too. He spoke softly and smiled often, a trait I had not expected in a man leading the commons in rebellion. He seemed to have an innate ability to soothe and persuade. Had I not already been partial to his cause, I would have been utterly convinced by his earnest, well-reasoned pleas. Glancing furtively at my husband, I wondered if his heart could also be changed.

"Master Aske, we are more than happy to indulge some of these demands: a general pardon, a full parliament, and the queen's coronation in York. These are simple affairs. The other things you ask us are more complex, but we see no reason to dismiss them outright. A compromise can be reached. However, we must discuss these matters with our advisors, taking the security of the whole of the kingdom into consideration, before making any firm promises."

"But you *shall* take them into consideration?" Aske inquired hopefully.

"Yes, of course, Master Aske. We did not ask you to come all this way just to deny you."

"Your Majesty is a gracious prince, and I am forever grateful to have been invited into your council." He paused uncertainly, his gaze alighting on the faces encircling the table. "It comes to my attention that the Lord Privy Seal is not amongst our number. Nor do I see his henchman, Sir Richard Rich. Would I be correct in assuming these men no longer influence Your Majesty's policies?"

Resting steepled fingers against the tight line of his lips, the king stared at the man. The air thickened with tension. Finally, he said, "We believe you have been given a false impression of Lord Cromwell. He does not—nor has he ever—influenced our policies. Still, he has worked wondrous miracles for our realm and deserves our utmost respect. He will be consulted if we deem it necessary."

Satisfied by these assurances, Master Aske took the king's extended hand. "I leave it to your wise counsel, my king."

"Now, Master Aske, let us proceed in good faith. Things in the north have not gone so far that they cannot be undone. All can be forgiven and put aright if only our people trust in us. Do you pledge your bond and fealty to your gracious lord and sovereign?"

"Yes, Your Majesty," Aske affirmed, getting up from his chair to kneel at the king's feet. "My loyalty belongs only to you."

"Then let us begin to repair this breach." The king beckoned my brother. "Thomas, fetch Master Aske's gift, please."

Tom flew from the room, returning a moment later with a jacket of crimson satin draped over his arm. Taking it from my brother, the king presented it to Aske with an effusive thump on the shoulder.

Awestruck, Aske traced the delicate embroidery. "This is too much, Your Majesty."

"The feast awaits, Master Aske. Put it on and let us join in the merriment. Afterward, we would like you to write a history of the events in the north so we can further discuss the terms of our peace."

Sitting in the great hall, I felt the warmth of contentment spread through me. After a season of bitterness and strife, the world was stitching itself back together. The Lady Mary had been restored at last. Her joyful laughter mingling with the minstrel's carols made beautiful music in my ears. And the king, so calm and assured. He was listening to Aske—*really listening.* Perhaps the man truly had convinced him that the religious houses should be restored. As the thought came to me, I noticed Margery Horsman out of the corner of my eye. Tamping down the flutter of guilt in my belly, I waved her off with a smile. *If Newbo is restored, I will find another way.*

When I turned back, the king and Master Aske were bent close, heads together as they laughed, and talked, and planned. Watching them, I knew all would be well. The king would keep his promises, I felt confident of it. When he came to my bed that night, I would welcome him wholeheartedly.

CHRISTMAS SPED TOWARDS New Year, our days tumbling from one pleasure to the next. The world was made anew in our celebrations. The dreadful months of our recent past were nothing more than a series of nightmares dissolving into the dawn of our joy. When the king wasn't closeted with Robert Aske and the rest of the northern delegates, hammering out the terms of their accord, we made cheer with all manner of feasts and revelry. Presiding over the crowd in the great hall, my husband was gallant and indulgent—the bluff king about whom courtiers from the early days of his reign reminisced.

I spent most of my time with the Lady Mary, passing the quieter hours with sewing or devotions, and our bond grew stronger with every moment lived in each other's company. Occasionally, the Lady Elizabeth joined us. On those days, the pair of them would curl up together in a cushion beneath the window, the elder sister reading from one of their father's books in the dappled winter sunlight. After the rest of the palace had gone to sleep, the king came to my rooms at night. Slowly my dread began to ebb away, and then, one evening, I discovered I was looking forward to his arrival.

The Henry who visited was a version I had never known before—not even while he was courting me. Back then, I had not wanted to engage with him; my refusals were genuine, despite what everyone said. Truthfully, I found his pursuit of me rather insulting. He had been married when it began—if not to Anne Boleyn, then certainly to Queen Catherine. After the latter's death, I continued to resist in fear of his fickle heart. It was Edward who insisted. Edward who assured me I would make a good match after the relationship was over. Then he involved Sir Francis Bryan and Nicholas Carew, and soon the king was set upon making me his wife. There had been no escaping it. Now, in the icy moonlight, enjoying his tender touch, I felt happy to have been so ensnared.

EMERALD

Fertility

JANUARY-MARCH 1537

MARGERY HORSMAN

GREENWICH

"Margery, where is my gown? You said Master Skutt would have it back in time. The wedding is tomorrow. What am I going to do?" Mary Arundell screeched from the bowels of her trunk. It was tipped to its side, bolts of silk and damask spilling across the floor while the top half of its owner writhed around inside.

"If you came out of there, you would see." I waved the gown like a flag of surrender, causing the other maids to giggle. "I had him add an edge of pearl. The earl can surely afford it, don't you think?" I wriggled my brow. More laughter.

Backing out of the trunk, Mary aimed a withering glare in my direction. "You will get me into trouble."

"I sincerely doubt it. The man is besotted with you." Taking the gown from my hands, Joan held it against her sister's figure for inspection. "Besides, he shall be so stunned by how beautiful you are, he will not care what it cost. Right, ladies?" Joan paused, waiting for our nods of agreement. "Now, try it on."

The Earl of Sussex could hardly contain his excitement watching Mary glide down the aisle, resplendent in her brocade and silver tinsel gown. With her flawless fair skin and sapphire eyes, the ultramarine hue gave her the appearance of a winter faerie, glistening in snow and ice. Her lower lip trembled with each step that delivered her closer to the aged man waiting at the altar, but her fate was sealed, and so she pressed on towards her fearful destiny.

"How fortunate you are, Margery," Mistress Ashley cooed in my ear. "Michael Lyster is still young. Handsome, too," she added as an afterthought.

When we returned to the dormitory, the empty spot that had contained Mary Arundell's belongings was filled once again. Standing nearby was our former compatriot's replacement—a woman I met recently when the queen sent me to Lady Anne Beauchamp's house with a girdle for her impending birth.

"Well met, Mistress Jerningham. It is good to see you again," I greeted her, smiling. "How fares Lady Beauchamp?"

The young lady fussed with the partlet covering her neckline. She clutched at the collar, attempting to hide any hint of skin that might be showing. "Mistress Horsey, right?"

One of the other maids threw a hand over her mouth, narrowly suppressing a peal of laughter.

"Hors*man*," Jane Ashley corrected, smirking.

"Soon I shall be Margery Lyster, and so it is no matter," I jumped in quickly, heading off further mockery. "You must be exhausted from your journey. Can I get you anything?"

She shook her head. "My apologies if I have offended anyone. I am afraid the last month has been a bit difficult. Lady Beauchamp is exceedingly uncomfortable and not in the best of moods. In truth, I think she did not want me to go."

"Then why are you here?" Mistress Ashley retorted. She had never been the most welcoming of our group, and change made her even less so.

"Lady Beauchamp said it was the only way I could make an acceptable marriage. It was a reward for my good service." The girl looked close to tears.

"Feel free to ignore Mistress Ashley. I always do." I jabbed Jane with my elbow before she could issue any other rude remarks. "Mother Stonor will confirm sleeping arrangements. In the meantime, I would like to offer you my bed, until you get more comfortable around us. It will be easier that way."

Joan Arundell gave me a look filled with gratitude. The first nights without her sister were bound to be the hardest. At least there would not be a stranger lying next to her.

"Thank you, Mistress Horsman. You can call me Eleanor if you wish." The girl offered a tremulous smile.

"We are slightly more formal than you are used to." I tilted my head towards the door. "Out there, we will call you Mistress Jerningham. In here, we can call you whatever you like."

"Then let it be Eleanor, for that is what my friends call me."

TO MARY ARUNDELL'S relief, the Earl of Sussex was sent to the fringes of Wales to maintain the king's order within days of their wedding. Wasting no time at all in establishing herself as head of the household in his absence, she took great pleasure in her newfound status. When they weren't serving the queen, the sisters kept company in the sumptuous rooms Mary shared with the earl. Occasionally, they invited the rest of us to supper, when the king and queen dined privately—something they were choosing to do more often in recent days.

Relations in the royal marriage had grown considerably warmer since the yuletide festivities. Queen Jane certainly seemed more at peace. There was colour in her cheeks again, a giddiness to her demeanour. The king, for his part, was in an expansive mood—gregarious and jovial. His limp was gone too. Were the storms past? Had he finally spilled enough blood to slake his thirst? I would never forget the terrible things he wrought, but the queen's evident happiness brought me comfort. I prayed it would continue, for her sake and ours.

While Sussex maintained the peace in Wales, Norfolk held the north tight in his grip. By all accounts, Robert Aske's visitation had been a rousing success. Still, the feeling at court was one of uncertain optimism. Aske managed to persuade the king; could he also convince the commons? When John Husee mentioned rumours that a man named Bigod was causing unrest, I began to have my doubts. Noting my discomfort, he moved on to a topic of which he never tired.

"Did the queen like her New Year gift? Lady Lisle said the beads were made from the purest gold she could find in Calais." Husee's breath clouded in the cold air. Approaching the ice-slicked cobblestones, he offered his arm.

"She liked the chain well enough, but I am afraid it will take more than that to get her daughters here." I reluctantly held on to him while we crossed the path. It unsettled me, being that near to him. Especially now.

"Lady Rutland says she will speak to the queen. In truth, I am not sure what good it will do if there are no openings. What day did you say you were getting married?"

I bit my lip to keep from snapping at him. How many times had I told him already? Were our conversations so unmemorable? "The wedding is on Saturday, but I will be keeping my position until after lent, at the very least."

"That soon? Have they read the banns already?"

"I told Michael to get a dispensation. I have not set foot in my home parish since I was a girl. Besides, I doubt anyone there would even care now that my father is gone. Why do you ask? Were you planning to object?"

"Curiosity is all." His ears went red. From embarrassment or the cold, I could not be certain. "And then Mistress Ashley is next?"

"Yes, she and Peter Meutas will be married after Easter." It was all Mistress Ashley could talk about lately. Peter this and Peter that. Though I supposed I wasn't much better. How many times had she been forced to discuss Michael? Countless. Despite our small cruelties to each other, I knew I would miss her when she left the dormitory to work in the privy chamber.

When we arrived at the queen's wardrobe, Husee bowed to take his leave. "Congratulations on your marriage, Mistress Margery. I wish you all the happiness in the world."

"You are just saying that so I will continue to help you," I teased, kicking a bit of snow at him. I reached for the door.

Grabbing my hand, he pulled me close. His lips brushed my cheek. "I mean it, Margery. Don't ever imagine otherwise."

It took every measure of strength I had not to run my fingers along the searing imprint left by his fading kiss.

ON THE DAY of my wedding, I awoke with a sour stomach, wondering if I had made the wrong decision. Michael said there was hope. I wasn't so sure. What if he grew to hate me for not being Bess? Perhaps I would never live up to his first wife. My belly churned as these terrible thoughts shook me, again and again.

It was Mother Stonor who finally convinced me to get dressed. "Margery, you have always believed that everyone else is better than you, and you have always been wrong. If you could see yourself through my eyes, you would know I speak the truth. Have faith in Master Lyster. Has he ever given you reason to doubt him?"

"No," I mewled, pulling my gown up over my hips.

"Then stop torturing yourself. It is your wedding day." She helped pin a brooch to my neckline, then pinched my cheeks for colour. "Much better. Go on, now. They are waiting."

With the roads out of London still buried beneath a sheet of ice, the queen insisted we hold the ceremony in her private closet at Greenwich. Michael and I wanted minimal fuss, so there were few witnesses and no celebratory feasts. Besides Queen Jane and her chaplain, only Michael's father attended. Though I recognized Sir Richard from his visits to court over the years, this was my first opportunity to properly meet him. Much as the pair of them looked alike, I was struck by the differences in how they carried themselves. Where Michael was open and friendly to every person he encountered, Sir Richard maintained his distance. He was reserved and quiet, though not unpleasant. After the ceremony ended, he called me daughter and wrapped me in a warm embrace.

My heart grew heavy thinking of my own father. I cupped the brooch at my breast, drawing strength from the enamelled gold flower once worn by my mother. How I wished they could have been here with me.

"Father insists upon enjoying a meal together before he departs for his estates." Michael leaned in to kiss me. "Happily, the queen has agreed to give you a respite from your duties, so we shall have the evening and tomorrow together." I thanked Queen Jane effusively when she came over to bid us farewell. I feared it was not enough. She had been exceedingly charitable to me these late months.

"Think nothing of it," she said kindly, admiring the circlet of gold on my finger. "I have done nothing more than my duty as your queen."

SIR RICHARD'S APARTMENTS were simply furnished, yet cosy and inviting. His table had already been set by the time we arrived, the savoury scent of roasted chicken wafting out to greet us. A stack of logs in the enormous hearth crackled merrily, chasing away the draught seeping through the windows. While we ate, Michael shared stories of his childhood, and then Sir Richard asked about my family.

"My father served Lady Salisbury years ago. He caught the sweat and died before I came to court. The countess took pity upon me and, being then in high favour with the Dowager Princess, secured my position." It pained me to use Queen Catherine's degraded title, but I deemed it safest. "She spoke for me when I had no one. My mother did not live past my eighth year."

Sir Richard gave me a sympathetic smile. "Michael lost his mother too. Fortunately, he was grown by the time she died. We had many wonderful years with her."

Taking a ring from his finger, Michael dropped it into my palm. The face of the silver circlet held an engraving of a skull. "It is a memento mori," he explained. "A reminder of the inevitability of death. It was once my grandfather's, and then my mother's. She passed it on to me, and I wear it in her memory."

Instead of giving the ring back, I removed my brooch, placing it in Michael's outstretched hand. "It doesn't contain a death's head, but I suppose you could call this my memento mori. It belonged to my mother."

"And so, they are both here with us," Sir Richard added. Setting down his napkin, he roused himself from the chair. "I best go, for I have a long ride ahead of me. Margery, it has been a pleasure spending this time with you. You are everything Michael has promised you would be. I cannot tell you how delighted I am to see him merry once again. It has been far too long."

Michael grinned when I caught him gazing at me. "Thank you, Father. God speed you on your journey."

After Sir Richard had gone, Michael wasted no time leading me to his bedchamber. "Please excuse the cramped quarters. We shall have our own rooms when we go back to London."

"Michael, this is grand compared to my lodgings. Do not forget I sleep with six other maids." I fought back a nervous giggle. "And since none of them are here, you are going to have to help me disrobe."

Unsure fingers pulled at my laces. "I hope I am not doing it wrong. I haven't done this in a while." His breath tickled my neck.

"You never undressed your mistresses?" My tone was light; inside, I was quaking.

"I have not been with a woman since Bess." He gave one last tug, and the bodice began to slip past my shoulders. I felt the heat of his lips on my bare skin.

My breath caught in my throat. "Oh."

"Forgive me if I am out of practice." Guiding me on to the bed, he caressed my cheek.

The pleasure that came from his tenderness seemed to engulf me. I grasped him tightly, pulling him closer and closer, our bodies colliding breathlessly. He moulded and shaped me to him, creating one being out of two until I was unsure where he ended, and I began. His kiss covered my gasp of pain. The discomfort became a dull ache and then an indescribable bliss. I surrendered to it.

Afterward, we laid together in the candlelight, wrapped in each other's arms. I felt at peace, content for the first time in my life. All the tragedies I had survived, all the people I had lost. Every moment of misery seemed to melt away under the power of his ministrations. Michael may have thought himself incapable of loving again, but his actions were proving otherwise. In time, all would be as it should—I just needed to have patience. And faith.

JANE SEYMOUR

GREENWICH AND

CHESTER PALACE ON THE STRAND

"Your Majesty? Pardon me for interrupting." Lady Mary's companion, Susan Clarencius, edged around the yeoman, her round honey-brown eyes peering at me from the doorway.

Waving off Mistress Arundell and her ewer of wine, I set down my knife and pushed away from the table. "Please come in, my lady Clarencius. Is there something I can do for you?"

Lady Clarencius stepped gingerly over the threshold, then bobbed a brisk curtsy. "The Lady Mary sent me to say she feels unable to join Your Majesty for vespers. She offers her deepest regrets and begs forgiveness."

Lady Mary always suffered at the onset of her courses; this month had been particularly brutal. "Have the tisanes helped at all? We could call the apothecary back."

"None of the medicines seem to work. She weeps in agony, swearing there are thorns in her womb." Lady Clarencius' face contorted, and a stream of tears burst forth. "Will you pray for her?"

"Yes, of course. I shall visit her this evening after the service."

"Thank you, Your Majesty," she sniffed. "I will inform my mistress."

"That will not be necessary, my lady." If Mary had warning, she would insist upon receiving me formally, regardless of how poorly she felt.

"Won't the Lady Mary be upset?"

"If she is, I shall shoulder the blame. Order a poultice from the kitchens and make sure she rests."

Lady Clarencius curtsied again, then dashed off to find a chamberer.

The king was restless during the service. More than once, I caught him plucking at the buttons on his shirt, staring irritably at the chaplain. The choir launched into another hymn, and he shifted his bulk, sighing heavily. His chair groaned beneath the strain. I ignored the sound but sensed him glowering beside me. At the altar, the chaplain felt it too and promptly concluded the sermon when the choristers ceased their song.

"What is the matter, Henry? You have been unsettled all evening." In truth, he had been out of sorts ever since Robert Aske went back north. Within days of the man's departure, every privy councillor who was not already at Greenwich had been summoned. Exiled during the festivities, Cromwell was back and ever-present. Eating with the king, worshipping with the king—given half the chance, he might have even accompanied the king to my bed. I cringed at the thought.

Henry cupped my chin, his thumb stroking the ledge of my bottom lip. "Dearest Jane, always fretting over me."

"Suffolk and the others are waiting, Your Grace," Cromwell interrupted, picking up the stack of letters he had set aside during the service. He looked pallid beneath his black cap, eyes red-rimmed and heavy with exhaustion. Cromwell had never been a small man, but his girth was rapidly approaching that of his master's. Too much administration and not enough sport. My husband's chief minister had been busy.

Rising from his seat, the king smiled apologetically. "These meetings do go on, don't they? You should go for a walk in the gallery while you wait. I have had your picture mounted on the wall."

Staring down at my hands, I avoided his gaze. How delighted Henry had been when Holbein arrived with the portrait, sending the artist on a tour of the palace to show it off. I was less than thrilled. Confronted with the evidence of my rash defiance, I felt ashamed. Why did I choose those clothes? Why did I wear that brooch? It had been petty and childish. With the happiness of the last month at the forefront of my mind, I struggled to remember why I had been angry. Summoning my courage, I looked up to reply and found that my husband had already gone.

BENEATH A MOUND of heavy quilts, the Lady Mary writhed in pain. Her pitiful groans, low and desperate, filled the air. A cluster of maids hovered nearby, gawking uselessly. Susan Clarencius was the first to look up and spot me in the doorway. Rushing to pay reverence, she nearly dropped the bowl she carried in her hand. The rest followed suit, and there was a great rustle of taffeta and damask as the girls sank to the ground. Lured by the commotion, Lady Mary lifted the covers and peered out. Seeing me, she began to wail.

I perched on the edge of the bed. Brushing the lanky strands of russet hair from her face, I wiped away hot tears. Her skin was flush and dampened with sweat, yet she did not feel feverish. I called for a cool rag. She whimpered when I held it to her brow, the tip of her tongue darting out to moisten the cracked surface of her lips. "When did you last drink, Lady Mary?"

"Not since yesterday morning, Your Majesty. She refuses to eat, as well." Lady Clarencius handed me the broth. "Maybe you could try?"

Lady Mary regarded the bowl suspiciously. "It made me retch last time."

I took a spoonful into my mouth. The broth had grown cold, but it was still flavourful—rich and savoury. "It is good, see? You try."

Lady Mary propped herself against the headboard, opening her mouth like a robin chick in the nest. She grimaced with the first swallow, but soon she was gulping it down. Lady Clarencius took the empty bowl when she finished, handing over a mug of small ale in return.

"Drink up," I instructed, certain from experience it would blunt the sharpest pangs.

She took a long pull from the mug and started to cry again. "I am embarrassed for Your Grace to see me in this condition."

"Lady Mary, a mother cares not for propriety when her child is hurting. Your suffering causes me great distress." I remembered my own lady mother wearing the badges of maternal love—blood, vomit, and all other manner of secretions—upon her clothing during our childhood. There were nurse-maids, of course. Another woman fed us from her breasts so that more siblings could be conceived. Still, Mother was ever involved in our rearing. I missed her constant presence, her warmth and compassion always sustaining me. Now, she seemed an entire world away.

Lady Mary's face crumpled, anguish suffusing every feature. She threw herself into my arms. The tears came hard and fast, her slight frame convulsing with the force of her despair. When she finally went limp, all her emotion spent, I laid her back on the bed, covering her with the quilt. "Can I call you Lady Mother?" she asked dreamily, drifting off to sleep.

She grew more robust with the passing days, and once her courses were over, she broke free the confines of her sickbed. We were walking together in the privy garden, admiring the newly bloomed snowdrops, when a messenger from my brother arrived with tidings of great joy: Lady Anne had been delivered of a baby girl. In hopes that I would accept the honour of acting as godmother, the child was to be named Jane.

THE MORNING OF the christening, I awoke at dawn with a violent desire to vomit. Like a wave, it crashed over me, soaking my body in sweat. Too slow with the piss pot, Mistress Norris stood by in horror as I drenched my nightgown and the bed, staining the sheets with last night's supper. Amid this scene, Margery Horsman appeared with the day's attire. Acting quickly, she threw my clothing over one of the chairs and gestured for the washbasin from the sideboard.

"Arms up, Your Grace." Carefully containing the mess, she pulled the nightgown over my head. When she stepped back, fabric bundled in her hands, nausea hit again. This time, Mistress Norris was ready.

Somehow, I managed to get out of bed. Trembling, I stood naked in the weak sunlight, my maids washing away the bile with water from the basin. Fretting over my distress, Margery ordered a bath. As I sank into the steaming water, the onslaught began anew, my revulsion rising with the heat.

"What do we do?" Mistress Norris moaned. "Should we call the physician?"

"Quiet. I am thinking." Margery tallied the days with her fingers. "When did I last bring linen for the queen's blood?"

Mistress Norris shook her head. "I don't remember. I must not have been in the chamber that day."

"Epiphany," I replied faintly, hanging over the side of the bayne. "It was Epiphany."

Margery locked eyes with me, a wide grin spreading across her face. "Nearly three weeks late, Your Grace."

Rolling to my back, I stared down at the swathe of flesh beneath the waterline—supple and colourless, vulnerable to every threat imaginable. "Keep this to yourselves. We must be certain."

The maids acquiesced with silent nods, but there was a growing uneasiness regarding my journey to Chester Place. Mistress Norris argued it would be best to go by boat, while Mistress Jerningham insisted horseback was safer. Margery wished I could call off my visit altogether but recognized the impracticality of it. My absence would only invite scrutiny, and I did not intend to miss my niece's christening. In the end, I chose the relative comfort and seclusion of the royal barge; bearing in mind travel down the Thames would be slow going with lingering ice floes still drifting on the tides.

Trussed up in fur-lined velvet, I met Thomas Cromwell and the Lady Mary on the water stair. Both had been named godparents and would accompany me to the service. Edward's choice in the Lady Mary was not at all surprising. Now that she was back in the king's graces, he was free to act on his fondness for her. His picking Cromwell was a bit more bewildering. Why not one of our brothers? Tom would not mind being overlooked, but what of Harry? If anything could tempt him out of the countryside, this would be it. In bestowing the honour upon the Lord Privy Seal, Edward signalled his preference for ambition over family. I was disgusted by it.

"Feeling well today, Majesty?" Cromwell interrupted my thoughts. "I saw the chamberers hauling water to your rooms."

I lowered my ermine muff to hide my stomach. "My bedchamber was quite chilly this morning. I thought it would be nice to have a hot soak." *What I do in my rooms is none of your concern, Lord Cromwell.*

"How snug." His gaze raked my body appraisingly. Stepping aside, he motioned us on to the barge. Under his intent observation, we settled into our seats. "If you need me, I shall be in the front with the captain."

I forced a smile, then turned my attention to the Lady Mary. "You look beautiful. Those emeralds suit your complexion."

Her face lit up. "I have Your Grace to thank. Without your intercession, I would have been utterly lost."

My meddling had almost killed her. It was she who saved herself from death. "Think not on these sad memories, Lady Mary. Today, we celebrate life."

TOM STOOD ON the dock at Chester Place—tall and lithe—his sandy hair whipping in the breeze. Eschewing all decorum, he squeezed me tightly, the scents of Wulfhall filling my lungs: wood smoke, leather, and sweet lavender. The odours made my stomach churn but reminded me of home. "You look sort of green," he remarked when we parted. "Are you ill? Queen or not, Lady Anne would send you down the river if you brought the plague to her home."

I poked his chest. "And they say you are the agreeable Seymour."

"Who in God's name says that?" He wrinkled his nose.

"Certainly not me," Cromwell cut in, eager to complete his duty and get back to court. "I prefer Lord Beauchamp. He doesn't feel the need to fill the silence with inane conversation."

Spurred by the insult, Tom kept up the chatter. Leading us through the palatial home, he pointed out all of Edward's building improvements. Leased from the Bishop of Chester, the property was my brother's most recent acquisition, and his family had only just taken up residence.

Despite having been dragged out of confinement days before her delivery, Lady Anne appeared jolly and well-contented when the Lady Mary and I visited her sumptuously appointed chamber. I was relieved to find her in such high spirits.

Mother dropped the pillow in her hands when she saw me. Her breath caught in her throat, emotion welling in her eyes. "My lovely Jane, a queen," she breathed. We flew to each other, our hearts pressed together as one. I spied my sister, Dorothy, over her shoulder. She hung back, timid and unsure, taking us in from afar.

"How are you, Dorothy? I cannot believe how much you have grown."

She crept forward. "My husband is kind and keeps me well. There is nothing more I could wish for."

"I am pleased to hear it. There is always a place in my household if you should ever feel inclined."

"Your Grace is most generous, but I am content at home." Dorothy's palm flattened against her waist. "Besides, Clement is keen to start our family. I doubt he would give permission."

"I am sure your sister understands, Dorothy. Even the grandest woman in the land must bend to her husband's will." Mother linked our hands, cocooning them within her own. "Now, let us not forget the reason we are all together—another Seymour girl craves our attention. How about we see to her and give Lady Anne a brief reprieve?"

Re-joining the men in the great hall, we processed to the chapel together. Though it was Edward's home, the Lady Mary and I took precedence, leading the way through the maze of corridors to the chapel stairs. Above the entrance, a porch had been erected with jewel-toned glass windows glittering on either side. Here the midwife met us, a tiny babe slumbering in the cradle of her arms. As godparents, it was our duty to speak for the child, and we did so when the priest asked if she would forsake the devil and all his works. Satisfied with our answer, he let us into the chapel to complete the ceremony.

I couldn't help but smile when I saw the font beneath the richly decorated canopy. Edward requested the one from our private chapel at Greenwich, and the king was only too happy to oblige—after some persistent supplication on my part. That evening was one of the sweetest I had spent with my husband. Had we conceived then? The infant wailed when the priest splashed holy water on her head, and I felt a surge of anticipation. Soon it would be my turn; pray God I carried a boy.

During the ensuing feast my brothers slunk off with Cromwell to discuss court business. With everyone else's attention fixated on the baby, I slipped out, hoping to catch Lady Anne alone in her chamber.

Rounding the corner, I heard Edward's voice. "...and what of Aske? Has he been arrested?"

Intrigued, I dipped into an empty closet just off the hall, out of sight.

"His Grace is not calling it an arrest," Cromwell replied, "Norfolk has merely taken him into custody. We cannot risk setting him free. Lord Darcy is also under suspicion. We intercepted one of his letters and have reason to believe he is re-fortifying Pontefract against us."

No, not Robert Aske. He pledged his fealty and swore to keep the king's peace. A man like Aske would never break his promise.

"Are Norfolk's forces to stay at Carlisle?" This time it was Tom.

"At least until he has finished carrying out the king's punishment." Cromwell laughed bitterly. "So far, seventy-four men have been hanged from the walls of the city, their bodies left to rot on all corners."

Tom gave a low whistle. "Seems excessive, doesn't it? The skirmish was doomed from the beginning since Bigod didn't have the support. Does the king also discipline men who did not take part?"

"Not just men. Norfolk's been ordered to administer justice without prejudice or pity."

What did he mean? Women and children too? Choking back a yelp, I gripped my belly.

Edward exhaled deeply. "What has the king decided about Reginald Pole? Is it true he is on his way to France?"

"We will know more once Thomas Wyatt has been installed at Francis' court. Wallop and Gardiner have been recalled for the time being. If it were up to His Grace, our dear cardinal would have never made it out of Italy. Perhaps he shall come to an untimely end on his journey."

Reginal Pole was a man of God and the king's cousin. How could they say such things? I could not listen to any more of this cruelty. My nausea returning, I fled in search of a stool closet.

MARGERY HORSMAN

GREENWICH

Michael brushed a crumb of food from his whiskers. Nudging his trencher aside, he bent to the ledger spread open on the table and jotted another mark in the margin. The book was too distant for me to read in its entirety, but I could make out a few of the headings. There were columns for Chabnor, Ivy Church, Alderbury, and Newbo. Training his eyes upon his work, he dunked the nib of his quill into the inkpot. The little bottle tilted, precariously wobbling until it fell back to its bottom with nary a droplet spilled.

"Almost finished? The chamberer is here to clear our plates." Removing the napkin from his shoulder, I leaned in close to nuzzle the delicate flesh below his ear. He patted my cheek absentmindedly, then scribbled some more numbers in the ledger. Near enough to read, I stole another glance. Below the property names, he had listed crops and animals. It was a census of his holdings. *Our holdings.*

Dismissing the servants, I retired to the bedchamber. The rumpled wool blankets were still piled at the end of the bed, evidence of our afternoon lovemaking. With Queen Jane gone from the court, attending her niece's christening on the Strand, we found time for a few precious hours together, and they had been well spent. Lulled by the balm of our intimacy, I toyed with the notion of telling Michael what I witnessed in the queen's rooms, but reason quickly overcame emotion. If I learned anything over the last year, it was that the covenant between husband and wife did not extend far when it came to matters of state. What would Michael do in the name of duty? I shared his board and his bed, yet in some ways he remained a stranger to me. In time I would unravel his mysteries; for now, it was wiser to exercise caution.

I was in the middle of loosening my gown when one of the candles sputtered out. Startled, I yanked the tie too forcefully, tightening the knot. Stumbling in the faint light of the second taper, I wrenched at it, succeeded only in making it worse.

"What is going on in there, Margery?" Michael yelled from the other room.

"Can you help me?" I called back. "I'm rather...stuck."

I heard a chair crash to the floor and then the patter of footsteps.

"Are you hurt? Why is it so dark in here?" Michael panted, having sprinted to my rescue.

"The candle went out," I flustered breathlessly. "I seem to have entrapped myself." I turned so he could see the lacings.

"God's blood, you frightened me. Hold on, let me grab some more candles." Stepping out, he returned with a pewter candlestick in each hand. This time, he was laughing.

"Well, I am glad one of us is amused," I huffed. He pulled a face at me, and my indignation melted away. "Just get me out of this gown."

Michael used one of the tapers to reignite the first candle, then set both on the table. Disappearing behind me, he began tugging at the ribbon. I felt it yield, the fabric of my gown loosening its grip around my bust. "We must hire a girl to help you with these things."

"I suppose you are right. I shall make some inquiries in the morning." Reaching for him too late, the fabric of his doublet slithered through my fingertips. "Aren't you coming to bed?"

He smiled at me from the doorway. "I have work to do, Margery. Get some sleep. I will be in soon."

A HANDFUL OF petitioners were already milling about the queen's watching chamber before dawn. One of them—a bedraggled man in torn hose—cried out when he saw me. "Norfolk took my son—my beloved boy. Strung him up like a traitor, though he never did no wrong. You must help me. Please, girl!"

Dodging his grasp, I ran headlong into another man, nearly knocking him to the floor. This one was worse off than the last. Thin as a waif, his skin hung from his bones. "The soldiers—they raided my stores. I have nothing left to feed my family. Tell the queen for me, please. Tell her good majesty—I know she is fair and just," he wept.

I scrambled for the door and the safety of the yeomen. The tallest of the guards on duty lunged forward, admonishing the men. "Keep the peace, or both shall lose your chance to see the queen today. Disturb one of her ladies again and reap the consequences. Understand?"

Backing away, the men offered their apologies. Their desperation frightened me, but I also pitied them. The men of the north had lost everything, and nothing could restore their families. Worse, their pleas would fall upon deaf ears. No one could wring a drop of grace from this merciless king, not even his wife.

In the bedchamber, the acrid stench of vomit burned my nose. The same ladies from yesterday were again in attendance. They hurried through the room, dumping the sick pail in the close stool, and fumbling with the latches on the windows. Their efforts did little to suppress the evidence. I understood the queen's desire to hide her pregnancy. I merely failed to see how it could be accomplished. When the rotation changed, it would be Jane Ashley and Joan Arundell sleeping on the pallet, and both loved to gossip. How soon before the secret was buzzing in every man's ear?

"How was Lady Beauchamp, Your Grace?" I asked cheerily, keeping the mood light. "I trust there was a fine celebration?"

The queen nodded weakly; her peaked skin marred by florid blotches. She ventured a sip of ale, blanching at the taste. "Lady Anne fares well and sends her regards. She will be back after the churching ceremony." Handing the cup to Mistress Jerningham, she stepped out of her nightgown. "Keep the ties loose, I beg of you. I cannot suffer tight lacings today."

Once she was dressed, I raided the jewel coffer, paying no mind to the drawer containing the cursed pearls. I fastened a chained pomander around the queen's waist and then lifted the spice-filled orb to her nose. "The sprigs of mint will help. Your Grace will need it to face the Northmen waiting in the watching chamber."

The queen's chin quivered. She rolled her bottom lip between her teeth. The rosy flesh re-emerged tattered with bite marks and ripped skin. "Tell my chamberlain I will not be giving an audience today."

"Yes, Your Grace. Anything else?"

She shook her head. "If the weather holds, I plan to walk in the privy garden this afternoon."

"I shall fetch Your Grace's cloak."

Back at the wardrobe, Master Lloyd was incandescent with rage. Spittle flying, he tore into Master Husee, the slam of his fist on the counter punctuating every word. "I have already told you. Lady Lisle must wait. The arras and carpet she requires remain at Chester Place with Lady Beauchamp."

Husee smiled calmly, undeterred by Lloyd's frenzy. "My good sir, it was never my intention to cause any upset. Master Kingston mentioned it might be possible to get a cloth of estate for the christening of my lady's child. That is all I am here to inquire. Lady Lisle has no desire to impose upon Lady Beauchamp and offers her sincere appreciation. If the answer is no, then I shall be on my way."

Master Lloyd seemed to shrink when he spied me in the entry. He took a few steps back, distancing himself from Husee. Crossing his arms, he lifted his chin. "I will see what I can arrange. No promises."

Husee grinned triumphantly. "I am forever in your debt, Master Lloyd."

Lloyd grunted in return. Snatching the laundry from my hands, he disappeared into the closet.

I followed Husee out to the courtyard. "He only made that concession because it was in my hearing. When the time comes, you won't be getting that cloth of estate."

He whirled around, face alight with anger and humiliation. "I know that, Margery. Do you take pleasure in reminding me?"

"That is not what I meant. I would never…"

Husee's shoulders slumped. He removed his cap. Pinching the bridge of his nose, he gathered himself. "I am sorry, that was unforgivably rude. My grievance is naught to do with you. I would never speak poorly of Lady Lisle, but the woman seems to think I can work miracles. Do this, Husee. Get me that, Husee. Bloody glorified errand boy that I am."

"Listen, I might be able to help you. Are you still looking to place one of Lady Lisle's daughters?"

He shook his head doubtfully. "I asked Lady Sussex if she would take Katherine. Unfortunately, she already has a girl in place."

"Yes, she hired a maid shortly after her wedding. She cannot take on another, but I can."

Husee met my gaze. "Truly? Are you certain?"

"My husband will have to give his approval, but I see no reason he wouldn't. Have Lady Lisle write to him."

"You will take Katherine before the queen? Make sure she is noticed?"

"As long as she is properly attired in the English style." I widened my eyes in mock horror. "Queen Jane has forbidden anything that might be worn in the French courts."

"And we are all the poorer for it." Husee laughed, relieved. "Thank you, Mistress Margery. You are a true friend."

"After all the bribes you have given me, it is the least I could do." Without thinking, I gave him a playful nudge. Husee paid the motion no heed. Still, I regretted it. The easy camaraderie between us was no longer appropriate, now that I was a married woman. "Go on ahead. I must go back for the queen's cloak. I shall tell Master Lyster to look out for that letter."

JANE SEYMOUR

GREENWICH AND YORK PLACE

The people of the north haunted my dreams. Stalking me in the murky shadows, they crashed through the forests, the rivers, and the fields. They screamed my name, pleading for mercy and compassion. They wept for the dead, shedding swollen tears of blood that threatened to drown me. The foul smell of the rotting flesh that hung from the walls of their towns filled my nostrils. Soon, I began to feel their ghostly presence during my waking hours too. Night poured into day, then day deepened into night, and one nightmare tumbled into another.

I wanted so much to speak with Lady Anne, to ask her for comfort or advice. Should I tell the king I was with-child in the hopes it would move him to clemency? Or should I wait until I was more certain? Would I be too late to save the lives of Robert Aske and the rest? Lying in bed awake, staring up at the sarcenet-covered tester, I considered my options. On the verge of deciding to postpone, I heard my ladies giggle on the pallet below. The sound reminded me that secrets never lasted long in these rooms. I had to act quickly before my husband learned of my condition from someone else. Ready or not, the time had come.

I celebrated lauds in private with my almoner, asking him to offer up prayers of thanksgiving for the life growing inside of me. His words soothed my worried mind and gave me the strength I needed to trust the signs my body gave me. Afterward, I sent a messenger to the king with an invitation to take supper in my privy chamber. I tried to eat a little and snatch a few hours of rest, but my thoughts churned like a ship in a storm. Henry would be thrilled when I told him the news, yet he would never forgive me if I turned out to be wrong. Worse loomed on the horizon if I was right and lost the child before its time. Once the king knew, there was no going back.

He arrived late and in a foul mood—the worst since before Christmas—bringing with him a litany of complaints against the King of Scots, the rebels, Reginald Pole, and the Duke of Norfolk. "He's far too lenient, and all he does is complain," he said about the latter. "If he's not lamenting the weather and his bodily aches, he bemoans my treatment of his daughter. Why should I grant her jointure? My son never consummated the union. Besides, I only agreed to the forsaken marriage for that wretched virago." He recoiled at the mention of her—the wife who came before. "Norfolk is fortunate I don't take his daughter's title away."

There was too much at stake to give in to the tentacles of dread tightening around my throat. I forced the words out before I lost my nerve. "Henry, I am with-child."

He continued ranting; my meek proclamation lost in the torrent of his rage.

"Henry? Are you listening?"

He glowered, eyes narrowing in irritation. "What is it, Jane? Do you have something more pressing to discuss?" The remark dripped with sarcasm.

I thought of Aske and his followers, the fortitude they displayed, protecting the church. The vision gave me courage. "Yes, dear husband, I think you will find what I have to say is far more important. I am pregnant, Henry. Six—maybe seven—weeks gone now."

He glared at me with such fury I began to wonder if I had made a terrible mistake. Slowly, the meaning of my words dawned, and the corners of his lips twitched upwards. "It is true, then? I heard murmurs but dared not believe them."

I granted Mistress Ashley a scowl of contempt. She withered under the heat. It was confirmation of what I already suspected: lover's confidences exchanged with Peter Meutas. Meutas served in the king's privy chamber and would have gone straight to his master. "It is true. I would have told you sooner. I merely wanted to be sure first."

"These are glorious tidings indeed," the king enthused, enfolding me in his arms. I felt small and insignificant under the weight of them. "This is proof of God's blessing. He is pleased we have brought the north to heel and restored glory to His church. His benevolence shines upon us both."

"Then you will release Robert Aske? Surely there is nothing more to fear from him."

Henry rested his hands on my waist, addressing his next words to the slight mound of my womb. "We shall see, Jane. We shall certainly see."

BY THE SECOND week of March, the last of the snow had thawed. The world outside was still damp and dreary, but the gardens were finally beginning to show signs of life. Lifting her skirts so as not to drag them on the sodden ground, the Lady Mary took a few tentative steps off the path. Carefully, she bent down to pluck a winter honeysuckle from a shrub laden with blooms. She returned, holding the milky-coloured blossom aloft in offering. "I wish I didn't have to go back to Hunsdon. It is so far away, and now you're..." She paused, gesturing at my stomach. "What if something goes wrong?"

"Try not to worry, Lady Mary. I am healthy and strong. Besides, if the worse were to happen, God forfend, there is nothing you could do to stop it. Just say you will keep me in your prayers." I inhaled the fragrant scent of the honeysuckle, attempting to reassure myself alongside the king's daughter.

"I will always pray for you, Your Grace."

How she had grown since the day we visited her at Hackney, not only in stature but also in confidence. She seemed more self-assured and willing to speak up. Each day, I grew more impressed with her capacity for forgiveness. She took a particular interest in Lady Rochford, giving her small tokens and gifts of black satin for her gowns. When I asked her why she showed such favour to a woman so closely connected to Anne Boleyn, a woman she regarded as her adversary, she merely shrugged. "Jesus calls us to forgive. Who am I to question His directives?" Her father benefitted from the same philosophy. When they were together, it was as though they had never been parted. Henry, for his part, returned the affection in kind. Still, I sensed an underlying uncertainty, and he refused to seriously consider any offers for her hand, even ones that did not require her to be legitimized.

A few days after our heartening walk in the garden, we departed for London. The Lady Mary stayed with us at York Place long enough to attend the churching of my brother's wife, then headed back to Hunsdon, where the Lady Elizabeth awaited her return. On the day she left, I visited the hospital of St Katherine by the Tower. Having appointed Gilbert Latham to its mastership recently, I was eager to meet him and see how the religious house was faring under the king's oppressive laws.

Master Latham welcomed me warmly. Beaming with pride, he took my ladies and me through the hospital. The rooms were overrun with the poor and downtrodden, those who would be turned loose and ignored if the house were to be suppressed. I asked him if there was enough money to continue his work of caring for the destitute, and he demurred, answering rather sheepishly that the first fruits payments to the crown had strained their finances more than he anticipated. I thanked him for his candour and promised to speak to the king on his behalf.

Taking advantage of Henry's fulsome excitement over my pregnancy, I broached the subject carefully that evening over supper. To my great surprise, he agreed to suspend their payments without reserve for as long as Latham was master. No mean favour, the king's gesture was meaningful and significant. In securing it, I discovered the breadth of my power. Carrying the heir granted a measure of influence thus far denied me, and I had no intention of squandering it.

The elation I felt over my success quickly dissipated when Edward swanned into my rooms, bearing a letter from our sister, Elizabeth. He handed it over with little ceremony. "You look slightly peaked this morning. Has your sickness abated at all?" he asked with the practiced concern of an elder sibling and a father several times over.

"Far from, in truth. It increases daily." I scanned the missive, searching for figures. If Elizabeth was writing our brother, it was because she wanted money. Instead, I found compliments and a mention of marriage. "What is this? Has the king proposed a match?" Elizabeth had been eager to find a second husband since the death of her first. Not because Sir Anthony Ughtred had treated her poorly, but because he left her with a pile of debts. While she would never admit it, I suspected her unpleasantness was due to Edward prioritizing my marriage prospects over hers. We had never been close, but at our last parting, I felt the depth of her loathing, and it saddened me.

"Not the king. This is Cromwell's doing...and mine." He did not attempt to hide his smug satisfaction. Edward always thought himself the cleverest man in the room. "She is to marry his son, Gregory."

"Edward, are you sure that is wise? We have both seen greater men fall from dizzier heights than Cromwell now occupies. One mistake and he will find himself reunited in death with his former master, Wolsey."

"Cromwell is the most powerful man in England, next to the king. Elizabeth knows this. That is why she has already asked for his help in getting some lands."

"Why did she not ask me? Am I not the queen?" My family seemed determined to undermine me at every turn. It had been this way long as I could remember. Edward had always been ahead of me, plotting and planning our lives. Once he was old enough, Tom joined in, though we were much closer in age, and I was far wiser. My senior place among the girls meant nothing, since I was not the prettiest nor most desirable.

I thought back to the day I lost William Dormer's hand. His parents had come to Wulfhall to seal the engagement and sign the jointure. Lady Dormer's thinly veiled contempt was obvious the moment her foot stirred from the carriage. She was searching for a reason to bow out and my brother obliged. "Why would you ever choose Jane?" he asked William's father, feigning ignorance. "Our sister, Elizabeth, is far livelier and the fairer of the two. Jane is so homely your son will prefer one of the servants. Your heirs will all prove bastards!" The Dormers had tittered as if it was all in good fun. When the time came to sign the jointure, they insisted upon forwarding the documents to their lawyer one last time. We never saw them again.

Edward folded his arms across his chest, giving me a look of disdain. "Of course, you are the queen. Do not be ridiculous. She didn't ask you because we all know your feelings about dissolving the monasteries. The land she wants once belonged to the church."

"I would have happily sent her money from my own privy purse."

Seeing my increasing distress, Edward tried to comfort me. "However generous you might have been, a sum once spent can never be replenished. The lands Elizabeth requested will supply her with a stream of income for as long as she owns them."

"I am not a simpleton, Edward. I just don't believe it is honourable to carve up and distribute what does not belong to us. I cannot understand why you do."

He gave an unconcerned shrug. "It is the king's prerogative to do whatever he likes in his realm. If it so happens to benefit our family, all the better."

"Even if it means haranguing men like the Bishop of Chester so that you can have the convenience of living closer to court? You have not changed, Edward. You only see things to your advantage, never to anyone else's."

Stung, Edward spun away. He went to the oriel window and stood in the embrasure, staring wordlessly at the parade of boats floating past. My ladies busied themselves with their sewing, their quiet chatter embroidering the heavy silence that hung in the air. When he turned back around, his eyes avoided mine. "That is enough for today. All this upset is harmful to you and the baby. My dearest wife plans to return to your service after Easter. As this pregnancy progresses, it might be helpful to have her experience and advice." He bowed low, and then he was gone.

Edward observed the usual rites of Holy Week and Easter alongside me, serving as the lone representative of the Seymour family, with Tom otherwise occupied at Dover and Harry keeping to his estates. He played the part of a dutiful brother as I washed feet, gave alms, and crawled on my knees towards the cross, but he kept his distance. He spoke to me only when necessary, his voice clipped and cold. Yet, for all his anger, he never wavered in his love or concern over my well-being. It was he who made sure I learned of Robert Aske's arrest in the most delicate way possible, and he who held me as I wept with fear and grief.

MARGERY HORSMAN

YORK PLACE

Michael hung his cloak on the nail by the door. He greeted me with a gentle kiss, his lips tasting of the sprig of mint he chewed on the road back to London. Kicking off his boots, he strode over to the hearth, where he warmed his hands before the blazing fire. "I am glad that is over. Can't say I have ever enjoyed taking part in those ghastly interrogations."

I handed him a mug of ale and draped a quilt over his stooped shoulders, giving them a brisk rub to loosen the tension. "Is that why you went to Stepney? Which wretched soul does the Lord Privy Seal have in his clutches this time?" I heard rumours about what happened to accused men in Cromwell's house at Stepney—terrible things people only dared whisper.

"A ruffian who broke into the king's chapel and stole some gold plate." He threw back his ale. Wiping his mouth, he laughed. "The fools hid their spoil in the woods at Tyburn. The keeper who found it was ecstatic until he saw the king's mark. Poor sod had to turn it all in."

"You didn't harm him, did you?" The thought of my husband taking part in a man's torture was unsettling and most unwelcome. I could not countenance hands that had caused harm touching me in the intimate way that Michael did. That sort of horror blighted a man's soul. It was akin to sleeping with an enemy.

Michael shook his head and pulled the quilt tighter around him. "I leave that sort of justice to Cromwell. I have no knowledge of what he does after I leave, nor do I care to." He took a deep breath. "Let us move on to more pleasant affairs, shall we? Have you secured the queen's permission to visit Chabnor? We should go soon before the commoners are up again. With Robert Aske and Lord Hussey remanded to the Tower, there is no telling what sort of grief they might cause."

The plan to leave for Michael's estate in Herefordshire had been in the making for nearly a fortnight, and I had yet to broach the subject with Queen Jane. She made merry when the eyes of the court were watching, but behind closed doors, she was still terribly ill. I was concerned for her and worried about the baby. I would not go until support arrived in the form of the formidable Anne Seymour. "Lady Beauchamp is due back tomorrow, so I shall ask first thing."

Tossing the quilt aside, Michael went to the table and began dishing up a helping of lamprey pie. He took a bite, watching me as he chewed. "I admire your loyalty to the queen, Margery, but you are a wife now and mother to little Richard. We have been married for four months, and the child hasn't even met you. You cannot put it off forever."

"What if he does not like me? I'm not sure how to be a proper mother."

Setting down his spoon, Michael grabbed my hand. "You won't know until you try. Now, promise you will ask in the morning."

The vow weighed heavily upon my mind. I tossed and turned throughout the night, wearily rising when daylight poured through the windows. Hurriedly, I dressed, ambling out of the room before my husband awoke. He was snoring when I shut the door. Our apartments at York Place were close to the queen's, so the walk was short, brief enough to contain my nerves. When the yeoman granted me access to the royal bedchamber, I was surprised to find Lady Anne Beauchamp already in attendance. She was holding back the queen's hair as she vomited.

"You must be careful," she warned in hushed tones. "You cannot lose this baby. Our lives depend upon it."

The queen retched violently, her body convulsing with the force of it.

Lady Beauchamp glanced up at me. "We have no need of you today, Mistress Lyster. You may go."

"Yes, my lady." I lingered in the doorway, hesitant to leave without fulfilling my promise to Michael.

"Is there something else you needed?" she barked, visibly irritated by my continued presence.

"Master Lyster would like to tarry at Chabnor for a time. May I be excused to accompany him?"

Queen Jane sat up to answer. Lady Beauchamp cut her off. "Yes, I think that would be good. Mother Stonor will take care of finding a suitable replacement until your return. Give our best to Master Lyster."

"Thank you, my lady." I curtsied. "Shall I send the other maids in?"

The queen's voice was gravelled and raw. "Not yet, Margery. I would have this time alone with my sister."

I knelt again, then hurried from the room. Michael was awake and breaking his fast by the time I returned. He was thrilled with the news. For the rest of the meal, he could talk of nothing but the delights awaiting us in Herefordshire: wooded parks teeming with game, a snug timbered manor house, and a green-eyed boy with golden hair who longed for a mother to call his own.

JANE SEYMOUR

YORK PLACE

rounded on Lady Anne the moment Margery Lyster departed. "You had no right to do that. I decide who has permission to leave my household, not you. Why is everyone so intent upon usurping my authority?" My mouth tasted of sour bile and more threatened at the back of my throat. I was parched and hungry, the pangs in my stomach serving only to make the nausea worse. I reached for the bowl again.

Lady Anne caught my hair in her fingers, just in time to avoid the splatter of sick. In one swift move, she knotted it at my neck, pinning it into place. "Calm yourself, Jane. The last woman in your position miscarried when she gave in to hysterics."

"Her name was Anne Boleyn, and don't you ever compare me to her," I roared. My face felt hot and damp. The room was spinning.

Lady Anne eased me on to the bed. She tried to pull the heavy counterpane over me. I kicked it away. She opened the window instead. The cool air felt pleasurable against my skin. "That is not what I meant," she said, sitting down next to me. "You are nothing like her."

"Why can you not say her name?" Tears streamed down my face, soaking the pillow beneath my head.

"Because I am afraid, even after all these months. What was done to her can be done to you. To us. If you lose the child…if it is born a girl…" She covered her mouth to stop the rest from spilling out: Anne Boleyn lay stiff and cold in an arrow chest, buried beneath the Chapel of St Peter, and still she exerted control over our lives.

Seized with a sudden sense of foreboding, I got up and found my footing. Stumbling to the jewel chest, I yanked the lid open. It lay there innocently enough, the source of our misfortune—a coil of pearls casting a soft glow on scarlet silk—yet it radiated a terrible beauty. I should have destroyed it long ago.

Lady Anne gasped when I held it aloft. "The king told Edward you had it broken apart."

"That is what he assumes. I have never corrected him." I threw the necklace down and snatched a silver candlestick from the table. Hefting it over my shoulder, I prepared to swing.

She stopped me before the blow landed. "Jane, this is not like you."

"What if Anne Boleyn cursed it? What if those pearls are causing our troubles? The rebellion? The death of Henry Fitzroy? The king insists she tried to poison him."

Taking the candlestick from my hand, Lady Anne led me to the bench at the foot of the bed. She retrieved a rag from the washbasin and wiped the sweat from my brow. She tilted my chin, and we locked eyes. "You don't truly believe that do you?"

I shook my head.

She stepped back, sighing. "If that woman had been capable of working such magic, she would still be here. I do not think the necklace is accursed, though I do wonder why you kept it."

Because the king was cruel, and I wanted to spite him. "It is not mine to destroy. It belongs to the Lady Elizabeth."

"You cannot keep it here." Lady Anne thought for a moment. "Can you trust one of your ladies to take custody and deliver it when she is older? Perhaps Lady Rochford?"

"No. The king already despises Lady Rochford. If he was to discover the necklace in her possession…" I shuddered.

A tenuous silence fell. We sat together, neither of us speaking a word. From its cage in the corner of the room, my linnet chirped softly and then began to sing. The mournful melody reminded me of home. Lady Anne's eyes found mine. "Who do you trust, Jane?"

I shook my head again. There was no one.

"What of Michael Lyster? He has been loyal to your family all this time. And Margery? Is she not keeper of the jewels? She could take it to Chabnor, and none would be the wiser. You know they would do anything you asked of them. They owe their happiness to you."

"Are they happy? Truly?" I asked. "Because I am starting to believe that marriage is nothing more than unceasing torment."

Lady Anne threaded her fingers through mine. She clenched them tightly, the sweat on my palms mingling with the sweat from hers. "Not all unions, Jane. And once you have a son, yours will get better too." She exhaled. "In the meantime, the necklace will be safer with the Lysters."

I nodded faintly. "But is it the right thing to do? Perhaps we would all be better off pretending Anne Boleyn never existed."

Lady Anne tucked a loose tendril of hair behind my ear, a gesture that brought both comfort and reassurance. "Search your conscience. You must do what is in your heart."

My heart had spoken of nothing but sorrow and enmity for so long. It was little wonder I struggled to know my own mind. I yearned for forgiveness—from those brought low in the name of my advancement and from the families they left behind. More than that, I wanted absolution. I may not have ordered the executions of Anne and George Boleyn, kind Sir Henry Norris, Brereton, Weston, and clever Marc Smeaton, but their deaths stained my hands. How could I find rest when I clung so tightly to memories of the departed?

"Summon the Lysters after evensong. I want the necklace gone before the week is out."

AMBER

Protection

APRIL–JUNE 1537

MARGERY HORSMAN

CHABNOR

The mare whickered as she picked her way through the mud, flicking her tail in annoyance at a cloud of flies. Overhead, a canopy of trees blocked out the sky, making it difficult to decipher just where the forest ended. Undaunted, Michael pushed ahead, leading our retinue over a road lost beneath a carpet of blackened leaves, soggy and rotted after a season of rain. He had traversed this path for almost a decade and would know the way in his sleep. We would have been mired and disoriented without him, stranded in the woods.

Exhausted from the previous day's ride, we moved at a languid pace. Last night's accommodations had been limited; the inns filled with travellers returning to London after an Easter spent at home. When we finally secured a bed, I found sleep impossible. Michael had taken precautions, locking up our valuables in an iron chest. I continued to fret, despite his many assurances. He had been uncharacteristically mum, since the queen charged us with safeguarding the only possession the Lady Elizabeth was likely to inherit from her mother. His refusal to discuss it further suited me well, for I was not prepared to divulge my previous connection to the necklace. The weeks it spent hidden away in my trunk seemed a lifetime ago, and I had no desire to revisit them.

At the edge of the park, Michael glanced back to check on me. He confirmed my position, then turned to his servant. Ned Cresset gave him a toothy grin. A steadfast and reliable man, Cresset captained our retinue and performed administrative duties on Michael's estates. He was proving to be gregarious and helpful at every turn. The men exchanged a few words, and Cresset signalled a halt. There were riders ahead of us; caution was required.

When the horses slowed, I dipped my hand into the saddlebag and was reassured when my fingers touched the satin purse containing the pearls. Michael had warned against removing them from the coffer but having them within reach felt safer somehow. He had indulged me, against his better judgment.

Cresset disappeared through the trees for further investigation. At length, he returned, convinced that the other riders posed no threat. He issued a low whistle and we continued. Soon the forest gave way to a broad valley dotted with verdant pastures; at its heart lay the small parish of Dilwyn.

"Welcome home, Margery," Michael called out as we neared a two-story black and white timbered manor covered in creeping ivy. One of the chimneys expelled a plume of smoke in greeting.

A passel of servants met us in the courtyard. They chattered excitedly, taking our cloaks, and offering refreshments. While Cresset saw to the baggage, Michael showed me the house. The rooms were cheery and inviting, richly decorated without being garish or extravagant. The hall was the most lavish, boasting two brick hearths and a series of intricately embroidered wall hangings. "Bess' work," he remarked, pointing at one depicting his late wife's heraldry. "I can have them removed if you wish."

"No, please don't. This was her home. They belong here." I offered a sympathetic smile. "Having lost my own mother, I can understand how comforting it must be to Richard. It is important to honour her memory."

Michael touched one of the birds stitched into the banner. "It's a martlet, a mark of cadency for the fourth son. The bird's lack of feet denotes the inability to walk on one's ancestral lands."

"Then it is most fortuitous."

"Why do you say that?" he asked. "I am sure there are many who would not find it so."

"My father was the fourth son, and I have yet to set foot on Horsman lands."

Michael stepped away from the banner, turning his attention towards me. "Where are these lands, Margery? You have never told me."

"The north." My answer came out more forceful than intended.

Michael's expression turned sombre. He moved closer, reaching for my hand. "Did your family participate in the uprisings? Is that why you kept it from me?"

"They are strangers to me. I have a cousin—Martin Hastings—but he contacted me only once. He wanted me to speak to Lord Cromwell on his behalf. It was a favour that cost me dearly." One the councillor had used to compel my testimony against the Boleyn siblings.

"They are all the poorer for having forsaken you."

I squeezed his fingers. "Enough of this sorrowful talk. I am anxious to meet your young man. Where is he?"

My husband's face lit up, the corners of his eyes crinkling with his grin. "Richard is with the chaplain, taking his lessons. I suppose it wouldn't hurt to interrupt."

Richard rose from his cushion the instant he saw his father. He sped across the room, spilling giggles of delight over the engraved tiles of the chapel floor. Michael fell to his knees. He caught the boy in a ferocious grip. When they parted, Richard graced me with an exaggerated bow. "Welcome to Chabnor," he said with well-practiced courtesy.

I knelt to meet his gaze. "You have the manners of a true gentleman, my good sir. How wonderful it is to make your acquaintance."

Richard pressed a pudgy hand to my cheek. "Papa has told me how kind you are. He says you make him very happy. That makes me happy, too."

My eyes grew damp. The emotion of the moment washed over me, warming the length of my body. "I hope I continue to do so, sweet Richard."

"You can call me Dickon if you like. Papa does."

"Then Dickon it is. What would you prefer to call me?"

Dickon grinned. "Why, Lady Mother, of course. What else would I call you?"

The chaplain cleared his throat and gestured for the boy to return to his books. "We must complete our lessons, Master Dickon."

"Run along now, son." Michael chucked the boy on the chin. "Starke does not like to be kept waiting."

Watching the pair of them, I was overcome by a feeling both familiar and foreign, unnameable yet known. It was a sensation treasured but lost, discovered once again. In the days to come, I would savour it, soaking in its sweetness.

JANE SEYMOUR

GREENWICH AND HAMPTON COURT PALACE

O n St Mark's Day, my belly stirred for the first time. It was the sparest of movements—a flick or flutter—faint enough to cause me to wonder if I had imagined it. I was on my knees in the privy garden at Greenwich, excising weeds from a patch of violet heart's ease. The flutter became a rumble, a lion's roar of hunger, so I ignored it and continued digging. It came again, this time more insistent than the last. A sequence of bubbles careening through my womb. I tugged Lady Anne to the ground, directing her palm to the ever-expanding mound beneath my kirtle. "Can you feel that?"

She pressed down hard, moving her hand across the width of my stomach. "Was it a kick? A punch? I don't feel anything."

I shook my head. "Gentler than that. I know not how to explain it."

"A promising sign. Still, keep it to yourself for now. There is no use celebrating until the quickening when there is no mistaking the movement." She scrabbled to her feet. "The king's meeting shall be over soon. We best get you cleaned up for supper."

I looked down at my hands, examining the half-moons of dirt wedged beneath my fingernails. How wonderful it was to touch the soil again, to breathe in the clean earthy scent. I had almost forgotten the inherent pleasure of coaxing a bud to bloom or seeing tender green shoots burst through the loam. "Would that I could spend every day this way."

"Consider yourself fortunate to have stolen this afternoon. Dr Butts will be none too pleased if he finds out." She eyed my maids doubtfully.

Shaking the clippings from my gown, I straightened. "Mother worked in the gardens at Wulfhall until she went into confinement. How dangerous could it be? Besides, those two will not say anything. They knew of my condition before anyone else and breathed not a word." At my gesture, Mistresses Norris and Jerningham trotted over with my cloak.

Lady Anne sighed. "Nevertheless, I would avoid inviting any of your other ladies on these excursions."

"You sound like Edward," I snapped, peevish over her fussing. The pair of them had been insufferable lately—watching what I ate, where I went, and to whom I spoke. In their learned opinion, everything I did was wrong. One would think Lady Anne was the only woman to ever have borne a child.

"You will thank me in the end," she replied, grimacing at the spot of mud on my hem. She bent to wipe it away. "You have stained it, I think."

"Margery will take care of it when she is back from Chabnor."

At the table, the king was exuberant with the prospect of naming a new Garter Knight. I listened to his bluster, that laudatory tone he always took when praising himself, but my mind was still in the garden, wandering amongst the flowers. My ears pricked to attention when he mentioned Thomas Boleyn.

"Is he back at court for good?" I asked, careful not to display my reticence on the matter. I shoved a heaping spoonful of mashed turnip into my mouth to keep from saying more.

"He leaves on the morrow for London to sit in judgment of Robert Aske, Lord Darcy, and the rebels. Having sat out the trials of his wayward children, it was the least he could do. I didn't allow him to retain his earldom so he could hide away at Hever."

Of course not. Why would one such as yourself do a thing out of mercy? I swallowed the turnip, felt it sink to the pit of my stomach. "Who have you decided upon for the garter?"

"The Earl of Cumberland will be installed. After his diligence in putting down the rebels, I found it fitting he should replace that traitor

Darcy." He ripped a bit of bread from the loaf. "Edward was keen for the position, but he is young yet. Give us a boy, and the next opening shall be his." The reminders were becoming more pointed: give us a boy, Jane, and we shall reward your family; give us a boy, Jane, and we shall allow you your head.

I should have begged clemency for both Aske and Sir Robert Constable, a kinsman of mine imprisoned alongside him. Instead, I bit my tongue. My pleadings would only lead to discord and further punishment for their families. Better I stay quiet and complicit in hopes it would spare them from the worst—in hopes it would spare me from the worst.

WHILE THE NORTHERNERS languished in the Tower, life beyond its stony precincts continued apace with preparations for the May Day celebrations. The festivities were muted, the jousts cancelled in consideration of the king's sore leg. Having Anne Boleyn's pearls removed from my coffers brought a measure of relief, and I found it far easier to push thoughts of her from my mind. Still, her ghostly presence endured on the anniversary of her fall, haunting the tiltyard where Henry abandoned her and the rooms that witnessed her arrest. Lady Rochford went about her duties in a daze. Pouring my evening wine, the ewer slipped from her trembling fingers, claret spraying us both. She stood frozen, staring at her empty hand in disbelief until one of the other ladies led her from the room.

Outside, a flock of dotterels scurried around the yard, oblivious to the fate awaiting them. A gift from the persistent Lady Lisle, the birds had already waxed lean by the time they arrived. With John Husee's usual compatriots—Lady Rutland and Mistress Margery—away from court, Master Long of the Privy Chamber had been roped into presenting them. Upon seeing the birds' frail condition, His Grace had them conveyed to the garden to be fattened for slaughter.

Sitting beneath the window sewing altar cloths for the chapel, Lady Anne mentioned that the Duchess of Suffolk had offered to take on Lisle's eldest daughter until there was another vacancy in my household.

"Is Honour Lisle bribing everyone now?" I asked, suddenly suspicious. "Don't tell me you support her."

Lady Anne tied off her stitch, snipping the excess thread with brutal efficiency. "It is nothing to me. I only suggest it because you will need to replace Mistress Ashley when she marries. I have already given you Mistress Jerningham. I cannot spare another."

I laid the embroidery frame in my lap and reached for another spool of thread. "I shall think on it. Meantime, Lady Bryan has asked me to write Lord Lisle in support of her cousin. Let us see how kindly they respond, then decide."

SLINGING A LEG over the sleek black courser, the king winced. He could go by barge, Chancellor Audley had told him last night at council. Edward said the king laughed it off, insisting he could sit a horse better than any other man, wounded or not. In the dusty light of the stable, it was clear His Grace was not about to back down, despite his obvious discomfort.

"Darling?" I asked sweetly. "Would it not be nicer to go by river?"

Hoisting himself into the saddle, he grunted. "No."

I tried again, pleading my own indisposition so that he could save face. "With this belly, I would be more comfortable—"

Another grunt and then a hiss of air through clenched teeth. "Then you take the barge," he growled.

The Master of Horse laid a hand on my palfrey's rump and shot me a questioning look: riding or not? I stepped on the block and hoisted myself into the saddle.

We rode in silence, my husband at the front of the column, the rest of us trailing behind. At Putney, he halted, beckoning me forward. I reined my horse up alongside him. He threw out his arms. "These are Crum's people. My most able councillor: a shearman. What do you suppose my father would think?" Before I could reply, he went on. "No point in answering. You never knew him."

"What was he like, your father?" A portrait of the man still hung above the hearth at Wulfhall, an ancient relic of a bygone era. From his perch on high, the elder Henry had watched the Seymour children scamper and play. Could he have ever imagined that the timid little girl with wild hair and dirty feet would one day carry his grandchild in her womb?

"Distant," the king answered. He spurred his courser, kicking up a cloud of dirt.

Evening shadows bathed the vermillion brick towers of Hampton Court by the time our retinue crested the hill overlooking the palace. The yard was empty, the workman having put off their tools to head inside for a warm meal and a few moments respite near the fire. They greeted us enthusiastically, sending up a cheer when the king burst into the hall.

"Go back to your supper, men," he boomed. "The rest of my courtiers will arrive on the morrow to disrupt your peace, and for that, we are heartily sorry." He snapped his fingers at my brother. "Tom, see that they get another round of ale."

Glancing up at my husband, one of the rosettes carved into the wooden screen behind him caught my attention. Inside it, the initials A and H had inexplicably escaped the carpenter's pick.

"Shall we, Jane?" he asked, taking my hand.

I lowered my eyes. "I am yours to command."

MARGERY HORSMAN

CHABNOR

Olwen brushed a tangle of umber curls from her forehead. A bead of sweat followed the curve of her hairline, pooling in the hollow of her collarbone. She gave the wad of linen in her hands a sharp twist, spraying a shower of water over the freshly mown grass. A quick jerk to shake the wrinkles from the sheet, and then she draped it over the line, using one of the clothespins wedged between her lips to hold it in place.

"Have you given my offer any more thought?" I asked, handing her a damp nightgown. Dickon peered around the freshly hung sheet wearing a mischievous grin. I smiled back. "The chaplain is looking for you, young man. He is coming this way." Dickon giggled and then tore off in the opposite direction, wisps of hair flying out beneath his cap.

"Mam says I should go, but she has been trying to find me a position for ages. Would it not be better to take someone with more experience than a laundress to be your lady's maid?" Olwen hung up the nightgown and reached for the next item. "Surely there is another better suited?"

"There is nothing wrong with being a laundress. Where do you think I got my start?" I overturned the emptied basket and watched the remaining liquid seep into the ground. Giving it a final shake to dislodge the dregs of lavender, I perched it on my hip while I awaited the girl's answer.

Curious, Olwen turned around. "You were employed in the laundry? How did you get a place in the royal household?"

"I worked hard. Made myself indispensable. I also had a champion—a woman loved by the queen."

"Are you beloved of the queen?" she asked.

I paused, considering my response. "I am not sure this queen loves anyone, in truth. She tends to keep most of her feelings hidden. Come to think of it, she has never really displayed favourites either. Cannot say I blame her after what happened to the last queen."

"Were you there for that nasty business?" Olwen leaned in, whispering conspiratorially. "Mam and I think it a farce. They say she entertained men within days of giving birth. Mam says there is no woman heated enough to take a man to bed that soon. She would know, being a midwife."

"Keep that between you and your mam. It's not safe to discuss such things at court."

Olwen went stiff, her almond-shaped eyes flicking side to side, looking for eavesdroppers. "Sounds like a dangerous place. Perhaps I shan't go, after all."

"It can be if you are not careful." I gave her the basket and turned on my heel. "I have no doubt you will get on well, but you must guard your tongue and try not to be so blunt."

"ARE YOU SURE you want to take Olwen?" Michael asked later as he readied for bed. A month of working like a ploughman had darkened the smattering of freckles across the bridge of his nose and toned the muscles in his shoulders. They moved beneath his skin when he shrugged the nightshirt over his head.

"I thought to have Lady Lisle's daughter, but she has made it quite clear that she prefers a viscountess at the very least." I groaned. "Why not Olwen? She has known your family for years. Did you not tell me her mother delivered Dickon?"

Michael blew out the candle and crossed to the bed. Pulling the hangings shut, he crawled beneath the quilt. "She is a fine girl and an able servant, but she has never been far from Wales. She is not one for flattery or false pleasantries."

"I like that about her." I nuzzled his cheek and laid back on the pillows. He snuggled closer, draping his arm around me.

"Things are different now. We must be more careful." He went quiet, and I wondered if he had fallen asleep. A chorus of crickets sang outside the window. I had just begun to doze when he picked up the conversation, his voice taking on an indignant tone. "I wish the queen had not asked this of us. I despised the woman while she lived. Why must I be charged with protecting her relic?" The necklace—Michael had not spoken of it since we left London. He didn't even want to know where I kept it hidden.

"How could you hate her?" I asked quietly. "You hardly knew her."

"Of course, I did. She was the queen, after all."

I wriggled free of his grasp, scooting towards the edge of the bed. "In all my time in her service, I never once saw you grace her rooms. Never saw you speak to her or pay her courtesy. How could you possibly know anything of her?"

"I know what people said about her," he sputtered. "What else matters?"

"Lies, most of it," I snapped, growing angrier with each word. "People say plenty of unkind things about me. Are you going to believe them too?" I tried to roll away. Michael pulled me back.

"What is wrong, Margery? Please tell me why this touches you so."

In the blackness, free from his judgmental gaze, I found the courage to tell him the truth. "It was my doing. Jealousy got the better of me, and I spoke out of turn. I never imagined they would die for it. It is all my fault."

Michael ripped open the curtains and stumbled out of bed. He crashed through the house looking for fire to relight the candle. When he returned, his face was bathed in its eerie glow. "What do you mean? How could you possibly bear any blame?"

I sat up, rubbing furiously at the salty tracks running down my face. "I was angry. I had worked to the point of exhaustion and still could not escape the wardrobe. I should have been a maid-of-honour, not an overweening laundress. The queen had her favourites, and I was not amongst them. One night, I had enough. I told Edward Baynton I was suspicious of her relationship with the musician, Marc Smeaton. I accused him of stepping outside the bounds of propriety. Smeaton was apprehended, taken to

Cromwell's. Soon after, Anne went to the Tower. I did it out of pure spite and jealousy. I just wanted them both to love me."

Michael set the candle down and took me in his arms. "Who did you want to love you?"

"I don't want to tell you," I wailed. Would he understand? How could I go on if he thought less of me? What if he repudiated me? My sobs grew louder.

Michael crushed me in his embrace. We began to rock slowly. "Margery, my love. Please unburden yourself to me. There is nothing you could say that would turn me away from you."

A tremor rippled up from the base of my spine. It struck through my limbs, causing my hands to tremble. I gulped a lungful of lavender-sweetened air, steeling my nerves. "I wanted Anne and her brother, George, to love me. I wanted to be her sister and closest companion. I wanted to marry George. But I was a fool. And I became a murderess."

Michael went quiet. The force of my words had stilled his swaying. I froze in his grip. After a moment, he tilted my chin, and we locked eyes. "Sweetheart, you are not a murderess. Or a fool for that matter. Your only fault is in being human. There are times we give in to weakness, and often it costs us. But be assured, their deaths were not caused by you. They never would have arrested the queen unless Smeaton gave them reason to do so."

"He must have been so frightened," I murmured. "He would have said anything if promised his life. You have been in those interrogations. You know what it is like. Tell me I am wrong."

Michael hugged me again, saying nothing. My heartbeat slowed, the steady rise and fall of his chest soothing me. "You are not wrong," he admitted after a long silence. "Still, you cannot blame yourself. You did not force Smeaton to say those things."

"It is my fault he came to Cromwell's attention. My fault Anne Boleyn and those other men are dead."

"They are dead because the king wanted it that way. There is nothing you could have done to save any of them."

"How must it feel to be married to such a man?" I replied bitterly. "Queen Jane took great risk sparing that necklace. If you must be angry about our charge, be angry with me."

"I do not think I could ever be angry with you, Margery." He kissed my forehead and cradled me until I succumbed to sleep.

Michael was already gone by the time I awoke. Peering out the window, I spied him striding across the yard with Cresset. They stopped at the fence line, my husband slinging a quiver of arrows over his shoulder, and then the woods swallowed them both. I turned away when I heard the door open. It was Olwen, come to dress me for the day.

"I have decided to go," she announced. "If I stay here, Mam will expect me to take up her trade, and I have no love for squalling babies."

In the hall, Dickon was at the table, shovelling porridge into his mouth. Setting aside his spoon, he watched me tear off a chunk of cheat loaf. His hand darted towards the plate of cheese. He swiped two wedges, offering me one. A servant bustled in with a jug of milk and a tray of fruit. I ate a berry, its sweet flavour bursting across my tongue. When I looked back at Dickon, his face was scrunched up. "Did you get a sour one?"

He nodded, reaching for the milk.

After breakfast, I went to the chapel to pray. Bent beneath the watchful gaze of Our Lady, I begged for absolution and the strength to carry on—if not for myself, then for the good of my newfound family. When I opened my eyes, Dickon stood near me, holding on to the pew. He climbed into my lap, burying his face against my chest. Kissing the crown of his head, I breathed deep. He smelled of leaves and sunshine.

JANE SEYMOUR

HAMPTON COURT

S ir John Russell strode into the great watching chamber, scattering a crowd of petitioners. "Lisle's man has just been here with a delivery, Your Grace." He bowed, pressing two fingers against his eyepatch to keep it from moving. "This batch should be more to your liking. I told Husee they needed to be fatter." He signalled a page hovering in the doorway. The boy lurched across the room, carrying an unwieldy crate in his arms.

"Only the best for my queen," Henry replied, reaching over the chair's armrest to curl his ring-bedecked fingers around my wrist. "Let us see them."

Wiry legs trembling, the page eased the crate to the floor. Lifting the lid with a grunt, he revealed a covey of dead quails. "I counted two dozen, Majesty, with more live ones on the way."

"Excellent." Henry produced two silver coins, dropping them into the page's outstretched hand. "Now, be a good lad and take half to the kitchen for roasting. We shall have the rest at supper."

When the last of the petitioners trickled out, we retreated to the privy chamber to eat. Watching the carver do his duty, my mouth watered. Slicing through the bird's crisp golden skin, he paused to let the juice trickle out to the platter, where it formed a steaming pool. He placed a generous portion on my plate, and I tucked in, devouring the first tender bite without regard for the king's precedence.

"Slow down, dear wife," my husband said, laughing. "There is plenty to go around."

I licked the grease from my fingers. "It is the child, Henry. His cravings are maddening." Since arriving at Hampton Court, I had thought of nothing but all manner of delicacies. Fresh cucumbers sprinkled with salt, strawberries drenched in sweet cream, savoury puddings, and meat pies—the kitchen brought them out fast as I could eat them. Still, there had been one thing I desired above all else: a plump, succulent quail. I had hoped the first batch from Calais would have been enough to satisfy my appetite. It only served to increase the intensity of my longing. Soon, it was all I wanted. I could not get enough.

Henry shook out his napkin. Ripping a leg from his bird, he gnawed at it delicately, sucking the meat off the bone. He did the same with the other leg before spearing a chunk of breast. I was already digging into my second bird. "I can compel Lord Lisle to continue supplying quails for your table, but his wife will come to expect certain favours." He paused to dab at the corner of his mouth. "She has already sent a diplomat to bend my ear with praise for her daughter, Anne. It got so tiresome that I agreed just to make him stop."

My stomach pitched. I swallowed the half-chewed lump of quail. "What of the elder sister?" I groped for an excuse. "Surely, we should consider her first?"

Henry stared at me. His eyes were alight with bemusement. "You can bring them both in, but they say Anne is prettiest. The more desirable." He flashed a grin that said Anne Bassett would be in my household whether I willed it or not.

I took a sip of wine. "Are you not concerned her French manners will set a bad example for the other maids?"

"Not with you at the helm. You have maintained far better control over your women than the last one. If this Anne exhibits any of the same tendencies, put an end to it."

"Can I at least meet them both? Perhaps the rumours are false, and Katherine is the fairer."

He brushed me off, rising from his seat. "If you must. Alas, I would not wager on it."

LATER, WHEN WE gathered in the chapel for vespers, I sat in the same closet where we were betrothed. On that day, the image of St Anne had laughed at me. Gazing at the window near the altar, I saw that she was gone—the stained glass depicting her having been removed. In her place stood St George carrying a gore-soaked sword, the slain dragon lying at his feet. Was I St George or the dragon? The vanquisher or the vanquished? Which did I want to be?

After the service, Henry bid me farewell. The execution of the rebels would commence on the morrow, and he wanted to meet with the council to discuss the details. Five men, two of them abbots, were to be drawn to Tyburn to suffer the most brutal punishment the king meted out. I tried to blot out their faces as I picked at the bones of the quails brought up by the kitchen for my supper, but the men invaded my thoughts. Martyrs, all of them, dead for their steadfast loyalty to the beliefs we had all agreed upon for time immemorial. Beliefs held to be right and true until my husband decided they were not and took them away. What sort of tragic legacy would our child inherit?

Pushing away from the table, I felt a powerful kick. And then another. And another. Each one was more forceful than the last. I seized the hand of the lady standing nearest me. "Get Lady Anne Beauchamp."

"Yes, Your Grace," Lady Rochford's voice cracked. When I looked up, her face was grey and devoid of emotion. She stared through me like I was invisible.

Lady Anne prodded my belly like a crone testing a melon for ripeness, her bony fingers digging into the soft folds of my skin, feeling for movement.

"You are not supposed to be touching me," I hissed through gritted teeth, trying to ignore the awkward stares of the maids who had been sent in to dress me.

"That is why we are in your bedchamber," she snapped. "Now, hold still." Her tongue worked at the corner of her mouth. She concentrated on the knoll beneath my nightgown. "You are sure it was not wind? What did you eat?"

I opened my mouth to respond, and the child kicked her hand.

"Praise be to God," she yelped, a broad grin spreading across her face. She started for the door.

I stopped her. "The feast of the Trinity will soon be upon us. What better holy day to tell the father that his son stirs?" I could not celebrate life while men waited to die—the news must be forestalled.

Ignorant of my real motivation, Lady Anne suppressed a smirk. Her bright eyes flashed. "You are learning, Jane. Succeed where others have failed, and your position shall be assured. Put a boy in that cradle and save us all."

ON THE APPOINTED day, we arose early to observe the solemnities. Before lauds, I took to my holy closet. Kneeling at the prie-dieu, I offered up prayers for the departed: the men who died at Tyburn and the woman burned at Smithfield. Margaret Bulmer's death seemed much crueller than the rest. She was a sacrificial lamb—a warning that women would not be spared the king's retribution. After the events of last May, I had trouble believing that the point was ever in doubt. No one could escape Henry's wrath, not even his wife.

Throughout the service and the meals that followed, I waited for the child to move. After a few tenuous hours, I pulled Lady Anne aside. Take a walk, she counselled. It had always helped during her pregnancy. Out in the privy garden, Henry was solicitous. He took my arm as the minstrels followed us down the path, slowing his stride when I grew winded. Heading back, we stopped at the fountain so I could watch the sunlight dancing on the water. That was when it came—another forceful thump. I arranged my face into an expression of astonishment. "The child quickens, Henry!"

The king's eyes lit up. He gestured at the minstrels to cease their song. "Are you certain?"

"Yes, my love. The child is strong." I placed his hand on my belly. The baby flailed again.

"Oh, the Lord is good," he exclaimed. "We must send word to London. I want Te Deums sung in the churches and bonfires in the streets with a hogshead of wine at each one."

"And prayers at St Paul's?" I needed all the intercession I could get.

"For you and my prince." Henry threw his arms around me. Pulling away, he looked up at the red brick wall of the palace. "How would you like a private gallery overlooking the garden? That way, when you stand at the window, you will always be reminded of this glorious day."

MARGERY HORSMAN

CHABNOR AND HAMPTON COURT

A bove the copse of trees bordering the entrance to Chabnor, a cloud of dust snaked across the sky. A rider was making his way down our lane. I had been expecting one for some time—an interloper come to drag us from our idyllic life in the countryside. I resented the man before he set foot on the property and briefly considered ignoring his knock. My heart sank when I remembered that Michael was in the yard. My husband would not fail to welcome the visitor, no matter the message he carried.

Clambering to the ground, the man dug a sheaf of paper from one of the tawny saddlebags strapped to his horse. From my perch at the window in our bedchamber, I watched Michael approach the animal with an apple he had taken for his dinner. The bay snatched it from his hand eagerly, bobbing its head as it chewed. The men exchanged a few words, and then the rider remounted, bolting out of the yard with a tip of his hat. An eternity seemed to pass while Michael stood in the grass reading the missive. With his back to the window, his reaction was hidden. What was the tenor of the note? Looking down at him, a worrisome thought struck me. Had the queen miscarried?

Throwing aside my embroidery frame, I rushed down the stairs. Olwen was at the bottom, a basket of linens wedged against her hip. Her eyes widened when I flew past, yet she made no remark. Her efforts to rein in her tongue had been successful as of late, despite her inability to conceal an occasional frown or smirk. In truth, I was not much better at containing my own emotions. We would have to muddle through together.

Michael's face darkened when he saw the concern on my face. "What is wrong? Where is Dickon?"

"He is in the kitchen with Cresset. Has something happened? Is the queen well?"

With a triumphant grin, Michael handed over the paper. Edward Seymour's signature was scribbled at the bottom. "Her Grace is healthy and in fine spirits. On Trinity Sunday, the child in her belly quickened. It seems we have missed a hearty celebration."

The rush of relief felt sweet. The first danger was past, pray God she carried to term. "That is joyful news. I am pleased to hear it."

"Lord Beauchamp says we must come back. The king is ready to go on progress."

"To Yorkshire this time? The north country?" I could hardly get the words out. It had been years since I last saw home. Was there anything left?

Michael shook his head. "That has been put off for now. The rebels won't thank him for it, but it's not safe to take the queen that far. He will make good on his promise once the prince is born, I am certain of it."

I PACKED THE trunks for our return journey, a dull ache settling within my chest. Each constricted breath felt like it might rip me from the inside out. I wondered if my ribs would crack and part, spilling bits of bone and flesh all over the rush mats on my bedchamber floor, my viscera splattered across the woollen window coverings like so many dye stains. Our days at Chabnor were so simple, uncomplicated. There was never a need for deceit or deception. A careless word was just that, and not an act of treason or aggression. The worst it could bring was a shower of tears or hurt feelings, not death and destruction. At court, we treaded on the knife's edge. One misjudged step could end a life or wipe an entire generation from existence. Those alluring, sumptuous apartments were nothing more than gilded prisons.

And what of the rebels? Yet another danger. If the king reneged on his promises, would they storm the capital?

"Mistress Lyster? You look awful." Olwen took the bonnet from my hand and pushed me on to a stool. "Can I get you anything? Some ale or maybe a bite of food?"

Shaking her off, I forced a laugh. The last thing I wanted to do was frighten her more than she was already. "Thank you, Olwen. I am sure it is nothing a drink cannot cure."

"I will be back." Setting the bonnet on the bed, she picked up a small coffer from the table beside it. "Meantime, sort through this and decide what you would like to take."

"What is it?" I asked, taking the box from her hand. The carved wood opened at a touch. Inside laid an assortment of jewels—modest adornments, nothing extravagant or ornate.

Olwen sucked in a breath. Her cheeks flushed. "Oh, I thought you knew. They belonged to Dickon's mother."

I shoved the coffer back towards her. "Why are you giving it to me?"

She yanked her hand away as though the container was a tinderbox aflame. "Master Lyster bid me. He said the jewels are yours now."

"He did?" I opened the coffer again, pulled out a string of amber beads.

"For mothers," Olwen explained, touching one of the brown orbs. "You wear it for protection during childbirth."

I pushed the beads back into the coffer. "Didn't do much good for poor Bess, did they?"

"She thought it an old crone's tale. Wouldn't wear the thing." Olwen snorted. "Sent Mam through the roof."

I stopped her before she could go on. "I would not mind that ale, Olwen." Once she was gone, I returned the coffer to the table. Regardless of my position, it felt wrong to plunder the memories of my husband's late wife. Even if he did grant them to me. For all my good intentions, I found myself retrieving the amber the night before we left for court. Old crone's tale or not, I wanted those beads when the queen's time came.

WE SET OFF for Hampton Court before daybreak. I peered over my shoulder to watch the warm, glowing windows of Chabnor fade into the cold, grey mist. I thought of Dickon snug under a coverlet, curled up on his pallet near the hearth. He put on a brave countenance when we exchanged farewells. It was the faint quiver in his lip when he hugged me goodnight that gave him away. Michael's servants did their best to keep him occupied, and he had his lessons with the chaplain every day. Still, he was keen for a brother and had asked mere days after our introduction when he could expect one. The hours could be long and lonely for an only child.

From Dilwyn to Molesey, Olwen vacillated between bewilderment and wonder. At each market town, Michael had to convince her to stay in the saddle and out of harm's way. The brightly coloured stalls of merchants cheerily hawking their wares proved tempting, but I feared that we would lose her in the crowd. In return, we promised a stop at Reading so that she could part with some of her newly earned wages. When the palace finally rose into view, she gasped in astonishment, and then the tears began coursing down her cheeks.

"Beautiful, is it not?" I beamed with unwarranted pride.

"And far from home," she sobbed, soaking the linen handkerchief her mother had sent along.

I felt the same during those early days in Queen Catherine's household. "You will get used to it. Eventually."

While Olwen got our things settled into the apartment, I traipsed out to base court to gather my bearings and visit the wardrobe. Joan Arundell bounded out the open door, carrying an armload of fabric. "Margery," she cried when she spied me. "By all the saints, am I relieved to see you."

"Is that a placard?" I gestured at the stiffened material laid atop the stack. It was a piece I had not seen before—deep indigo damask embroidered with gold thread and seed pearls.

"The queen uses them all the time now." Mistress Arundell's laugh was shrill, cutting. "Wait until you see her belly. It truly is something to behold."

"Surely, it cannot be that big."

Joan puffed up her cheeks and fixed me with a wide-eyed stare. Parting her lips to release the air, she said, "I blame the quails, not the child."

"Have you spoken to Skutt about letting out her gowns? That should have been done weeks ago. I can send for him tomorrow, but—"

"Skutt's wife is dead, Margery," Joan interrupted. "Lost in childbirth. He won't be taking new commissions."

"The poor man. And the child?"

"The girl lives but only just. We do not speak of it in the queen's presence." She leaned in, adopting a confidential tone. "At night, after we have gone quiet and she thinks us asleep, Her Grace weeps until she can hardly draw breath. It is most pitiful."

Biting words, small cruelties—I had forgotten how much courtiers enjoyed wounding one another. Watching Mistress Arundell skip gaily across the courtyard, I found myself desperately longing to return to the comforting embrace of Chabnor. This place was no longer my home.

AMETHYST

Relief

JULY–SEPTEMBER 1537

JANE SEYMOUR

THE SUMMER PROGRESS

AT WOKING, HENRY informed me of his intention to restore one of the nunneries in the north and re-establish the dissolved monastery of Chertsey at Bisham. We were in the chapel for evensong, the fragrant scent of incense thick in the air. The soaring stone arches bore down, trapping us together. Had I wings, they would have beaten against the cage.

My husband sat like a child, enraptured and tremulous with glee. Behind my saintly smile, I fumed. Benevolent though the king imagined his intentions, the offering felt more like a droplet of balm given to the victim of a stake burning. When the faithful begged for the same kindnesses, he spurned them, named them traitors and rebels, and drenched their fields in gore. What good is concession when the opponent has already rotted on the gibbet?

By the time I returned to the chapel for morning mass, the leaders of the pilgrimage were dead: Lord Darcy felled on Tower Hill and Robert Aske hanged in chains at York. His body swung for weeks, desiccated and rotten from starvation and the elements. There he would stay, his soul wandering Purgatory until the king would allow a burial. My cousin, Sir Robert Constable, suffered a similar fate at Hull. Had my womb been empty, I may have succumbed to hysterics; such was my distress. But the memory of Anne Boleyn's miscarriage kept me from breaking apart. The child might have lived had she not crumbled at news of the king's jousting accident. Yet for all my inner resolve, another danger lurked in the shadows.

On Wednesday evening, Sir John Russell accompanied the king to supper. They lingered over the threshold conversing, Henry's bluster drowning out the courtier's more serious tone. When Russell realized I was listening, he clammed up and waited for his master to take the lead.

Henry kissed me. "Sir John will be on his way. He was just telling me of Crum's unfortunate turn. One in his household has taken ill."

"Please pass along my condolences."

The king cleared his throat. "You can tell him yourself in a day or two."

Sir John looked to his shoes.

My chest hollowed. Perspiration beaded across my brow. "Are you not afraid of contagion? Surely, business can wait?" During plague season, all caution must be taken, especially with a prince on the way.

Henry flicked his ring-bedecked fingers in irritation. "Crum shows no sign of sickness, so I would have him here with us to make merry. Off you go, Russell. Tell the Lord Privy Seal I am expecting him."

Throughout the meal, the king ate like a man starved, while my plate sat untouched. When he excused himself, I summoned my brother.

To my dismay, Edward appeared less shocked than I expected. He strode into my rooms, preoccupied with preparations for our sister's upcoming nuptials. "Elizabeth and Gregory will be married in less than a month. I am not going to risk the father of the groom's displeasure by asking him to stay away from court." He pulled a face, wrinkling his blunted nose. "I cannot entertain her at Twickenham much longer. She orders the servants about as if she runs the place. I have already had two threaten to quit."

"Something must be done. You know the risks as well as I do."

Edward threw his hands up. "I shall stop by Lord Russell's room before I retire. But no promises."

"Thank you, Edward." I reached out, tucked a loose strand of hair behind his ear. The gesture felt too intimate, so I backed away. By God's bones, I was tired of being unceasingly mindful. "In truth, Lord Cromwell should be grateful. My successful delivery of a healthy baby boy is in his best interest, now that our families are to be forever linked in matrimony." My earlier apprehension at the match had melted away when I realized this convenient truth during the lush spring days at Hampton

Court. My position was the most secure it had ever been, but only a male heir would keep me there.

After a broken sleep and mumbled prayers at the prie-dieu, the king arrived to accompany me to mass. "Sweetheart," he cooed, stroking the back of my hand with featherlight touches, the blue lapis on his finger shining in the sunlight. "Upon deeper reflection, it may be best if Crum lodges with some of the other lords. He will join me on the hunt while remaining without the bounds of court."

"How wise you are, my love." I turned my face up to his for a kiss. How pliable he could be when led in the right way.

MUCH AS I tried to evade it, the roasted quails served at the afternoon meal brought with it another round of earnest pleadings, this time from two of my senior ladies. It seemed no one was immune to the relentless stream of gifts Honour Lisle shipped across the channel. Lady Rutland was the most vocal, no doubt due to the elaborate brooch nestled at her breast. How did Lady Lisle afford it when her husband incessantly pled poverty?

"We hear nothing but good report of both girls, Your Grace." Lady Sussex chimed in, eyes wide and searching over the rim of her goblet. Since her marriage to the earl, she was thoroughly enjoying her promotion from mere maid-of-honour. "Mistress Anne is most accomplished and the fairest. Yet, the elder sister also has her charms. Katherine is biddable and has a sweet disposition. Either would serve Your Grace well."

One of the maids glided over with more wine. If our discussion over her possible replacement caused any discomfort, she gave no indication. Humming a tune under her breath, she seemed somewhere far off, likely thinking about her recent betrothal. Another girl shuffled off, given over to the king's friends and courtiers alike. Who would have taken me had Henry not expressed interest?

"...and she speaks perfect French. Would that not be helpful during your audiences with Ambassador Chapuys?" Lady Rutland continued, determinedly listing off Anne Bassett's considerable attributes.

"Our brother, Edward, knows the language as well, and we are not asking him to serve in our household."

Heat rose to Lady Rutland's face. "Your Grace is sure to make the wisest choice, whichever sister is selected." She passed me a bowl filled with ripe strawberries and blackberries of the deepest violet. "Would you like some cream?"

Discussing my predicament during our nightly bedtime rituals, Margery Lyster was more circumspect. "Master Husee has assured me that both Lady Lisle's daughters are upstanding young women. I understand Your Grace does not think all that highly of their mother, but neither girl has spent much time with her. Your Grace may find the ladies vastly different than their forebear," she said, catching her comb on a snarl.

Margery made a reasonable point. None of the many women in the Seymour household were alike. When my father would arrive home after a day in the fields with his tenants, he would jest that he never knew what sort of wrens would be occupying the nest. I waited for Mistress Lyster to detangle the knot. Rubbing at the sore spot where my hair pulled, I asked if she trusted Husee.

Rapping the comb against the palm of her hand, she thought for a moment. "He has never given me reason to doubt him." Was the glint of regret in her eyes real or just my imagination?

WHEN THE HUNTING dried up at Woking, we moved on to East Hampstead and Sunninghill. I longed to be outside with my husband—sitting astride a horse, the wind tearing at my hood—instead, I spent my days holed up indoors, breathing stale incensed air and staring listlessly out the window. I was proud of my belly, thrilled by each kick that rocked my womb. Still, it held me hostage. With little else to occupy my mind, I spent an excessive amount of time worrying about the plague. Lady Rutland had to be excused when a gentleman of her house died of the wretched illness, and Cranmer wrote of the men perishing daily outside his gates. London seethed with disease.

Edward appeared exasperated when I informed him that I had no intention of attending our sister's wedding at Cromwell's Mortlake house. "We will not go anywhere near the city," he argued. "Everyone expects you to be there."

"I shall extend my congratulations when Cromwell comes to Windsor for the Garter election," I answered, resolute in my decision.

"Has the king mentioned who might take Lord Darcy's place?" He fiddled with a button on his doublet.

I did not have the stomach to tell him he had been overlooked once again. "You know he does not tell me such things," I lied. "Besides, I thought it was decided upon by vote?"

"Yes, by vote," he echoed, the slight lilt of a frown marring his features. He looked down at his feet. When he raised his eyes again, all hint of displeasure had been erased. "If you insist on missing the wedding, then a suitable gift must be sent to avoid offense. Perhaps one of the religious houses so recently vacated."

My hand involuntarily twitched, itching to connect with his face. "When the progress is over, and we return to Hampton Court, it would be best if you tarried at Wulfhall. Take Tom. The pair of you are getting far mightier than I would like. Do not forget that I am queen, Edward. You may have ordered me around as a child, but those days are gone. I shall not endure your arrogance any longer."

MARGERY HORSMAN

HAMPTON COURT

T he small brown and white spaniel tread gingerly across the lawn, pausing every few steps to nose the dew-laced grass. Queen Jane's hand dropped to her side, a curt snap issuing from her fingertips. "Clary, come," she commanded. Dappled ears perking, the dog trotted closer to her mistress' heel.

Mary Norris and Eleanor Jerningham chittered behind me; their high voices carried above my head on the cool late morning breeze. With the recent marriage of Mistress Ashley top of mind, the two maids were engaged in a lively debate over which Bassett sister would take her place. When I glanced back at them, Mistress Jerningham gave me a timid smile. "When is your sitting with Master Holbein?" she asked.

In a show of generosity, the queen had recalled the artist to court. She wanted portraits drawn of her ladies—a gift before she went into confinement for the birth of her child. "It is tomorrow. Hopefully, not too early. I have not slept well since Michael left for Wulfhall." My excuse was only partially true. I had found rest elusive since my husband's departure with the queen's brothers, but my morning sickness was the real reason I did not want Holbein calling upon me before mid-day. The vomiting had arrived with a vengeance earlier in the week, shortly after I realized my courses had stopped. Not even Michael was aware that life had sprouted within my womb.

"What do you suppose they are doing right now?" Mistress Norris wondered aloud.

"Michael took a pack of hounds with him, so I imagine they are chasing game out of the Savernake," I answered. The queen muttered something indecipherable under her breath.

Leaving the privy garden, the spaniel loosened a ferocious bark. Having picked up the trail of a small animal, she tore off towards the palace. "Margery, would you?" The queen gestured helplessly at her escaping pet. Even if royal protocol had not forbidden it, her immense belly would have been enough to keep her from chasing after.

I crossed the lawn in hot pursuit. Near the cloisters, the dog disappeared. Stopping to catch my breath, I heard voices outside the chapel. I peered around the corner. A tall man, powerfully built, leaned against one of the pillars. There was something familiar about him that I could not place initially. When I moved closer for a better view, recognition dawned. He was Harry Parker's groom—the pleasant one who helped me when searching for Cromwell. His appearance had changed somewhat since that day in the great hall. His arms were thick, muscles straining the fabric of his doublet; the healed remnant of a deep gash was etched across the bridge of his nose. Harry Parker's men were sent north during the rebellion; had his groom also seen battle?

The man bent forward, grasping the hands of some unseen figure. "I cannot bear to see you this way. What happened to the brave young woman who pushed me into the fishpond and ordered me around? You have become like a ghost."

"That girl is gone, Hugh," came the reply. "She died on the scaffold with George."

"He would have never wanted this for you. Can you not see that?"

Lady Rochford. Tears pricked at my eyes. How much more could the woman endure?

"What would you have me do?" she asked. "Throw off my mourning clothes and dance the galliard? I cannot. Grief weakens me."

Hugh touched her cheek. "You are so much stronger than you know. Do not lose faith in yourself, Jane."

Lady Rochford pushed his hand away. "I must go, Master Wynter. The queen will be back from her walk shortly. I would rather not be discovered this way."

She darted into the chapel, leaving the man to catch me lurking in the shadows. "The maid who drank my ale," he muttered. "Didn't know you were an eavesdropper as well."

I swallowed hard. "It was not my intention, Master Wynter. I was looking for the queen's lapdog."

"Isn't that you? Off to tell her what you witnessed?" The insult stung, but it was not unwarranted.

"I have done Lady Rochford harm enough," I answered quietly. "You seem to know her better than anyone. What can I do to repair the damage?"

"Good to know you are not all irredeemable. After the maids turned on their last queen, I had given you lot up for lost causes." The anger in his tone ebbed away.

"My sins are manifold, but Lady Rochford is the only one to whom I can make amends."

"Then you must do so. When the others are cruel, be kind. Remind her that she is not alone."

"And if she refuses my friendship? What then?"

The cleft in his chin deepened when he smiled. "Then you do as I have these long years. You offer it up again and again." He dipped a bow and was gone.

I found Clary at the entrance to the queen's lodgings. Scooping her up, I carefully removed the squirming—but mostly uninjured—mouse from her jaws. "Naughty dog," I scolded.

PREFERRING LIGHT FROM the morning sun, Master Holbein instructed me to meet him in the long gallery shortly after prime. I protested, feigning prior commitments to the queen. The painter was adamant. Mercifully, I had squirreled away a stash of ginger, and the root managed to curb the worst of the nausea. He sat across from me, studying my face intently, then he began to draw. Deep in concentration, the tip of his tongue worked diligently at the downturned corner of his mouth. This early in the day, the gallery was still deserted, so the sound of his voice in the hushed silence startled me.

"You do not mind if I draw a trio of marguerites on your hood, no?" he asked.

I traced the smooth fabric border of my headdress. "I am not wearing jewels on this one. Still, I suppose it would be fitting. Why should I take offense?"

He rocked back in his seat, choosing his next words carefully. "The decoration *could* symbolize your name. However, this particular flower is known to have another meaning."

"Yes, I know the French refer to pearls as marguerites. But if you aim to portray me as an innocent, you are woefully misguided."

The painter smirked behind his hand. He cleared his throat. "Excellent, Mistress Margery. Pearls are indeed representative of purity. Still, there is yet another message they convey. Marguerites tell the observer that the subject is soon to be a mother."

I nearly fell out of my chair. "You are mistaken, Master Holbein. Do I appear pregnant to you?"

He considered my figure. "It is early days. And yet, the signs are all there if one knows what to look for."

"You must not share this news with anyone," I sputtered, stunned the painter could have been so astute. I tried to suck in my gut. The effort pushed vomit up into my throat. "I have not yet told my husband."

"Marguerites also symbolize secrets. I suspect you have those in abundance." Holbein gave a conspiratorial wink. "That is something we have in common."

I SAT WITH the painter for the next three days. On the afternoon of the fourth, a messenger burst in near the end of our session to inform me Michael had returned from his hunting trip.

"Go, Mistress Margery. Tell your beloved," Holbein said, rushing me out the door. "I have enough to finish on my own."

Michael was already abed when I got to our rooms, a strangled groan emanating from somewhere beneath the pile of blankets. His boots—still caked with mud from the road—hung over the side, dangerously close to the counterpane. When I bent to remove them, a soft snore escaped his throat.

While my husband slept, I wandered down to the riverside. A burnished bronze sun hung low on the horizon; its reflection set the water ablaze with light. At the end of the dock, John Russell's barge bobbed gently on the tide. I watched one of the boatmen carry off a parcel of goods. Behind him strode John Husee.

"What a pleasant surprise, Mistress Margery," he called out, approaching at his customarily brisk pace. He held a bottle of wine in one hand; a cage of chirping linnets dangled from the other.

"The industrious Master Husee. Never a spare moment for yourself."

Husee grinned. "You know Lady Lisle charges me with only her most important tasks."

"Well, your next one had better be conveying her daughters over here with all due haste," I relieved him of the wine bottle. "The queen takes to her chamber in less than a fortnight. If they are not here in time, they shall be returned on the next ship back to France."

"They are preparing to disembark as we speak. It took a bit longer than expected to get their wardrobes in order." Queen Jane's exacting specifications. Not even Anne Boleyn had been quite so particular.

"I hope they make a good show, for your sake."

"That makes the pair of us." Husee snorted. "Sometimes I wish I had continued my father's trade. I could be making wine for the great and the good instead of merely delivering it like a giddy page."

"Surely it is not all bad. We would have never met had you not come to court."

Husee touched the brim of his cap, the trace of a smile on his lips. "How horrid to imagine such a thing. I'll ask you not to say the like ever again."

"Impertinent man. Take your wine." I shoved the bottle back towards his hand.

"Keep it," Husee said, turning on his heel. "When you drink it, think of me."

RETURNING TO OUR apartment after vespers, I found my husband awake and sitting at the table. I brushed my lips against his brow and took my place in the empty chair beside him. Despite the exhaustion on his face, he brightened when he saw me. "I have missed you, Margery."

"And I you, my love." I patted his knee. "How was the hunting?"

Michael shrugged. "One of my hounds took down a rather hearty stag. It looked like good eating, but we never got to taste it. Edward sent it to the Imperial Ambassador."

"Was the pursuit pleasurable, at least?"

His nose wrinkled with disdain. "Most of the time was spent discussing politics and Edward's plans for the child in his sister's belly. In all honesty, I found it all rather tedious."

Lord Beauchamp was one of Michael's oldest friends. His ambivalence over the man's success surprised me. "Are you not happy for him? Surely this bodes well for us."

Michael levered himself from the chair. He stood before the fire, watching the flames gambol in the hearth. "I am not much of a courtier, Margery. And neither was Edward years ago. He is different now. I still prefer life at home with my boy."

Being of the same mind, I saw my opening. "We could go back, you know. We have a reason to return home. Once I inform the queen, she may even insist upon it."

"Inform her of what?" Hoisting me from the chair, Michael gave me a look filled with trepidation. He cupped my face in his hands.

"I am pregnant, Michael."

Michael's arms enfolded me. Sudden deep sobs wracked his chest.

"I thought you would be overjoyed," I cried. "Please stop, Michael. You are scaring me."

He gulped a lungful of air, stilling the shudder of his ribcage long enough to answer. "I am, Margery. Oh, I am. Yet, there is much I fear. What if the Lord takes you as he took Bess?" My mind had not even dared go to that forbidden place. The possibility of it was not worth considering. The Lord would never punish Michael in the same way twice, would he?

"Let's beg leave, my love. We can head back to Chabnor in the morning, be there before the week is out."

"You cannot tell the queen, Margery." Michael sniffed. "We cannot risk upsetting her before she goes into confinement. Besides, Edward will not countenance my leaving until the child is born. He needs me here, should it have the misfortune of coming into the world a girl. Difficult though it may be, we must wait."

Michael had a point. The king would be incensed if his wife failed to give him the son for which he had torn Christendom apart. There would be carnage. Heads rotting upon pikes. Bodies swinging from gibbets. Death, destruction, and turmoil.

If the worst happened, would Queen Jane survive it?

JANE SEYMOUR

HAMPTON COURT

B eneath an ornately woven cloth of estate, I sat in judgment of the two young ladies standing before me. The pair—so utterly alike in countenance—could not have been any more opposite in demeanour. They were like dresses made of the same pattern yet cut from contrasting cloth. I had expected to prefer the elder with her quiet and meek nature. Instead, the captivating girl beside her bewitched me. When Anne Bassett spoke, I found myself leaning closer, hanging on her every word.

"Madame de Bours kept an extremely strict household. She never allowed time for indolence or frippery. Between Mass and meals, our days were occupied with music lessons and embroidery; prayers for the unfortunate and confession every morning." The girl lowered her lashes deferentially. "As Your Grace certainly knows, France has a reputation for vice and licentiousness. I can assure Your Grace nothing of the sort tarnished Madame's family."

"And what of you, Mistress Katherine?" I forced myself to acknowledge the other sister. "How did you fare under de Bours?"

Katherine Bassett reddened under my gaze. She chewed her lip nervously. "Mother insisted I stay in Calais. She thought she could find me a place in Queen Anne's household." A tortured gasp escaped when she realized her mistake. "The Lady Pembroke's household, I mean," she corrected.

"We call her plain Mistress Boleyn here," Mistress Arundell chirped from her cushion.

Katherine's hand flew to her mouth. "I am deeply sorry," she mumbled. Her sister looked on, mortified.

When I stood up, the maids perched on the floor found their footing. "You leave us with much to think on. We shall take the evening to decide, and whoever is chosen will be sworn to our service on the morrow. Until then, please enjoy Lady Rutland's hospitality."

The supper plates had hardly been placed on the table before my brother's wife began her line of inquiry. What had I thought of the girls? Did I prefer one over the other? Which one would the king choose?

"Lady Anne, you tire me already. Is Edward not content to await my decision like everyone else?" I waved Mistress Norris over. "Bring me a stool, please." The girl blanched at the swollen stalks straining the seams of my stockings. Elevating my feet relieved the discomfort somewhat, but the throbbing in my lower back continued unabated. Carrying a child was weary work. How had Mother been able to do it so many times? God-willing, the babe would be a prince. Then what? There was no end—next would come the spare. I would be expected to deliver babies until my womb fell out. The servants could carry the organ around on a litter, propping it up during state occasions.

"Edward has never willingly waited for anything. Just tell me so that I can spare you the annoyance of his trudging down here himself." Lady Anne folded her arms across her chest. In the glow of the setting sun, her features were softened. Delicate. A pretty girl, grown into a beautiful woman. I envied her.

"Katherine is the more prudent choice and less likely to attract the king's attention. However, there is something alluring about Anne. She is confident, though not insufferably so. Intelligent without being smug. By all appearances, pious and devout. Trustworthy."

Lady Anne grinned. "I am glad Your Grace is finally seeing reason."

Edward hated Lord Lisle. Why his wife wanted to support the man's stepdaughter was beyond my comprehension. I started to ask then stopped, suddenly realizing that I did not care to know the answer. All relationships

at court operated in much the same manner, always messy and complicated. One day friends, the next enemies. Round and round it went in an
unending coil of mistrust. It was exhausting. "Tell Lady Rutland I will take
Anne. She can wear out the gowns she brought, but she must have a proper
bonnet. No French hoods."

SUNDAY MORNING BROUGHT with it a tempest of heavy rain.
Standing in the embrasure, I watched weeping clouds scud across the sky.
Grey light filtered through the leaded glass window, pooling on the deco-
rative tile that was soon to be covered with expensive Turkish carpets and
a pallet dressed to welcome a prince. The poor weather seemed an ominous
portent of disaster to come. Drawing my robe tighter, I tried to push the
unsettling thought away.

Doubt chased me like a shadow, laughing mockingly in my nightmares and robbing the breath from my lungs. I could give it purchase
no longer. Left unchecked, it would lurk in the corners of the birthing
chamber, threatening my happiness. The babe would be a boy, I was sure
of it. I had been a faithful and devoted daughter; Christ would not let
me fail.

Margery pushed the door open with a grunt. Struggling beneath the
weight of the damask and cloth of gold gown in her arms, she stumbled to
the bed. Crimson fabric spilled atop the counterpane.

"I should have chosen a different colour. Something more auspicious
than red."

Margery's brow furrowed. Had her face grown more rounded? "I can
see if there is another in the wardrobe, but I do not think there is anything
else so fine. Perhaps Your Grace would like to wear the amethyst brooch
instead of the ruby. Something to cool the flame?" *And ward off as much
pain as possible.*

"A wonderful idea. Henry's mother wore it on her wedding day." I
parted my lips in the approximation of a smile.

The king awaited me outside the chapel. Rocking impatiently on his
heels, he pounced the moment my coterie stepped through the archway.

He kissed my hand. "My queen. It has been far too long since we last saw your face. How fares our prince?"

I choked back a retort. Henry had returned to Hampton Court from his progress nearly a week ago. If he missed me, he could have visited earlier. "The child gives me no rest. He is strong like his father, and just as determined."

After a long and drawn-out mass that nearly put me to sleep, the entire royal household processed back to my apartments to partake in a course of spices and wine. Already drowsy from a lullaby of hymns, my head began to nod when the hippocras warmed my belly. Tom noticed and gathered up Archbishop Cranmer for final prayers. I felt relieved to leave the ordeal behind, flanked on either side by the two most eminent peers of the realm. They led me to my bedchamber, then bid their farewells. I would not see them again until after I became a mother. The day of my reckoning seemed so close and yet so far away.

Having sworn her oath the day prior, Anne Bassett was allowed into the bedchamber to help me out of my clothes. When she knelt, the curve of her breasts skimmed the border framing the neckline of her gown. *Too much. Too impertinent.* I would have to send Margery to John Husee. No French hoods and no French gowns either.

"Can I get Your Grace anything else? Food? More wine?" Mistress Bassett's liquid amber eyes peered up at me.

"It feels stuffy in here. Open a window." The massive tapestries that had been hung on the wall while I was away at Mass closed in on me. They depicted the life of the Roman general Pompey—an inexplicable choice of decoration for a birthing chamber. Hadn't his wife died in childbirth? I would have to ask Margery. I collapsed on the bed, like a casualty of war, and closed my eyes. The heat from the fire raked the tips of my toes. Sweat dripped behind my ears. The maid said something else, but her words were lost in the thrum of rain lashing against the glass. I would not leave this room for the next month. In the untamed forest of my mind, I was free.

SAPPHIRE

Peace

OCTOBER & NOVEMBER 1537

*And then they saw the God of Israel and under His feet there
appeared to be a pavement of sapphire, as clear as the sky itself.*
—EXODUS 24:10

MARGERY HORSMAN

HAMPTON COURT

"Master Husee! Wait!" Moisture from last night's storm seeped through the soft soles of my slippers as my feet slapped the damp flagstones. Having no previous intentions of leaving the comfort of the palace, I had not given much thought to my choice in shoes when I charged after Husee. More than a fortnight had passed since I last saw him, kitted out in a new doublet for the queen's lying-in ceremonies. Since that day, Her Grace's instructions regarding Anne Bassett's clothing had changed. I was tasked with delivering the message. Each day, Queen Jane demanded to know why Mistress Bassett still wore her French apparel. And each day, I patiently explained Husee's absence from court. To no avail. She grew restless, ever riddled with worry. It took little to nothing to set her off. In my desperation, I flew into action the moment I caught sight of the man passing beneath her window.

Husee paused halfway across the courtyard. He turned, giving a small wave. "To what do I owe the honour, Mistress Margery?"

Stepping in a puddle, water sloshed over my toes. I recoiled. "You won't like it. Lady Lisle will be giving you fits when she hears."

Husee smiled sheepishly. "I confess to having grown accustomed to it." He brushed a wayward strand of hair out of his eyes, then adjusted his cap. "So, what is it I can do for you?"

"It is the queen. She cannot bear Mistress Anne's gowns. They remind her of..." I trailed off.

He nodded, understanding. "I wondered how long that would last. What should I order instead?"

"She needs a black gown of satin and velvet; another in tawny. The queen also insists her smocks and sleeves be made with better cloth and that she orders another bonnet or two. With an edge of pearl."

Husee repeated the list back, ticking off each request on his fingers. He held up his hand. "Only five. That is manageable."

I scrunched up my face. "And she must have them by the queen's churching."

He grimaced as if in pain. "Less manageable, but by no means impossible. I shall see what can be accomplished."

"Thank you, Master Husee." I turned to leave.

"Wait," he said. "Something has changed in you. You seem to glow from within. Happy news?"

Afraid I would give myself up, I continued to stare ahead rather than turn to face him. "Not yet, Master Husee. I must go now. The queen will be calling for me."

The herald brayed my name from his perch outside the bedchamber door. He kept his eyes averted, lest his gaze inadvertently fall upon his mistress and violate the sanctity of her birthing room. It was just as well he did because the great tester bed's thick arras hangings were thrown open to let in the last rays of sunlight. Queen Jane scuttled backward, her unwieldy belly swaying as she struggled to hoist herself up against the headboard. "Herald," she barked. "Be gone and close that infernal door." The chamberer tending to the fire scurried around me, fleeing. Mistress Jerningham returned to the psalter laying open in her lap. "That is enough for today," the queen continued, stopping the maid mid-sentence. The maid pursed her lips, closing the book dutifully.

"I have delivered your directive to Master Husee." I curtsied. "All shall be accomplished imminently."

Queen Jane nodded, a pained expression marring her visage. "They tell me I must close the windows, but I cannot abide this darkness. Why shouldn't I see God's creation?" She clutched at the bed linens, her knuckles going white. A soft grunt passed her lips. Besides being dim, the room was infernally hot. My undergarments grew sticky with perspiration.

"Does it hurt, Your Grace?" This was the first time I had ever been allowed in the birthing chamber. I had no expectations of the experience for either Her Grace or myself.

Queen Jane's grip relaxed, her hand falling limply beside mine. Our fingertips brushed. "It is not the same for every woman, so do not fret over what you see in here. Your time may be different." She sighed, glancing pointedly at my waist. I felt my face redden. Was I showing already? Noting my discomfort, she went on. "Once this is all over, I shall grant your leave. In the meantime, take as much rest as you need. I have plenty of other maids to see to my demands." Her lip twitched in disgust when she looked towards the corner where Mistress Bassett sat working an embroidery hoop.

"I have never been better," I assured her with more confidence than I felt. "Now, let me remove that gown and get Your Grace into something much more comfortable. I trust Master Lloyd has sent up the sarcenet-lined robes we ordered. I am certain this night will be a cold one." We couldn't have the queen catching a chill.

THUNDER RUMBLED SOMEWHERE off in the distance, a low rolling grumble stretching wide across the deer park and rattling the windows. I awoke with a start in the early morning twilight, the deep ache of a full bladder urging me from the warmth of my bed. Groggy from a restless sleep, I groped for the piss pot underneath the bed. The noise alerted Olwen, who hurried in to light a candle.

I waited until she left before padding over to the corner to relieve myself. Finishing, I felt a sharp pinch in my abdomen. I stilled, waiting for the pain to pass. With fear pulsing through me, I reached down to check for blood. My hand came back unstained. I carried the pot to the table that held the washbasin, setting it aside to clean my hands. That was when I saw it in the candlelight—a thin vermillion thread, suspended in the urine.

I crawled back into bed, curling my body against Michael's. His solid, comforting presence did not stop the dread gnawing at my belly. He was already terrified of what childbirth would bring. I resolved to keep this new development to myself for as long as possible.

Queen Jane was up and about by the time I reached her apartments. She stared out the window, watching the wind batter the last vestiges of her beloved garden. Across the room, Dr Butts argued with the midwife. "Her Grace must return to bed. Should she suffer to take ill or catch cold, the child will be in grave danger."

The old woman brushed him off. "Drivel! Movement will help speed labour. I encourage all my patients to walk in the days leading up to birth. Haven't lost one yet."

Butts' face grew red, his eyes widening in disbelief. "The queen is not your patient," he sputtered. "As royal physician to our dread sovereign King Henry, it is I who has charge of her care."

"What do you know about delivering babies?" the woman huffed. "I was there when the Princess Mary took her first breaths. Where were you?"

Seething, Butts jabbed his finger towards the door. "Out! Her Grace has no need of you."

The midwife grunted but did as she was told. I slipped out behind her while the rest of the maids rushed to comply with Butts' orders to cover the windows and get the queen off her feet. I caught up to the woman in the corridor. She listened as I told her about the spotting. "Have you experienced this before or is this the first time?" she asked.

"My first," I whispered. "First time and first pregnancy."

She caught my hands in her gnarled fingers, giving them a reassuring squeeze. "What you have described is nothing for concern. Keep a vigilant watch and send your maid to fetch me should the bleeding continue or become heavier."

"Where would I find you? Dr Butts has banished you from the queen's rooms."

"Ah, but not from court." She tapped the side of her nose and gave me a wink. "I shall stay nearby. Her Grace will require me when these *learned men* botch things."

Nestled among the heavy furs now strewn about the royal bed, Queen Jane appeared forlorn. She attempted a wan smile when I pulled up a stool beside her. "Dr Butts is right," she croaked through parched lips. "He should be the one to deliver the prince."

"How much longer until Your Grace's reckoning?" I asked, hoping her travail was nearing its end. How dreary it must be, locked in this room day after day—pure torment for a woman who loved the outdoors such as Queen Jane.

"Soon, I hope," she whimpered.

THE DAYS PLODDED on, each bloated hour lasting an eternity. We waited patiently, watching for the signs. A yelp of pain, a heaving grunt, a strangled moan—any abnormal utterance brought a crowd to the royal bed. "Get them out of here!" the queen screamed at Mother Stonor on more than one occasion. Despite her irritation, custom dictated our presence; our attendance was deemed even more imperative due to the lack of available noblewomen. Ladies Sussex and Rutland were both considered too far gone with-child themselves, and several others were kept from court for fear of the plague. Lady Anne Beauchamp joined us at Hampton Court, but she also carried life in her womb and could not be counted upon to stay the course.

The queen slept fitfully, taking rest when she could. It was not enough. She grew weak from lying abed so long and nearly collapsed when she got up to use the close stool. When we pulled her upright, a great gush of water rushed out beneath her nightgown, splashing our feet.

"Get Lady Anne Beauchamp," I called to Mistress Ashley. "I will find Lady Rochford."

I went first to the sparse rooms Jane Rochford called her own. They were far less comfortable than the ones she had used as the wife of George Boleyn. I curled my tongue around his name, marvelling that the sound of it no longer caused a sharp jab in my chest. I had not thought of him since we were at Chabnor. Was I starting to forget? The sound of his voice, the cadence of his footsteps, the scent that lingered in his wake; I could no longer recall them. Perhaps my love for him had been nothing more than an infatuation, borne out of desperation. If it were genuine affection, I would have been able to summon those long-dead relics as if I had experienced them yesterday. How George's memory must torment his widow. It was little wonder she retreated inside herself.

A lady's maid named Lucy met me at the door. "Lady Rochford went for a walk in the long gallery. She has been gone for quite some time. I expect her to return at any moment."

"The queen's labour has begun. There is no time to tarry. We must get her."

Lucy scurried out behind me.

Approaching the entrance to the gallery, we heard an exchange of laughter. "Do you see that?" came one high-pitched voice. "I cannot believe she has fallen asleep. How mortifying."

"Saddled by such guilt, it is a wonder she gets any rest at all," chimed another. "I hear it was she who told old Cromwell about her husband's lusty romps with his sister. Too bad she got nothing for her trouble."

In the centre of the leering circle, Lady Rochford lay slumped on a bench, snoring softly. Lucy quivered with fury beside me. I cleared my throat loudly enough to draw curious stares from the end of the hall. "Show some respect for your betters," I snarled at the brace of girls, all minor lady's-maids to the titled women serving the queen. "You know nothing of Lady Rochford and the trials she has suffered. Now, be gone. Else I shall tell your mistresses what trouble you have been causing."

The girl in the middle eyed me brazenly. "Lady Monteagle says she is nothing but a traitor's bawd. I shall suffer no recrimination from her."

When I stepped towards the girl, the others instinctively shrunk back. "Nevertheless, Lady Rochford is a great favourite of the queen. You do not want to be caught on the wrong side of Her Grace. In just a few short hours, she will birth the heir. Her power and influence will be so great that none will challenge her." *From my lips to God's ears*, I prayed.

The girl shifted her weight, uncertainty filling her face. She glanced at the others, making up her mind in the span of a moment. "I shall make haste to inform my lady."

Lady Rochford stirred. "Lucy? What are you doing here?" She bristled when she caught sight of me. "What is it now, Margery?"

"It is the queen," I answered, taking her by the hand. "The child is on its way."

JANE SEYMOUR

HAMPTON COURT

P ain seized me like the devil clutching a soul, my womb contracting in a vice. Wave upon wave washed over me. I kicked for the surface, but relief proved futile. I drowned in agony. Disembodied voices floated in the deep around me. Why had all the candles been extinguished? Could they not see my anguish? I cried out, "Get us some light, you fool!"

"Open your eyes, Majesty." With great effort, I pried them open. At the foot of my bed, Dr Butts was bathed in candlelight. "If Your Grace permits, I would like to do an examination. See how the child progresses."

"Do as you must." Another surge swelled within me. I clawed at the sheets, choking back a scream. The doctor's hands were cold and cruel. His bony fingers prodded at the secret parts no man, save the king, had ever touched. Each poke elicited another jolt, another stab, another cramp. Mother had not prepared me for such indignities.

Finishing, Butts pulled the quilt back down to cover my feet. "I am afraid Your Grace still has far to go. I have been told these things take time. Perhaps by the morrow, we shall have a prince."

He had been told? Had he no experience? "Call the midwife," I spat. "Get us one who knows what they are doing."

Butts shook his head apologetically. "I am under strict orders from the king. Only the royal physicians may attend Your Grace."

Overtaken by another spasm, I slumped against the headboard. What ignorance was this? A birthing chamber was the realm of midwives, not physicians. I gave Lady Anne a pleading look.

"Thank you, Dr Butts," she said, hurrying the man from my room. "Perhaps the queen should rest awhile. We shall call for you if the child stirs."

I looked over at the tapestry-covered windows, wondering if the sun still shone outside them. I was unsure how many hours had passed since my waters had soiled the carpets. It seemed to have happened so terribly long ago, and yet I knew it was no more than a day. My belly ached for sustenance. The last thing I ate had been a fat partridge, basted in its juices. I promptly voided it in a sea of vomit when hit by the first pangs of birth. The thought of it turned my stomach again.

Lady Anne knelt at my bedside. She smiled at me before folding her hands in prayer. Her lips moved wordlessly. My brother's wife should have been home, tending to her own child and preparing for the birth of another. She was still relatively early in her pregnancy—one would never know she was with-child just by looking at her—but I could see how tired she was. I resolved to send her back to Chester Place after the christening.

I closed my eyes when the pain returned. My insides clenched hard, shuddering again and again. Biting my tongue to keep from crying out, tears streamed down my face. I grasped at Lady Anne's arm, squeezing hard. When the wave finally subsided, she managed to wrest me from the bed to a pallet on the floor.

Crouched on the low mattress, I laboured on my hands and knees into the vast expanse of night. The hours had never seemed so still and oppressive. I wondered if I had ever felt such torment before in my life. The pain seeped into my marrow, speeding through bone and veins like fire or poison. My body instinctively curled inward. The maids pulled me apart again. "The baby cannot escape that way," they said. They meant only to help. Yet, I heard condemnation in their voices. Did they think I knew nothing of childbirth?

Margery brought a wet rag when I collapsed in exhaustion. The cool water soothed my burning skin. "Should we try to get her on the stool?"

Lady Anne poured ale down my scorched throat. Concern shadowed her face. "She is too weak. If this continues, she shall not have the strength to expel the child. Send for Dr Butts."

"Yes, send for Dr Butts," I echoed faintly. We must have the king's trusted physician to make sure nothing underhanded occurred. God forfend one of my women tried to substitute a changeling if the new-born proved a princess. I would die by that man's hands. Closing my eyes, I sank into oblivion.

When I awoke, Butts stood in the corner with my brother's wife, deep in conversation. He glanced over, marking my movement with interest. Lady Anne rushed to my side. "He says there has been no progress. The baby is lodged firmly inside your womb."

"What is there to be done?" Mistress Norris worried, blinking back tears. Searching the crowd of faces, I noted a proliferation of swollen eyes. All the maids had been crying.

Lady Anne sighed. "We can do nothing, save wait."

While the court prayed for a safe delivery, I writhed and panted on the sweat-soaked, bloodstained mattress. Delirious from hunger and exhaustion, I flitted in and out of consciousness. In my weakest moments, I wondered if I had died already. Trapped in Hell, my throat burned. I cried out for water. Jesus brought me a pitcher and I drank deeply, realizing later that it was not my saviour, and I was not in Hell. The angel who quenched my thirst was Lady Rochford, her golden hair a halo around her head. Oh, what horrible things had been done to her family to bring me to this place. When my death finally came, would God forgive me, or would I indeed be sentenced to eternal damnation in the never-ending fires of Hell?

Without notion of time, I lost track of how many days had passed. Was it a week or a month? Had it been only minutes? I did not know. All certainty had fled. Perhaps there was no child at all, a mere figment of my imagination. Eventually, voices cajoled me into pushing. I strained to relieve the heaviness in my groin. With each push, the child pressed back. Undaunted, I continued to bear down until I felt something wet and slick slither out from between my legs. Another gush of fluid and viscera followed. The room stank of sulphur and metal. I held my breath. An ear-splitting cry broke the silence, and then came the words I longed to hear: *It is a boy, Your Grace.*

At last, England had a prince.

MARGERY HORSMAN

HAMPTON COURT

T endrils of dawn wrapped around the stone colonnades of the cloister. Outside the chapel door, I heard rustling coming from within— Archbishop Cranmer preparing for lauds. A swirl of incense welcomed me inside. When the smoke cleared, I saw the true source of the noise. It was not the expected churchman, but the sturdy form of Lady Rochford huddled at the altar. I crept closer, quietly so as not to disturb her prayers. Only when I reached the edge of the dais could I make out her whispered words.

"It should have been you, my darling Anne. That should have been your prince."

Feeling like an intruder, I backed away, stumbling in my haste. When I reached out to steady myself, I sent one of the silver candlesticks clattering to the floor.

"Who is there?" Lady Rochford's voice was tinged with sorrow. She stood and spun around to face me. Her ruddy cheeks were soaked.

"Excuse me, my lady. I seek not to bother you. I intend only to go and leave you in peace." I took another step backward.

"Wait," she said, after a moment of uncomfortable silence. "Would you pray with me? I do not want to be alone."

Heeding Hugh Wynter's words of advice encouraging me to offer up my friendship, I extended my hand, and together we unburdened our souls to the Almighty.

When the carpenters arrived to build the scaffold for the baptismal ceremonies, Lady Rochford and I parted ways. She went off to her lonely apartments while I returned to the cosy rooms where my loving husband awaited.

MICHAEL ROSE FROM the table. He gave me a broad grin, then pressed his lips to mine. They tasted of sweet wine. When he pulled back, I noticed we had a visitor. Tom Seymour remained seated, touching the brim of his cap in greeting. Triumph sparkled in his eyes. A man like Tom knew precisely what rewards awaited the Seymour family and their supporters, now that his sister had given the king an heir. Is that why he was here?

"Tom has just informed me that we are to be knighted," Michael exclaimed. They both looked to me for a reaction.

I feigned delight. "How wonderful, my love. 'Tis a great honour to be raised so high." Inwardly, my heart contracted with worry. Knighthood came with an increase in expenses and more responsibilities, which pushed my dream of returning to Chabnor as a family further from my grasp. Even so, I could not express my disappointment and risk wounding Michael's pride. Yet, for all the playacting, my husband was not convinced. When Seymour left, he followed me into the bedchamber.

"What is the matter, Margery?" he asked, ushering Olwen from the room. The maid glanced back at me helplessly.

Laying back on the bed, I rested my hand on the slight hill beneath my bodice. The child had not yet quickened, but already I was protective of the seedling. It would be best not to provoke an argument and risk upsetting myself. "I am tired, that is all. A day of rest would do me a world of good."

Michael crawled in beside me. Slipping his hand beneath my back, he pulled me close. I relaxed into his embrace, feeling safe and at ease. "I promised you that we would go home. Being knighted does not change that. I shall always keep my word, no matter the honours heaped upon me. The recognition pleases me, but my place is at Chabnor with you and Dickon." He touched my belly tenderly. "And the little life you carry inside."

My fears allayed, I snuggled deeper into his arms. The rhythmic thud of his heart lulled me to sleep.

THE MORNING OF the prince's christening, I awakened with a jolt. The remains of last night's supper gurgled in my stomach. The sour taste of bile lay heavy in the back of my throat. Although the morning sickness had subsided for the most part, some days were worse than others. Still, there was no time to be spent miserable in bed. Olwen helped me into the new livery I had been gifted for the celebrations and then brought my jewels. When I opened the box, a string of amber beads flashed at me accusingly. The birthing girdle. Having meant to give it to the queen, I had forgotten it in the ensuing chaos of her labour.

Seeing my distress, Olwen rescued the box from my grasp. She snapped it shut. "It is not worth a second thought. Those beads would not have saved your mistress her travail, you likely spared her from a worse fate. I think the bedevilled things are accursed."

I touched a finger to her lips. "Speak not your heresies, Olwen. There are churchmen prowling the court who would not hesitate to put one such as yourself to the flames." Rolling her eyes dramatically, she stilled her tongue. "You can say whatever you like when we return home," I continued, "until then, watch your words."

A plague outbreak in London meant that precautions had to be taken. Anyone who may have been exposed, no matter their rank, was banned from the festivities. This meant that the Marchioness of Dorset would not be carrying the prince to the font as invited. Queen Jane burst into tears when informed of the news. Since the birth, a heaviness hung about her. When the clerk brought the birth announcement for signature, her fingers trembled ever so slightly around the quill. The poor woman had to have been exhausted beyond all repair to appear so forlorn while the celebrations raged outside the palace walls. In any case, Dorset was replaced by the Marchioness of Exeter. We gathered in the courtyard at dusk to follow her and the precious bundle into the chapel to seal his dedication to God and country.

Amongst this group of revellers, the Earl of Wiltshire stood by solemnly, carrying out his duty. The flame on the taper in his hand quivered and danced with each shallow breath he exhaled. I wondered at the thoughts racing through his mind. Did he imagine himself in Edward Seymour's place, escorting the Princess Elizabeth to the altar with the chrisom? Did he picture his son, George, bearing the canopy in place of Tom Seymour? What a waste it was: a man's future obliterated by his monarch's caprice. His children sunk in the ground, shrivelling to dust.

After the ceremony and *Te Deum*, we processed through the court and into the royal apartments where the king and queen awaited their son, now proclaimed Prince Edward—Duke of Cornwall and Earl of Chester. Queen Jane sat propped up on a couch in the great watching chamber, supported by a heap of luxurious furs and quilts of velvet, her milky skin stark and corpselike against the rich colours of her attire. She startled at the outburst of trumpets, then arranged her face into a smile to cover her unease. Queen Jane had succeeded where others failed. Now was the time for celebration. Despite the discomfort she surely felt, the woman forced herself on.

Later that night, drunk on wine and full bellies, Michael and I settled into bed, our limbs a tangle beneath the sheets. As I dozed off, my husband's deep voice caressed my ear. "There is something wrong with the queen. I fear Her Grace is not long for this world."

JANE SEYMOUR

HAMPTON COURT

M y breasts ached at the infant's wails; an expression of warm milk wet the linen beneath my furs. Tempted by the scent, my son burrowed his head into the fabric, rooting for its source. Lady Anne nudged me discreetly. Queens did not nurse their children. I had forgotten this critical detail. The king's minions gawped at me like a broodmare, my value much raised by the foal in my arms. This was my triumph, and yet I felt exceedingly empty.

The king bent to kiss the baby's mottled forehead. Naming the boy Edward had been his decision, and I chose not to fight him on the matter. It was not due to disbelief in my success—for any request was in my grasp now—I merely lacked enthusiasm for the challenge. There was no strength left within me. Much as I was irritated by my brother's pleasure in it, Edward would have to suffice. I preferred John, after our father.

The courtiers lingered long after the prince was returned to the nursery, the last one traipsing out in the early morning hours. Eyelids heavy, I wobbled on my feet. My husband instructed a pair of grooms to carry me back to my bedchamber. When they left, Mistress Norris and Mistress Bassett changed my bloody linens. The maids exchanged a worrisome glance. "Seems a lot," Mistress Bassett muttered under her breath. I was gratified to see her hair properly covered for once. No more French attire.

Climbing into bed felt like getting into a hot bath, and I found myself emerging hours later covered in a sheen of sweat. I thrust the quilts aside, gasping. The maids wiped down my limbs, then shoved me under the covers again. When next I awoke, the room was flooded with sunlight. Feeling much revived, my cravings returned. "Is there any quail to be had?" I asked Margery when she came for my soiled laundry.

Throughout the day, I sent the maids scuttling to the kitchens for whatever dish stirred my desires. I was mother to the future king. Who would dare deny me? Veal cutlets and roasted turnips were brought afore noon, with stewed apples and venison pie following behind. By compline, I had consumed more food than I was accustomed to eating in an entire week. None of it filled the void hollowing my body. I spent the evening in the close stool, purging. Emptied and weak, I stumbled back to bed. Lady Anne sent for Dr Butts.

When I surfaced from my dreams, shivering violently against the cold, the physician's hand was upon my forehead. "The Bishop of Carlisle is on his way to administer extreme unction," I heard him say.

I struggled to rise. "There is no need. I am much amended."

Butts jerked back in surprise. He had given me up for lost. "Do not get up, Your Grace. You must take care."

"Inform the bishop his services are not needed," I heaved, breathless from the exertion. Had everyone gone mad? Unction was for the dying.

Lady Anne eased me against the pillows. "Let us see how Your Grace fares when he gets here," she soothed, knitted brows giving away her barely concealed worry. "There is no harm in hearing his prayers."

"No harm," I repeated weakly, the creamy half-moon of her face already fading into the blackness that edged my vision.

THE ENTIRETY OF a day had passed by the time I finally came around again. Lady Anne rushed to my bedside when she noticed me stirring. "Bring warm water and a rag," she commanded a nearby chamberer. She grabbed a gilt cup from the table and held it to my lips. The ale burned as it coated my throat. Parched, I gulped it down.

"How is Edward?" I asked when I found my voice. Much to my shame, I had forgotten about the child in my delirium. *My son, my boy.*

Lady Anne sighed. "I told him it was in poor taste to go forward with the ceremony, but both he and Tom insisted. The pair of them would not even have their new honours if not for you." My grimace of confusion brought about an abrupt pause. "My apologies, Your Grace meant the prince. He is a goodly boy, fair and plump. Strong enough to carry the weight of the throne on his shoulders."

The remark elicited a smile from me. I had done my duty to the king. Then I remembered the bishop. "Why was Butts preparing me for unction? Is that not too extreme for a bit of exhaustion?" I considered commenting upon the greed of my brothers, flaunting their rewards while believing I was in such dire straits, but could not summon the effort. It was not worth the argument it would provoke. Besides, I would always lose.

Lady Anne's expression softened. She held my hand. "Sister, you were near death. The fever burned so hot, there were moments we could not revive you."

Fear rattled my chest, a heaviness settling in. I could not remember any of it. "What say the doctors now? Am I beyond danger?"

"Butts believes so." She kissed my palm. "Think not on these things. You must get some rest."

Drifting off, another question teased my mind. "What honour did you say my brother received?"

Lady Anne brushed a strand of hair from my face before rising from the stool. "Edward has been named Earl of Hertford. He is most pleased." The urgency of the ceremony suddenly made sense—he wanted to secure his earldom before I died.

CONVINCED THE FEVER was finally gone, Henry came to visit with Cromwell in tow. The minister hung back to give us the appearance of privacy, but he watched me with interest, measuring each shallow breath I took. He looked like the spectre of death in his black robes. All he lacked was a scythe. The king fawned over me, making sure I had every comfort available. Yet, he spoke only of our child. He did not ask how I felt. He did not ask what I needed. He merely assumed what would be best. What

I wanted was my son. "Plenty of time for that, my dearest sweetheart," he answered when I worked up the courage to make my request. "We must be sure you are well and truly on the mend." After the pair left, I began to sob.

Margery Lyster appeared at my bedside, a seraph of mercy. She laid her hand on the sheet. "Can I do anything for Your Grace?"

Remembering her own delicate state, I endeavoured to dam the flood. "Oh, there is nothing to be done. I have merely been in this bed far too long. Perhaps I could get up?" I attempted to swing my legs over the floor, but they would not budge. Try as I might, I could not move them. Flustered, I fell back against the headboard.

"Give it another day, Your Grace," Margery said kindly. "Butts will be here tomorrow. He can help."

I laid awake all night, thinking of my child. I tried to remember what his hair smelled like and how it felt to cradle his heft in my arms. What colour were his eyes? Had I remembered to count the number of his fingers and toes? I yearned to hold him and nuzzle my lips against the silky expanse of skin that stretched across his forehead, inhaling his sweet baby scent. I wanted to treasure my time with him before his father sent him to Wales with his own household. The king's brother, Arthur, had gone there and never returned. Not my Edward. I would force one of my brothers to go along. Not the two graspers here at court, but Harry. Harry would watch over him.

Despite his better judgment and my evident weakness, the doctor consented the next afternoon when I insisted upon getting up. He positioned a maid on either side, and they levered me to my feet, escorting me carefully to the close stool. I sat astride the gaping hole, my insides turning to liquid. The maids cleaned away the mess when I finished and led me back to bed.

Butts was pleased. "I believe Your Grace has turned the corner," he enthused, pulling the quilt up to my chin. He murmured at his assistant, and the small man flew from the room. "The king will be very glad to hear of it. I see no reason to keep the prince away any longer."

My heart soared. "I shall send to the nursery. I would have him with me immediately."

Butts put a restraining hand on my shoulder. "There is no need. Once the king gives his approval, I shall escort the child myself. Rest now. Your Grace must conserve herself."

Satisfied, I closed my eyes and slipped into a deep slumber.

I AWOKE DRENCHED in sweat and shivering uncontrollably. Something felt wrong. The room was dark as night. Had the fire gone out? Where were my ladies? I heard voices above me. They were shouting for my confessor. I tried to call out, but my throat made no sound. I clawed at the sheets.

Someone! Please!

The voices rose higher. I heard them say I was dying.

No! I am supposed to see my son! I began to cry. No one seemed to notice.

Another voice, this one more familiar—my confessor. "Let us pray," he said.

I willed my body to move. It remained immobile, like an empty, useless shell. My mind screamed his name: *Edward!* I fought to hold on to him, despair tearing at my heart. I thought of the wife who came before me. *Was this how it felt, Anne? How could you bear those days in the Tower knowing you would never see your child again?* She had once said that she was Princess Mary's death, and that Mary was hers. In truth, I was Anne Boleyn's death, and now she would be mine. My guilty soul was damned, and God's judgment rained down upon me. Shrouded in terror, I groped for my saviour's hand. His fingers closed around mine, and I felt myself drifting away. A sudden burst of light swallowed the darkness, and I saw Him standing before me. He turned, beckoning me with a slight tilt of the head. On trembling knees, I followed Him towards redemption.

MARGERY HORSMAN

HAMPTON COURT AND WESTMINSTER PALACE

T he black mourning habit hung limply over a chair near the fireplace. Olwen had placed it there every evening, hoping it would be warmed through when I donned it again each morning, but the fabric felt ever more frigid whenever it touched my skin. I hated to wear it.

Michael reached for my hand. "Not much longer, my love. Once the queen is buried, we can set off for home. Ned Cresset says he and Dickon have been carving a wooden horse for the baby. They hope you will be pleased."

"I am sure it is beautiful." It seemed profane to speak of such things before Queen Jane had been laid to rest. The poor soul would never see her son ride a horse, wooden or otherwise.

"Who will be sitting vigil with you? Not Joan Arundell, I hope." Joan's constant wailing had caused significant disquiet among the ladies. Her outpouring of grief was exceeded only by the Lady Mary. The pair of them together was enough to drive even the most composed of us to the edge of despair. For a woman in my state, it was dangerous. Michael would not have me risk upset.

"Lady Rochford will be my companion. She has hardly spoken a word, so you have little to worry about."

My husband exhaled in relief. "Good. That is good. I shall let you get changed."

JANE ASHLEY AND Mary Norris awaited me in the presence chamber. It had been a long night for them. Mistress Norris rubbed her eyes. "I can wait if you would like," she offered charitably.

I smiled at her. "Get some rest. You shall need it for tomorrow." In their departing wake, a chamberer arrived to change out the tapers and refresh the fire. The disruption allowed me an opportunity to check over the queen's body. She looked peaceful, lying there in repose. I retied a lace that had come loose and adjusted her sapphire brooch. When my mother died, Father had tried to comfort me with a pretty tale about the blue stones paving the streets of Heaven. I thought the jewel an apt choice when dressing her to lie in state. I hoped Father was right; my mother and my queens would tread the very same road.

Task completed, I took up my position on the bench and bowed my head to pray. When I lifted my chin, Lady Rochford was seated beside me, her gaze settled upon the bier holding the corpse of her former mistress. "Are they? Ah…" she began haltingly, her voice trailing off for a moment. "George and Anne, I mean," she started again. "Are they together now? With her?"

"Perhaps." My mind conjured an image of the dead queens, face to face in the black abyss of Purgatory. Cloaked in robes the colour of blood—a symbol of their martyrdom—both had been sacrificed for King Henry's most ardent desire: a son. "Do you suppose Anne will torment her in the afterlife?"

Lady Rochford shook her head. "No. Anne knows what it feels like."

"To what?" I asked.

"To lose everything."

AT THE END of a long, cheerless procession, Queen Jane was interred in St George's Chapel at Windsor. Despite the pomp and ceremony, it was not lost on any of us how unnatural it was to hold such proceedings when an heir was in the cradle. Where there should have been dancing and music, feasting and laughter, there was sorrow and regret.

"Can you believe Cromwell is blaming us?" Mistress Ashley threw a handful of aiguillettes into the jewel coffer with such force several bounced free, rolling across the floor.

"Careful! I have to account for all of those." I knelt to retrieve them, narrowly avoiding the table ledge when I stood up again. I placed them in the compartment. "How many was that?"

"Fifteen," she replied, slumping on the stool.

I did a quick recount, then marked the amount in my inventory book. I still needed to visit the wardrobe, but that would have to wait until tomorrow. Nightfall approached, and I was tired. "Will Peter send you home to his estates?"

"He wants to keep me with him in London. I think he is eager for his own heir." She shuddered. "How strange it is to be married. In one way, it is comforting to have the protection of a man. And yet, in another, it is terrifying. I cannot explain it."

"It is because you are at his whim and command," I explained quietly. "He could abandon you at any moment."

"Even after you give him what he wants." Mistress Ashley poked at a coil of turquoise beads, pushing them into a drawer. "Do you suppose the king will notice that dreaded necklace of Anne Boleyn's is gone? What did Holbein do with it, anyway?"

The necklace. I had forgotten all about it. "The queen had it broken down and remade into a brooch. Remember?"

Mistress Ashley snorted. "Hopefully, His Grace believes that. You are not fooling the rest of us, Margery. The brooch Jane Seymour wore in her portrait belonged to Queen Catherine."

My mind replayed her words repeatedly, reigniting that old fear of discovery. By the time Michael and I were summoned to Westminster Palace with the jewels, my gowns had grown loose with my incessant vomiting. Olwen attempted to hide the evidence with more layers beneath my skirts. I blamed the pregnancy. Michael remained unconvinced. "Regardless of whether the king grants me leave, you are going back to Chabnor," he insisted.

We found the monarch in the privy garden, staring dejectedly at the rotting leaves that littered the dirt pathways between bare rosebushes. He was fatter than the last time I saw him, fleeing from his wife's sickbed, abandoning her to fate. Beneath the furs, his black velvet doublet stretched to accommodate his widening girth. I had never seen him in mourning clothes, despite his being a widower thrice over. He acknowledged us with a nod, then addressed Master Holbein. "It shall be the grandest mural we have ever commissioned. Spare no expense in its creation. We want the entire world to know the Tudor line is secure and will rule for centuries to come."

"Leave it with me, humble prince." Holbein gave me a knowing glance.

The king turned to us. "Ah, yes. My wife's jewels."

Trapped in his cold blue gaze, I felt a chill take hold of me. The downy hair on my arm strained against the fabric of my sleeves. What would he say when he opened the coffer? Would he notice? I gingerly held the box aloft, fingers trembling against the gilt edges. He reached for it, and I held my breath.

His Grace lifted the lid, prodding at the contents. He peeked in the drawers, all the while mumbling to himself. At last, he closed everything up and handed the coffer to Holbein. "Take it to the jewel tower. We cannot bear to look at it any longer." When the artist left us, he eyed my belly warily. "We heard you were with-child, Lady Lyster. You must be eager to leave the court."

I measured my words carefully. "Only if Your Grace wills it so."

A tense silence fell. Michael went rigid beside me. He had wanted me to tell the truth about the necklace. It would be safer if we returned it, he reasoned. I balked, refusing to flout Queen Jane's express commandment. We had argued until the early morning hours. Once dawn broke, Michael relented. He would not force me, but he could not lie either. His conscience would not allow it. Our fate was left to God.

"You have my blessing," the king said finally. "Go, be fruitful. I shall call you both back once my council settles upon a new wife."

OLWEN CRAMMED A stack of linen undergarments into the already overstuffed trunk, giving the room one last look before she called for a groom. "I think that is everything, my lady." She snapped her fingers, and the young man heaved the parcel into his wagon to be taken out to the waiting carriage.

"You do that with such ease, my girl. Court life agrees with you," I chided. "How will you ever manage to live in the country again?"

The maid gave me a side-long glance. "I imagine Mam will have me delivering that baby of yours, and then maybe she will find me a husband." She laughed. "Or not. Such trouble men are."

"Oh, we are not all bad." Michael strode into the room, carrying our household books under his arm. He caressed my face with his free hand, kissing me on the cheek. "Much happiness can be found in the right match."

Olwen smiled. "I have always found Master Cresset an interesting fellow."

"Now that is something to consider." Michael grasped my hand, and then we walked out into the sunlight together.

Master Husee stood in the courtyard, deep in conversation with one of the great ladies, no doubt attempting to secure new positions for his mistress' daughters. The king had never lost a wife without having one waiting to take her place. We were in unprecedented times. Where would all the unmarried maids go? Husee tipped his hat when we passed. Was it remorse in his eyes, or had I imagined it?

"May God keep you safe in your travail," the lady trilled. The death of Queen Jane had made us even more acutely aware of dangers awaiting us in childbirth. However, I refused to dwell on the possibilities.

"Thank you, my lady. All the best to you both."

Helping me into the carriage, Michael caressed my belly. He would ride ahead of us on his horse. "The lady of the house shall be welcomed home with open arms," he said. "By none more so than her family. Dickon and I will be eagerly anticipating your arrival."

I embraced him tightly. Home. Family. The two things I thought forever out of reach. Now that they were mine, I would never let them go.

EPILOGUE

Nine Years Later

FEBRUARY 1547

MARGERY HORSMAN

CHABNOR AND WHITEHALL

"Not like that, Charles. You must never lose sight of the target. Let us try again. Shoulders back and let the bow rest in your hand. Do not forget to breathe." Dickon gently adjusted his brother's stance, careful not to overwhelm the boy with too much correction and risk undermining his confidence. Having been in the world for a mere eight years, Charles was still at a tender age. One which required much encouragement. Dickon, as the elder of the two, handled the boy masterfully. He always knew when to be tough and how to be kind. It gave his father and me much hope for the future. Young as he was, he would be a good husband when the time came for him to wed. A match had already been nearly two years in the making.

Cresting the hill at the end of the road, Michael's horse cantered into view. He was accompanied by three other men, messengers from London by the looks of their livery. They staked their horses in the yard and approached, hats in hand. Michael handed me a basket filled with dead rabbits. He had spent the afternoon hawking, and his cheeks were chapped from the brisk air. "Word from the court, my love. King Henry is dead."

A familiar face among the trio stepped forward. "Lady Lyster, how good it is to see you."

"Master Hugh! I almost did not recognize you."

He smiled, a slight blush colouring his face. "It is Sir Hugh Wynter now, my lady. I bring with me compatriots from the battlefield—Sir Matthew Brady and Sir Ezra Kirk. Knighted for our service at the siege of Boulogne."

Ezra, a most Biblical name. Our chaplain called him the scribe of the law of God in Heaven. "You must be famished. Come break bread with us. We have more than enough." I waved Dickon over. "Tell Olwen to have the table set for three more. We have honoured guests."

Clearing their plates, the knights told us of the king's death. How it had been kept secret until his son could be brought to the Tower to prepare for his coronation. Young Edward would take the throne. Queen Jane's death bringing him forth had not been in vain. Sir Hugh produced the summons from his bag. I glanced out the window at the gathering dusk while Michael looked it over. "It says the boy will be crowned in twenty days. Who has been named regent?"

Sir Matthew leaned back in his chair. "No one, in truth. In practice, the power falls to the Seymours."

"And they already tear at the child like wolves on a carcass," Sir Ezra growled, tossing his bread aside in disgust.

He would be as a lamb led to the slaughter. I could not bear to hear more. "Night creeps upon us," I interrupted. "Say that you will stay until the morrow. There is room enough for the three of you."

"If my lady insists," Sir Hugh answered, his azure eyes shining in the torchlight.

The next morning, after we broke our fast, I cornered the knight outside the stable. In the simmering dawn, he appeared worn and weary. "Please accept my sincere condolences, Sir Hugh. I still cannot believe Lady Rochford is no longer with us. It must have been difficult to hear of her execution."

Sir Hugh tugged at his cloak. I noted the threadbare fabric and loose threads of embroidery. "Witnessing it proved harder," he murmured.

"The blood of many women stained the last king's hands. I pray he pays for his murderous deeds in death."

Sir Hugh pressed his lips into my palm. "I appreciate your kindness,

Lady Lyster. I am certain Lady Rochford did as well. She was dealt a cruel hand, but she is with her beloved George now. The time for sadness has passed."

"Fare thee well, Sir Hugh. May God keep you in his favour."

The knight bowed, and then he was gone.

A WEEK FLEW by, and then another. And soon, it was time to set off on that long journey to court for the coronation festivities. Olwen helped me set out my best gowns and left the rest of the packing to the lower servants. She had gamely tried her hand at baby-catching when Charles was born but found the gore and trauma abhorrent. Despite her mother's pleas, she took up with a Scotsman who lived in a neighbouring town. When they married, I convinced Michael to take on the pair of them. Olwen led the household while her husband, James MacNaught, cared for the horses. Of all the help, she was the one I trusted most and the only other person who knew of the secret hidden beneath the floorboards.

I waited until the last trunk was full, acting quickly before the chamberers arrived to carry it out. Reaching beneath the bed, I rubbed my hands along the plank seams until my thumbnail caught on a notch in the wood. I loosened the slab, raising it just high enough to retrieve a small satin purse. Ear against the floor, I heard footsteps approaching. Scrambling backward, I managed to tuck the parcel into the trunk and secure the latch before Michael appeared in the doorway. "Are you ready?" he asked.

The frigid winter air chilled to the bone, but the scene that lay before us displayed all the wonder of God's heavenly touch. The trees wore coats of thick frost that glittered like the gems I cared for in Queen Jane's service. Hawks circled lazily above, eyeing the auburn-furred foxes darting amongst the snow-laced stumps. High on the hill, a graceful hind stood sentry, watching our party move through its territory with interest.

We stopped often, staying at several inns along the way to conserve the horses and warm ourselves for the night. When we finally made it to London, the celebrations were already underway. The streets were hung with brightly coloured pennants and banners. On every corner, crowds cheered merrily around dancing bonfires, their faces pinked by the wine flowing freely from fountains decorated with the king's arms. At White-hall, Michael's father greeted us with fresh clothes and a hot meal.

The palace was much changed since its days as York Place. Yet, I could not help being reminded of all that had happened within its stone walls. Marriages made and torn asunder. Lives lived and sacrificed. Who would they be—Henry's wives—had they been spared? What would become of their memory?

I found my answer in a high, bright voice echoing down the corridor. "Oh, Kat!" the young woman exclaimed, laughing. "You are hopeless, and yet I love you beyond all reason. When I am Queen, I shall always keep you close. Even when you are old and grey." Though crowned with the fiery red hair of the Tudors, she was her mother's daughter in every other way. From her flashing dark eyes to the very tips of her long delicate fingers, the Princess Elizabeth exuded the same intoxicating charm and charisma Anne Boleyn had when she captured the heart of the king. Confident and alluring, the princess was no longer a child. She was the Boleyn legacy and spoke with the determination characteristic of their house.

Kat Champernowne rounded on her charge. "Careful, Your Grace," she chided. "We cannot have the privy councillors accusing you of treason."

"I was born for greater things, dear Kat." She sighed. "Besides, Edward adores me. He would never allow any harm to come my way."

"The king is yet a boy. Much hangs in the balance until he reaches his majority. And what of the Princess Mary? She is next in line."

Elizabeth flicked her wrist dismissively. "Edward and I have a pact. He says he will name me successor. But I shall take your warning under advisement. No need stirring up my sister."

I followed the princess and her chaperone into the chapel, my fin-gers clasped tightly around the satin purse hanging from my girdle. Through the fabric, the pearls seemed to vibrate in my hand. Now was my moment—the time had come. Elizabeth knelt, with Kat following suit after she set her psalter in the choir stall. Quietly, I slipped behind them, stopping short to lay my purse atop the open book. The image on the page was one of St Anne with an inscription that read: blessed is the one whose transgressions are forgiven, whose sins are covered.

As the chapel doors closed behind me, I felt the weight of a thousand regrets melt away. I was free. Unshackled. Pandora had been content to keep it hidden away in her box, but hope was meant to hang upon the world like a strand of pearls reminding us of all the good in it. Sacrifice, charity, innocence, and tenderness—the brilliant jewels of a mother's pure love.

AUTHOR'S NOTE

T he idea to write a novel about Jane Seymour was birthed in much the same circumstances as those endured during its creation. The first year after The Raven's Widow's publication was one of great turmoil and anxiety—a time of momentous change that almost derailed my writing career. Thankfully, I persevered. For, it is in telling Jane and Margery's story that I found healing from the profound grief that would dominate my life in the years that followed.

I had never been overly fond of Jane Seymour. Never cared to know anything about her or allow her into my heart the way I did Anne Boleyn. The instigation for writing this novel came from my inability to detach from the other Jane in my life—I just couldn't let Lady Rochford go. Seymour wasn't even the main protagonist to begin with. It was Margery Horsman who led the way. Alas, there just wasn't enough information on the woman to fill an entire book. She needed someone to play off—someone who could offer a different perspective. That's where Henry's third wife came in.

It has been said that what we know about Mary Boleyn could fit on a postcard with room to spare. The same could be said for Margery. We don't know when or where she was born or died. We don't know how she got to court or precisely what she did there, excepting her years serving Jane. Researching her, the theories have run the gamut. She was younger/older. She was Catholic/Reformed. She was friends/enemies with Anne Boleyn. She may have served in Catherine of Aragon's Household and gone to Calais in 1520…or she may have started out as Mistress of the Robes for Anne Boleyn in 1534. We just don't know. I tried to take a little bit from each as I crafted her story.

It is certain that Margery was at court from 1534-1537. During that time, she married Michael Lyster and they jointly served as Keeper of the Jewels to Jane Seymour. The Abbey at Newbo was gifted to her shortly after the wedding. A year later, Henry decided to give it to another courtier, but she had already sold it off. It's likely that she never even visited it. She did give some evidence during the investigation into Anne Boleyn, but seemingly changed her mind and clammed up, annoying Sir Edward Baynton. Why? No one knows. She had a great relationship with John Husee and served as something of a bridge between the courtier and her royal mistresses. She makes many appearances in his letters to Lady Lisle and their easy comradery has inspired my rendering of their relationship. One of her letters is still in existence—a missive to Thomas Cromwell asking his assistance for a cousin of hers. These are the bare bones. Everything else is conjecture.

In the absence of knowledge, authors tend to write what we know. Well—I know worry, regret, longing, and sorrow...the emotions that form the basis for much of Margery's experience. The fact that her relations are impossible to source and the dispensation she and Michael requested against the reading of the banns of their marriage led me to believe that either she had been abandoned/orphaned by her family or, at the very least, distant from them. It is an experience I am familiar with. It is for these reasons that, out of all my protagonists, Margery is most like me.

In the absence of family, Margery must have had a connection to someone at court with influence. So, I have chosen one of the great ladies who wielded such in Catherine of Aragon's household. The idea to place Anne's iconic necklace into the maid's hands was one of divine inspiration. I honestly cannot recall how it came to me, only that it spilled out on the page when I began writing. Several years later, Hever Castle's Assistant Curator, Kate McCaffrey, released the findings of her brilliant research into Anne's Book of Hours, confirming my belief that the disgraced queen had secret supporters stowing away these lovely relics of her life.

We know a bit more about Jane and it's safe to say that most readers of my novel will be familiar enough to pick out what is true and what is fictitious in this story, so I won't go into exhaustive detail. When it comes to Jane's inner beliefs and motivations is where we are left to our own devices. Who brought her to the attention of Henry and why? How much did she know about the plot to bring about Anne's downfall and what was her role in it? What did she think of the wife-murdering tyrant she found herself married to? We will likely never know. For that reason, I allowed the recent events of the #MeToo movement and spate of allegations against powerful men to inform my artistic choices regarding Jane's thoughts and emotions.

Jane's relationship with her brothers could be debated for centuries, so I tried to write them as authentically as possible, the push and pull of power a never-ending cycle. The dynamic being particularly difficult due to Edward's position as the de facto head of the family, which Jane should have assumed upon her marriage to the king. The discovery that their father had died a year earlier than thought explained many of the choices these siblings made. Did Edward scupper the match with William Dormer? Doubtful, but my rendering of it is just the thing an elder brother would do to cement his authority. It wasn't all bad though, and according to Susan Higginbotham's meticulous research into Anne Stanhope, the child born in the early months of 1537 was a daughter named Jane.

Whether true or not, Jane is often seen as Henry's "true love." She likely was…but only because she birthed his hard-won heir and then died before he could grow tired of her. Until that point, the groom had been happy to denigrate his new wife publicly on many occasions. When his actions are viewed through the lens of the #MeToo Movement, we start to see the evidence of a truly toxic marriage. Imagine, if you will, the gaslighting and abuse that went on behind closed doors with a narcissist like Henry. It is chilling.

My final note relates to the renaming of two maids and the inspiration behind my fictional characters. With so many similar names, Elizabeth Jerningham became Eleanor and Jane Arundell became Joan. It was just too confusing otherwise. Readers of *The Raven's Widow* will recognize Lucy (Lady Rochford's maid) and Hugh Wynter. For those who don't already know, Hugh is based upon my sweet friend, Jeff White—who insists I tell you my version is much idealized (It's not. He really is that kind). Margery's maid, Olwen, is based upon my delightfully snarky Siamese Twin, Olga Hughes. A co-conspirator in my quest to change the way readers perceive hidden and maligned women, she also has no love for squalling babies. The jester at the Christmas festivities is based upon my boss, Jason Doneth. He made me promise to put him in my novel, so I did. He wears a lot of blue and broke his front tooth riding a scooter. He also thinks it's hilarious I wrote him as the Lord of Misrule. He really loves the Lord part! Sir Ezra Kirk and Sir William Brady are the hosts of a *Game of Thrones* podcast called *Bend the Knee*. For all their support, I gave them cameos.

ACKNOWLEDGMENTS

I t is February 19, 2022. As I sit—propped up on the couch—in the living room of my cosy town home, staring at a blinking cursor, I can't help but feel a catch in my throat when I pause to consider all the things that have happened to me during the genesis of this novel. I've gone through a pandemic and a divorce; experienced the crumble and shifting of what was once solid ground, thrusting me into a new world not of my own making. I lost the home where this novel was conceived, forced to sell it in order to begin life anew. I learned that the man I loved and trusted above all others was a liar and a cheat; an imposter who gaslit me to a breaking point. I discovered that I was not the woman I believed I was. I had always seen myself as weak, alone. A victim of my anxiety. Now, I know the truth. I am strong and loved. A survivor. For that reason, I begin by thanking the woman whose body lays buried alongside her abuser's: Jane Seymour. She managed to reach through the veil of the afterlife and save me, one word at a time. Through her story, I found peace and healing—hope that my trauma would not define me. And indeed, it does not - as it should not define her.

For all the pain my marriage wrought, it gave me the most wonderful gift of all: my son. It is he who I must acknowledge next. Logan, you are my moon and my stars. The infinite light of my universe. Thank you for keeping me sane and grounded. For giving me unconditional love. For offering up that silken forehead of yours for me to blanket with kisses. You make everything in my life lovely and I am endlessly proud of you. You are the worthiest prince in all of Christendom.

Throughout the writing of this book, I was blessed to have the most amazing readers. My sincere appreciation goes to Olga Hughes for being my alpha—the first reader and co-creator. She offered such insightful, detailed feedback on the sections as they came together; rough and unpolished as they were. She's also served as an inexhaustible champion of my work, and I am forever grateful for her support and friendship. Thank you to my betas: Laura Ann Riddling, James Nutter, Breeanna Judy, Shannon Marshall, Nikkole Fuscaldo, Theresa Whisenhunt, and Danielle Wagner. I am so appreciative of you all. I am also exceedingly thankful for my fellow authors who took time from their own projects to offer constructive critiques and write such lovely reviews: Owen Emmerson, Gareth Russell, and Wendy J. Dunn.

I'd like to thank my copyeditors and proof-readers, Katie Belliel and Brett Miller for making my manuscript shine. Love and appreciation to my designer, Domini Dragoone, for my gorgeous cover and interior. Domini experienced loss of her own during the creation of this novel—the death of her beloved mother. I know she is looking down, beaming with pride for her daughter's warm, generous spirit. I'd also like to thank another beautiful soul I encountered on this book's journey: Apprentice Agent, Maggie Sadler. I am deeply grateful for her encouragement and coaching. The suggestions she made took Jane and Margery's story to the next level. She is the sort of person every writer needs in their corner. Thank you to my team at GreyLondon Press for all they have done to bring my book baby out into the world.

Along the way, I have been endlessly supported by an entire cast of kind-hearted, magnanimous friends who have showered me with love and encouragement. Christine Seabury, my chosen sister and Best Friend for Life. Sandra Vasoli, my chosen mom and partner-in-crime. Catherine Brooks, my therapist and bonne amie across the narrow sea. Derek Gilbert, my confidant and eternal cheerleader. Elena Kuhnhenn, my HLM and fellow Hogwarts Alum. Annie England Noblin, my rescuer from bad dates and bad agents. And the to the lovely crew at my day job - My D&S Family: where would I be without you?

They say social media is a bad thing but without it, I would have never met these wonderful kind people: Amy Licence, Amy Lovett Logan, Annechien Foeth, Beth von Staats, Caroline Angus, Charlie Fenton, Claire

Ridgway, Elizabeth Figler, Heather Teysko, Heidi Malagisi, James Peacock, David Lee Barreto, Janet Wertman, Kathryn Holeman, Dr Lauren Mackay, Natalie Grueninger, Kristin Bundesen, Rebecca Larson, Sharon Conrad, Mary Wood, Allison Merkle, Sarah Mueller, Shauna Stone Johnston, Nicole Smith, Jehnna Louise, Rebecca Monet, Mallory Cole, Kristie Dean, Natalia Richards, Sara Thompson, Michael Blanding, Carol Ann Lloyd-Stanger, and many of those I have already mentioned in the paragraphs above. Thank you for having me on your podcasts and blogs, for writing such thoughtful and detailed reviews of my novels, for sharing your brilliant research, for promoting my work and offering advice and encouragement, for sending me sweet notes when I was struggling, for cheering my successes and allowing me into your lives to cheer on yours. I see every single like and comment and share. I see all your posts in the Tudor Groups recommending my books and telling others about how my research on Jane Boleyn impacted your perception of her. You have all lifted me up at one time or another, sometimes without even knowing it. I am blessed to call you friends.

Thank you to David Ebershoff for being such a lovely dinner companion at the 2017 HNS Conference in Portland. He was one of the first people I spoke to about this project, and I am still pinching myself that the author of such brilliant historical fiction cared one fig about what I was writing. That night, I feasted amongst giants of the genre. My heartfelt gratitude to Dominic Bruce-Binney, Dee Atkinson, and Aly Stott for inviting us to Wulfhall. I cannot adequately express how much it meant to be so welcomed by a Seymour descendant on land that bore witness to the rise and fall of one of my favourite Tudor queens. Looking out upon the windswept hills, I heard Jane's voice whispering to me. I sensed her footsteps on the excavated tiles laying in the archaeological trenches. I got chills sitting across from her many times great-grand-nephew, who with his deep-set eyes and dark features, was the very image of a young Edward Seymour. It was an experience I shall never forget.

Finally, I feel the need to acknowledge the many frogs I kissed during the writing of this novel. As my readers know, when I am creating a personality for figures of which we know nothing about, I often use people in my life as a template. As such, Michael Lyster went through something of a metamorphosis, having originally been based upon my now ex-husband. In the end, I drew him to be not like a man I knew, but one I wanted and needed in my life. One that I hope to one day base future characters upon. The moral: don't be afraid to change the prince in your story. Sometimes, they were frogs all along.

ABOUT THE AUTHOR

A drienne Dillard is a BA graduate in Liberal Studies with emphasis in History, Poli-Sci, and Economics from Montana State University-Northern. Her previous works include best-selling novels, *Cor Rotto: A Novel of Catherine Carey* and *The Raven's Widow: A Novel of Jane Boleyn*. When she isn't writing, Adrienne works as an administrative assistant in the financial services industry and enjoys spending time with her son, Logan, at their home in the Pacific Northwest.

CPSIA information can be obtained
at www.ICGtesting.com
Printed in the USA
LVHW022209280922
729514LV00003B/41